HIS FOR
CHRISTMAS

HIS FOR CHRISTMAS

**SHARON KENDRICK
NIKKI LOGAN
AMY ANDREWS**

First Published in Great Britain 2017
By Mills & Boon, an imprint of HarperCollins*Publishers*
1 London Bridge Street, London, SE1 9GF

HIS FOR CHRISTMAS © 2017 Harlequin Books S.A.

Christmas in Da Conti's Bed © 2014 Sharon Kendrick
His Until Midnight © 2013 Nikki Logan
The Most Expensive Night of Her Life © 2013 Amy Andrews

ISBN: 978-0-263-93170-9

9-1117

Printed and bound in Spain
by CPI, Barcelona

CHRISTMAS IN DA CONTI'S BED

SHARON KENDRICK

This book lovingly acknowledges the feisty and wonderful McCormick women – and most especially, Joan and Eileen.

Sharon Kendrick once won a national writing competition by describing her ideal date: being flown to an exotic island by a gorgeous and powerful man. Little did she realise that she'd just wandered into her dream job! Today she writes for Mills & Boon, featuring often stubborn but always to die for heroes and the women who bring them to their knees. She believes that the best books are those you never want to end. Just like life…

CHAPTER ONE

NICCOLÒ DA CONTI hated marriage, Christmas and love—but most of all he hated it when people didn't do what he wanted them to.

An unfamiliar feeling of frustration made him bite back a graphic expletive as he paced the floor of the vast New York hotel suite. Outside, skyscrapers and stars glittered against the deepening indigo sky, though not nearly as brightly as the Christmas lights which were already adorning the city.

But Niccolò was oblivious to the party atmosphere, or even to the onset of this most hated time of year. All he could think about was his only sister and wondering why she was being so damned *disobedient*.

'I do not want,' he said, sucking in a ragged breath in an attempt to control his rapidly spiralling temper, 'some tacky topless model acting as your bridesmaid. I have worked long and hard to establish a degree of respectability in your life, Michela. Do you understand what I'm saying? It cannot be allowed to happen, and what is more—I will not allow it to happen.'

From the other side of the glitzy New York hotel penthouse suite, Michela's expression remained unchanged as she looked at him.

'But you can't stop me from having her, Niccolò,' she said stubbornly. 'I'm the bride and it's my decision. That's the thing.'

'You think so?' His mouth hardened and he felt another hot flicker of rage. 'I could refuse to pay for this wedding for a start.'

'But the man I'm marrying is rich enough to carry the cost of the marriage if you decide to take such drastic action.' Michela hesitated. 'Though I'm sure you wouldn't want the world to know that Niccolò da Conti had refused to finance his only sister's wedding, just because he doesn't approve of her choice of bridesmaid. Wouldn't that be a step too far in the modern world—even for a man as old-fashioned as you?'

Niccolò flexed and then relaxed his fingers, wishing there were a nearby punch-bag on which he could vent his mounting frustrations. The world usually ran according to his wishes and he was not used to having them questioned. Bad enough that Alekto Sarantos was acting like some kind of prima donna...without having to cope with the bombshell that Alannah Collins was here.

His mouth tightened with anger as he thought about his sister and the sacrifices he had made. For too long he had fought to keep their tiny family unit intact and he was not prepared to relinquish control over her just yet. Because old habits died hard. He had faced shame and tragedy and had seen them off. He had protected Michela as much as was within his power to do so, and now she was about to enter into marriage, which would see her secure for life. His careful vetting of would-be suitors had paid dividends and she was about to marry into one of the most powerful Italian-American families in New York. She would have the sanctity he had always wished for her and nothing would be allowed to tarnish the occasion. Nothing and no one.

Especially not Alannah Collins.

Even the *thought* of the minxy little tramp made his body react in a complicated way he found difficult to control—and he was a man who prided himself on control. A powerful combination of lust and regret flooded over him, although his overriding emotion was one of rage, and that was the one he hung onto.

'I cannot believe that she has had the nerve to show her face,' he bit out. 'I can't believe she's even here.'

'Well, she is. I invited her.'

'I thought you hadn't seen her since I withdrew you from that appalling school.'

Michela hesitated. 'Actually, we've…well, we've stayed in touch over the years,' she said. 'We emailed and phoned—and I used to see her whenever I was in England. And last year she came to New York and we took a trip to the Keys and it was just like old times. She was my best friend at school, Niccolò. We go back a long way.'

'And yet you told me nothing of this before?' he demanded. 'You maintain a secret friendship and then spring it on me on the eve of your marriage? Didn't you stop to consider how it might look—to have someone as notorious as this tawdry exhibitionist playing a major role in your wedding?'

Michela lifted her hands up to the sides of her head

in a gesture of frustration. 'Are you surprised I didn't tell you, when this is the kind of reaction I get?'

'What does Lucas say about your connection with her?' he demanded.

'It happened a long time ago. It's history, Niccolò. Most people in the States haven't even heard of *Stacked* magazine—it folded ages ago. And yes, I know that a video of the original shoot seems to have found its way onto YouTube—'

'What?' he exploded.

'But it's really quite tame by modern standards,' said Michela quickly. 'If you compare it to some of the music videos you see these days—well, it's almost suitable for the kindergarten! And Alannah doesn't do that kind of stuff any more. You've got her all wrong, Niccolò, she's—'

'She is a tramp!' he gritted out, his Sicilian accent becoming more pronounced as his temper rose once again. 'A precocious little tramp, who shouldn't be allowed within ten feet of decent society. When will you get it into your head, Michela, that Alannah Collins is—'

'Whoops!' A cool voice cut into his angry tirade and Niccolò turned to see a woman strolling into the room without bothering to knock and suddenly his words were forgotten. If somebody had asked him his name right then, he thought he might have trouble remembering it. And yet for a moment he almost didn't recognise her—because in his memory she was wearing very little and the woman in front of him had barely an inch of flesh on show. It was the sound of her naturally sultry voice which kick-started his memory and his libido. But it didn't take long for his eyes to reacquaint themselves with her magnificent body—nor to acknowledge the natural sensuality which seemed to shimmer from it in almost tangible waves.

She was wearing jeans and a white shirt with a high collar, but the concealing nature of her outfit did nothing to disguise the luscious curves beneath. Thick black hair like lustrous jet hung over her shoulders, and eyes the colour of denim were studying him with a hint of mockery in their depths. Niccolò swallowed. He had forgotten the pale creaminess of her complexion and the rosiness of her lips. He had forgotten that this half-Irish temptress with an unknown father could burrow underneath his skin, without even trying.

As she moved he could see the glitter of a little blue dragonfly brooch gleaming on her shirt-collar, which matched the amazing colour of her eyes. And even though he despised her, he could do nothing about the leap of desire which made his body grow tense. She made him think of things he'd rather not think about—but mostly she made him think about sex.

'Did I just hear my name being taken in vain?' she questioned lightly. 'Would you like me to walk back out and come in again?'

'Feel free to walk out any time you like,' he answered coldly. 'But why don't you do us all a favour, and skip the second part of the suggestion?'

She tilted her chin in a way which made her black hair ripple down her back, like an ebony waterfall. But the smile she slanted at him didn't quite reach her eyes.

'I see you've lost none of your natural charm,

Niccolò,' she observed acidly. 'I'd forgotten how you could take the word "insult" and give it a whole new meaning.'

Niccolò felt a pulse begin to pound in his temple as his blood grew heated. But much worse was the jerk of lust which made his groin feel unbearably hard. Which made him want to crush his mouth down over her lips and kiss all those insolent words away and then to drive deep inside her until she screamed out his name, over and over again.

Damn her, he thought viciously. Damn her, with all her easy confidence and her louche morals. And damn those sinful curves, which would compel a grown man to crawl over broken glass just to have the chance of touching them.

'Forgive me,' he drawled, 'but for a moment I didn't recognise you with your clothes on.'

He saw the brief discomfiture which crossed her face and something primitive gave him a heady rush of pleasure to think that he might have touched a nerve and hurt her. Hurt her as she had once hurt his family and threatened to ruin their name.

But she turned the look into a bright and meaningless smile. 'I'm not going to rise to that,' she said as she turned instead to his sister. 'Are you ready for your fitting, Michela?'

Michela nodded, but her eyes were still fixed nervously on Niccolò. 'I wish you two could be civil to each other—at least until the wedding is over. Couldn't you do that for me—just this once? Then you never need see one another again!'

Niccolò met Alannah's speculative gaze and the thought of her smiling serenely in a bridesmaid gown made his blood boil. Didn't she recognise that it was hypocritical for her to play the wide-eyed innocent on an important occasion such as this? Couldn't she see that it would suit everyone's agenda if she simply faded into the background, instead of taking on a major role? He thought of the powerful bridegroom's elderly grandparents and how they might react if they realised that this was the same woman who had massaged her own peaking nipples, while wearing a dishevelled schoolgirl hockey kit. His mouth hardened. How much would it take to persuade her that she was persona non grata?

He flickered his sister a brief smile. 'Why don't you let Alannah and I have a word or two in private, *mia sorella*? And let's see if we can sort out this matter to everyone's satisfaction.'

Michela gave her friend a questioning look, but Alannah nodded.

'It's okay,' she said. 'You're quite safe to leave me alone with your brother, Michela—I'm sure he doesn't bite.'

Niccolò stiffened as Michela left the suite and his unwanted feeling of desire escalated into a dark and unremitting tide. He wondered if Alannah had made that remark to be deliberately provocative. He would certainly like to bite *her*. He'd like to sink his teeth into that slender neck and suck hungrily on that soft and creamy skin.

Her eyes were fixed on him—with that infuriating look of mild amusement still lingering in their smoky depths.

'So come on, then, Niccolò,' she said insouciantly. 'Do your worst. Why don't you get whatever is bugging you off your chest so that we can clear the air and give your sister the kind of wedding she deserves?'

'At least we are agreed on something,' he snapped. 'My sister does deserve a perfect wedding—one which will not involve a woman who will attract all the wrong kind of publicity. You have always been wild—even before you decided to strip for the cameras. And I don't think it's acceptable for every man at the ceremony to be mentally undressing the brides-maid, instead of concentrating on the solemn vows being made between the bride and groom.'

'For someone who seems to have spent all his life avoiding commitment, I applaud your sudden dedi-cation to the marriage service.' Her cool smile didn't slip. 'But I don't think most men are as obsessed with my past as you are.'

'You think I'm obsessed by your past?' His voice hardened. 'Oh, but you flatter yourself if you imag-ine that I've given you anything more than a fleeting thought in the years since you led my sister astray.' His gaze moved over her and he wondered if the lie showed in his face because he had never forgotten her, nor the effect she'd had on him. For a long time he had dreamt of her soft body and her sweet kiss—before waking up in a cold sweat as he remembered what he had nearly done to her. 'I thought you were out of her life,' he said. 'Which is where I would pre-fer you to stay.'

Calmly, Alannah returned his stare and told herself not to react, no matter what the provocation. Didn't matter how angry he got, she would just blank it. She'd seen enough of the world to know that remain-ing calm—or, at least, *appearing* to—was the most effective weapon in dealing with an adversary. And Niccolò da Conti was being *very* adversarial.

She knew he blamed her for being a bad influence on his beloved sister, so maybe she shouldn't be surprised that he still seemed to bear a grudge. She remembered reading something about him in the press—about him not being the kind of man who forgot easily. Just as he wasn't the kind of man who was easily forgotten, that was for sure. He wore his wealth lightly; his power less so. He could silence a room by entering it. He could make a woman look at him and want him, even if he was currently staring at her as if she were something which had just crawled out from underneath a rock. What right did he have to look at her like that, after all these years? Because she'd once done something which had appalled his straight-laced sensibilities—something she'd lived to regret ever since? She was a different person now and he had no right to judge her.

Yet it was working, wasn't it? The contempt in his eyes was curiously affecting. That cold black light was threatening to destabilise a poise she'd spent years trying to perfect. And if she wasn't careful, he would try to crush her. *So tell him to keep his outdated opinions to himself. Tell him you're not interested in what he has to say.*

But her indignation was beginning to evaporate, because he was loosening the top button of his shirt and drawing attention to his body. Was he doing that on purpose? she wondered weakly, hating the way her stomach had suddenly turned to liquid. Was he deliberately reminding her of a potent sexuality which had once blown her away?

She became aware that her heart was pounding like mad and that her cheeks had grown hot. She might not like him. She might consider him the most controlling person she'd ever met—but that didn't stop her from wanting him in a way she'd never wanted anyone else. Didn't seem to matter how many times she tried to block out what had happened, or tried to play it down—it made no difference. All they'd shared had been one dance and one kiss—but it had been the most erotic experience of her life and she'd never forgotten it. It had made every other man she'd met seem as insubstantial as a shadow when the fierce midday sun moved over it. It had made every other kiss seem about as exciting as kissing your teddy bear.

She ran her gaze over him, wishing he were one of those men who had developed a soft paunch in the intervening years, or that his jaw had grown slack and jowly. But not Niccolò. No way. He still had the kind of powerful physique which looked as if he could fell a tree with the single stroke of an axe. He still had the kind of looks which made people turn their heads and stare. His rugged features stopped short of being classically beautiful, but his lips looked as if they had been made with kissing in mind—even if their soft sensuality was at odds with the hostile glitter in his eyes.

She hadn't seen him for ten years and ten years could be a lifetime. In that time she'd achieved a notoriety she couldn't seem to shake off, no matter how much she tried. She'd grown used to men treating her as an object—their eyes fixed firmly on her generous breasts whenever they were talking to her.

In those ten years she'd seen her mother get sick

and die and had woken up the day after the funeral to realise she was completely alone in the world. And that had been when she'd sat down and taken stock of her life. She'd realised that she had to walk away and leave the tawdry world of glamour modelling behind. She had reached out to try something new and it hadn't been easy, but she had tried. She was still trying—still dreaming of the big break, just like everyone else. Still trying to bolster up her fragile ego and hold her head up high and make out she was strong and proud, even if inside she sometimes felt as lost and frightened as a little girl. She'd made a lot of mistakes, but she'd paid for every one of them—and she wasn't going to let Niccolò da Conti dismiss her as if she were of no consequence.

And suddenly, she was finding it difficult to do 'calm', when he was staring at her in that contemptuous way. A flicker of rebellion sparked inside her as she met his disdainful gaze.

'While you, of course, are whiter than the driven snow?' she questioned sarcastically. 'The last thing I read was that you were dating some Norwegian banker, who you then dumped in the most horrible way possible. Apparently, you have a reputation for doing that, Niccolò. The article quoted her as saying how cruel you'd been—though I guess that shouldn't have really surprised me.'

'I prefer to think of it as honesty rather than cruelty, Alannah,' he answered carelessly. 'Some women just can't accept that a relationship has run its natural course and I'm afraid Lise was one of them. But it's interesting to know you've been keeping tabs on me all this time.' He gave her a coolly mocking smile. 'I guess single billionaires must have a certain appeal to women like you, who would do pretty much anything for money. Tell me, do you track their progress as a gambler would study the form of the most promising horses in the field? Is that how it works?'

Alannah tensed. Now he'd made it sound as if she'd been *stalking* him. He was trying to make her feel bad about herself *and she wasn't going to let him*. 'Now who's flattering themselves?' she said. 'You're best friends with the Sultan of Qurhah, aren't you? And if you go out for dinner with royalty, then the photos tend to make it into the tabloids—along with speculation about why your date was seen sobbing outside your apartment the following morning. So please don't lecture me on morality, Niccolò—when you know nothing of my life.'

'And I would prefer to keep it that way,' he said. 'In fact, I'd like to keep you as far away from any member of the da Conti family as possible. So why don't we get down to business?'

She blinked at him, momentarily disconcerted. 'Business?'

'Sure. Don't look so startled—you're a big girl now, Alannah. You know how these things work. You and I need to have a little talk and we might as well do it in some degree of comfort.' He waved his hand in the direction of the cocktail cabinet which stood at the far end of the glittering hotel suite. 'Would you like a drink? Don't good-time girls always go for champagne? I can't guarantee a high-heeled shoe for you to sip it from, but I can vouch for an extremely good vintage.'

Don't rise to it, she told herself, before fixing a

weary smile to her lips. 'I hate to challenge your ste-reotype, but I'm not crazy about champagne and even if I was I certainly wouldn't want to drink it with you. That might imply a cordiality we both know doesn't exist. So why don't you say whatever it is you're de-termined to say? And then we can end this conversa-tion as quickly as possible so that I can concentrate on fitting Michela's wedding gown.'

He didn't answer for a moment, but instead leaned back against one of the giant sofas and looked at her, his arms folded across his broad chest. Yet for all his supposedly casual stance, Alannah felt a chill of fore-boding as his eyes met hers. There was a patina of power surrounding him which she hadn't noticed in that long-ago nightclub. There was a hardness about him which you didn't find in your average man. Sud-denly he looked formidable—as if he was determined to remind her just who she was dealing with.

'I think we both know a simple way to resolve this,' he said softly. 'All you have to do is step out of the spotlight right now. Do that and there will be no problem. Michela is about to marry a very powerful man. She is about to take on an important role as a new wife. In time, she hopes to have children and her friends will be role models to them. And...'

'And?' she questioned, but she knew what was coming. It was crystal clear from the look on his face.

'You are not an appropriate role model,' he said. 'You're not the kind of woman I want fraternising with my nephews and nieces.'

Her heart was beating very fast. 'Don't you dare judge me,' she said, but her voice wasn't quite steady.

'Then why not make it easy for yourself? Tell Michela you've changed your mind about acting as her bridesmaid.'

'Too late!' Forcing herself to stay strong, she held up her palms in front of her, like a policeman stepping into the road to stop the traffic. 'I've made my own dress, which is currently swathed in plastic in my room, waiting for me to put it on just before noon tomorrow. I'm wearing scarlet silk to emphasise the wedding's winter theme,' she added chattily.

'But it's not going to happen,' he said repressively. 'Do you really think I would let it?'

For a moment Alannah felt another shimmer of doubt flicker into the equation. The quiet resolution of his voice scared her and so did the forthright expression in his eyes. Somehow he was making her feel...vulnerable. *And she wasn't going to let that happen.* Because she didn't do vulnerable. Not any more. Vulnerable got you nowhere. It made you fall down when life landed one of its killer punches and think you'd never be able to get back up again. It made you easy prey to powerful predators like Niccolò da Conti. 'How wicked you make me sound,' she said.

'Not wicked,' he corrected silkily. 'Just misguided, out-of-control and sexually precocious. And I don't want any publicity generated by the presence of *Stacked* magazine's most popular pin-up.'

'But nobody—'

'Michela has already mistakenly tried to tell me that nobody will know,' he interrupted impatiently. 'But they will. The magazines you stripped for have become collectors' items and back issues now change hands for thousands of dollars. And I've just been informed that a film of you has made its way onto YouTube, raising your public profile even further. It doesn't matter what you wear or what you don't wear—you still have the kind of body which occupies a fertile part of the male imagination. Men still look at you and find themselves thinking of one thing— and only one thing.'

Alannah tried not to cringe, but unfortunately his words struck home. Clever, cruel Niccolò had— unwittingly or not—tapped into her biggest insecurity. He made her feel like an object. Like a *thing*. Not a woman at all, but some two-dimensional image in a magazine—put there simply for men to lust over.

The person she was now wouldn't dream of letting her nipples peek out from behind her splayed fingers, while she pouted at the camera. These days she would rather die than hook her thumbs in her panties and thrust her pelvis in the direction of the lens. *But she'd needed to do it, for all kinds of reasons. Reasons the uptight Niccolò da Conti wouldn't understand in a million years.*

'You were *notorious*, Alannah,' he continued. 'And that kind of notoriety doesn't just go away. It sticks like mud.'

She looked at him in despair. He was telling *her* that? Didn't he realise that she'd been living with the consequences of that job ever since? No, of course he didn't. He saw what he wanted to see and no more— he didn't have the imagination to put himself in someone else's shoes and think what their life might be like. He was protected by his wealth and position and his arrogance.

She wanted to go up and shake *him* and tell him

to think outside the box. To wipe that judgemental look from his face and to start seeing her as a person, instead of someone who'd once behaved rashly. She could see exactly why Michela had been so scared of him when they'd been at school together. Was it any wonder that the Italian girl had rebelled from the moment he'd dropped her off at the exclusive Swiss finishing school where Alannah's mother had worked as school matron?

'The most important thing for me,' she said slowly, 'is that Michela wants me there. It's her day and she's the bride. So, short of tying me up and kidnapping me—I intend to be there tomorrow.'

'Unless we come to some kind of mutually beneficial arrangement,' he said.

'Oh?' She tilted her head. 'Tell me more.'

'Oh, come on, Alannah.' He smiled. 'You're a streetwise woman. You've been around. There must be something in your life that you'd...*like*.'

'Something in my life that I'd like?' she repeated. 'You mean like a cure for the common cold, or an alarm that doesn't make you want to smash the phone every time you hear it?'

'Very amusing. No, nothing like that.' He paused, and his black eyes glittered. 'I am a very wealthy man—and I'm willing to make it worth your while to tell Michela that you've changed your mind.'

She stared at him in disbelief.

'Let me get this straight,' she said. 'You're offering me *money* to stay away from your sister and not be her bridesmaid?'

'Why not?' He gave a cold smile. 'In my experience, if you want something badly enough you can usually get it. The tricky thing is negotiating the right price—but that is something I should imagine you're very good at.'

'But that's…bribery.'

'Try thinking of it as common sense,' he suggested softly.

She was shaking her head. 'You know, Michela used to tell me how unbelievably controlling you were,' she said. 'And part of me thought she might have been exaggerating. But now I can see that every word was true.'

'I am not seeking your approval of my character,' he clipped out. 'Just think why I'm making you this offer.'

'Because you're a control freak?'

'Because Michela means everything to me,' he said, and suddenly his voice grew harsh as he remembered how he'd fought to protect his sister from the sins of their father. *And their mother.* He thought of their flight from Sicily—his mother pregnant with Michela and not knowing what lay ahead. Niccolò had been only ten, but he had been the one everyone had relied on. He had been the man around the house. And it was hard to relinquish that kind of role or those kinds of expectations…

'Michela is the only family I have left in the world and I would do anything for her,' he ground out.

'Except give her the freedom which a woman of her age has the right to expect?' she retorted. 'Well, I'm *glad* she's had the courage to stand up to you. To maybe make you realise that you can't keep snapping your fingers and expecting everyone else to just leap to attention. I'm not going anywhere until after the wedding. Better deal with it, Niccolò.'

Their gazes clashed and Niccolò felt the flicker of something unknown as he returned her stare. Oh, but she was a one-off. She took defiance to a whole new level and made it seem erotic. She made him want to take her in his arms and dominate her—to show her that he could not and would not be thwarted. He took a step towards her and a primitive surge of pleasure rippled over him as he watched her eyes darken. Because she still wanted him, he realised. Maybe not quite as much as he wanted her—but the desire he could read in her eyes was unmistakable.

And couldn't desire be the most powerful weapon of all? Didn't sex give a man power over a woman who wanted it?

'Why don't you think about what I've said?' he suggested. 'So that by the time I see you at the pre-wedding dinner later, you'll have had the sense to change your mind about my offer.'

Her eyes narrowed. 'But…'

He raised his eyebrows. Suddenly, she didn't look quite so defiant. Suddenly she looked almost unsure of herself. 'But?'

'I…' She shrugged her shoulders. 'It's just that… well, Michela said you were probably going to skip the dinner and that we wouldn't see you until tomorrow. Something to do with a business deal. Some new apartment block you've recently built in London.'

'Is that what she said?' He smiled. 'Well, not any more. I've decided business can wait, because something much more important has come up.' There was a pause as he looked at her and suddenly it was easy to forget the pressing needs of his billionaire clients and friends. 'What is it they say? Keep your friends close but your enemies closer. And I want you *very* close for all kinds of reasons, Alannah. You'd better believe that.'

CHAPTER TWO

ALANNAH PULLED UP the zip of her cocktail dress and stared at her pale-faced reflection in the mirror. She'd tried deep breathing and she'd done a quick bout of yoga, but her hands were still trembling and she knew why. Slipping on a pair of high-heeled shoes, she felt a wave of self-recrimination washing over her.

She thought about the things Niccolò had said to her earlier. The way he'd insulted her and looked down his proud, patrician nose. He'd been judging her in the most negative way possible, but that hadn't stopped her wanting him. She shuddered. Where was the self-respect she'd worked so hard to get back? She wondered what had happened to the cool, calm Alannah who wasn't going to let him get under her skin. How had he managed to puncture her self-possession with nothing more than a heated ebony gaze, which reminded her of things she'd rather forget?

Because memory was a funny thing, that was why—and sometimes you had no control over it. It flipped and jerked and jumped around like a flapping fish on the end of a hook. It took you to places you didn't want to visit. It could make ten years seem like a minute, or a minute seem like an hour.

It could put you back inside the skin of the person you'd once been.

And suddenly she was a teenager again. Seventeen years old and about to break the rules. Off to a party wearing the make-up which her Swiss finishing school strictly forbade, when really she should have been tucked up in bed in the dormitory. Wearing a tiny little micro-mini because she had been young and carefree—because back then she hadn't realised that a woman's body could become her enemy, instead of her friend...

By rights, someone like her shouldn't have been a pupil at the exclusive all-girls academy, tucked high in the beautiful mountains of Switzerland. She wasn't rich. She wasn't well-connected. She was just the illegitimate daughter of a single-parent mother who happened to be Matron at the fancy boarding school. And while this meant that Alannah got herself a great education, her 'charity' status meant that most of the girls simply tolerated her.

Michela da Conti was different. She was the only one who had held out the hand of genuine friendship—maybe because they had something in common, despite their rich-girl/poor-girl pairing. Alannah had spent her life rebelling against her super-strict mother while Michela had known real tragedy in her short life, plus she wanted to escape the strictures of her controlling brother, Niccolò.

Their youthful rebellion usually stretched no further than going out for illicit under-age drinks in one of the nearby bars after lights-out, or hanging out of the dormitory window, trying to inhale cigarettes without being sick.

But one night they heard about a party. A glitzy twenty-first birthday celebration for one of Niccolò's godsons—which was being held in one of the neighbouring mountain valleys.

'And we're going!' declared Michela excitedly.

Alannah remembered frowning. 'But what about your brother? Won't he be there?'

'You're kidding.' Michela had given a smile of satisfaction. 'Apparently, he's miles away in some obscenely expensive resort in Barbados, with his latest ghastly supermodel girlfriend. So we're safe.'

Alannah remembered walking into the crowded room, where coloured lights were flashing and music was blaring out loudly. Her borrowed silver minidress was clinging to her body like honey and she was getting lots of requests to dance, but she turned down every one because all the boys seemed too loud and too brash to be interesting.

She did her best to enjoy herself. She sipped a soft drink and admired the snowy view. Found a sleeping kitten on her way back from the loo and spent an enjoyable ten minutes stroking its furry tummy and wishing she could go home. When eventually she went back into the main room to find Michela to suggest they got a cab back to school, she couldn't find her anywhere. So she went and stood in a quiet corner of the room, losing herself in the shadows while everyone else partied—and that was when she saw him.

Him.

She had never forgotten that moment. It was like being struck by something with no sense of warning that it was coming. As if a velvet sledgehammer had hit her very hard. She was aware that he was tall and his hair was as black as the night sky. His eyes were black too—even from this distance she could see that. He was dressed in a dark suit, which made him look outwardly sophisticated, but she could sense something *primitive* about him. There was something predatory in the gleam of his eyes, which should have scared her as he began to walk towards her, with a sense of purpose in his step.

But she wasn't scared.

It was the most illogical thought she'd ever had, but at that moment she felt as if she'd been waiting all her life for him to arrive, and here he was.

Here he was.

He looked her up and down—as if it was his right to study a strange woman as he might study a car he was thinking of buying. But surely no car would make him smile like that—a smile which seemed to come from somewhere deep inside him, one that pierced her heart and made her knees feel as if they might have difficulty supporting her.

'I think you need to dance,' he said.

'I'm not a very good dancer.'

'That's because you've never danced with me. So come here and let me teach you how.'

Later, she would remonstrate with herself at the eagerness with which she fell into his arms. At the way she let him slide his hands around her back as if she'd known him for years. His hand moved to her hair and he started stroking it and suddenly she wanted to purr as loudly as that kitten had done earlier.

They said very little. The party was too loud for conversation and, anyway, it didn't seem to be conversation which was dominating Alannah's thoughts right then. Or his. Words seemed superfluous as he pulled her closer and, although the music was fast, they danced so slowly that they barely moved. Their bodies felt as if they were glued together and Alannah almost wept with the sheer pleasure of it all. Did he sense her enjoyment? Was that why he dipped his mouth to her ear, so that she could feel the warmth of his breath fanning her skin?

'You,' he said, his velvety voice underpinned with an accent which she recognised as Sicilian, 'are very beautiful.'

Wasn't it funny how some people you just seemed to spark off? So that she—inexperienced and raw as she was—didn't respond in a conventional way. She didn't blush and tell him she wasn't beautiful at all— but instead came out with something which sounded almost slick.

'And you,' she cooed back, looking straight into his black eyes, 'are very handsome.'

He smiled. 'A perfect match, then?'

She tipped her head back. 'Aren't you getting a little ahead of yourself?'

'Probably.' He leaned forward, so that her face was bathed in the dark spotlight of his gaze. 'Especially as we haven't even kissed. Don't you think that's a shocking omission, my beauty? So shocking that I think we ought to remedy it right now.'

She remembered the way her heart had crashed loudly against her ribcage. The way her mouth had dried with anticipation and the words had just come tumbling out of her mouth. 'Who says I'm going to kiss you?'

'I do.'

And he did.

In that shadowy corner of some anonymous house in the Swiss mountains, while outside flakes of snow floated past the window like big, white feathers, he kissed her.

He kissed her so intensely that Alannah thought she might faint. He kissed her for so long that she wanted him never to stop. It was like that pile of bone-dry sticks she'd once built on a long-ago holiday to Ireland—she remembered the way they'd combusted into flames the moment her aunt had put a match to them. Well, it was a bit like that now.

She was on fire.

His thumb brushed over her breast and Alannah wriggled with excitement. Because surely this was what she had been made for—to stand in this man's arms and be touched by him. To have him look at her as if she were the most beautiful woman in the world. He deepened the kiss to one of added intimacy and as he pushed his thigh between hers the atmosphere suddenly changed. It became charged. She could feel the flood of liquid heat to her groin and the sudden, almost painful hardening of her nipples as they pushed insistently against his chest. His breath was unsteady as he pulled away from her and there was a primitive emotion on his face which she didn't recognise.

'We'd better think about moving somewhere more comfortable,' he said roughly. 'Somewhere with a bed.'

Alannah never had a chance to reply because suddenly the mood was broken by some kind of commotion at the door. She felt him tense as Michela burst into the room with snow melting on her raven hair, and the guilty look on her friend's face when she saw Niccolò told its own story.

It was unfortunate that Michela was surrounded by the miasma of sickly-sweet marijuana smoke—and even more unfortunate when Niccolò's discreet enquiries the next day yielded up the information that both girls were already on a formal warning from the school. A small matter of the building's elaborate fire-alarm system having been set off by the two of them hanging out of a dormitory window, smoking.

Alannah would never forget the look of passion dying on Niccolò's face, only to see it being replaced with one of disgust as he looked at her. She remembered wanting to wither beneath it.

'You are my sister's friend?' he questioned incredulously. 'Her *school friend*?'

'Y-yes.'

'How old are you?'

'Seventeen.'

All the colour drained from his face and he looked as if she'd hit him. 'So Michela associates with a *puttana*, does she?' he hissed. 'A cheap little tart who puts out for strangers at parties.'

'I d-don't remember you objecting,' she stammered, stung into defending herself, even if deep down she felt she had no real defence to offer.

'No man objects when a woman offers herself to him on a plate like that,' he snapped.

The following day he had withdrawn Michela from the school and shortly afterwards the head teacher had summoned Alannah and her mother to her office. The head had clearly been furious at the prospect of having to say goodbye to Niccolò da Conti's generous donations to the school. She had told Alannah that her behaviour was unacceptable and her mother had pre-empted the inevitable expulsion by offering up her resignation.

'I'm not having my girl scapegoated by some rich financier,' she'd said fiercely. 'If you're going to heap all the blame on her, then this is not the kind of school for her.'

Of course, that was not an end to it—merely the beginning of a nightmare which put the whole Niccolò incident to the back of her mind.

But she'd never grassed up Michela and Michela had remained loyal to her ever since.

Her thoughts cleared and she saw her friend looking at her in the dressing-table mirror, her face still glowing from her pre-wedding facial, and Alannah sighed as she met Michela's questioning gaze. 'Maybe it would be better if I just bowed out, if it's going to cause a massive row between you and your brother. I'll just stand at the back like everyone else and throw rose petals. I can live with that.'

Michela glared as she put her hairbrush down.

'And let Niccolò have his own way? I don't think so. You've been the best of friends to me, Alannah—and I want you there. In fact, it'll probably do Niccolò good on all kinds of levels. I've never heard *anyone* speak to him the way you do.' She smirked. 'Nobody else would dare.'

Alannah wondered what Michela would say if she realised how much of her reaction to her powerful brother was bravado. That her feelings for him were... *complicated*. Would she be shocked if she knew the truth? That she only had to look at him to want to rip the shirt from his body and feast her eyes on all that silken olive flesh? That somehow he brought out a wildness in her which frightened her. Which she knew was wrong. And not only wrong…she knew only too well that those supposedly seamless sexual fantasies were nothing but an illusion.

She forced a smile. 'Okay, if you insist…it'll be business as usual. In which case, we'd better get going. I know it's traditional for the bride to keep her groom waiting on the big day, but not on the eve-of-wedding dinner!'

They took the elevator down to the iconic Midnight Room, where a large clock was set permanently at the witching hour. It was a spectacular party room designed by Emma Constantinides, the hotel owner's wife—and had won countless industry prizes since its opening. Circular tables had been set for dinner and the dark velvet ceiling was punctured with tiny lights, so that it resembled a star-filled sky. In the silvery light from hundreds of candles, people in evening dress stood drinking champagne as the scent of dark blue hyacinths wafted through the air.

A roar of delight greeted the bride-to-be's appearance and Alannah leaned forward to whisper in Michela's ear as people began to surge towards them. 'You go and sparkle,' she said. 'Anything you need me to check?'

Michela shook her head. She had already spotted Lucas on the opposite side of the room, talking to his mother. 'No. You go and sparkle too,' she said. 'And for goodness' sake, have a very large cocktail before we sit down to dinner. You look completely washed out, Alannah.'

But Alannah refused a drink. A drink on an empty stomach was a recipe for disaster and hers was already in knots. All she had to do was to get through the next thirty-six hours without crumbling, and surely she could do that.

And then she looked around the room and saw Niccolò—and every empowering thought flew straight from her mind as her gaze focused on him.

He was standing talking to a blonde whose sequined dress left little to the imagination and Alannah found herself thinking that he didn't seem to have a problem with *that*. The woman was gazing up at him and nodding intently, as if nothing but pearls of wisdom were falling from those cruel and kissable lips. There were other women clustering nearby, too—as if he were a dark shark and they were all hungry little pilot fish, just waiting for whatever scraps he cared to leave for them.

He lifted his head as if he had sensed her watching him—glancing across the room to where she stood. And suddenly it was too late to look away. His gaze captured hers and held it and it felt as if some fierce dark light were piercing through her skin. She felt sensitive. Exposed and raw. Terrified he would see through to the dark mass of insecurities hidden beneath her cool exterior, she tried to look away, but she couldn't. *She couldn't.* He seemed to be drawing her in by the force of his formidable will.

Desperately, she tried to compose herself. To concentrate on something other than how beautifully the dark suit caressed his hard body, but she failed at that, too. Instead she found herself staring at the snowy edge of his dinner-shirt and the way his olive skin gleamed like burnished gold above it.

He bent his head to say something to the blonde, who turned to look at her, and Alannah thought she saw faint surprise clouding the other woman's eyes. Had her uncomfortable stance given her away—making the woman guess that she was the outsider here?

She forced herself to turn away to talk to some of the other guests, who seemed genuinely charmed by her English accent, and for a while she allowed herself to relax before the bell rang for dinner. But a glance at the seating plan showed her that she was next to Niccolò—*of course she was,* for hadn't Michela made it clear that she wanted the two of them to get along better? She wondered when her friend was going to realise that it simply wasn't going to happen. Or at least, not in this lifetime. Her heart began thumping painfully as she made her way towards the top table.

She felt his presence behind her even before his shadow fell over the table. The palms of her hands were clammy and the race of her heart was thready, but somehow she managed to fix a wide smile to her lips as she turned to look at him.

'Niccolò!' she said brightly.

'Just the person you wanted to sit beside, right?'

'How did you guess?' Solely for the benefit of the other guests, she maintained that brittle rictus of a smile. 'You were right at the top of my list.'

But Alannah tensed as he leaned forward to kiss her on both cheeks, just as he would have done to any other female guest. She wondered if any other female guest would have reacted the way she did, with a pulse which was threatening to rocket out of control and a desire to tip her head up so that his mouth would meet hers, instead of grazing the innocent surface of her cheek. She found herself longing to reach up to touch that hard, chiselled jaw and to feel it scrape against her fingertips. She wanted to press her lips against his ear and kiss it. And how crazy was that? How could you want a man so much when you didn't even *like* him?

Stop it, she told herself as he pulled out her chair with an exaggerated courtesy, which seemed to be at odds with the mockery gleaming from his eyes. Did he know what kind of effect he had on her? Did he realise that her legs were weak and her breasts growing heavy? He sat down next to her and she could smell his warm, male flesh—as subtle and spicy as sandalwood—and all she wanted to do was to breathe it in. Reaching out, she picked up her champagne flute and took a gulp.

She could feel him watching as she drank the cold, fizzy wine but the champagne tasted as sour as a remedy you might take for an upset stomach. She put down her glass and looked at him, because they couldn't go on like this. Not with a whole day and a half to get through.

'I think Michela has sat us together deliberately,' she said.

He raised his eyebrows. 'Because?'

'I think she's hoping that we're going to declare some sort of truce.'

'Why—are we engaged in some sort of battle?'

'Please don't be disingenuous, Niccolò. You know we are. We've done nothing but argue since we reconnected.' She shrugged. 'And while that seems to be what you seem to want—I'd prefer it, and your sister would prefer it, if we could manage to be non-confrontational. At least, in public.'

Niccolò met her denim-blue eyes and gave a small dissenting shake of his head—thinking how wrong she'd got it. Because battle was the last thing he wanted. His needs around Alannah Collins were much more fundamental. He might even have contemplated a more conventional route by asking her out on a date, if she hadn't been the kind of woman he despised.

Yet there was nothing of the precocious teenager or sexy glamour model about her tonight. The image she presented was almost *demure*. Her navy silk dress was high-necked and the hemline showed nothing more than a couple of inches of slender knee. A small, glittering brooch in the shape of a fluttering moth was her only jewellery. Her most magnificent assets—the breasts which had once so captured the imagination of the British public—were only hinted at and certainly not on show. All he could see was the occasional glimpse of a soft curve as the material brushed against them. He swallowed. Was she aware that it was just as provocative to conceal something, as to reveal it?

Of course she was.

Trading on her own sexuality had been her stock-in-trade, hadn't it? She knew everything there was to know about how to pull in the punters and leave them slavering for more.

Shaking out his napkin, he placed it in his lap and scowled, recalling the first time he'd seen her at his godson's birthday party.

He remembered looking in amazement at the silver dress, which had clung to her curvy body like melted butter, and thinking that he'd never seen anyone looking quite so alluring. Had he been frustrated? Too long without a woman? Unlikely. All he knew was that he hadn't been able to tear his eyes away from her.

The look which had passed between them had been timeless. The lust which had overwhelmed him had been almost tangible. He had never experienced anything like it in his life—not before, nor since. The hardness at his groin had been almost unbearable as he had danced with her. Something elemental had caught him in its grip and he'd felt almost...*lost*. The dance had been simply a formality—paving the way for their first kiss. He had kissed her for a long time, tempted by a need to pull her into a dark and anonymous corner and just *take* her. And even though he detested being out of control...even though his own history had warned him this was not the way to go— it hadn't been enough to deter him from acting on it.

He had been just about to drive her back to his hotel, when there had been some sort of commotion by the door. He remembered turning to see Michela giggling as she'd entered the room, accompanied by a group of boys. His *sister*. Large flakes of snow had been melting on her raven hair and her look of guilt when she had seen him had told its own story.

And that was when Niccolò had discovered that Alannah Collins wasn't some twenty-something party guest, but the teenage best friend of his only sister. A wild-child who had been threatening to ruin Michela's reputation and bring shame on the da Conti name, after he'd spent years meticulously dragging it from the mud.

Was it any wonder that he despised her?

Was it any wonder that he despised himself, knowing what he had nearly done to her?

What he still wanted to do to her.

He leaned back in his chair, paying little attention to the plates of smoked salmon which were being placed in front of them. 'Did you ever tell Michela what happened between us?' he questioned suddenly.

She stiffened a little before turning to look at him, her eyes narrowing warily. 'But nothing did happen.'

'Oh, come on.' He gave a harsh laugh. 'It might as well have done. It would have done, if my sister hadn't arrived. I've never had a dance quite so erotic as the one I had with you. It was a dance which was headed straight for the bedroom.'

'Oh, for heaven's sake—'

'Does Michela realise that you would have spent the night with me if she hadn't turned up when she did?'

'You can't know that.'

'Yes, I can. And so can you. Why don't you try being honest with yourself for once, Alannah?' He leaned forward and his voice roughened. 'I know enough about women to realise when they want a man to make love to them—and you were screaming out to have me do it to you that night.'

'Really?' She took a nervous sip of her drink.

'And you've avoided answering my question,' he persisted. 'What exactly did you tell Michela?'

There was a pause. 'I didn't tell her anything.'

'Why not?'

Alannah shrugged, reluctant to admit the truth—
that she'd been too ashamed of her own reaction to
want to acknowledge it to anyone and certainly not
to her best friend. That she'd felt dirty and cheap.
Michela had warned her that her big brother was a
'player'. That he changed his women nearly as often
as he changed his shirts. She remembered the two of
them agreeing that any woman who went out with a
man like him was *sad*. But she'd nearly been one of
those women, hadn't she? Because he was right. If Michela hadn't walked in right then, she would have...

Briefly, she let her eyes close. She'd been so in
thrall to him that he probably could have taken her
outside and taken her virginity pressed up against a
cold and snowy tree. She had certainly been up for
going back to his hotel with him.

She opened her eyes and looked at him. 'Why not?
Because even though Michela has always thought you
a total control freak, she absolutely idolised you—and
I knew you were the only family she had. It wasn't
for me to disillusion her by telling her that you'd been
hitting on her best friend.'

'Hitting on her best friend?' He gave a cynical
smile. 'Oh, please. Unfortunately, I didn't realise I
was dealing with *jailbait* at the time. You kept that
one crucial fact to yourself.'

'Is that why you got me expelled?' she said, without missing a beat.

He shook his head. 'I didn't mention your name
when I withdrew Michela from the school.'

Her eyes narrowed. 'Are you serious?'

He shrugged. 'There was no need. I thought I was
removing Michela from your bad example—what I

didn't realise was that you were going to continue the friendship behind my back.'

Alannah ran her fingertip down over her champagne glass, leaving behind a transparent stripe in the condensation. 'But all that happened a long time ago,' she said slowly.

'I guess it did.' He leaned back in his chair. 'And since your role seems to be non-negotiable, I guess I'm just going to have to be nice to you.'

'Is that possible?'

'Me being nice?' He watched the golden flicker of candlelight playing on her pale skin. 'You don't think so?'

'Not really. I think it would be like someone hand-rearing a baby tiger and then expecting it to lap contentedly from a saucer of milk when it reaches adulthood. Naïve and unrealistic.'

'And nobody could ever accuse you of that.'

'Certainly not someone with as cutting a tongue as you, Niccolò.'

He laughed, his gaze drifting over fingers which he noticed were bare of rings. 'So what has been happening to you in the last ten years? Bring me up to speed.'

Alannah didn't answer for a moment. He didn't want to know that her life had imploded like a dark star when her mother had died and that for a long time she had felt completely empty. Men like Niccolò weren't interested in other people's sadness or ambition. They asked polite questions at dinner parties because that was what they had been taught to do—and all they required was something fairly meaningless in response.

She shook her head at the waitress who was offering her a basket heaped with different breads. 'I'm an interior designer these days.'

'Oh?' He waited while the pretty waitress stood close to him for slightly longer than was necessary, before reluctantly moving away. 'How did that happen? Did you wake up one morning and decide you were an expert on soft furnishings?'

'That's a very patronising comment.'

'I have experience of interior designers,' he said wryly. 'And of rich, bored women who decide to set themselves up as experts.'

'Well, I'm neither rich, nor bored. And I think you'll find there's more to the job than that. I studied fashion at art school and was planning to make dresses, but the fashion world is notoriously tough—and it's difficult to get funding.' Especially when you had the kind of past which meant that people formed negative judgements about you.

'So what did you do?'

'I worked for a big fashion chain for a while,' she continued, pushing her fork aimlessly around her plate. 'Before I realised that what I was best at was putting together a "look". I liked putting colours and fabrics together and creating interesting interiors. I spent a few years working for a large interiors company to gain experience and recently I took the plunge and set up on my own.'

'And are you any good?' he questioned. 'How come I've never heard of you?'

'I think I'm good—have a look at my website and decide for yourself,' she said. 'And the reason you haven't heard of me is because there are a million other designers out there. I'm still waiting for my big break.'

'And your topless modelling career?' he questioned idly. 'Did that fall by the wayside?'

Alannah tried not to flinch, terrified he would see how much his question had hurt. For a minute back then she'd actually thought they were sticking to their truce and talking to each other like two normal human beings. 'This is you being "nice", is it, Niccolò? Behaving as if I was something you'd found on the sole of your shoe?'

His eyes didn't leave her face. 'All I'm doing is asking a perfectly legitimate question about your former career.'

'Which you can't seem to do without that expression of disgust on your face.'

'Wouldn't anyone be disgusted?' he demanded hotly. 'Isn't the idea of a woman peddling her flesh to the highest bidder abhorrent to any man with a shred of decency in his bones? Although I suspect the end-product must have been spectacular.' There was a pause before he spoke. 'Alannah Collins *shaking her booty.*'

His last few words were murmured—and Alannah thought how unexpected the colloquialism sounded when spoken in that sexy Sicilian accent of his. But his words reminded her that what you saw wasn't necessarily what you got. Despite his cosmopolitan appearance and lifestyle, Niccolò da Conti was as traditional as they came. His views and his morals came straight from another age. No wonder his sister had been so terrified of him. No wonder she'd gone off the rails when she had been freed from his claustrophobic presence and judgemental assessment.

'Those photographs were stills,' she said tonelessly. 'I never *shook* anything.'

'Ah, but surely you're just splitting hairs.' He gave a dangerous smile, his finger idly circling the rim of his untouched champagne glass. 'Unless you're trying to tell me that cupping your breasts and simulating sexual provocation for the camera while wearing a school uniform is a respectable job for a woman?'

Alannah managed to twist a sliver of smoked salmon onto the end of her fork, but the food never made it to her mouth. 'Shall I tell you why I did that job?'

'Easy money, I'm guessing.'

She put the fork back down. Oh, what was the point? she thought tiredly. He didn't *care* what had motivated her. He had judged her—he was still judging her—on the person she appeared to be. Someone who had danced too intimately with a stranger at a party. Someone who had gone off the rails with his beloved sister. Someone who had discovered that the only way to keep hope alive had been by taking off her clothes...

Who could blame him for despising her—for not realising that she was so much more than that?

She dabbed at her lips with her napkin. 'On second thoughts, I don't think polite interaction is going to be possible after all. There's actually too much history between us.'

'Or not enough?' he challenged and suddenly his voice grew silky. 'Don't you think it might be a good idea to forge some new memories, Alannah? Something which might cancel out all the frustrations of the past?'

Alannah stiffened. Was he suggesting what she *thought* he was suggesting? Was he *flirting* with her? She swallowed. And if he were? If he were, she needed to nip it in the bud. To show him she respected herself and her body.

She slanted him a smile. 'I don't think that's going to happen. I think we need to avoid each other as much as possible. We'll support Michela all the way and try not to let our mutual animosity show, but nothing more than that. So why don't you do me a favour and talk to the woman on your other side? She's been trying to get your attention since you first sat down and she's very beautiful.' She picked up her wine glass and took a sip, her eyes surveying him coolly over the rim. 'I'm surprised you hadn't noticed that, Niccolò.'

CHAPTER THREE

IT WAS THE worst night he'd had in a long time, or maybe it was just that Niccolò couldn't remember ever losing sleep over a woman before. He lay tossing and turning in the king-size bed of his hotel room, trying to convince himself that Alannah had been right and the less time they spent together, the better. But every time he thought about distancing himself from those denim-blue eyes and that pouting, provocative mouth he felt an uncomfortable ache deep inside him.

What was the matter with him?

Kicking away the rumpled sheet, he told himself she wasn't his kind of woman—that she represented everything he despised in a sometimes trashy and disposable society.

Abandoning all further attempts to sleep, he dealt with his emails and spoke to his assistant in London, who informed him that Alekto Sarantos was still unhappy with the interior of the penthouse suite. The Greek billionaire had let it be known that the apartment's design was too 'bland' for his tastes and, despite a close association going back years, he was now considering pulling out of the deal and buying in Paris instead. Niccolò silently cursed his temperamental friend as he terminated the phone-call and wondered how soon he could decently leave after the wedding to return to work.

Pulling on his gym gear, he went for a run in Central Park, where the bare trees were etched dramatically against the winter sky. Despite his restless night and the fact that little was in bloom, his senses seemed unusually receptive to the beauty which surrounded him on this cold winter morning. There were ducks and gulls on the lakes and woodpeckers were tapping in the trees. Other runners were already out pounding the paths and an exquisite-looking blonde smiled hopefully at him, slowing down as he approached. But he didn't even bother giving her a second look. Her eyes were glacial green, not denim blue—and it was that particular hue which had been haunting his sleep last night.

The run took the edge off his restlessness, even if it didn't quell it completely, and after he'd showered and dressed he found a series of increasingly frantic texts from his sister queuing up on his smartphone. The final one was followed by a wobbly voicemail message, demanding to know where he was.

He went along the corridor and knocked at her door—stupidly unprepared for the sight of Alannah opening the door, even though he'd known she was sharing a suite with his sister. He felt almost *high* as he looked at her and could feel the aching throb of longing which stabbed at his groin. She was wearing a denim shirt-dress which matched her eyes and a tiny ladybird brooch which twinkled red and black on the high collar. For a moment it occurred to him that she was dressed as sedately as a schoolteacher and he watched as a complicated series of expressions flitted across her face as she looked at him, before producing a smile which was clearly forced.

'Hi,' she said.

'Hi.' He tried his own version of that fake smile. 'Sleep well?'

She raised her eyebrows. 'You're here to enquire how I slept?'

No, I'm here because I'd like to take your panties down and put my tongue between your thighs. He shrugged. 'Michela has been bombarding my phone with texts. Is she here?'

'She's...' cocking her head in the direction of one of the closed doors behind her, she pulled a face '...in the bathroom.'

'Is something wrong?'

'She's broken a nail.'

He frowned. 'Is that supposed to be some kind of a joke?'

'No, Niccolò, it's not a joke. It's the finger her wedding ring will go on and everyone will notice. To a bride who's just hours away from the ceremony, something like this is nothing short of a catastrophe. I've called the manicurist, who's on her way up.'

'First World problems,' he said caustically. 'So everything is under control?'

'Well, that depends how you look at it.' She met his gaze and seemed to be steeling herself to say something. 'Her nerves aren't helped by the worry that you're going to lose your temper at some point today.'

'What makes her think that?'

'Heaven only knows,' she said sarcastically, 'when you have a reputation for being so mild-mannered and accommodating. Could it have something to do with the fact that you and I were at loggerheads throughout dinner last night, and she noticed?'

He raised his eyebrows. 'So what does she want us to do—kiss and make up?'

'Hardly,' she snapped. 'That might be stretching credibility a little too far.'

'Oh, I think I could manage to put on a convincing enough performance,' he drawled. 'How about you?'

So she *hadn't* been imagining it last night. Alannah stiffened. He really *was* flirting. And she was going to have to put on the performance of a lifetime if she wanted to convince him that it wasn't working.

She raised her eyebrows. 'So can I tell Michela that you're planning to be a good boy today? Do you think you're a competent enough actor to simulate enjoyment and behave yourself for the duration of the wedding?'

'I don't usually have to simulate anything—and I've never been called a *good boy* in my life,' he answered softly. 'But if Michela wants reassurance that I'm going to behave myself, then tell her yes. I will be extremely virtuous. And I will be back here at three, to take you both down to the wedding.'

Alannah gave a brief nod and her cool, careful smile didn't slip until she had shut the door on him, though her pulse was pounding loudly.

At least an air of calm had descended by the time the manicurist arrived to repair the tattered nail and the mood was elevated still further as Alannah helped Michela slide into her delicate white gown. Because this was *her* territory, she reminded herself fiercely.

She was proud of the dress she'd made for the bride and she wasn't going to let Niccolò da Conti whittle away at her confidence.

Her movements became sure and confident as she smoothed down the fine layers of tulle and soon she felt like herself again—Alannah Collins, who was living life according to her own rules, and ignoring the false perceptions of other people.

But the moment Niccolò arrived all that composure deserted her. She was aware of his piercing gaze as he watched her adjusting the floral circlet which held Michela's veil in place and it was difficult to keep her fingers steady. She could feel his dark eyes moving over her and the only comfort she got was by reminding herself that after this day was over, she need never see him again.

So why did that make her heart plummet, as if someone had dropped it to the bottom of a lift-shaft?

'You look beautiful, *mia sorella*,' he said, and Michela gave a smile of delight as she did a twirl.

'*Do* I?'

'Indeed you do.' His voice was indulgent. 'Lucas is a very lucky man.'

'Well, I have Alannah to thank for my appearance,' said Michela brightly. 'She's the one who made the dress. It's gorgeous, isn't it, Niccolò?'

Alannah wanted to tell her friend to stop trying so hard. To tell her that she and her brother were never going to achieve anything more than a forced civility. But she maintained the fiction necessary to soothe the bride's frazzled nerves by smiling at him in what she hoped looked like a friendly way.

'It is indeed a very beautiful dress,' he agreed

softly, his eyes gleaming out a silent message which she didn't dare analyse.

Alannah tried to relax as she handed Michela her bouquet and the three of them made their way to the Pembroke's celebrated wedding room, where the assembled guests were waiting. A harpist began to play and Alannah saw the sudden look of tension which hardened Niccolò's features into a grim mask as he gave his sister away to be married.

Maybe he just didn't like weddings, she thought.

She tried not to stare at him as the vows were made and to ignore the women who were clearly trying to catch his eye. And after the rings had been exchanged, Alannah tried to be the best guest she possibly could. She chatted to the groom's sister and offered to suggest some new colour schemes for her house in Gramercy Park. After the wedding breakfast, she took time to play with several of the frilly-dressed little girls from Lucas's huge extended family. And when they were all worn out, she lined them all up to twist their long hair into intricate styles, which made them squeal with delight.

By the time the tables had been cleared and the band had struck up for the first dance, Alannah felt able to relax at last. Her duties had been performed to everyone's satisfaction and the wedding had gone off without a hitch. Drink in hand, she stood on the edge of the dance-floor and watched Michela dancing in the arms of Lucas—soft white tulle floating around her slender body and a dreamy smile on her face as she looked up at her new husband.

Alannah felt her heart contract and wished it wouldn't. She didn't want to feel *wistful,* not today—

of all days. To wonder why some people found love easy while others seemed to have a perpetual struggle with it. Or to question why all that stuff had never happened to her.

'How come I always find you standing alone on the dance-floor?'

Alannah's heart clenched at the sound of Niccolò's Sicilian accent, but she didn't turn round. She just carried on standing there until he walked up to stand beside her.

'I'm just watching the happy couple,' she said conversationally.

He followed the direction of her gaze and for a moment they stood in silence as Lucas whirled Michela round in his arms.

'Do you think they'll stay happy?' he asked suddenly.

The question surprised her. 'Don't you?'

'If they are contented to work with what they've got and to build on it, then, yes, they have a chance. But if they start to believe in all the hype...' His voice grew hard. 'If they want stardust and spangles, then they will be disappointed.'

'You obviously don't rate marriage very highly.'

'I don't. The odds against it are too high. It's a big gamble—and I am not a gambling man.'

'And love?' she questioned as she turned at last to look at him. 'What about love?'

His mouth hardened and for a moment she thought she saw something bleak flaring at the depths of his black eyes.

'Love is a weakness,' he said bitterly, 'which brings out the worst in people.'

'That's a little—'

'Dance with me,' he said suddenly, his words cutting over hers, and Alannah tensed as his fingers curled over her bare arm.

They were a variation on the words he'd spoken all those years ago. Words which had once turned her head. But she was older now and hopefully wiser— or maybe she was just disillusioned. She no longer interpreted his imperious command as masterful— but more as an arrogant demonstration of the control which was never far from the surface.

She lifted her face to his. 'Do I get a choice in the matter?'

'No.' Removing the glass from her hand, he placed it on the tray of a passing waitress, before sliding his hand proprietorially around her waist and propelling her towards the dance floor. 'I'm afraid you don't.'

She told herself that she didn't have to do this. She could excuse herself and walk away. Because he was unlikely to start behaving like a cave-man by dragging her onto the dance-floor—not with all his new in-laws around.

Except that she left it a split second too long and suddenly it was too late for objections. Suddenly, she was on the dance-floor and his arms were round her waist and the worst thing of all was that she *liked* it. She liked it way too much.

'You can't do this, Niccolò,' she said breathlessly. 'It's over-the-top alpha behaviour.'

'But I just can't help myself,' he said mockingly. 'I'm an over-the-top alpha man. Surely you knew that, Alannah.'

Oh, yes. She knew that. A block of stone would

have known that. Alannah swallowed because his hands were tightening around her waist and making her feel there was no place else she would rather be. She told herself it would cause a scene and reflect badly on both of them if she pulled away from him. *So endure it. One dance and it will all be over.*

She tried to relax as they began to move in time with the music and for a while they said nothing. But it wasn't easy to pretend that it meant nothing to be wrapped in his arms again. Actually, it was close to impossible. His body was so hard and his arms were so strong. His unique scent of sandalwood and raw masculinity seemed to call out to something deep inside her—to touch her on a subliminal level which no one else had even come close to. She could hear the thunder of her heart as he lowered his head to her ear and even his voice seemed to flood over her like velvety-dark chocolate.

'Enjoying yourself?' he said.

She swallowed. 'I was before you forced me into this farce of pretending we have a civilised enough relationship to be dancing together.'

'But surely you can't have any complaints about what we're doing, *mia tentatrice*. Aren't I behaving like a perfect gentleman?'

'Not with...' Her words tailed away, because now he had moved his hands upwards and his fingers were spanning her back. She could feel their imprint burning through the delicate material of her bridesmaid dress and her throat constricted.

'With what?'

'You're holding me too tightly,' she croaked.

'I'm barely holding you at all.'

'You are a master of misinterpretation.'

'I am a master of many things,' came the silken boast, 'but misinterpretation wouldn't have been top of my list.'

She looked up from where she had been staring resolutely at his black tie and forced herself to meet the mocking light in his eyes. 'Why are you doing this?' she whispered.

'Dancing with you? Isn't it customary for the brother of the bride to dance with the bridesmaid at some point—particularly if both of them are single? Or were you holding out for the best man?'

'I'm not holding out for anyone. And I don't remember telling you I was single.'

'But you are, aren't you? And if you're not, then you might as well be.' He met her eyes. 'Because you are responding like a woman who hasn't been touched by a man for a very long time.'

She was tempted to snap back at him with indignation, but how could she? Because he was right. It *was* a long time since she had been touched by a man. It was a long time since she had danced with a man too, and it had never felt like this. Not with anyone. *It had only ever felt like this with him.*

'I don't understand what it is you want,' she said. 'Why you're dancing with me. Taunting me. Trying to get underneath my skin. Especially when you don't even *like* me—and the feeling is mutual.'

He pulled her closer. 'But not liking doesn't stop us *wanting*, does it, Alannah? Desire doesn't require affection in order to flourish. On the contrary, sometimes it works better without it. Don't you find that, *mia tentatrice*?' He stroked a reflective finger along her waist. 'That sex can be *so* much more exciting when there is a frisson of animosity between a man and a woman?'

Her skin still tingling from the lazy caress of his finger, she pulled away from him, trying to focus on the presumptuous things he was saying, rather than the way her body was reacting. 'Stop it,' she said weakly.

'But you haven't answered my question.'

'And I don't have to. Just as I don't have to stand here and take any more provocative comments. My duty dance is over.' With a monumental effort, she pulled away from him. 'Thanks for reminding me what a consummate player you are, Niccolò. And thanks for reminding me that ten years might have passed but you don't seem to have changed. You still treat the opposite sex as if—'

'I wouldn't generalise if I were you,' he interjected and now his voice was edged with steel. 'Because you have no idea how I treat women. And believe me when I tell you that I've never had any complaints.'

The sexual boast was blatant and Alannah suddenly felt as if her skin were too tight for her body. As if her flesh wanted to burst out of her bridesmaid dress. Her breasts were tingling and she knew she had to get away from him before she did something she regretted—or said something she would never live down. 'Goodnight, Niccolò,' she said, turning away and beginning to walk across the dance-floor. 'I think we can officially declare our truce to be over.'

Niccolò watched her go and felt frustration mount inside him, along with an even greater feeling of disbelief. She had gone. She had walked away with her head held high and her shoulders stiff and proud, and all his hunter instincts were aroused as he watched the retreating sway of her silk-covered bottom.

He swallowed.

He had played it wrong.

Or maybe he had just read her wrong.

She had been right. He didn't particularly like her and he certainly didn't *respect* her. But what did that have to do with anything? He still wanted her in a way he'd never wanted anyone else.

And tomorrow she would be gone. Leaving New York and going back to her life in London. And even though they lived in the same city, their paths would never cross, because their two lives were worlds apart. He would never know what it was like to possess her. To feel those creamy curves beneath his fingers and her soft flesh parting as he thrust deep inside. He would never know what sound she made when she gasped out her orgasm, nor the powerful pleasure of spurting his seed deep inside her. She might be the wrong type of woman for him on so many levels—but not, he suspected, in bed.

Still mesmerised by the sway of her bottom, he began to follow her across the dance-floor, catching up with her by one of the bars, where she was refusing a cocktail.

She barely gave him a glance as he walked up beside her.

'You're not leaving?' he said.

'I can't leave. At least, not until Michela has thrown her bouquet and driven off into the night with Lucas. But after that, you won't see me for dust, I promise.'

'Before you make any promises—I have a proposition you might like to hear.'

'I don't need to hear it,' she said flatly. 'I wouldn't need to be a genius to work out what you might have in mind, after the things you said on the dance-floor and the way you were holding me. And it doesn't make any difference.' She sucked in a deep breath and met his gaze. 'I'm not interested in having sex with you, Niccolò—got that?'

Niccolò wondered if she knew how blatantly her nipples were contradicting her words—but maybe now wasn't the time to tell her.

'But what if it was a business proposition?' he questioned.

Her eyes narrowed. 'What kind of business proposition?'

He looked at the waxy white flowers which were woven into her hair and he wanted to reach out and crush them between his fingers. He wanted to press his lips on hers. He wanted to undress her and feast his eyes on that soft, creamy body. In a world where he had managed to achieve every single one of his objectives, he suddenly recognised that Alannah Collins had been a residual thorn in his flesh. A faint but lingering memory of a pleasure which had eluded him.

But not for much longer.

He smiled. 'You said you were an interior designer and suggested I have a look at your website, which I did. And you *are* good. In fact, you are very good. Which means that you have a skill and I have a need,' he said.

Her mouth thinned into a prudish line. 'I don't think that your needs are the kind I necessarily cater for.'

'I think we're talking at cross purposes, Alannah. This has nothing to do with sex.' He slanted her a thoughtful look. 'Does the name Park View ring any bells?'

'You mean that enormous new apartment block overlooking Hyde Park which has been disrupting the Knightsbridge traffic for months?'

'That's the one.'

'What about it?'

'It's mine. I own it. I built it.'

Alannah blinked. 'But it's the most…'

'Don't be shy, Alannah,' he said softly as her voice tailed off. 'One should never be shy when talking about money. It's the most expensive building of its kind in the world—isn't that what you were going to say?'

She shrugged. 'I fail to see how your property portfolio could possibly interest me.'

'Then hear me out. A friend of mine—a brilliant Greek named Alekto Sarantos—is about to complete one of the penthouse apartments.'

She lifted her hand to adjust a stray petal on her headdress. 'And is there a problem?'

'*Sì.* Or at least—he certainly seems to think there is.' A note of irritation entered his voice. 'The problem is that Alekto doesn't like the décor, even though it has been overseen by one of the most popular designers in the city.'

'Let me guess.' She raised her eyebrows. 'Cream walls? Bowls of big pebbles lying around the place? Lots of glass and neutral-coloured blinds?'

He frowned. 'You must have seen photos.'

'I don't need to, but I'd recognise a bandwagon

anywhere—and every interior designer in the business seems to be jumping on it. Presumably this friend of yours doesn't do bland and that's why he doesn't like it.'

'No, Alekto doesn't do bland—in fact, he is the antithesis of bland. He described the décor to my assistant as a "tsunami of beige" and unless I can transform the place to his satisfaction before the Greek new year, then he says he'll pull out of the deal and go to Paris instead. It has become a matter of pride for me that he chooses London.' He gave a hard smile. 'And maybe that's where you could come in.'

'Me?'

'You want a break, don't you? I don't imagine they get much bigger than this.'

'But…' Somehow she managed to keep the tremble of excitement from her voice. 'Why me? There must be a million other designers itching to accept a job like this.'

His gaze swept over her like an icy black searchlight—objective, speculative and entirely without emotion.

'Because I like your style,' he said unexpectedly. 'I like the way you dress and the way you look. I always have. And if you can satisfy my exacting friend with your designs—then the job is yours.'

Alannah felt ridiculously thrilled by his praise, yet she didn't want to be thrilled. She wanted to feel nothing. To give nothing and take nothing. She met his dark gaze. 'And the fact that you want to go to bed with me has nothing to do with your offer, I suppose?'

He gave a soft laugh. 'Oh, but it has everything to do with it, *mia sirena*,' he said. 'As you said yourself, there are a million interior designers out there, but your desirability gives you a distinctive edge over your competitors. I cannot deny that I want you or that I intend to have you.' His black eyes gleamed. 'But I wouldn't dream of offering you the job unless I thought you were capable of delivering.'

CHAPTER FOUR

'NICCOLÒ WILL SEE you in just a moment, Alannah.'
The redhead sitting outside Niccolò's office wore a
silk blouse the colour of the lilies on her desk and
when she smiled her lips were a neat coral curve. 'My
name's Kirsty, by the way—and I'm one of Niccolò's
assistants. Take a seat over there. Can I get you a coffee? Some tea perhaps?'

'No. I'm fine, thanks.' Carefully putting down her
mood-boards, Alannah sank onto a seat, wondering if
any of her reservations showed in her face. Whether
her nerves or sick dread were visible to the impar-
tial observer.

Ever since she'd left New York, she had listed all
the reasons why she should say no to Niccolò's offer of
work and during the cramped flight she had checked
them off on her fingers. He was arrogant. Tick. He
was dangerous. Double tick. He was also completely
unapologetic about wanting to take her to bed. Only
he hadn't even said *that* in a flattering way. He'd made
it sound as if she was just something he needed to
get out of his system. Like an itch. Or a fever. She bit
her lip because his attitude brought too many memories flooding back. She hated men who regarded a

woman as some kind of *object*, so surely self-respect and pride should have made her turn his offer down, no matter how lucrative?

But he was offering her work—legitimate work. His proposition had been like a cool drink when your throat was parched. Like finding a crumpled ten-pound note in your jeans before you washed them. She thought about the scarcity of jobs in her highly competitive field, and the ridiculously high mortgage on her tiny bedsit. She couldn't *afford* to turn him down—which was why she'd spent all weekend coming up with ideas she thought might appeal to a Greek billionaire who didn't like beige. And through it all she had realised that this was the vital springboard her career needed and she was going to grab at it with both hands.

She stared at the cream lilies on Kirsty's desk, trying to concentrate on their stark beauty, but all she could think about was the way Niccolò had stroked his finger over her when they'd been dancing at the wedding. Her heart began to pound. It had been an almost *innocent* touch and yet her response had been anything but innocent. The intensity of her feelings had shocked her. She had wanted him to peel the bridesmaid dress from her body and touch her properly. She had wanted him to kiss her the way he'd done all those years before—only this time not to stop.

And that was the problem.

She still wanted him.

She had done her best to quash that thought when she'd emailed him some suggestions. And had attempted to ignore her spiralling feeling of excitement when his reply came winging into her inbox late last night.

These are good. Be at my offices tomorrow at 7p.m.

It hadn't been the most fulsome praise she'd ever received, but it was clear he considered her good enough for the job and that pleased her more than it should have done. And hot on the heels of professional pride came a rather more unexpected feeling of gratitude. She had stared at his email and realised that, no matter what his motives might be, Niccolò was giving her the chance to make something of herself.

So she'd better show him that his faith had not been misplaced.

A buzzer sounded on Kirsty's desk and she rose to her feet, opening a set of double doors directly behind her.

'Niccolò is ready for you now, Alannah.' She smiled. 'If you'd like to come this way.'

Alannah picked up her mood-boards and followed Kirsty into a huge and airy office, blinking a little as she looked around her, because she'd never been anywhere like this before. She gulped. It was...*spectacular.* One wall consisted entirely of glass and overlooked some of London's more familiar landmarks and Alannah was so dazzled by the view that it took a moment for her to notice Niccolò sitting there and to realise that he wasn't alone.

Her first thought was how at home he looked in the luxury of his palatial surroundings. Long legs stretched out in front of him, he was reclining on a large leather sofa in one corner of the vast office—and opposite him was a man with black hair and the bluest eyes she'd ever seen. This must be Alekto Sarantos, Alannah thought, but she barely noticed him. Despite his unmistakable gorgeousness, it was Niccolò who captured her attention. Niccolò whose outwardly relaxed stance couldn't quite disguise the tension in his powerful body as their gazes clashed and held. She could read the mockery in his eyes. *I know how much you want me,* they seemed to say. And suddenly she wished that the floor could swallow her up or that the nerves which were building up inside her would show her some mercy and leave her alone.

'Ah, Alannah. Here you are.' Black eyes glittered with faint amusement as he looked her up and down. 'Not jet-lagged, I hope?'

'Not at all,' she lied politely.

'Let me introduce you to Alekto Sarantos. Alekto—this is Alannah Collins, the very talented designer I was telling you about.'

Alannah gave an uncertain smile, wondering exactly *what* he'd said about her. They were friends, weren't they? And didn't men boast to their mates about what they'd done with a woman? She could feel her cheeks growing slightly warm as she looked at Alekto. 'I'm very pleased to meet you.'

'Do sit down,' he said, in a gravelly Greek accent.

Alannah saw Niccolò pat the space beside him on the sofa—and she thought it looked a bit like someone encouraging a dog to leap up. But she forced herself to smile as she sat down next to him, unwinding the vivid green pashmina which was looped around her neck.

Alekto turned his startling blue gaze on her. 'So…

Niccolò assures me that you are the person who can replace the existing décor with something a little more imaginative.' He grimaced. 'Although frankly, a piece of wood could have produced something more eye-catching than the existing scheme.'

'I'm confident I can, Mr Sarantos.'

'No. *Parakalo*—you must call me Alekto,' he said, a hint of impatience hardening his voice, before giving a swift smile. 'I always like to hear a beautiful woman saying my name.'

Beautiful? No woman ever thought she was beautiful and that certainly hadn't been the effect Alannah had been striving for today. She'd aimed for a functional, rather than a decorative appearance—tying her hair back in a thick plait to stop it being whipped up by the fierce December wind. She had wanted to project style and taste as well as hoping her clothes would be like armour—protecting her from Niccolò's heated gaze.

Her Japanese-inspired grey dress bore the high neckline which had become her trademark and the fitted waist provided structure. A glittering scarab beetle brooch and funky ankle-boots added the unconventional twists which she knew were necessary to transform the ordinary into something different. It was the detail which counted. Everyone knew that.

'If you insist,' she said, with another polite smile. 'Alekto.'

Niccolò raised his eyebrows. 'Perhaps you'd like to show *Alekto* what ideas you have in mind for his apartment, while he concentrates on your undoubted beauty,' he suggested drily.

Trying to ignore the sarcasm in his voice, Alannah

spread out the mood-boards she'd been working on and watched as Alekto began to study them. Squares of contemporary brocade were pasted next to splashes of paint colour, and different swatches of velvet and silk added to the textural diversity she had in mind.

'We could go either traditional or contemporary,' she said. 'But I definitely think you need something a little bolder in terms of colour. The walls would work well in greeny-greys and muted blues—which would provide a perfect backdrop for these fabrics and textiles and reflect your love of the sea.'

'Did Niccolò tell you that I love the sea?' questioned Alekto idly.

'No. I searched your name on the Internet and had a look at your various homes around the world. You do seem rather fond of sea views and that gave me a few ideas.'

'Enterprising,' Alekto commented, flicking through each page, before lifting his head. 'Neh. This is perfect. All of it. You have chosen well, Niccolò. This is a huge improvement. You have pleased me, Alannah—and a woman who pleases a man should always be rewarded. I think I shall take you out for dinner tonight, to thank you.'

'I'm sure Alannah would love nothing more,' interjected Niccolò smoothly, 'but, unfortunately, she is already committed this evening.'

'Really?' Alekto raised dark and imperious brows. 'I'm sure she could cancel whatever it is she is *committed* to.'

'Possibly.' Niccolò shrugged. 'But only if you are prepared to wait for your apartment to be completed, my friend. Time is of the essence if you expect it to be ready for your new year party. Isn't that what you wanted?'

The gazes of the two men clashed and Alekto's eyes suddenly hardened with comprehension.

'Ah,' he said softly as he rose to his feet. 'Suddenly, I begin to understand. You have always been a great connoisseur of beauty, Niccolò. And since good friends do not poach, I shall leave you in peace.' His blue eyes glittered. 'Enjoy.'

Alekto's chauvinistic innuendo took Alannah by surprise but she reminded herself that she was simply working for him—she wasn't planning on having him as her friend. Keeping her lips clamped into a tight smile, she stood up to let him shake her hand, before Niccolò led him into the outer office.

She waited until the Sicilian had returned and closed the door behind him before she turned on him.

'What was that all about?' she questioned quietly.

'What?' He walked over to his desk, stabbing at a button on his telephone pad, so that a red light appeared. 'The fact that your designs pleased him? Alekto is one of the wealthiest men I know. You should be delighted. The patronage of a man like that is more priceless than rubies.' He looked at her, his eyes curiously flat and assessing. 'Who knows what kind of opportunities could now come your way, Alannah. Especially since he clearly finds you so attractive.'

'No, none of that!' She shook her head—hating the way he was looking at her. Hating the way he was talking about her. 'I don't care that he's rich—other than it means I will have a very generous budget to work with. And I don't care whether or not he finds me attractive. I'd like it if for once we could keep my looks out of it, since I'm supposed to be here on merit.' She stared at him. 'What I'm talking about is you telling him I was busy and couldn't have dinner with him tonight.'

'Did you want to have dinner with him?'

'That's beside the point.'

He slanted her a look. 'I'm not sure what your point is.'

'That I don't want you or anyone else answering for me because I like to make my own decisions. And...' she hesitated '...you have no right to be territorial about me.'

'No,' he said slowly. 'I realise that.'

She narrowed her eyes warily. 'You mean you're agreeing with me?'

He shrugged. 'For a man to behave in a territorial way towards a woman implies that she is his. That she has given herself to him in some way. And you haven't, have you, Alannah?' The eyes which a moment ago had looked so flat now gleamed like polished jet. 'Of course, that is something which could be changed in a heartbeat. We both know that.'

Alannah stiffened as his gaze travelled over her and she could feel her throat growing dry. And wasn't it crazy that, no matter how much her mind protested, she couldn't seem to stop her body from responding to his lazy scrutiny. She found herself thinking how easy it would be to go along with his suggestion. To surrender to the ache deep inside her and have him take all her frustration away. All she had to do was smile—a quick, complicit smile—and that would be the only green light he needed.

And then what?

She swallowed. A mindless coupling with someone who'd made no secret of his contempt for her? An act which would inevitably leave him triumphant and her, what? *Empty*, that was what.

A lifetime of turning down sexual invitations meant that she knew exactly how to produce the kind of brisk smile which would destabilise the situation without causing a scene. But for once, it took a real effort.

'I think not,' she said, scooping up her pashmina from the sofa. 'I have a self-protective instinct which warns me off intimacy with a certain kind of man, and I'm afraid you're one of them. The things I require from you are purely practical, Niccolò. I need a list of craftsmen—painters and decorators—who you use on your properties and who I assume will be available to work for me—and to work very quickly if we're to get this job in on time.'

The impatient wave of his hand told her that painters and decorators were of no interest to him. 'Speak to Kirsty about it.'

'I will.' She hitched the strap of her bag further over her shoulder. 'And if that's everything—I'll get going.'

He nodded. 'I'll drive you home.'

'That won't be necessary.'

'You have your own car?'

Was he kidding? Didn't he realise that car parking costs in London put motoring way beyond the reach of mere mortals? Alannah shook her head. 'I always use public transport.'

'Then I will take you. I insist.' His eyes met hers

with cool challenge. 'Unless you'd prefer to travel by train on a freezing December night, rather than in the warm comfort of my car?'

'You're boxing me into a corner, Niccolò.'

'I know I am. But you'll find it's a very comfortable box.' He took his car keys from his jacket pocket. 'Come.'

In the elevator, she kept her distance. Just as she kept her gaze trained on the flashing arrow as it took them down to the underground car park, where his car was waiting.

He punched her postcode into his satnav and didn't say another word as they drove along the busy streets of Knightsbridge, where Christmas shoppers were crowding the frosty pavements. Alannah peered out of the window. Everywhere was bright with coloured lights and gifts and people looking at the seasonal displays in Harrods's windows.

The car turned into Trafalgar Square and the famous Christmas tree loomed into view and suddenly Alannah felt the painful twist of her heart. It was funny how grief hit you when you least expected it—in a fierce wave which made your eyes grow all wet and salty. She remembered coming here with her mother, when they were waiting for the result of her biopsy. When standing looking up at a giant tree on an icy winter night had seemed like the perfect city outing. There'd been hardly any money in their purses, but they'd still had hope. Until a half-hour session with a man in a white coat had quashed that hope and they'd never been able to get it back again.

She blinked away the tears as the car began to speed towards West London, hoping that Niccolò's concentration on the traffic meant he hadn't noticed. He reached out to put some music on—something Italian and passionate, which filled the air and made her heart clench again, but this time with a mixture of pleasure and pain.

Closing her eyes, she let the powerful notes wash over her and when she opened them again the landscape had altered dramatically. The houses in this part of the city were much closer together and as Niccolò turned off the main road a few stray traces of garbage fluttered like ghosts along the pavement.

'Is this where you live?' he questioned.

She heard the faint incredulity in his voice and realised that this was exactly why she hadn't wanted this lift. *Because he will judge you. He will judge you and find you wanting, just as he's always done.* 'That's right,' she said.

He killed the engine and turned to look at her, his dark features brooding in the shadowed light.

'It's not what I expected.'

Her question was light, almost coquettish. She wondered if he could tell she'd been practising saying it in her head. 'And what *did* you expect?'

For a moment Niccolò didn't answer, because once again she had confounded his expectations. He had imagined a pricey location—a fortified mansion flat bought on the proceeds of the money she'd earned from *Stacked* magazine. Or a cute little mews cottage in Holland Park. Somewhere brimming with the kind of wealthy men who might enjoy dabbling with a woman as beautiful as her.

But *this*…

The unmistakable signs of poverty were all around

them. The rubbish on the pavement. A battered car with its wing-mirror missing. The shadowy group of youths in their hoodies, who stood watching their car with silent menace.

'What happened to all your money?' he questioned suddenly. 'You must have earned—'

'Stacks?' she questioned pointedly.

His smile was brief as he acknowledged the pun. 'A lot.'

She stared down at her handbag. 'It was a short-lived career—it didn't exactly provide me with a gold-plated pension.'

'So what did you do with it?'

I paid for my mother's medical bills. I chased a miracle which was never going to happen. I chased it until the pot was almost empty though the outcome hadn't changed one bit. She shrugged, tempted to tell him that it was none of his business—but she sensed that here was a man who wouldn't give up. Who would dig away until he had extracted everything he needed to know. She tried to keep her words light and flippant, but suddenly it wasn't easy. 'Oh, I frittered it all away. As you do.'

Niccolò looked at the unexpected tremble of her lips and frowned, because that sudden streak of vulnerability she was trying so hard to disguise was completely unexpected. Was she regretting the money she had squandered? Did she lay awake at night and wonder how the hell she had ended up in a place like this? He tried and failed to imagine how she fitted in here. Despite all her attempts to subdue her innate sensuality and tame her voluptuous appearance, she must still stand out like a lily tossed carelessly into a muddy gutter.

And suddenly he wanted to kiss her. The streetlight was casting an unworldly orange light over her creamy skin, so that she looked like a ripe peach just begging to be eaten. He felt temptation swelling up inside him, like a slow and insistent storm. Almost without thinking, he found himself reaching out to touch her cheek, wondering if it felt as velvety-soft as it appeared. And it did. Oh, God, it did. A whisper of longing licked over his skin.

'What…what do you think you're doing?' she whispered.

'You know damned well what I'm doing,' he said unsteadily. 'I'm giving into something which has always been there and which is refusing to die. Something which gets stronger each time we see each another. So why don't we just give into it, Alannah— and see where it takes us?'

She knew it was coming. Of course she did. She'd been kissed by enough men to recognise the sudden roughening of his voice and opaque smoulder of his black eyes. But no man had ever kissed her the way Niccolò did.

Time slowed as he bent his face towards hers and she realised he was giving her enough time to stop him. But she didn't. How could she when she wanted this so much? She just let him anchor her with the masterful slide of his hands as they captured the back of her head, before he crushed his lips down on hers.

Instantly, she moaned. It was ten long years since he'd kissed her and already she was on fire. She felt *consumed* by it. Powered by it. Need washed over her as she splayed her palms against his chest as his tongue licked its way into her mouth—her lips opened greedily, as if urging him to go deeper. She heard his responding murmur, as if her eagerness pleased him, and something made her bunch her hands into fists and drum them against his torso—resenting and wanting him all at the same time.

He raised his head, dark eyes burning into her like fire. But there were no subtle nuances to his voice now—just a mocking question in an accent which suddenly sounded harsh and *very* Sicilian. 'Are you trying to hurt me, *bella*?'

'I—yes! *Yes!*' She wanted to hurt him first—before he had the chance to do it to her.

He gave a soft laugh—as if recognising his own power and exulting in it. 'But I am not going to let you,' he said softly. 'We are going to give each other pleasure, not pain.'

Alannah's head tipped back as he reached down to cup her breast through the heavy silk of her dress. And she let him. Actually, she did more than let him. Her breathless sighs encouraged him to go even further, and he did.

He kissed her neck as his hand crept down to alight on one stockinged knee. And wasn't it shameful that she had parted her knees—praying he would move his hand higher to where the ache was growing unbearable? But he didn't—at least, not at first. For a while he seemed content to tease her. To bring her to such a pitch of excitement that she squirmed with impatience—wriggling restlessly until at last he moved his hand to skate it lightly over her thigh. She heard him suck in a breath of approval as he encountered the bare skin above her stocking top and she shivered as she felt his fingers curl possessively over the goose-pimpled flesh.

'I am pleased to see that despite the rather staid outfits you seem to favour, you still dress to tantalise underneath,' he said. 'And I need to undress you very quickly, before I go out of my mind with longing. I need to see that beautiful body for myself.'

His words killed it. Just like that. They shattered the spell he'd woven and wiped out all the desire—replacing it with a dawning horror of what she'd almost allowed to happen.

Allowed?

Who was she kidding? She might as well have presented herself to him in glittery paper all tied up with a gift ribbon. He'd given her a lift home and just assumed...*assumed*...

He'd assumed he could start treating her like a pin-up instead of a person. Somewhere along the way she had stopped being Alannah and had become a body he simply wanted to ogle. Why had she thought he was different from every other man?

'What am I doing?' she demanded, jerking away from him and lifting her fingertips to her lips in horror. 'What am I *thinking* of?'

'Oh, come on, Alannah.' He began to tap his finger impatiently against the steering wheel. 'We're both a little too *seasoned* to play this kind of game, surely? You might *just* have got away with the outraged virgin scenario a decade ago, but not any more. I'm pretty sure your track record must be almost as extensive as mine. So why the sudden shutdown at exactly the wrong moment, when we both know we want it?'

It took everything she had for Alannah not to fly at
him until she remembered that, in spite of everything,
he was still her boss. She realised she couldn't keep
blaming him for leaping to such unflattering conclusions, because why *wouldn't* he think she'd been
around the block several times? Nice girls didn't take
off their clothes for the camera, did they? And nice
girls didn't part their legs for a man who didn't respect them.

'You might have a reputation as one of the world's
greatest lovers, Niccolò,' she said, 'but right now, it's
difficult to see why.'

She saw his brows knit together as he glowered at
her. 'What are you talking about?'

Grabbing the handle, she pushed open the car door
and a blast of cold air came rushing inside, mercifully
cooling her heated face. 'Making out in the front of
cars is what teenagers do,' she bit out. 'I thought you
had a little bit more finesse than that. Most men at
least offer dinner.'

CHAPTER FIVE

EVERY TIME NICCOLÒ closed his eyes he could imagine those lips lingering on a certain part of his anatomy. He could picture it with a clarity which was like a prolonged and exquisite torture. He gave a groan of frustration and slammed his fist into the pillow. Was Alannah Collins aware that she was driving him crazy with need?

Turning onto his back, he stared up at the ceiling. Of course she was. Her *profession*—if you could call it that—had been pandering to male fantasy. She must have learnt that men were turned on by stockings—and socks. By tousled hair and little-girl pouts. By big blue eyes and beautiful breasts.

Had she subsequently learnt as she'd grown older that teasing and concealment could be almost as much of a turn-on? That to a man used to having everything he wanted, even the *idea* of a woman refusing sex was enough to make his body burn with a hunger which was pretty close to unbearable. Did she often let men caress the bare and silky skin of her thigh and then push them away just when they were in tantalising reach of far more intimate contact?

Frustratedly running his fingers through his hair, he got out of bed and headed for the bathroom.

If she hadn't been such a damned hypocrite when she'd slammed her way out of his car last night, then he wouldn't be feeling this way. If she'd been honest enough to admit what she really wanted, he wouldn't have woken up feeling aching and empty. She could have invited him in and turned those denim-blue eyes on him and let nature take its course. They could have spent the night together and he would have got her out of his system, once and for all.

He turned on the shower, welcoming the icy water which lashed over his heated skin.

True, her home hadn't looked particularly *inviting*. It didn't look big enough to accommodate much more than a single bed, let alone any degree of comfort. But that was okay. His mouth hardened. Mightn't the sheer *ordinariness* of the environment have added a piquant layer of excitement to a situation he resented himself for wanting?

Agitatedly, he rubbed shampoo into his hair, thinking that she made him want to break every rule in the book and he didn't like it. The women he dated were chosen as carefully as his suits and he didn't do *bad girls*. His taste tended towards corporate bankers. Or lawyers. He liked them blonde and he liked them cool. He liked the kind of woman who never sweated…

Not like Alannah Collins. He swallowed as the water sluiced down over his heated skin. He could imagine *her* sweating. He closed his eyes and imagined her riding him—her long black hair damp with exertion as it swung around her luscious breasts. He turned off the shower, trying to convince himself that the experience would be fleeting and shallow. It would be like eating fast food after you'd been on a health kick. The first greasy mouthful would taste like heaven but by the time you'd eaten the last crumb, you'd be longing for something pure and simple.

So why not forget her?

He got ready for the office and spent the rest of the week trying to do just that. He didn't go near Alekto's apartment, just listened to daily progress reports from Kirsty. He kept himself busy, successfully bidding for a new-build a few blocks from the Pembroke in New York. He held a series of back-to-back meetings about his beach development in Uruguay; he lunched with a group of developers who were over from the Middle East—then took them to a nightclub until the early hours. Then he flew to Paris and had dinner with a beautiful Australian model he'd met at last year's Melbourne Cup.

But Paris didn't work and neither did the model. For once the magic of the city failed to cast its spell on him. Overnight it had surrendered to the monster which was Christmas and spread its glittering tentacles everywhere. The golden lights which were strung in the trees along the Champs Élysées seemed garish. The decorated tree in his hotel seemed like a giant monument to bad taste and the pile of faux-presents which rested at its base made his mouth harden with disdain. Even the famous shops were stuffed with seasonal reminders of reindeer and Santa, which marred their usual elegance.

And all this was underpinned by the disturbing fact that nothing was working; he couldn't seem to get Alannah out of his mind. *Even now.* He realised that something about her was making him act out of character. There were plenty of other people whose style he liked, yet he had hired her without reference and only the most cursory of glances at her work. Governed by a need to possess her, he had ignored all reason and common sense and done something he'd sworn never to do.

He had taken a gamble on her.

He felt the icy finger of fear whispering over his spine.

He had taken a gamble on her and he never gambled.

He ordered his driver to take him to the towering block which rose up over Hyde Park. But for once he didn't take pride in the futuristic building which had been his brainchild, and which had won all kinds of awards since its inception. All he could think about was the slow build of hunger which was burning away inside him and which was now refusing to be silenced.

His heart was thudding as he took the elevator up to the penthouse, his key-card quietly clicking the door open. Silently, he walked through the bare apartment, which smelt strongly of paint, and into the main reception room where he found Alannah perched on a stepladder, a tape measure in her hand.

His heart skipped a beat. She wore a loose, checked shirt and her hair was caught back in a ponytail. He didn't know what he'd been planning to say but before he had a chance to say anything she turned round and saw him. The stepladder swayed and he walked across the room to steady it and some insane part of him wished it would topple properly, so that he could catch her in his arms and feel the soft crush of her breasts against him.

'N-Niccolò,' she said, her fingers curling around one of the ladder's rungs.

'Me,' he agreed.

She licked her lips. 'I wasn't expecting you.'

'Should I have rung to make an appointment?'

'Of...of course not,' she said stiffly. 'What can I do for you?'

His eyes narrowed. She was acting as if they were strangers—like two people who'd met briefly at a party. Had she forgotten the last time he'd seen her, when their mouths had been hot and hungry and they'd been itching to get inside each other's clothes? Judging from the look on her face, it might as well have been a figment of his imagination. He forced himself to look around the room—as if he were remotely interested in what she was doing with it. 'I thought I'd better see how work is progressing.'

'Yes, of course.' She began to clamber down the ladder, stuffing the tape measure into the pocket of her jeans. 'I know it doesn't look like very much at the moment, but it will all come together when everything's in place. That...' Her finger was shaking a little as she pointed. 'That charcoal shade is a perfect backdrop for some of the paintings which Alekto is having shipped over from Greece.'

'Good. What else?' He began to walk through the apartment and she followed him, her canvas shoes squeaking a little on the polished wooden floors.

'Here, in the study, I've used Aegean Almond as a colour base,' she said. 'I thought it was kind of appropriate.'

'Aegean Almond?' he echoed. 'What kind of luna-
tic comes up with a name like that?'

'You'd better not go into the bathroom, then,' she
warned, her lips twitching. 'Because you'll find Cigarette Smoke everywhere.'

'There's really a paint called Cigarette Smoke?'

'I'm afraid there is.'

He started to laugh and Alannah found herself
joining in, before hurriedly clamping her mouth shut.
Because humour was dangerous and just because he'd
been amused by something she'd said it didn't mean
he'd suddenly undergone a personality transplant.
He had an *agenda*. A selfish agenda, which didn't
take any of *her* wishes into account and that was because he was a selfish man. Niccolò got what Niccolò
wanted and it was vital she didn't allow herself to be
added to his long list of acquisitions.

She realised he was still looking at her.

'So everything's running according to schedule?'
he said.

She nodded. 'I've ordered velvet sofas and sourced
lamps and smaller pieces of furniture.'

'Good.'

Was that enough? she wondered. How much detail
did he need to know to be convinced she was doing a
good job? Because no matter what he thought about
her past, he needed to know she wasn't going to let
him down. She cleared her throat. 'And I've picked
up some gorgeous stuff on the King's Road.'

'You've obviously got everything under control.'

'I hope so. That is what you're paying me for.'

Niccolò walked over to the window and stared out
at the uninterrupted view of Hyde Park. The wintry

trees were bare and the pewter sky seemed heavy with the threat of snow. It seemed as if his hunch about her ability had been right. It seemed she was talented, as well as beautiful.

And suddenly he realised he couldn't keep taking his anger out on her. Who *cared* what kind of life she'd led? Who cared about anything except possessing her? Composing his face into the kind of expression which was usually guaranteed to get him exactly what he wanted, Niccolò smiled.

'It looks perfect,' he said. 'You must let me buy you dinner.'

She shook her head. 'Honestly, you don't have to do that.'

'No?' He raised his eyebrows in mocking question. 'The other night you seemed to imply you felt short-changed because I'd made a pass at you without jumping through the necessary social hoops first.'

'That was different.'

'How?'

She lifted her hand to fiddle unnecessarily with her ponytail. 'I made the comment in response to a situation.'

'A situation which won't seem to go away.' His black eyes lanced into her. 'Unless something has changed and you're going to deny that you want me?'

She sighed. 'I don't think I'm a good enough actress to do that, Niccolò. But wanting you doesn't automatically mean that I'm going to do anything about it. You must have women wanting you every day of the week.'

'But we're not talking about other women. What if I just wanted the opportunity to redeem myself?

To show you that I am really just a…what is it you say?' He lifted his shoulders and his hands in an exaggerated gesture of incomprehension. 'Ah, yes. A regular guy.'

'Of course you are.' She laughed, in spite of herself. 'Describing you as a regular guy would be like calling a thirty-carat diamond a trinket.'

'Oh, come on, Alannah,' he urged softly. 'One dinner between a boss and his employee. What's the harm in that?'

Alannah could think of at least ten answers, but the trouble was that when he asked her like that, with those black eyes blazing into her, all her reservations slipped right out of her mind. Which was how she found herself in the back of a big black limousine later that evening, heading for central London. She was sitting as far away from Niccolò as possible but even so—her palms were still clammy with nerves and her heart racing with excitement.

'So where are we going?' she questioned, looking at the burly set of the driver's shoulders through the tinted glass screen which divided them.

'The Vinoly,' Niccolò said. 'Do you know it?'

She shook her head. She'd heard about it, of course. Currently London's most fashionable venue, it was famous for being impossible to get a table though Niccolò was greeted with the kind of delight which suggested that he might be a regular.

The affluence of the place was undeniable. The women wore designer and diamonds while the men seemed to have at least three mobile phones lined up neatly beside their bread plates and their gazes kept straying to them.

Alannah told herself she wasn't going to be intimidated even though she still couldn't quite believe she'd agreed to come. As she'd got ready she had tried to convince herself that exposure to Niccolò's arrogance might be enough to kill her desire for him, once and for all.

But the reality was turning out to be nothing like she'd imagined. Why hadn't she taken into account his charisma—or at least prepared herself for a great onslaught of it? Because suddenly there seemed nothing in her armoury to help her withstand it.

She had never been with a man who commanded quite so much attention. She saw the pianist nodding to him, with a smile. She saw other diners casting surreptitious glances at him, even though they were pretending not to. But it was more than his obvious wealth which drew people's gaze, like a magnet. Beneath the sophisticated exterior, he radiated a raw masculinity which radiated from his powerful body like a dark aura.

They sat down at a discreet table but suddenly the complex menu seemed too rich for a stomach which was sick with nerves. Alannah found herself wishing she were eating an omelette at her own kitchen table rather than subjecting herself to a maelstrom of emotions which were making her feel most peculiar.

'What are you going to have?' asked Niccolò as the waiter appeared.

The words on the menu had blurred into incomprehensible lines and she lifted her gaze to him. 'I don't know. You order for me,' she said recklessly.

He raised his eyebrows before giving their order but once the waiter had gone he turned to study her, his black eyes thoughtful. 'Are you usually quite so accommodating?'

'Not usually, no.' She smoothed her napkin. 'But then, this isn't what you'd call *usual*, is it?'

'In what way?'

'Well.' She shrugged. 'You made it sound like a working dinner, but it feels a bit like a date.'

'And what if we pretended it was a date—would that help you relax a little more?'

'To be honest, it's been so long since I've been on a date that I've almost forgotten what it's like,' she said slowly.

He took a sip of water which didn't quite disguise the sudden cynicism of his smile. 'I find that very difficult to believe.'

She laughed. 'I'm sure you do—given your apparent love of stereotypes. What's the matter, Niccolò—doesn't that fit in with your image of me? You think that because I once took off my clothes for the camera, that I have men queuing up outside the bedroom door?'

'Do you?'

'Not half as many as you, I bet,' she said drily.

They were staring at one another across the table, their eyes locked in silent battle, when suddenly he leaned towards her, his words so low that only she could hear them.

'Why did you do it, Alannah?' he questioned roughly. 'Wasn't it bad enough that you were kicked out of school for smoking dope and playing truant? Why the hell did you cheapen yourself by stripping off?'

The waiter chose precisely that moment to light the

small candle at the centre of the table. And that short gap provided Alannah with enough time for rebellion to flare into life inside her.

'Why do you think I did it?' she demanded. 'Why do people usually do jobs like that? Because I needed the money.'

'For what?' His lips curled. 'To end up in a poky apartment in one of the tougher ends of town?'

'Oh, you're so quick to judge, aren't you, Niccolò? So eager to take the moral high ground, when you don't have a clue what was going on in my life and you never did! Did you know that when my mother handed in her notice, she never found another job to match that one—probably because the reference the school gave her was so grudging. Did you know that they got all their clever lawyers to pick over her contract and that she lost all her rights?'

His eyes narrowed. 'What kind of rights?'

'There was no pension provision made for her and the salary she got in lieu of notice was soon swallowed up by the cost of settling back in England. She couldn't find another live-in job, so she became an agency nurse—with no fixed contract. I had to go to a local sixth-form college to take my exams and at first, I hated it. But we were just beginning to pick ourselves up again when...'

Her voice tailed off and his words broke into the silence.

'What happened?' he demanded.

She shook her head. 'It doesn't matter.'

'It *does*.'

Alannah hesitated, not wanting to appear vulnerable—because vulnerability made you weak. But wasn't anything better than having him look at her with that look of utter *condemnation* on his face? Shouldn't Niccolò da Conti learn that it was wise to discover all the facts before you condemned someone outright?

'She got cancer,' she said baldly. 'She'd actually had it for quite a long time but she'd been ignoring the symptoms so she didn't have to take any unnecessary time off work. By the time she went to see the doctor, the disease was advanced and she was scared,' she said, swallowing down the sudden lump in her throat. They'd both been scared. 'There was nobody but me and her. She was only a relatively young woman and she didn't want...' The lump seemed to have grown bigger. 'She didn't want to die.'

'Alannah—'

But she shook her head, because she didn't want his sympathy. She didn't *need* his sympathy.

'Our doctor told us about an experimental drug trial which was being done in the States,' she said. 'And early indications were that the treatment was looking hopeful, but it was prohibitively expensive and impossible to get funding for it.'

And suddenly Niccolò understood. Against the snowy tablecloth, he clenched his hands into tight fists. *'Bedda matri!'* he said raggedly. 'You did those photos to pay for your mother to go to America?'

'Bravo,' she said shakily. 'Now do you see? It gave me power—the power to help her. The thought of all that money was beyond my wildest dreams and there was no way I could have turned it down.' *No matter how many men had leered in her face afterwards. No matter that people like Niccolò judged her*

*and looked down their noses at her or thought that
she'd be up for easy sex because of it.* 'My unique
selling point was that I'd left one of the most exclusive Swiss finishing schools under rather ignomini-
ous circumstances and I guess I can't blame them
for wanting to capitalise on that. They told me that
plenty of men were turned on by girls in school uniform, and they were right. That's why that issue became their best-seller.'

Alarmed by the sudden whiteness of her face, he
pushed the wine glass towards her, but she shook her
head.

'It wasn't narcissism which motivated me, Niccolò—or a desire to flash my breasts like the exhibitionist you accused me of being. I did it because it's
the only way I could raise the money. I did it even
though I sometimes felt sick to the stomach with all
those men perving over me. But I hid my feelings
because I wanted to bring a miracle to my mother,
only the miracle never happened.' Her voice wavered
and it took a moment or two before she could steady
it enough to speak. 'She died the following spring.'

She did pick up her glass then, swilling down a
generous mouthful of red wine and choking a little.
But when she put the glass back down, she had to
lace her fingers together on the table-top, because she
couldn't seem to stop them from trembling.

'Alannah—'

'It's history,' she said, with a brisk shake of her
head. 'None of it matters now. I'm just telling you
what happened. I used the rest of the money to put
myself through art school and to put down a deposit
on a home. But property is expensive in London.

That's why I live where I do. That's why I chose to live in one of the "tougher" parts of London.'

Niccolò put his glass down with a hand which was uncharacteristically unsteady as a powerful wave of remorse washed over him. It was as if he was seeing her clearly for the first time—without the distortion of his own bigotry. He had judged her unfairly. He saw how she must have fought against the odds to free herself from a trap from which there had been no escaping. He'd fought against the odds himself, hadn't he? Though he realised now that his own choices had been far less stark than hers. And although he hated the solution she had chosen, he couldn't seem to stop himself from wanting to comfort her.

'I'm sorry,' he said huskily. 'For what happened and for the choices you had to make.'

She shrugged. 'Like I said, it's history.'

'Your mother was lucky to have a daughter like you, fighting for her like that,' he said suddenly. He found himself thinking that anyone would be glad to have her in their corner.

Her head was bent. 'Don't say any more,' she whispered. 'Please.'

He stared down at the plateful of cooling risotto which lay before him. 'Alannah?'

'What?'

Reluctantly, she lifted her head and he could see that her eyes were unnaturally bright. He thought how pale and wan she looked as he picked up his fork and scooped up some rice before guiding it towards her mouth. 'Open,' he instructed softly.

She shook her head. 'I'm not hungry.'

'Open,' he said again.

'Niccolò—'

'You need to eat something,' he said fiercely. 'Trust me. The food will make you feel better. Now eat the risotto.'

And although Alannah was reluctant, she was no match for his determination. She let him feed her that first forkful—all warm and buttery and fragrant with herbs—and then another. She felt some of the tension seep away from her, and then a little more. She ate in silence with his black eyes fixed on her and it felt like a curiously intimate thing for him to do, to feed her like that. Almost *tender*. Almost *protective*. And she needed to remember it was neither. It was just Niccolò appeasing his conscience. Maybe he'd finally realised that he'd been unnecessarily harsh towards her. This was probably just as much about repairing his image, as much as trying to brush over his own misjudgement.

And he was right about the food. Of course he was. It *did* make her feel much better. She could feel warmth creeping through her veins and the comforting flush of colour in her cheeks. She even smiled as he swopped plates and ate some himself while she sat back and watched him.

He dabbed at his lips with a napkin. 'Feel better now?'

'Yes.'

'But probably not in the mood to sit here and make small talk or to decide whether or not your waistline can cope with dessert?'

'You've got it in one,' she said.

'Then why don't I get the check, and we'll go?'

She'd assumed he would take her straight back to

Acton but once they were back in the car he made the driver wait. Outside, fairy lights twinkled in the two bay trees on either side of the restaurant door, but inside the car it was dark and shadowy. He turned to study her and all she could see was the gleam of his eyes as his gaze flickered over her face.

'I could take you home now,' he said. 'But I don't want the evening to end this way. It still feels...unfinished.'

'I'm not in the mood for a nightcap.'

'Neither am I.' He lifted his hand to her face and pushed back a thick strand of hair. 'I'm in the mood to touch you, but that seems unavoidable whenever you're near me.'

'Niccolò—'

'Don't,' he said unsteadily. 'Don't say a word.'

And stupidly, she didn't. She just sat there as he began to stroke her cheek and for some crazy reason she found that almost as reassuring as the way he'd fed her dinner. Was she so hungry for human comfort that she would take anything from a man she suspected could offer nothing but heartbreak?

'Niccolò—'

This time he silenced her protest with the touch of his lips against hers. A barely-there kiss which started her senses quivering. She realised that he was teasing her. Playing with her and tantalising her. And it was working. Oh, yes, it was working. She had to fight to keep her hands in her lap and not cling onto him like someone who'd found themselves a handy rock in a rough sea.

He drew away and looked into her face and Alannah realised that this was a Niccolò she'd never seen before. His face was grave, almost…assessing. She imagined this was how he might look in the board-room, before making a big decision.

'Now we could pretend that nothing's happening,' he said, as calmly as if he were discussing the mar-kets. 'Or we could decide to be very grown-up about this thing between us—'

'Thing?' she put in indignantly, but his fingers were still on her face and she was shivering. And now the pad of his thumb had begun to trace a line across her lower lip and that was shivering, too.

'Desire. Lust. Whatever you want to call it. Maybe I just want to lay to rest a ghost which has haunted me for ten long years, and maybe you do, too.'

It was his candour which clinched it—the bald truth which was her undoing. He wasn't dressing up his suggestion with sentimental words which didn't mean anything. He wasn't insulting her intelligence by pretending she was the love of his life or that there was some kind of future in what he was proposing. He was saying something which had been on her mind since Michela's wedding. Because he was right. This *thing* between them wouldn't seem to go away. No matter how much she tried, she couldn't stop want-ing him.

She wondered if he could read the answer in her eyes. Was that why he leaned forward to tap briefly on the glass which separated them from the driver, before taking her in his arms and starting to kiss her?

And once he had done that, she was left with no choice at all.

CHAPTER SIX

HE DIDN'T OFFER her a coffee, nor a drink. He didn't even put the lamps on. Alannah didn't know whether Niccolò had intended a slow seduction—but it didn't look as if she was going to get one. Because from the moment the front door of his Mayfair apartment slammed shut on them, he started acting like a man who had lost control.

His hands were in her hair, he was tugging her coat from her shoulders so that it slid unnoticed to the ground and his mouth was pressing down on hers. It was breathless. It was hot. It was...*hungry.* Alannah gasped as he caught her in his arms. He was burying his mouth in her hair and muttering urgent little words in Sicilian and, although her Italian was good, she didn't understand any of them. But she didn't need to. You wouldn't have to be a linguist to understand what Niccolò was saying to her. The raw, primitive sounds of need were international, weren't they?

He placed his hands on either side of her hips and drew her closer, so that she could feel the hard cradle of him pressing against her. He kissed her again and as the kiss became deeper and more urgent she felt him moving her, until suddenly she felt the hard

surface of the wall pressed against her back and her
eyelids flew open.

He drew back, his eyes blazing. 'I want you,' he
said. 'I want to eat you. To suck you. To bite you. To
lick you.'

She found his blatantly erotic words more than a
little intimidating and momentarily she stiffened—
wondering if she should confess that she wasn't very
good at this. But now his palms were skating over her
dress to mould the outline of her hips and the words
simply wouldn't come. She felt his hand moving over
her belly. She heard him suck in a ragged breath of
pleasure as he began to ruck up her dress.

'Niccolò,' she said uncertainly.

'I want you,' he ground out. 'For ten years I have
longed for this moment and now that it is here, I don't
think I can wait a second longer.'

Niccolò closed his eyes as he reached her panties
and impatiently pushed the flimsy little panel aside,
because she was wet. She was very wet. He could
detect the musky aroma of her sex as he slid his fingers against her heated flesh and began to move them
against her with practised ease.

'Niccolò,' she whispered again.

'I want to see your breasts,' he said, moving his
shaking fingers to the lapels of her silky dress and
beginning to unbutton it. Within seconds two luscious
mounds were revealed—their creamy flesh spilling
over the edge of her bra. He narrowed his eyes to
look at them. *'Madre di Dio,'* he breathed, his fingertips brushing over the soft skin. 'In the flesh it is
even better. You have the most beautiful body I have
ever seen.'

And suddenly he knew he really couldn't wait a second longer. Besides, she seemed more than ready for him. He felt as if something had taken hold of him and made him into someone he didn't recognise. As if this wasn't him at all but an imposter who'd entered his body. Unsteadily, he unzipped himself and he wanted to explode even before he positioned himself against her honeyed warmth.

She went very still as he entered her and for a moment he paused, afraid that he might come straight away—and when had *that* ever happened? But somehow he managed to keep it together, drawing in a deep breath and expelling it on another shuddering sigh as he began to move.

One hand was spread over her bare bottom as he hooked her legs around his hips and drove into her as if there were no tomorrow. As if there had been no yesterday. Her nails were digging into his neck as he kissed her, but he barely noticed the discomfort. He tried to hold back—to wait for her orgasm before letting go himself—but suddenly it was impossible and he knew he was going to come.

'Alannah!' he said, on a note of disbelief—and suddenly it was too late.

Wave after wave took him under. His frame was racked with spasms as he gasped out her name, caught up in a feeling so intense that he thought he might die from it. It felt like the first orgasm he'd ever had. He closed his eyes. The only orgasm he'd ever had. And it wasn't until his body had grown completely still that he noticed how silent and how still she was.

He froze.

Of course she was.

Remorse filled him as she put her hand against his chest and pushed him away. And although withdrawing from her succulent heat was the last thing he felt like doing he could see from the tight expression on her face that she wanted him to. And who could blame her?

There had been no answering cry of fulfilment from her, had there? He had given her no real *pleasure.*

With a grimace, he eased himself from her sticky warmth, bending to pull up his trousers before carefully zipping them up. 'Alannah?'

She didn't answer straight away—she was too busy fastening her dress, her fingers fumbling to slide the buttons back in place. He went to help her, but her voice was sharp.

'Don't.'

He waited until she'd finished buttoning and whatever little insect brooch she was wearing was surveying him with baleful eyes, before he lifted her chin with his finger, so that their eyes were locked on a collision course. 'I'm sorry,' he said.

She shook her head. 'It doesn't matter.'

'It does.' He heard the flatness in her voice. 'I'm not usually so...out of control.'

She gave a wry smile. 'Don't worry, Niccolò. I won't tell anyone. Your reputation is safe with me.'

His mouth hardened and his body tensed. It was her cool response which made something inside him flare into life—a feeling of anger as much as desire. A feeling set off by wounded male pride and an urgent need to put things right. This had never happened to him before. He was usually the master of control. He had always prided himself on his lovemaking skills; his ability to give women physical pleasure—even if he could never satisfy them emotionally.

A shudder of comprehension made his blood run cold.

Did he really want her to walk away thinking of him as a selfish lover? As a man who took, but gave nothing back? Was that how he wanted her to remember him?

'Let's hope you don't have to,' he said, his voice full of sudden resolution as he bent down to slide his arm behind her knees and then lifted her up.

'What...what the hell do you think you're doing?' she spluttered as he began to carry her along the wide corridor.

'I'm taking you to bed.'

'Put me down! I don't want to go to bed. I want to go home.'

'I don't think so,' he said, kicking open his bedroom door and walking over to the vast bed, before setting her down in the centre of the mattress. His knees straddling her hips, he began to unbutton her dress, but she slapped his hand away and he realised that his normal methods of seduction weren't going to work with her. Come to think of it, nothing felt remotely normal with her—and right now, this felt a million miles away from seduction.

He smoothed the tousled hair away from her face, staring down into the reproachful belligerence of her blue eyes, before slowly lowering his head to kiss her.

It wasn't a kiss, so much as a duel.

For a few seconds she held back, as if he were kissing some cold, marble statue. She lay there like a human sacrifice. He could sense her anger and frustration, so he forced himself to take it slowly—so slowly that it nearly killed him. He explored her lips with a thoroughness which was new to him—until he felt he knew them almost better than his own. And as she gradually opened them up to him—when she had relaxed enough to let his tongue slide inside her mouth—it felt like one of the most intimate acts he'd ever taken part in.

Her hands reached for his shoulders and he took the opportunity to press his body close to hers, but the shudder of delight as their bodies crushed against each other was entirely new to him. And still he took it slowly—still feasting on her lips until he was certain that her own desire was strong enough to make her wriggle against him with a wordless message of frustration.

He didn't speak. He didn't dare. Something told him that she didn't want him to undress her and he suspected that doing so would shatter a mood which was already dangerously fragile. His hands were trembling as they slid beneath her dress to reacquaint themselves with the hot, moist flesh beneath her panties. He heard her give a little moan—a sound of pleasure and submission—and his heart hammered as he unzipped himself and tugged her panties down over her knees.

He was only vaguely aware of the awkward rumpling of their unfastened clothing, because by then he was caught up with a hunger so powerful that he groaned helplessly as he slid inside her for a second time. It felt… For a moment he didn't move. It felt out of this world. He looked down to see an unmistakable flare of wonder in her eyes as he filled her, but just as quickly her dark lashes fluttered down to veil them. As if she was reluctantly granting him access to her body—but not to her thoughts.

He moved slowly. He kept her on the edge for a long time—until she was relaxed enough to let go. She wrapped her legs and her arms around him and held him close and Niccolò thought he'd never been quite so careful before. He'd learnt a lot about women's bodies during a long and comprehensive sexual education, but with Alannah it became about much more than technique.

Her body began to change. He could feel the tension building until it was stretched so tightly that it could only shatter—and when it did, she made a series of gasping little sighs, before she started to convulse helplessly around him. He was dimly aware of the groan he gave before he too let go, his every spasm matching hers, and he could feel her heart beating very fast against his as his arms tightened around her.

He must have fallen asleep, because when he next became aware of his surroundings it was to feel her shifting out from under him. His fingers curled automatically around her waist. 'What are you doing?' he questioned sleepily, moving his head so that her lips were automatically redirected to his and his voice was indistinct as his tongue slid into her mouth. 'Mmm?'

She let him kiss her for a moment before putting distance between them. He felt her lips ungluing themselves from his as she moved away.

'It's late, Niccolò—and this is a school night.'

He knew what she was doing. She was giving him

the opportunity to end the evening now, without either of them losing face. He wondered if this was what she normally did—give into a hot and mindless lust without much forethought, before following it up with a cool smile as if nothing had happened?

Without much forethought.

The words struck him and imprinted themselves on his consciousness. Suddenly he went hot and then cold as he realised their implication and he stared at her with growing horror.

'You know what we've just done?' he questioned and there was a note in his voice he'd never heard before.

She tilted her chin, but he could see the way she had instinctively started to bite her lip. 'Of course. We've just had sex. Twice.'

His fingers dug into her forearms, his voice suddenly urgent. 'Are you on the pill?'

He saw the exact moment that it registered. That would be the moment when her blue eyes widened and her lips began to tremble.

'We…' she whispered. 'We've…'

'Yes,' he completed grimly. 'We've just had unprotected sex.'

She swallowed. 'Oh, God,' she breathed. 'What are we going to do?'

He didn't answer at once. It was pointless to concentrate on the anger and frustration which were building up inside him, because he could see that harsh words of recrimination would serve no useful purpose. His mouth hardened. He should have known better. How could he have failed to take contraception into account?

'I think that there is only one thing we can do,' he said. 'We wait.'

'I...guess so.'

He frowned as he noticed that her teeth had started to chatter. 'You're shivering. You need to get into bed.'

'I don't—'

'I'm not listening to any objections,' he said emphatically. 'I'm going to undress you and put you to bed and then I'm going to make you tea.'

She wriggled. 'Why don't you go and make the tea and I'll undress myself?'

He frowned, and there was a heartbeat of a pause. 'Alannah, are you *shy*?'

She attempted a light little laugh, which didn't quite come off. 'Me? Shy? Don't be ridiculous. How could I possibly be shy when I've exposed my body to the harsh glare of the camera?'

Placing his palms on either side of her face, he stared down into her wide blue eyes. 'But stripping for a camera is a very anonymous thing to do,' he said slowly. 'While stripping for a man is intensely personal.'

She pulled a face. 'Stick with the day job, Niccolò—I don't think analysis is really your thing.'

Niccolò frowned. No, it wasn't his thing at all. Normally he ran a million miles from trying to work out what was going on in a woman's head. But most women weren't perplexing enigmas, were they? They didn't answer one question and immediately make you want to ask them a hundred more.

'You're shy,' he repeated. 'Are you going to tell me why?'

Alannah stifled a sigh as she looked at him, because telling Niccolò anything was the last thing she wanted. His lovemaking had left her feeling soft and vulnerable enough to have her defences weakened. And she wasn't stupid. She might despise the men who persisted in thinking of her as nothing but a body—yet surely that was the main attraction for Niccolò, no matter how much he might try to deny it. Wouldn't he be disappointed to discover the mundane truth about her?

Because iconic glamour models were supposed to typify sexuality, not belong to a band of women who had always found sex rather overrated until now.

'Yes, I'm shy,' she admitted grudgingly. 'I don't really like men looking at my body. I'm hung up about it. I hate being thought of as nothing but a pair of gravity-defying breasts. That's probably why I'm not usually able to relax very much. Why my sex life has been...'

Her words tailed off as she became aware that she'd said too much and she braced herself as she waited for him to distance himself, like a man who thought he'd bought a racy sports-car—only to find that he'd landed himself with a second-hand model which kept breaking down.

'Why your sex life has been, what?' he prompted softly.

She pulled a face. 'You really want me to spell it out for you? Isn't your ego healthy enough already without the added boost of me telling you how good you are in bed?'

He took her hand and lifted it to his lips, unable to hide his slow, curving smile of satisfaction. 'Am I?'

'You know you are.' She pulled her hand away. 'I'm sure I'm not the first woman to tell you that.'

'No, but you're the first woman who is such a mass of contradictions that you have my head spinning. You have a wildness...'

'Niccolò—'

He silenced her with a long kiss and when he finally raised his head, it was to subject her to a look of narrow-eyed thoughtfulness. 'I think we've done the subject to death for tonight,' he said. 'You're tired and so am I, and you're right—it *is* a school night. Bedtime,' he added firmly.

'I'm not sure,' she said.

'Well, I am. Relax, *mia tentatrice.*'

He was unbuttoning her dress again and suddenly Alannah had no desire to stop him. She lay there as he slid the silky garment from her body until she was left in just her hold-ups and her bra and, automatically, her palms moved towards her breasts—to protect them from his seeking gaze. But to her surprise he wasn't even looking at her breasts. He was sliding down her hold-ups as impersonally as if he'd been undressing a child who had been caught in a storm. Even her bra was removed with nothing but deft efficiency, so that she was naked and snuggled beneath the warm duvet almost before she'd realised it.

She blinked as he captured her in that searing ebony gaze.

'Now...was that so traumatic?' he questioned silkily.

She shook her head. 'I wasn't expecting...' Her words tailed off.

'You thought I would be unable to resist drooling

as I ogled your breasts? That you find yourself surprised by my sensitivity?'

'Something like that,' she mumbled.

He smiled, the pad of his thumb trailing a path over her bottom lip and causing it to tremble. 'You and me both,' he said drily, before getting up to let himself quietly out of the room.

While he was gone, Alannah took the opportunity to look around what was one of the most impersonal bedrooms she'd ever seen. There were no photos on display. No real hints as to what kind of man Niccolò really was. She knew his parents were dead—but there was no misty-eyed memorial of their wedding day. She remembered Michela clamming up whenever anyone had asked her about her folks—and hadn't she been a bit like that herself if people wanted to know about *her* father? It had seemed too crass to tell them the truth. *Oh, my mother was fresh out of Ireland and she had her drink spiked...*

She hadn't found out the whole story until three days before her mother had died. That Bridget Collins had woken up in her dingy hostel room with a splitting headache and vague, shifting memories of what had happened the night before—as well as a terrible soreness between her legs. She'd never seen the man again and the shame of it was that she didn't even know his surname. Nine months later Alannah had been born and her mother's over-protectiveness had kicked in.

Alannah stared at the photograph opposite the bed—a smoky, atmospheric monochrome study of a brooding Mount Vesuvius. If she'd known all that stuff before...if she'd been able to make sense of why her mother had been so unbelievably strict with her—would it have changed anything?

Probably not. And even if it had—it was all irrelevant now. Because you could never go back. You could never wipe out the things you'd done. Everyone knew that.

She was almost asleep by the time Niccolò returned, carrying a tray of camomile tea. Her eyelashes fluttered open as he sat down and the bed sank beneath his weight.

'This will help you sleep,' he said.

She didn't think she needed any help, but she drank the flower-filled brew anyway and then settled back down against the bank of pillows while Niccolò gently stroked her hair.

She wriggled her bare toes and stretched out her body and at that precise moment she didn't think she'd ever felt quite so blissfully content. Until a dark memory flickered into her mind like an evil imp—reinforcing the disturbing thought that they hadn't remembered to use protection....

CHAPTER SEVEN

'ANYONE WOULD THINK,' said Niccolò slowly, 'that you were trying to avoid me.'

Alannah looked up to find herself caught in the spotlight of a pair of ebony eyes, which cut into her like dark twin lasers. Winter light was flooding into the main reception room of the still bare Sarantos apartment, emphasising its vast and elegant dimensions. She had been there all morning, sitting on the newly upholstered window seat and sewing tassels onto a cushion, but the sight of the Sicilian standing in the doorway made her suspend her needle in mid-air.

She tried to compose herself and to say the right thing. Just as she'd been trying to do the right thing, ever since she'd crazily decided to have sex with him. She needed to treat what had happened as a one-off, and keeping their relationship on a purely professional footing was the only sane solution.

For both of them.

She put the needle down and pushed her empty coffee mug along the floor with the tip of her sneaker. 'Of course I'm not trying to avoid you,' she said lightly. 'You're my boss—I wouldn't dare.'

'Is that so?' He walked towards her. 'So why wouldn't you have dinner with me last night?'

'I explained that,' she protested. 'I had to travel to Somerset to buy some paintings and the man who owned the shop was just about to close up for the holidays, so it was the only day I could go. And then on the way back, there were loads of leaves on the line so the train was delayed. Didn't you get my voicemail message?'

'Oh, yes, I got your voicemail message,' he said impatiently. He stood looking down at her, feeling perplexed and more than a little frustrated. This had never happened to him before. Usually he had to barricade his bedroom once a woman had been granted access to it—he couldn't remember a lover ever being so reluctant to return. His mouth tightened. 'But the fact remains that on Tuesday we had sex and I've barely seen you since.'

She shrugged. 'That's just the way it's worked out. You're employing me to get this apartment done in a hurry and that's what I'm trying to do. That's my primary role, isn't it? You're not paying me to keep appearing at your office door and haunting you.'

Niccolò felt his mouth dry. He wouldn't mind her appearing at his office door. She was making him think of a few very creative uses for his desk… He swallowed. 'Am I going to see you later?'

Alannah sucked in a breath, trying not to be flattered at his persistence, but it wasn't easy. Because she had been dreading this meeting. Dreading and yet longing for it, all at the same time. Ever since she'd slipped out of his Mayfair apartment on Tuesday she'd told herself that it would be safer to stay away from Niccolò and not pursue the affair any further. She liked him. She liked him way more than was sensible for what she was sure he'd only ever intended to be a casual hook-up. And she didn't do casual. Just as she didn't do the kind of affair which would end up with her getting her heart smashed into a hundred little pieces.

'You're my boss, Niccolò,' she said.

'I haven't lost sight of that fact, *mia tentatrice*. But what does that have to do with anything?'

'You know very well. It's…unprofessional.'

He gave a soft laugh. 'You don't think we might already have crossed that boundary when you lay gasping underneath me for most of the night?' He narrowed his eyes. 'And on top of me at one point, if my memory serves me well.'

'Stop it,' she whispered, feeling colour flooding into her cheeks. 'That's exactly what I'm talking about. It blurs the lines and confuses things. I'm trying to concentrate on my work and I can't when you—'

'Can't stop wanting a rerun?'

'A rerun is what you do with movies. And it's a bad idea.'

'Why?'

She sighed. 'What happened last week was…' Her words tailed off. How best to describe it? The most amazing sex she'd ever had? Well, yes. She had certainly never realised it could be so intense, or so powerful. But there had been another blissful side to that night which was far more worrying. She'd realised that she could get used to waking up with Niccolò lying asleep beside her, his arms wrapped tightly around her. Just as she could get used to thinking about him at odd moments of the day and wishing he were there to kiss her. And those kind of daydreams would get her nowhere.

Because where would that leave her when the whole thing imploded? She'd just be another heart-broken woman crying into her gin and tonic, trying to resist the urge to send him a 'casual' late-night text. She would run the risk of making herself vulnerable and she wasn't going to let that happen. She felt a new resolve steal over her. 'A mistake,' she said.

'A mistake,' he repeated.

'Maybe that's a bad way to put it. It was obviously very enjoyable.' She pushed the cushion away and forced herself to face the truth, no matter how un-palatable it was. 'But the fact remains that you don't really like me. You told me that.'

He smiled. 'I like you a lot more now.'

'You described what you felt for me as, and I quote—"a wildness". You made me sound like a mild version of the bubonic plague.'

'I don't think any plague feels quite like this—ex-cept maybe for the fever in my blood when I close my eyes at night and find it impossible to sleep because I can't get you out of my mind.' His eyes gleamed. 'And you look incredibly beautiful when you're being defiant. Do you do it because you know how much it turns me on?'

'It's not defiance for the sake of it,' she said. 'It's defiance for a reason. I'm not doing it to try to entice you.' She forced herself to say it. To put the words out there instead of having them nagging away in-side her. 'This relationship isn't going anywhere. We both know that.'

'So you're not pregnant?'

His words completely shattered her fragile façade and she stared at him, her heart pounding. During the day, when she was busy working, it was easy to push that thought to the back of her mind. It was at night-time when it became impossible. That was when the fear flooded through her body as she tried to imagine just how she would cope with having Niccolò da Conti's baby. That was when she had to fight to stop herself imagining a downy little black head, glugging away contentedly at her breast.

'I don't know,' she said. 'It's too early to do a test.'

'Which means we may be about to be parents to-gether, *si*? I think that constitutes some sort of rela-tionship, don't you?'

'Not the best kind,' she said.

'Maybe not. But I need to know that if you are pregnant—*if you are*—whether I am the only man in the frame who could be the father.' His black eyes burned into her, but he must have seen her flinch be-cause his voice softened by a fraction. 'Is that such an unreasonable request?'

She met his gaze, telling herself that in the cir-cumstances he had every right to ask. But that didn't make it hurt any less and some of that hurt came spilling out.

'Yes. You are the only man in the frame. Did you think that because of my previous line of work that there would be a whole load of contenders?' She shook her head in despair. 'You really are fond of stereotypes, aren't you, Niccolò? Well, for your infor-mation, there isn't. If you really must know, I could count my previous lovers on one hand and still have

some fingers free—and there's been no one in my life
for the last three years.'

Niccolò let out the breath he'd been holding, unprepared for the powerful hit of pleasure which flooded
through his body in response to her words. *He was
the only man in the frame. There had been no one
else in her life for the past three years.*

He stared at her, his eyes taking in the way she
was illuminated in the harsh winter light. Her thick
hair looked blue-black, like the feathers of a raven.
He swallowed. *Dai capelli corvini.*

In her jeans and loose shirt she shouldn't have
looked anything special, but somehow she looked unbelievably beautiful. Against her hair, her skin was
creamy and her pallor emphasised the dramatic blue
of her eyes. A little brooch in the shape of a dragonfly glittered on her lapel and suddenly he found himself envying the proximity of that worthless piece of
jewellery to her body.

What if there were a baby?

His mouth hardened.

He would cross that bridge when he came to it.

The shrill sound of the doorbell shattered the silence.

'That'll be one of the painters,' she said. 'He rang
up to say he'd left his keys behind.' Rising to her
feet, she walked over and picked up a shoal of silver
keys from where they lay on another window seat. 'I
won't be long.'

Alannah was aware of his eyes burning into her as
she left the room. Her shoes were squeaking as she
went to open the front door where one of the painters stood. There were four of them in total and they'd

been working around the clock—and although she'd stopped short of making cups of tea for them, she'd been friendly enough. This one had plaster dust in his hair and he was grinning.

She forced a smile as she held out the clump of keys. 'Here you go, Gary.'

But after he'd taken them and shoved them into his dust-covered jeans, he caught hold of her wrist. His big, calloused fingers curled around her skin and his face had suddenly gone very pink. 'I didn't realise you were *the* Alannah Collins,' he said suddenly.

Her heart sank as she snatched her hand away because she knew what was coming next. She wondered if it would be better to call his bluff or to slam the door in his face. But there were only a few days of the project left and it *was* nearly Christmas...why alienate one of the workforce unless it was absolutely necessary?

'Will there be anything else?' she questioned pointedly. 'Because I have work to do.'

'The schoolgirl,' he said thickly. 'With the big—'

A figure seemed to propel itself out of nowhere and it took a moment for Alannah to realise it was Niccolò and he was launching himself at Gary with a look of undiluted rage on his face.

Grabbing hold of the workman's shirt collar, he half lifted him from the ground and shoved his face very close.

'Che talii bastardu?' he spat out. *'Ti scippo locchi e o core!'*

'Niccolò!' protested Alannah faintly, but he didn't seem to be listening.

'How dare you speak to a woman like that?' he demanded. 'What's your name?'

The man blanched. 'G-Gary.'

'Gary what?'

'G-Gary Harkness.'

'Well, take it from me that you won't ever work in this city again, Gary Harkness—I shall make sure of that.' Releasing the shirt collar, Niccolò pushed him away and the man staggered a little. 'Now get out of here—get out before I beat your worthless body to a piece of pulp.'

Alannah didn't think she'd ever seen anyone look so petrified as the workman turned and ran down the corridor towards the elevator.

She lifted her gaze to Niccolò and met the furious blaze firing from his eyes as he clicked the door shut.

'What was that you said to him in Sicilian?'

'I asked him what he was looking at.' He paused as he steadied his breath. 'And I told him I would wrench out his eyes and his heart.'

Alannah gulped. 'You don't think that was a little…over the top?'

'I think he's lucky he didn't end up in hospital,' he ground out and his jaw tightened as he stared at her. 'How often does that happen?'

'Not much. Not these days.' She shrugged as she began to walk back into the main reception room, aware that he was following her. Aware that her heart was pounding. This wasn't a conversation she usually had—not with anyone—but maybe Niccolò was someone who needed to hear it. She turned to look at him. 'It used to be a lot worse. People only ever seemed able to have a conversation with my breasts—

or think that I would instantly want to fall into bed with them.'

Guilt whispered over his skin and Niccolò swallowed down the sudden dryness in his throat. Because hadn't he done something very similar? Hadn't he judged her without really knowing the facts and assumed a promiscuity which simply wasn't true?

'And I did the same,' he said slowly.

Her gaze was fearless. 'Yes, you did.'

'That was why you suddenly froze in the hallway of my house when I was making love to you, wasn't it?' he questioned suddenly.

His perception was nearly as alarming as the realisation that the conversation had taken an even more intimate twist. Despite her determination to stay strong, Alannah couldn't prevent the rush of heat to her cheeks. 'Yes,' she said quietly.

She started to turn her head away, but suddenly he was right there in front of her and his fingers were on her arm. They felt good on her arm, she thought inconsequentially.

'Tell me,' he urged.

It was hard to get the words out. Baring her soul wasn't something she normally did—and she had never imagined herself confiding in Niccolò da Conti like this. But for once his gaze was understanding and his voice was soft and Alannah found herself wanting to analyse the way she'd reacted—not just because he'd asked, but because she needed to make sense of it herself. 'I just remember you saying something about my body being even better in the flesh and I started to feel like an object. Like I wasn't a real person—

just a two-dimensional image in a magazine, with a
staple in her navel. Like I was *invisible*.'

'That was not my intention,' he said slowly. 'I think
I found myself overwhelmed by the realisation that I
was finally making love to you after so many years
of thinking about it.' There was a pause as he looked
at her. 'Do you think you can forgive me for that, *mia
tentatrice*?'

She studied him, and the flicker of a smile nudged
at her lips because it was strange seeing him in this
conciliatory mood. 'I'll think about it.'

Niccolò pulled her into his arms and she didn't object. She didn't object when he bent his head to kiss
her either. Her breath was warm and flavoured with
coffee and he wanted to groan with pleasure. She
tasted as good as he remembered—in fact, she tasted
even better—and there seemed something awfully
decadent about kissing her in the near-empty apartment. This wasn't the kind of thing he usually did between meetings, was it? His heart skipped a beat as
his fingertips skated over her breast, feeling it swell
as he cupped it, and he heard her breath quicken as
he began to unbutton her shirt.

It pleased him that she let him. That she really
did seem to have forgiven him for his out-of-control
behaviour of the other night. That she was relaxed
enough not to freeze again.

He deepened the kiss, rubbing at her taut nipple
with his thumb, and she gave a little sigh of pleasure.
He kissed her for a long time until she was squirm-
ing impatiently and kissing him back. Until he forced
himself to pull away from her, his voice unsteady as
he looked into the darkening of her denim eyes and

he felt a rush of triumph fuse with the headiness of sexual hunger.

'I would like to lay you down on the bare floor and make love to you, but I am short of time and must go straight from here to a meeting. And I don't feel it would do my reputation much good if I walked in so dishevelled.' He grimaced as he remembered that time in the hallway of his apartment, when he had shown all the finesse of a teenage boy. 'And I am aware that perhaps you like your lovemaking to be a little more slow and considered.'

'I…thought I did.'

He heard the reluctance in her voice but noticed she was still gripping tightly onto his arms. Her lips were trembling, even though she was biting down on them in an effort to stop it—and he realised just how turned on she was.

'Of course…' He moved his hand down to the ridge of hard denim between her legs. 'I probably do have enough time for other things. Things which you might enjoy.'

'Niccolò,' she said breathlessly.

'What do you think?' he said as he edged his middle finger forward and began to stroke her. 'Yes, or no?'

'Y-yes,' she gasped.

'Keep still,' he urged—but to his delight she didn't obey him. Or maybe she just couldn't. Her head was tipping back and suddenly she didn't look remotely shy…she looked *wild*. Beautiful. He felt her thighs part and heard her moaning softly as he increased the relentless pressure of his finger.

She came very quickly, tightening her arms around

his neck and making that shuddering little crescendo of sighs with which he'd become so familiar on Tuesday night. As he kissed her again her fingers began to claw at his shirt, as if she wanted to tear it from his chest, and for a moment he thought about changing his mind and taking her in the most fundamental way possible.

Temptation rushed over him in a dark wave. Impatiently, his hand strayed to the belt of his trousers, until some remaining shred of reason forced him to play out the ensuring scene. What did he have in mind? Rushing into his meeting with his shirt creased and a telltale flush darkening his skin? Using Alekto's apartment to have sex with a woman—wouldn't that be kind of *cheap*? On every single level, it wouldn't work—but that didn't make it any easier to pull away from her.

She started buttoning her shirt back up with trembling fingers and he walked over to the window to compose himself, willing his frustration to subside.

Outside, a light flurry of snowflakes was whirling down and he felt a sudden sense of restlessness. He thought about the impending holiday and what he would be forced to endure, because one thing he'd learned was that unless you were prepared to live in a cave—it was impossible to ignore Christmas. Already there was a glittering tree which he'd been unable to ban from the main reception of his offices. He thought about the horrendous staff party he'd been forced to attend last night, with those stodgy mince pies they were so fond of eating and several drunken secretaries tottering over to him with glassy smiles and bunches of mistletoe.

He turned round. Alannah had finished buttoning up her shirt, though he noticed her hands were shaking and her cheeks still flushed.

'What are you doing for Christmas?' he questioned suddenly.

'Oh, I'm wavering between an invitation to eat nut roast with some committed vegans, or having an alternative celebration all of my own.' She glanced over his shoulder at the snowflakes. 'Like pretending that nothing's happening and eating beans on toast, followed by an overdose of chocolate and trash TV. What about you?'

He shrugged. 'I have an invitation to ski with some friends in Klosters, but unfortunately my schedule doesn't allow it. I hate Christmas. What I would really like is to fast-forward the calendar and wake up to find it was the new year.'

'Oh, dear,' she said softly.

His eyes met hers and another wave of desire washed over him. 'But since we are both at a loose end, it seems a pity not to capitalise on that. We could ignore the seasonal madness and just please ourselves.'

She opened her eyes very wide. 'Are you asking me to spend Christmas with you, Niccolò?'

There was a pause. 'It seems I am.' He gave a cool smile. 'So why don't you speak to Kirsty and have her give you one of my credit cards? You can book us into the best suite in the best hotel in the city—somewhere you've always wanted to stay. Forget the nut roast and the beans on toast—you can have as much caviar and champagne as you like.' He gave a slow smile as he touched his fingertips to her raven hair. 'Maybe I can make some of your Christmas wishes come true.'

* * *

Alannah felt like taking her sharpest pair of scissors and snipping the small square of plastic into tiny pieces. She thought about what Niccolò had said to her. Make her wishes come true. *Really?* Did he honestly think that staying in a fancy hotel suite was the sum total of her life's ambition, when right now her biggest wish would be to tell him that she didn't need his fancy platinum credit card and she'd rather spend Christmas day alone than spend it with him?

Except that it wouldn't be true, would it? She might *want* it to be true, but it wasn't. Why else would she be sitting hunched in front of her computer, about to book a two-night break in a London hotel? She wondered what had happened to her determination to forget the night she'd spent with him and maintain a professional relationship.

She bit her lip. It had been shattered by Niccolò's resolve—that was what had happened. She had been lost the moment he'd kissed her. A single touch had been enough to make all her good intentions crumble. All her silent vows had been a complete waste of time—because she'd gone up in flames the moment he'd taken her in his arms.

She remembered the way his fingertip had whispered over the crotch of her jeans and her face grew hot. She hadn't been so shy then, had she? He'd soon had her bucking beneath him, and he hadn't even had to remove a single item of clothing. And still in that dreamy, post-orgasmic state she had agreed to spend Christmas with him.

That was something it was hard to get her head round. There must be millions of things he could be doing for the holiday—but he wanted to spend it with her. *Her.* Didn't that mean something? Her mouth grew dry. Surely it *had* to.

She stared at the credit card, which Kirsty had crisply informed her had no upper limit. Imagine that. Imagine having enough money to buy whatever you wanted. *The best suite in the best hotel.* How fancy would a hotel have to be for Niccolò not to have seen it all before, and be jaded by it? She ran through a list of possibilities. The Savoy. The Ritz. The Granchester. London had heaps of gorgeous hotels and she'd bet that he'd stayed in all of them. Had constant exposure to high-end affluence helped contribute to his inbuilt cynicism?

She was just about to click onto the Granchester when something made her hesitate. Perhaps it was a desire to shift him out of his comfort zone—away from the usual protective barriers which surrounded him. He had knocked down some of her defences, so why shouldn't she do the same with him? Why *shouldn't* she try to find out more about the real Niccolò da Conti?

She thought of a fancy hotel dining room and all the other people who would be congregated there. People who had no real place to go, who just wanted the holiday to be over. Or even worse—the wink-wink attitude of Room Service if they started asking for turkey sandwiches and champagne to be brought to their room.

An idea popped into her mind and it started to grow more attractive by the minute. She stared at the long number on the credit card. She might not have much money of her own, but she did have her imagination. Surely she was capable of surprising him with something unexpected. Something simple yet meaningful, which would incorporate the true meaning of Christmas.

His power and privilege always gave him an edge of superiority and that couldn't be good for him. An expensive tab in a smart hotel would only reinforce the differences between them. Wouldn't it be great to feel more like his *equal* for a change?

Because what if she *was* pregnant? She was going to have to get to know him better, no matter what the outcome. Her heart gave a painful lurch as she waited for that intrusive yet strangely compelling image of Niccolò da Conti's baby to subside.

She waited a minute before typing *cute Christmas cottage* into her browser. Because cute was exactly what she needed right now, she told herself. Cute stood a chance of making a cynical man melt so you might be able to work out what made him tick. Scrolling down, she stared at the clutch of country cottages which appeared on the screen.

Perfect.

CHAPTER EIGHT

THE FLURRIES WERE getting stronger and Niccolò cursed as he headed along the narrow country lane.

Why could nothing ever be straightforward? Glancing in his rear-view mirror at the swirl of snowflakes which was obscuring his view, he scowled. He'd given Alannah a credit card and told her to book a hotel in town and she'd done the exact opposite—directing him to some godforsaken spot deep in the countryside, while she went on ahead earlier.

Well, in terms of distance he wasn't actually *that* far from London but he might as well be in middle of his friend Murat's Qurhahian desert for all the sense he could make of his bearings. The sudden onset of heavy snow had made the world look like an alien place and it was difficult to get his bearings. Familiar landmarks had disappeared. The main roads were little more than white wastelands and the narrow lanes had begun to resemble twisting snakes of snow.

Glancing at his satnav, he could see he was only four minutes away, but he was damned if he could see any hotel. He'd passed the last chocolate-boxy village some way back and now an arrow was indicating he take the left fork in the road, through an impenetrable-looking line of trees.

Still cursing, he turned off the road, his powerful headlights illuminating the swirling snowflakes and turning them golden. Some people might have considered the scene pretty, but he wasn't in the mood for pretty scenery. He wanted a drink, a shower and sex in exactly that order and he wanted them now.

Following the moving red arrow, he drove slowly until at last he could see a lighted building in the distance, but it looked too small to be a hotel. His mouth hardened. Something that small could only ever be described as a cottage.

He could see a thatched roof covered with a thick dusting of snow and an old-fashioned lamp lit outside a front door, on which hung a festive wreath of holly and ivy. Through latticed windows a woman was moving around—her fall of raven hair visible, even from this distance. His hands tightened around the steering wheel as he brought the car to a halt and got out—his shoes sinking noiselessly into the soft, virgin carpet.

He rang the bell—one of those old-fashioned bells you only ever saw on ships, or in movies. He could hear the sudden scurrying of movement and footsteps approaching and then the door opened and Alannah stood there, bathed in muted rainbow light.

His body tensing, he stepped inside and the door swung violently shut behind him. His senses were immediately bombarded by the scene in front of him but, even so, the first thing he noticed was her dress. Who could fail to notice a dress like that?

It wasn't so much the golden silk, which skimmed

her curves and made her look like a living treasure, it was the scooped neck showing unfamiliar inches of creamy skin and the soft swell of her breasts. She had even positioned the glittery grasshopper brooch so that it looked poised to hop straight onto her nipple. Had she started to relax enough to stop covering her body up in that old puritanical way? he wondered.

But even this wasn't enough to hold his attention for long. His gaze moved behind her, where a fire was blazing—with two wing chairs on either side. Sprigs of holly had been placed above the paintings and, yes, there was the inevitable sprig of mistletoe dangling from the ceiling. On a low table a bowl was filled with clementines and in the air he could scent something cooking, rich with the scent of cinnamon and spice. But it was the Christmas tree which jarred most. A fresh fir tree with coloured lights looped all over the fragrant branches from which hung matching baubles of gold.

He flinched, but she didn't seem to notice as she wound her arms around his neck and positioned her lips over his. 'Merry Christmas,' she whispered.

Like a drowning man he fought against her feminine softness and the faint drift of pomegranate which clung to her skin. Disentangling her arms, he took a step back as he felt the clutch of ice around his heart.

'What's going on?' he questioned.

She blinked, as if something in his voice had alerted her to the fact that all was not well. 'It's a surprise.'

'I don't like surprises.'

Her eyes now held a faint sense of panic. Was she realising just how wrong she'd got it? he wondered grimly. He could see her licking her lips and the anger inside him seemed to bubble and grow.

'I thought about booking a hotel in London,' she said quickly. 'But I thought you'd probably stayed in all those places before, or somewhere like them. And then I thought about creating a real Christmas, right here in the countryside.'

'A *real* Christmas,' he repeated slowly.

'That's right.' She gestured towards a box of truffles on the table, as if the sight of chocolate were going to make him have a sudden change of heart. 'I went online at Selfridges and ordered a mass of stuff from their food hall. It was still much cheaper than a hotel. That's a ham you can smell cooking and I've bought fish too, because I know in Europe you like to eat fish at Christmas. Oh, and mince pies, of course.'

'I hate mince pies.'

'You don't…' Her voice faltered, as if she could no longer ignore the harsh note of censure in his voice. 'You don't *have* to eat them.'

'I hate Christmas, full stop,' he said viciously. 'I already told you that, Alannah—so which part of the sentence did you fail to understand?'

Her fingers flew over her lips and, with the silky dress clinging to her curves, she looked so like a medieval damsel in distress that he was momentarily tempted to pull her into his arms and blot out everything with sex.

But only momentarily. Because then he looked up and saw the Christmas angel on top of the tree and something about those gossamer-fine wings made his heart clench with pain. He felt the walls of the tiny cottage closing in on him as a dark tide of unwanted emotion washed over him.

'Which part, Alannah?' he repeated.

She held out the palms of her hands in a gesture of appeal. 'I thought—'

'What did you think?' he interrupted savagely. 'That you could treat me like your tame puppet? Playing happy couples around the Christmas tree and indulging in some happy-ever-after fantasy, just because we've had sex and I asked to spend the holidays with you, since we were both at a loose end?'

'Actually,' she said, walking over to the blaze of the fire and turning back to stare at him, 'I thought about how soulless it might be—having a corporate Christmas in some horrible anonymous hotel. I thought that with the kind of life you lead, you might like some home cooking for a change.'

'But I don't *do* home. Don't you get that?' he questioned savagely. He saw a small, rectangular present lying on the table and realised he hadn't even bought her a gift. *It wasn't supposed to be that kind of Christmas.* He shook his head. 'I can't stay here, Alannah. I'm sorry if you've gone to a lot of trouble but it's going to be wasted. So pack everything up while I put out the fire. We're going back to town.'

'No,' she said quietly.

His eyes narrowed. 'What do you mean...*no*?'

'You go if you want to, but I'm staying here.'

There was a pause. 'On your own?'

Alannah felt a sudden kick of rebellion as she met the incredulity in his eyes. 'You find that so surprising?' she demanded. 'You think I'm scared? Well, think again, Niccolò. I live on my own. I've spent pretty much the last seven years on my own. I don't need a man to protect me and look after me—and I certainly don't want to drive back to London with someone who can misinterpret a simple gesture with your kind of cynicism. So go to your anonymous hotel and spend the next few days splashing your cash and telling yourself how much you hate Christmas. I'll be perfectly happy here with my chocolate and mulled wine.'

His black eyes glittered. 'I'm telling you now that if you're calling my bluff, it won't work. I'm not staying here, but I'm not leaving without you, either.'

'I'm afraid you don't have a choice,' she said, walking across to the cocktail cabinet and pouring herself a glass of wine with a trembling hand. 'Like I said, I'm not going anywhere—and I don't imagine that even you are macho enough to drag me out by my hair. So leave. Go on. Just *leave*!'

Silently, they faced each other off before he pulled open the door and a fierce gust of wind brought a great flurry of snowflakes whirling into the room, before it slammed shut behind him.

Alannah didn't move as she heard the sound of his car starting up and then slowly pulling away on the snowy path. Her fingers tightened around her wine glass as she wondered how she could have judged him so badly. Had she thought that, because he'd murmured soft words in Sicilian when he'd been deep inside her, he'd lost the elements of ruthlessness and control which defined him?

Or was he right? Had she been naïve enough to imagine that a homespun meal might make him crave an intimacy which extended beyond the bedroom?

Her heart pounded.

Yes, she had.

Walking over to the sink, she threw away the wine, washing out the glass and putting it on the side to dry. She drew the curtains on the snowy darkness of the night and switched on the radio, just in time to hear the traditional Christmas service being broadcast from King's College, Cambridge. And as soon as the sound of carols filled the room she felt tears spring to her eyes, because it was so heartbreakingly beautiful.

She thought about the nativity scene—the helpless little child in a manger, and briefly she closed her eyes. She'd got it so wrong, hadn't she? She had taken him as her lover and ignored all the warning bells which had sounded so loudly in her ears. She had conveniently forgotten that everything was supposed to be on *his* terms and she'd tried to turn it into something it wasn't. Something it could never be. What had she been thinking of? She'd even bought herself a new and more revealing dress to send out the silent message that he had liberated her from some of her inhibitions. And she was almost as grateful to him for that as she was about the job he'd given her.

But he had thrown the offer back in her face.

She was cold now and ran upstairs to find a sweater, her heart contracting painfully as she looked around the bedroom. She had thought he would be charmed by the antique iron bedstead and the broderie-anglais linen. She'd imagined him picking up that old-fashioned jug and studying it—or telling her that he liked the view out into the snow-covered woods at the back of the house. She had planned to run him a bath when he arrived, and to light some of the scented candles she'd had delivered from London. She had pictured washing his back. Maybe even joining him, if he could persuade her to do so. She'd never shared a bath with anyone before.

What a fool she was, she thought viciously, dragging a mismatched blue sweater over the golden dress, and shaking her hair free. It wasn't as if she'd had no experience of life and the cruel lessons it could teach you. Hadn't she learnt that you had to just accept what you were given—warts and all? She should have taken what was already on the table and been satisfied with that. But she had been greedy, hadn't she? Niccolò had offered her something, but it hadn't been enough. She had wanted more. And still more.

The sound of the front door clicking open and closing again made her heart race with a sudden fear which made a mockery of her defiant words to Niccolò. Why the hell hadn't she locked it after he'd left—or was she hoping to extend an open invitation to any passing burglar? Except that no self-respecting burglar would be out on a snowy Christmas Eve like this. Even burglars probably had someone to share the holiday with.

'Who is it?' she called.

'Who do you think it is? Father Christmas?'

The sardonic Sicilian voice echoed round the small cottage and Alannah went to the top of the stairs to see Niccolò standing in the sitting room, snow clinging like frozen sugar to his black hair and cashmere coat. He looked up.

'It's me,' he said.

'I can see that. What happened?' she questioned

sarcastically as she began to walk downstairs. 'Did you change your mind about the mince pies?'

He was pulling off his coat and snow was falling in little white showers to the ground. She reached the bottom stair just as the poignant strains of 'Silent Night' poured from the radio. Quickly, she turned it off, so that all she could hear was the crackling of the fire and the sound of her own heartbeat as she stared at him. 'Why did you come back?'

There was a pause. His black eyes became suddenly hooded. 'It's a filthy night. I couldn't face leaving you here on your own.'

'And I told you that I would be fine. I'm not scared of the dark.' *I'm much more scared of the way you make me feel when you kiss me.*

'I'm not about to change my mind,' he said. 'I'm staying, and I need a drink.'

'Help yourself.'

He walked over to the bottle she'd opened earlier. 'You?'

A drink would choke me. 'No, thanks.'

She went and sat by the fire, wondering how she was going to get through the next few hours. How the hell did you pass the time when you were stuck somewhere with someone who didn't want to be there? After a couple of moments Niccolò walked over and handed her a glass of wine, but she shook her head.

'I said I didn't want one.'

'Take it, Alannah. Your face is pale.'

'My face is always pale.' But she took it anyway and drank a mouthful as he sat down in the other chair. 'And you still haven't really told me why you came back.'

Niccolò drank some of his wine and for a moment he said nothing. His natural instinct would be to tell her that he didn't have to justify his actions to her. To anyone. But something strange had happened as he'd driven his car down the snowy lane. Instead of the freedom he'd been expecting, he had felt nothing but a heavy weight settling somewhere deep in his chest. It had occurred to him that he could go and stay in a hotel. That if the truth were known, he could easily get a flight and join his friends and their skiing party. He could pretty much get a plane to anywhere, because the hosts of the many parties he'd declined would have been delighted if he'd turned up unexpectedly.

But then he'd thought of Alannah. Curled up alone by the fire with her raven hair aglow, while beside her that corny Christmas tree glittered. All that trouble she'd taken to create some sort of occasion and he'd just callously thrown it back in her face. What kind of a man did that? He thought of how much he'd anticipated making love to her again. How he'd spent the day aching to possess her and wanting to feel her arms wrapped tightly around him. What was *wrong* with him?

He put down his glass and his face was sombre as he turned to look at her.

'I came back because I realised I was behaving like an idiot,' he said. 'I shouldn't have taken it out on you and I'm sorry.'

Alannah sensed that sorry wasn't a word which usually featured highly in his vocabulary, but she wasn't letting him off that lightly. Did he think that a single word could wash away all the hurt he'd inflicted?' 'But you did.'

'Yes. I did.'

'Because you always have to be in charge don't you, Niccolò?' she demanded, her anger starting to bubble up. 'You decided how you wanted Christmas to play out and that was it as far as you were concerned. What *you* want is paramount, and everyone else's wishes can just go hang. This is exactly what happened at Michela's wedding, isn't it? Niccolò wants it this way—so this is the way it must be.'

'That was different.'

'How?' she demanded. 'How was it different? How did you ever get to be so damned...*controlling*?'

The flames were flickering over his brooding features and illuminating his ebony hair, so that it glowed like fire-touched coal.

'How?' He gave a short laugh. 'You don't have any ideas?'

'Because you're Sicilian?'

'But I'm not,' he said unexpectedly. 'I'm only half Sicilian. My blood is not "pure". I am half Corsican.' He frowned. 'You didn't know that?'

She shook her head and suddenly his almost swashbuckling appearance made sense. 'No. I had no idea. Michela never really talked about that kind of thing. Boarding school is about reinvention—and escape. About painting yourself in the best possible light so that nobody feels sorry for you. All we knew was that you were unbelievably strict.' She put her glass down. 'Although you did used to take her to the Bahamas for Christmas every year, and we used to get pretty jealous about that.'

'She never told you why?'

'I knew that your parents were dead.' She hesitated. 'But nobody wants to talk about that kind of stuff, do they?'

Niccolò felt his mouth dry. No, they didn't. They definitely didn't. And when death was connected with shame, it made you want to turn your back on it even more. To keep it hidden. To create some kind of distance and move as far away from it as you could. He'd done that for Michela, but he'd done it for himself, too. Because some things were easier to forget than to remember.

Yet even though she was doing her best to disguise it, Alannah was looking at him with such hurt and confusion on her face that he felt it stab at his conscience. All she'd done was to try to make his Christmas good and he had thrown it back in her face in a way she didn't deserve. He'd given her a lot of stuff she didn't deserve, he realised—and didn't he owe her some kind of explanation?

'Mine was a very…unusual upbringing,' he said, at last. 'My mother came from a powerful Sicilian family who disowned her when she married my father.'

She raised her eyebrows. 'Wasn't that a little… dramatic?'

He shrugged. 'Depends which point of view you take. Her family was one of the wealthiest on the island—and my father was an itinerant Corsican with a dodgy background, who worked in the kitchens of one of her family hotels. It was never going to be thought of as an ideal match—not by any stretch of the imagination.' His gaze fixed on the flames which danced around one of the logs. 'My father was completely uneducated but he possessed a tremendous charisma.' He gave a bitter laugh. 'Along with a massive gambling addiction and a love of the finer things in life. My mother told me that her parents did everything in their power to prevent the marriage and when they couldn't—they told her she would only ever be welcome if she parted from him. Which for a strictly traditional Sicilian family was a pretty big deal.'

Alannah stared at him. 'So what did she do?'

'She defied them and married him anyway. She loved him. And she let that *love*—' His voice took the word and distorted it—so that when it left his lips it sounded like something dark and savage. 'She let it blind her to everything. His infidelity. His habitual absences. The fact that he was probably more in love with her inheritance, than with her. They took the boat to Italy when my mother was pregnant with me and we lived in some style in Rome—while my father flew to casinos all over the world and spent her money. My mother used to talk to me all the time about Sicily and I guess I became a typical immigrant child. I knew far more about the place of my birth than I did about my adopted homeland.'

Alannah leaned forward to throw another log on the fire as his words tailed off. 'Go on,' she said.

He watched the flames leap into life. 'When I was old enough, she used to leave me in charge of Michela so she could go travelling with him. She used to sit in casinos, just watching him—though I suspect it was mainly to keep the other women at bay. But he liked the attention—the idea that this rich and wealthy woman had given up everything to be with him. He used to tell her that she was his lucky charm. And I guess for a while that was okay—I mean, the situation certainly wasn't perfect, but it was bearable. Just that beneath the surface everything was crumbling and there was nothing I could do to stop it.'

She heard the sudden darkness in his voice. 'How?'

Leaning his head back against the chair, he half closed his eyes. 'My mother's inheritance was almost gone. The rent on our fancy apartment in Parioli was due and the creditors were circling like vultures. I remember her mounting sense of panic when she confided the bitter truth to me. I was eighteen and working towards going to college, though something told me that was never going to happen. My father found out about a big tournament in Monaco and they drove to France so that he could take part in it.' There was a pause. 'It was supposed to be the solution to all their problems.'

She heard the sudden break in his voice. 'What happened?'

'Oh, he won,' he said. 'In fact, he cleaned up big time. Enough to clear all his debts and guarantee them the kind of future my mother had prayed for.'

'But?' She sensed there was a *but* coming. It hung in the air like a heavy weight about to topple. He lowered his head to look at her and Alannah almost recoiled from the sudden bleakness in his eyes.

'That night they celebrated with too much champagne and decided to set off for Rome, instead of waiting until the morning. They were driving through the Italian alps when they took a bend too fast. They hit the side of the mountain and the car was destroyed.' He didn't speak for a moment and when he did, his words sounded as if they had been carved from stone.

'Neither of them would have known anything about it. At least, that's what the doctors told me.'

'Oh, Niccolò,' she breathed. 'I'm so sorry. Michela told me they'd died in a car crash, but I didn't know the background to the story.'

'Because I kept as much from her as I could. The post-mortem was inconclusive.' His voice hardened. 'Determining the level of alcohol in a…cadaver is always difficult. And no child should have the shame of knowing her father killed her mother because he was on a drunken high after winning at cards.'

She thought how *cold* he sounded—and how ruthless. But that was his default position, wasn't it—and wasn't it somehow understandable in the circumstances? Wasn't much of his behaviour explained by his dreadful legacy? 'You still must have been devastated?' she ventured.

He gave a bitter laugh. 'Do you want the truth? The real and shocking truth? My overriding emotion was one of relief that my father had won so big and that somehow the money got to me intact. It meant that I could pay the rent and clear the debts. It meant that I could send Michela away to school—at thirteen she was getting too much for me to handle. And it meant that I could live my own life. That I could capitalise on his win and make it even bigger. And that's what I did. I bought my first property with that money and by the end of that first year, I had acquired three.'

Alannah nodded. It was funny how when you joined up the dots the bigger picture emerged. Suddenly, she realised why he'd always been so strict with his sister. She saw now that his own controlling nature must have developed as an antidote to his father's recklessness. Financial insecurity had led him to go on and make himself a colossal fortune which nobody could ever bleed away. His wealth was protected, but in protecting it he had set himself in a world apart from other men.

'And did this all happen at Christmas?' she questioned suddenly. 'Is that why you hate the holidays so much?'

'No. That would have been neat, wouldn't it?' He gave a wry smile. 'It's just that Christmas came to symbolise the bleak epicentre of our family life. For me, it was always such an empty festival. My mother would spend vast amounts of money decking out the rooms of our apartment, but she was never there. Even on Christmas Eve she would be sitting like some passive fool on the sidelines while my father played cards. Supposedly bringing him luck, but in reality—checking out that some buxom hostess wasn't coming onto him.'

She winced at the phrase, but suddenly she could understand some of his prejudice towards her, too. For him, buxom women in skimpy clothes were the ones who threatened his parents' relationship. Yet in the end, his puritanical disapproval of her chosen career had done nothing to destroy his powerful lust for her, which must have confused him. And Niccolò didn't do confusion. She'd always known that. Black and white, with nothing in between.

'To me, Christmas always felt as if I'd walked onto a stage set,' he said. 'As if all the props were in place, but nobody knew which lines to say.'

And Alannah realised that she'd done exactly the same. She had tried to create the perfect Christmas.

She'd bought the tree and hung the holly and the mistletoe—but what she had created had been no more real than the empty Christmases of his past.

'Oh, Niccolò—I'm sorry,' she said. 'I had no idea.'

He looked at her and some of the harshness left his face. 'How would you have done? I've never talked about it. Not to anyone.'

'Maybe some time, it might be good to sit down and discuss it with Michela?' she ventured.

'And destroy her memories?'

'False memories are dangerous. And so are secrets. My mother waited until she was dying to tell me that her drink had been spiked and she didn't even know my father's name. I wish she'd shared it with me sooner. I would have liked to have let her know how much I admired her for keeping me.'

His eyes narrowed. 'She sounds an amazing woman.'

'She was.' His words pleased her but she felt vulnerable with his black eyes looking at her in that curiously assessing way. In an effort to distract herself, she got up and went to look out of the window. 'I'm afraid the snow shows no sign of melting?'

'No.'

She turned round. 'I suppose on a practical level we could take down all the decorations if that would make you feel better—and then we could watch that programme on TV which has been generating so much publicity. Have you heard about it? It's called "*Stuff Christmas*".'

Without warning, he rose from the chair and walked over to her, his shadow enveloping her and suddenly making her feel very small. His ebony gaze flickered over her and she saw that the bitterness in his eyes had been replaced by the much more familiar flicker of desire.

'Or we could do something else, *mia fata*,' he said softly. 'Something much more appealing. Something which I have been aching to do since I walked back in here. I could take you upstairs to bed and make love to you.'

His features were soft with lust and Alannah thought she'd never seen him looking quite so gorgeous. She wanted him just as she always wanted him, but this time her desire was underpinned with something else—something powerful and inexplicable. A need to hold him and comfort him, after everything he'd told her. A need to want to reach out and protect him.

But he'd only told her because of the situation in which they found themselves and she needed to face the truth. He wanted her for sex—*that was all*— and she needed to protect her own vulnerable heart. Maybe it was time to distance herself from him for a while. Give them both a little space.

But by then he was kissing her and it was too late to say anything. Because when he kissed her like that, she was lost.

CHAPTER NINE

SLOWLY, NICCOLÒ LICKED at the delicious rosy flesh of Alannah's nipple until eventually she began to stir. Raising her arms above her head, she stretched languorously as the silky tumble of her hair rippled over the pillow like a black banner.

'Niccolò,' she murmured, dark lashes fluttering open to reveal the sleepy denim eyes beneath.

He gave a smile of satisfaction as she somehow turned his name into a breathy little sigh—a variation of the different ways she'd said it throughout the night. She had gasped it. Moaned it. At one point she had even screamed it—her fingernails clawing frantically at his sweat-sheened body as she'd bucked beneath him. He remembered her flopping back onto the pillow afterwards and asking if was it always like this. But he hadn't answered her. He hadn't dared. For once there had been no words in his vocabulary to describe a night which had surpassed any other in his experience. He had come over and over again... in her and on her. And this time he'd remembered to use protection. Hell. Even doing *that* had felt as if it should be included in the pages of the Kama Sutra. He swallowed as he felt the renewed jerk of desire just from thinking about it. No orgasm had ever felt more powerful; no kisses that deep.

He was still trying to work out why. Because he had allowed her to glimpse the bleak landscape of his past—or because he had waited what seemed like a whole lifetime to possess her? He gave another lick. Maybe it was simply that he was discovering she was nothing like the woman he'd thought her to be.

'Niccolò?' she said again.

'Mmm?'

'Is it morning?'

'I think so.' His tongue traced a sinuous path over the creamy flesh and he felt her shiver. 'Though right now I don't really care. Do you?'

'I don't…' He could hear the note of dreamy submission in her voice. 'I don't think so.'

'Good.' He moved his tongue down over her body, feeling himself harden as it trailed a moist path to her belly. But the anatomical significance of that particular spot suddenly began to stab at his conscience and the thought he'd been trying to block now came rushing into his mind. *Was* she pregnant? He felt the painful contraction of his heart until he reminded himself that was a possibility, not a fact—and he only ever dealt with facts. There was nothing he could do about it right now—so why not continue tracking his tongue down over her salty skin and obliterating the nagging darkness of his thoughts with the brief amnesia of pleasure?

He wriggled down the bed and knelt over her, his legs straddling her as he parted her thighs and put his head between them. The dark triangle of hair at their apex was soft and for a moment he just teased at the curly strands with his teeth. She began to writhe as he flickered his tongue with featherlight accuracy against her clitoris, and the fingernails which had begun to claw restlessly at the sheet now moved to grip his shoulders.

She tasted warm and wet against his mouth and her urgent little cries only increased when he captured her circling hips and pinned them firmly against the mattress, so that he could increase the unremitting pressure of his tongue. He could hear her calling his name out. He could feel her spiralling out of control. And suddenly he felt her begin to spasm helplessly against his mouth.

'N-Niccolò!' she breathed. 'Oh, Niccolò.'

His mind and his body were at such a fever-pitch of hunger that he couldn't speak and, urgently, he reached for a condom and eased himself into her slick warmth.

He groaned. She felt so *tight*. Or maybe it was because he felt so big—as if he wanted to explode from the moment he thrust inside her. As if he wanted to come, over and over again. And yet surely she had drained every seed from his body, so that there was nothing left to give?

It seemed she had not. He drove into her until he didn't know where he ended and she began. Until her back began to arch and her eyes to close—each exquisite spasm racking through his body as time seemed to suspend itself, leaving him dazed and breathless.

The silence of the room was broken only by the sound of his own muffled heartbeat.

'I don't know how much more pleasure I can take,' she said eventually and he felt her face pressing against his shoulder.

He turned his head and blew a soft breath onto her cheek. 'Don't you know that you can never have too much pleasure, *mia tentatrice*?'

But Alannah wrinkled her nose as she stared up at the ceiling because she didn't agree. You could. You definitely could. There was always a snake in the garden of Eden—everyone knew that. She thought about all the things he'd confided in her last night. Her heart had softened when she'd heard his story. She'd felt so close to him—and flattered that he had trusted her enough to tell her all that stuff about his past. But that was dangerous, too. If she wasn't careful she could start weaving hopeless fantasies about something which was never intended to last.

She looked over at the window where bright light was shining against the closed curtains. And she realised that it was Christmas morning and last night he'd wanted to leave. She watched as he got out of bed and walked over to the window to pull back the curtains and she blinked as she gazed outside. Thick snow lay everywhere. Branches and bushes were blanketed with the stuff. Against a dove-grey sky the world looked blindingly white and not a sound could be heard and Alannah knew she mustn't let the fairy-tale perfection of the scene in front of her blind her to the reality of their situation.

She put her hands beneath the duvet, her warm belly instinctively recoiling from the icy touch of her fingers.

'We haven't really discussed what's going to happen if I'm pregnant.'

The words hung and shimmered in the air, like the baubles on the unwanted Christmas tree downstairs.

He seemed to choose his words carefully, as if he was walking through a minefield of possibilities.

'Obviously, if such a situation arises—then I will be forced to consider marrying you.'

Alannah did her best not to recoil because he made it sound like someone being forced to drink a bitter draught of poison. She didn't say anything for a moment and when she did, she chose her words as carefully as he had done.

'Before you do, I think there's something you should take into account,' she said quietly. 'Gone are the days when women could be forced to marry against their will—because there's a baby on the way. If I *am* pregnant, then I want my baby to have love— real love. I would want my baby to put contentment before wealth—and satisfaction before ambition. I would want my baby to grow up to be a warm and grounded individual—and, obviously, none of those things would be possible with you as a cynical role model. So don't worry, Niccolò—I won't be dragging you up the aisle any time soon.'

She had expected anger, or a righteous indignation—but she got neither. Instead, his expression remained cool and non-committal. She almost thought she saw a flicker of amusement in those ebony eyes.

'Have you finished?' he said.

She shrugged, wishing she didn't want him so much. 'I guess.'

'Then I'll make coffee.'

He didn't just make coffee. After a bath which

seemed to take for ever to fill, Alannah dressed and went downstairs to find him deftly cracking eggs into a bowl with one hand.

He glanced up. 'Breakfast?'

She grimaced. 'I don't know if I can face eggs.'

'You really should eat something.'

'I suppose so.' She sat down and took the cup of coffee he poured for her and, after a couple of minutes, a plate of scrambled eggs was pushed across the table. She must have been hungrier than she'd thought because she ate it all, before putting her fork down and watching while he finished his own. She thought how he could even make eating look sexy. *Keep your mind fixed on practicalities,* she told herself. 'We ought to investigate the roads,' she said. 'Maybe we can dig ourselves out.'

'Not yet.' His eyes were thoughtful as they surveyed her over the rim of his coffee cup. 'I think we should go for a walk. You look as if you could do with some colour in your cheeks.'

'That's what blusher is supposed to be for.'

He smiled. 'There's a cupboard below the stairs packed with boots and waterproof jackets—why don't we go and investigate?'

They found coats and wrapped up warm and as Niccolò buttoned up her coat Alannah kept reinforcing the same mantra which had been playing in her head all morning. That none of this meant anything. They were just two people who happened to be alone at Christmas, who happened to enjoy having sex with each other.

But the moment they stepped out into the snow, it

was impossible to keep things in perspective. It felt as if nature were conspiring against her. How could she not be affected when it felt as if she'd been transplanted into a magical world, with a man who made her feel so *alive*?

They walked along, their footsteps sinking into the virgin tracks, and she was surprised when he took her hand as they walked along. Funny how something so insignificant could feel so meaningful—especially when she thought about the many greater intimacies they'd shared. Because holding hands could easily masquerade as tenderness and tenderness was shot with its own special kind of danger...

As occasional stray flakes drifted down on their bare heads they talked about their lives. About the reasons he'd come to live in London and her summer holidays in Ireland. She asked how he'd met Alekto Sarantos, and he told her about their mutual friend Murat, the Sultan of Qurhah, and a long-ago skiing trip, when four very alpha men had challenged each other on the slopes.

'I didn't realise you knew Luis Martinez,' she said. 'That *is* Luis Martinez the world-champion racing driver?'

'Ex world champion,' he said, a little testily—and Alannah realised how competitive the four friends must have been.

He told her he hated litter and cars which hogged the middle lane of the motorway and she confided her dislike of drugs and people who ignored shop assistants by talking on their mobile phones. It was as if they had made an unspoken decision to keep the conversation strictly neutral and, unexpectedly, Alannah found herself relaxing. To anyone observing them, they probably looked like an ordinary couple who'd chosen to escape the mad rush of the city to create a dream holiday for themselves. And that was all it was, she reminded herself fiercely. A dream.

'Are you finding this…impossible?' she said. 'Being stuck here with this manufactured Christmas everywhere, when last night you were desperate to leave?'

He kicked at some snow, so that it created a powdery white explosion before falling to the ground. 'No,' he said eventually. 'It's easier than I imagined. You're actually very good company. In fact, I think I enjoy talking to you almost as much as I enjoy kissing you.' His eyes gleamed. 'Although, on second thoughts…'

She turned away, blinking her eyes furiously because kindness was nearly as dangerous as tenderness in helping you to distort reality. But he was getting to her—even though she didn't want him to. Wasn't it funny how a few kind words had the power to make everything seem different? The world suddenly looked bright and vivid, even though it had been bleached of colour. The snow made the berries on the holly bushes stand out like drops of blood and Alannah reached up to bend back a tree branch, watching as it sent a shower of snow arcing through the air, and something bubbled up inside her and made her giggle.

She turned around to find Niccolò watching her, his eyes narrowed against the bright light, and her mouth grew dry as she saw an instantly recognisable hunger in their black depths.

'What...what are we going to do if it doesn't melt?' she said, suddenly breathless.

He leaned forward to touch a gloved finger to her lips. 'Guess,' he said, and his voice was rough.

CHAPTER TEN

HE MADE LOVE to her as soon as they got back—while her cheeks were still cold from the snowy air and her eager fingers icy against his chest as she burrowed beneath his sweater. Alannah lay on the rug in front of the fire, with her arms stretched above her head, wearing nothing but a pair of knickers. And all her shyness and hang-ups seemed like a distant memory as he trailed his lips over every inch of her body.

His fingertips explored her skin with a curiously rapt attention and she found herself reaching for him with a sudden urgency, drawing in a shuddering breath as he eased into her and letting the breath out again like a slow surrender as he lowered his mouth to hers. She loved the contrast of their bodies—his so olive-skinned and dark against her own milky pallor. She liked watching the flicker of flames gilding his flesh and the way his limbs interlocked so perfectly with her own. She loved the way he tipped his head back when he came—and made that low and shuddered moan of delight.

Much later, he pulled his sweater over her head and set about cooking lunch, while she curled up on the sofa and watched him, and suddenly she felt relaxed.

Really and properly relaxed. The cushion behind her back was soft and feathery and her bare toes were warm in the fire's glow.

'It seems *weird*,' she said as he tipped a pile of clean vegetables from the chopping board into a saucepan, 'to see you in the kitchen, looking like you know exactly what you're doing.'

'That's because I do. It isn't exactly rocket science,' he answered drily. 'Unless you think cooking is too complicated for a mere man and that women are naturally superior in the kitchen?'

'Women are naturally superior at many things,' she said airily. 'Though not necessarily at cooking. And you know what I mean. You're a billionaire businessman who runs an international empire. It's strange to see you *scraping carrots*.'

Niccolò gave a soft laugh as he grabbed a handful of fresh herbs, though he recognised that she'd touched a nerve. Just because he *could* cook, didn't mean he did—and it was a long time since he'd done anything like this. Yet wasn't there something uniquely *comforting* about creating a meal from scratch? He'd cooked for his sister in those early days of loss but as she'd got older his responsibilities towards her had lessened. When he had sent her away to school, only the vacations had required his hands-on guardianship. But he had enjoyed his role as quasi-parent and he'd made sure that he carried it out to the best of his ability—the way he tackled everything in his life.

He remembered the trips to the famous Campagna Amica market, near the Circus Maximus. He had taken Michela with him and shown the sulky teenager how to select the freshest vegetables and the finest pieces of fruit. And all the stall-owners had made a fuss of her—slipping her a ripe pear or a small bunch of perfect grapes.

When Michela had finally left home, he had filled every available hour with work—building up his property portfolio with a determination to underpin his life with the kind of security he'd never had. And as his wealth had grown, so had his ability to delegate. These days he always ate out, unless a woman was trying to impress him with her culinary repertoire. His Mayfair fridge was bare, save for coffee and champagne. His apartment was nothing but a base with a bed. It wasn't a home because he didn't *do* home. But as he squeezed lemon juice over the grilled fish he realised how much he had missed the simple routine of the kitchen.

He glanced up to find Alannah still watching him, her bare legs tucked up beneath her. His sweater was much too big for her and it had the effect of making her look unbelievably fragile. Her black hair was spilling down over her shoulders and her blue eyes were shining and something about that almost innocent look of eagerness made his heart contract.

Deliberately, he turned away, reaching for a bottle of prosecco and two glasses. *She's just someone you're trying to get out of your system,* he reminded himself grimly.

His face was composed by the time he handed her a glass. 'Happy Christmas,' he said.

They drank prosecco, lit candles and ate lunch. Afterwards, he made love to her again and they fell asleep on the sofa—and when they awoke, the can-

dles were almost burnt down and outside the starry
sky was dark and clear.

Alannah walked over to the window and he wondered if she was aware that her bare bottom was revealed with every step she took.

'I think the snow might be melting,' she said.

He heard the unmistakable note of disappointment
in her voice and something inside him hardened. Did
she think they could exist in this little bubble for ever,
and pretend the rest of the world wasn't out there?

He insisted on loading the dishwasher and making
tea to eat with their chocolate. Because any kind of
activity was better than sitting there letting his mind
keep working overtime.

But action couldn't permanently silence the nagging thoughts which were building inside him and he
thought about what she'd said earlier. About putting
contentment before wealth and satisfaction before ambition. About not wanting to drag him up the aisle.

Because that was not a decision she alone could
make. And if there *was* a baby, then surely there was
only one sensible solution, and that solution was marriage.

His jaw tightened. Obviously it was something he'd
thought about, in the same way that the young sometimes thought about getting old—as if it would never
happen to them. He liked children—and was godfa-
ther to several. Deep down, he'd recognised that one
day he wanted to be a father and would select a suitable woman to bear his child.

He'd imagined she would be blonde and slightly
aloof. Maybe one of those American women who had
been brought up on milk and honey and could trace

their roots back over generations. The type who kept their emotions on an even keel. The type who didn't believe in fairy tales. The type he felt safe with. It wasn't their trust funds which excited him, but the satisfaction of knowing that they would unknowingly welcome the son of a Corsican bandit into their rarefied drawing rooms.

He stared across the room at Alannah. In no way was she aloof; he had never seen a woman looking quite so accessible. Even with her fingers wrapped chastely around a mug of herb tea, she looked...wild. He felt his throat dry. She touched something deep inside him, something which felt...*dangerous*. Something which took him to the very edges of his self-control. She always had. She spoke to him as nobody else did. She treated him in a way which no one else would dare try.

But the fact remained that she had a background even more unsettled than his own. He had already taken a gamble on her—but surely there was no need to take another. He might not have learnt many lessons at the knee of his father, but one thing he knew was that the more you gambled—the greater your chance of losing. The most sensible thing he could do would be to walk away from her. To keep on walking, without looking back.

He swallowed. Yet if she carried his child—he could walk nowhere. What choice would he have other than to stay with her? To tie himself to someone who no way fitted the image of the kind of woman he wanted to marry. Two mismatched people united by a single incident of careless passion. What future was there in that?

She looked up and her expression grew wary.

'Why are you frowning at me?'

'I didn't realise I was.'

'Actually, frowning isn't really accurate. You were glaring.'

'Was I?' He leaned back in his chair and studied her. 'I've been thinking.'

'Sounds ominous,' she said.

'You do realise that despite all your words of rebellion this morning—I'm going to marry you if you're having my baby?'

Her creamy skin went pink. He saw her fingertips flutter up to touch the base of her neck.

'What…what made you suddenly think of that?'

He saw the flare of hope in her eyes and knew he mustn't feed it, because that wasn't fair. He had a responsibility to tell her the truth and the last thing he wanted was her thinking he was capable of the same emotions as other men. He mustn't fool her into thinking that his icy heart might be about to melt. His mouth hardened. Because that was never going to happen.

'I suddenly realised,' he said slowly, 'that I could never tolerate my son or daughter growing up and calling another man Father.'

'Even though I am the last kind of person you would consider marrying under normal circumstances.'

He met her eyes—but hadn't he always been completely honest with her? Wouldn't she see through a placatory lie to try to make her feel better? 'I guess.'

She put her cup down quickly, as if she was afraid she was going to spill it. 'So this is all about possession?'

'Why wouldn't it be? This child is half mine.'

'*This child* might not even exist!' she choked out. 'Don't you think we ought to wait until we know, before we start having arguments about parental rights?'

'When *can* you find out?'

'I'll do the test when I get back to London,' she said, jumping up from the sofa and dabbing furiously at her eyes with shaking and fisted hands.

The warm and easy atmosphere of earlier had vanished. And how.

Alannah stormed upstairs to splash cold water onto her face and to try to stem the hot tears from springing to her eyes, and yet all she could feel was a growing sense of frustration. She didn't *want* to be like this. She couldn't blame him for what he'd said, just because it didn't fit in with her fantasies. He was only being straight with her. So maybe this was a wake-up call to start protecting herself. To start facing up to facts.

Their fairy-tale Christmas was over.

She went back downstairs and turned on the TV, giving an exaggerated sigh of relief when she heard the weatherman announce that a warm weather front was pushing up from Spain, and the snow was expected to have thawed by late morning.

'Great news,' she said. 'London here we come.'

Niccolò watched as she stomped out of her chair to throw away the untouched mince pies and chocolates and every attempt he made to start a conversation was met with a monosyllabic response. He realised that he'd never been given such cool treatment by a woman before.

But that didn't stop them having sex that night. Very good sex, as it happened. Their angry words momentarily forgotten, he reached for her in the darkness with a passion which she more than matched. In a room washed silver by the full moon, he watched as she arched beneath him and called out his name.

He awoke to the sound of dripping outside the window to find the weatherman's predictions had been accurate and that the snow was melting. Leaving Alannah sleeping, he packed everything up, made a pot of coffee, then went along the lane to find his car.

By the time he drove back to the cottage, she was up and dressed, standing in the middle of the sitting room, clutching a mug—her face pale and her mouth set. He noticed she'd turned the tree lights off and that the room now looked dull and lacklustre.

'Christmas is over,' she said brightly, as if he were a stranger. As if she hadn't been going down on him just a few sweet hours before.

'What about the tree?'

'The woman I hired the cottage from supplied it. She said she'll take it away.'

'Alannah—'

'No,' she said quietly. 'I don't want any protracted stuff, or silly goodbyes. I just want to get back to London and finish up the job you've employed me to do.'

Niccolò felt a flicker of irritation at her suddenly stubborn and uncompromising attitude, but there didn't seem to be a damned thing he could do about it. She was almost completely silent on the journey back as the car slushed its way through the unnaturally quiet streets and, for some reason, the passionate opera he usually favoured while driving now seemed completely inappropriate.

He drove her to Acton and parked up outside her

home, where most of the small nearby houses seemed to be decked with the most garish tinsel imaginable. Someone had even put an inflatable Santa in their cramped front yard.

'Thanks for the lift,' she said, as she reached for the door handle.

'Aren't you going to invite me in?'

She gave him a steady stare. 'Why would I do that?'

'Maybe because we've been sleeping together and I might like to see where you live?'

Alannah hesitated and hated herself for that hesitation. She wondered if secretly she was ashamed of her little home and fearful of how judgemental he might be. Or was it simply an instinctive reaction, because she was unwilling to expose any more of herself to him?

'Okay, come in, then,' she said grudgingly.

'Grazie,' came his sardonic reply.

It was shiveringly cold as she unlocked the door. She'd turned the heating down low before the taxi had arrived to take her to the cottage and now the place felt like an ice-box. Niccolò stood in the centre of her small sitting room as she adjusted the thermostat, looking around him like a man who had just found himself in a foreign country and wasn't quite sure what to do. She wondered how he managed to make her furniture look as if it would be better suited to a doll's house.

'Would you like a guided tour?' she said.

'Why not?'

The cramped dimensions meant she needed to be vigilant about tidiness and Alannah was glad there were no discarded pieces of clothing strewn around her bedroom and that the tiny bathroom was neat. But it still felt excruciating as she led him through an apartment in which she'd tried to maximise all available light in order to give an illusion of space. She'd made all the drapes herself from sari material she'd picked up at the local market, and the artwork which hung on the walls was her own. A friend from college had feng-shuied every room, there were pots of herbs lined up on the window sill in the kitchen, and she found the place both restful and creative.

But she wondered how it must seem through Niccolò's eyes, when you could practically fit the entire place into his downstairs cloakroom back in Mayfair.

They walked back into the sitting room and, rather awkwardly, she stood in front of him. He really did seem like a stranger now, she thought—and a terrible sense of sadness washed over her. How weird to think that just a few hours ago he was deep inside her body—making her feel as if she was closer to him than she'd ever been to anyone.

'I would offer you coffee,' she said. 'But I really do want to get on. If Alekto is going to have the apartment ready for his New Year's Eve party, then I need to get cracking.'

'You're planning to work *today*?'

'Of course. What did you think I'd be doing?' she questioned. 'Sobbing into my hankie because our cosy Christmas is over? I enjoyed it, Niccolò. It was an… interesting experience. And you're a great cook as well as a great lover. But you probably know that.'

She made a polite gesture in the direction of the door but he suddenly caught hold of her wrist, and all pretence of civility had gone.

'Haven't you forgotten something?' he iced out, his eyes glittering with unfeigned hostility.

She snatched her hand away, swallowing as she met his gaze. 'No, I haven't. It's not the kind of thing you can easily forget, is it? Don't worry, Niccolò. I'll let you know whether I'm pregnant or not.'

CHAPTER ELEVEN

'I'M NOT PREGNANT.'

Alannah's voice sounded distorted—as if it were coming from a long way away, instead of just the other side of his desk—and Niccolò didn't say anything—at least, not straight away. He wondered why his heart had contracted with something which felt like pain. Whether he'd imagined the cold taste of disappointment which was making his mouth bitter. He must have done. Because wasn't this the news he'd been longing for? The only sane solution to a problem which should never have arisen?

He focused his eyes to where Alannah sat perched on the edge of a chair opposite him and thought how pale she looked. Paler than the thick white lanes through which they'd walked on Christmas Day, when the snow had trapped them in that false little bubble. Her blue eyes were ringed with dark shadows, as if she hadn't been sleeping.

Had she?

Or had she—like he—been lying wide-eyed in the depths of the night, remembering what it had felt like when they'd made love and then fallen asleep with their limbs tangled warmly together?

He flattened the palms of his hands flat on the surface of his desk. 'You're sure?'

'One hundred per cent.'

He wondered why she had chosen to tell him here, and now. Why she had come to his office after successfully negotiating a ten-minute slot in his diary with Kirsty. And Kirsty hadn't even checked with him first!

'Couldn't you have chosen a more suitable time and place to tell me, rather than bursting into my office and getting my assistant to collude with you?' he questioned impatiently. 'Or is it just a continuation of your determination to keep me at arm's length?'

'I've been busy.'

That was usually *his* excuse. He leaned back in his chair and studied her. 'You won't even have dinner with me,' he observed coolly.

'I'm sure you'll get over it,' she said lightly.

His gaze didn't waver. 'I thought you said you'd enjoyed our "experiment" over Christmas—so why not run with it a little longer? Come on, Alannah.' A smile curved his lips. 'What harm could it do?'

Alannah stared at him. What *harm* could it do? Was he serious? But that was the trouble—he was. Unemotional, cynical and governed by nothing but sexual hunger—Niccolò obviously saw no reason why they shouldn't continue with the affair. Because it meant different things to each of them. For him, it was clearly just an enjoyable diversion, while for her it felt as if someone had chipped away a little bit of her heart every time she saw him. *It was being chipped away right now.*

She had chosen his office and a deliberately short

appointment in which to tell him her news in order to avoid just this kind of scene. She'd actually considered telling him by phone but had instinctively felt that such a move would have been counterproductive. That he might have insisted on coming round to confront her face to face and her defences would have been down.

It was bad enough trying to stay neutral now—even with the safety of his big oak desk between them. Sitting there in his crisp white shirt and tailored suit, Niccolò's face was glowing with health and vitality and she just wanted to go and put her arms around him. She wanted to lean on him and have him tell her that everything was going to be okay. But he didn't want a woman like her leaning on him and anyway—she was independent and strong. She didn't need a man who could never give her what she wanted, and what she wanted from him was love. *Join the queue,* she thought bitterly.

'You haven't *done* anything,' she said. 'You haven't made or broken any promises. Everything is how it's supposed to be, Niccolò. What happened between us was great but it was never intended to last. And it hasn't.'

'But what if...?' He picked up the golden pen which was lying on top of the letters he'd been signing and stared at it as if he had never really seen it before. He lifted his gaze to hers. 'What if I wanted it to last—at least for a little while longer? What then?'

Alannah tensed as fear and yearning washed over her—yet of the two emotions, the yearning was by far the deadlier.

'And how long did you have in mind?' she questioned sweetly. 'One week? Two? Would it be presumptuous to expect it might even continue for a *whole month*?'

He slammed the pen down. 'Does it matter?' he demanded. 'Not every relationship between a man and a woman lasts for ever.'

'But most relationships don't start out with a discussion about when it's going to end!' She sucked in a breath and prayed she could hold onto her equilibrium for a while longer. 'Look, nothing has changed. I'm still the same woman I always was—except that I have you to thank for helping me lose some of my inhibitions. But I still don't know who my father was and I still have the kind of CV which would make someone with your sensitive social antennae recoil in horror. Appearances matter to you, Niccolò. You know they do. So why don't you just celebrate the fact that you had a lucky escape and that we aren't going to be forced together by some random act of nature.' She rose to her feet. 'And leave me to finish off Alekto's apartment in time for his party. The caterers are arriving tomorrow, and there are still some last-minute touches which need fixing.'

'Sit down,' he said. 'I haven't finished yet.'

'Well, I have. We've said everything which needs to be said. It's over, Niccolò. I'm not so stupid that I want to hang around having sex with a man who despises everything I stand for!'

'I don't despise what you stand for. I made a lot of judgements about you and some of them were wrong.'

'Only *some* of them?' she demanded.

'Why can't you just accept what I'm offering? Why do you have to want more?'

'Because I'm worth it.' She hitched the strap of her handbag over her shoulder. 'And I'm going now.'

He rose to his feet. 'I don't want you to go!' he gritted out.

'Tough. I'm out of here. *Ciao*.'

And to Niccolò's amazement she picked up her handbag and walked out of his office without a backward glance.

For a moment he stood there, stunned—as the door slammed behind her. He thought about rushing after her, about pulling her into his arms and kissing her and *then* seeing whether she was so damned certain their relationship was over. But that would make it all about sex, wouldn't it? And sex had always been the least troublesome part of this equation. Besides, Kirsty was buzzing through to tell him that his eleven o'clock had arrived, so he was forced to concentrate on listening to what his architect was saying, rather than on a pair of stubborn pink lips he still wanted to crush beneath his own.

By seven o'clock that evening, he decided that Alannah had been right. Better to end it now, before she got in too deep—because it wouldn't be fair to break her heart as he had broken so many others. She would start falling in love with him. She would want more from him than he was capable of giving. Better they both recognised his limitations now.

He glanced up at the clock again. Maybe he should start as he meant to go on. Dinner with someone new would surely be the way to go. A civilised dinner with someone who didn't get under his skin the way she did.

He flicked through his address book, but none of the long list of names excited him enough to pick up the phone. He had his driver drop him home and worked in his study until way past midnight. But still he couldn't sleep. He kept remembering when Alannah had spent the night with him there and, even though the linen had been laundered, he thought he could still detect the unique scent of her skin on his sheets. He thought about the cottage. About the tree-lights and the snow. About that unreal sense of quiet satisfaction as he had cooked her Christmas lunch. The way they had fallen asleep on the sofa after they'd made love. Hadn't that been like the closest thing to peace he'd felt in a long, long time?

And that was all make-believe, he told himself fiercely. As insubstantial as Christmas itself.

He lay and watched the luminous numbers on his clock changing slowly and just before his alarm was due to go off a text arrived from Alekto Sarantos.

Don't be late for my party! Beautiful women and a beautiful apartment—what better way to see in the new year? A

Niccolò stared blankly at the screen of his mobile phone, telling himself that a party was exactly what he needed, and didn't Alekto throw some of the best parties he'd ever been to? But just the thought of it left him cold. Tugging on his running gear, he got ready for the gym and wondered why his eyes looked so shadowed and haunted.

But deep down, he knew exactly why.

'It is *spectacular.*' Alekto Sarantos smiled as he looked around the main reception room, his blue eyes gleaming. 'You have transformed my apartment, Alannah—and you have worked against the clock to get it done in time for my party. *Efkaristo poli.* I thank you.'

Alannah smiled back, even though just smiling seemed to take a massive effort these days. It was true that the place *did* look pretty amazing—especially when she thought back to the sea of beige it had been before. The woman who had made the curtains had got very excited about it and she had told someone, who had told someone else. Even during the short period between Christmas and new year, word had soon got round in an industry which survived by constantly seeking out new ideas and new faces. Already Alannah had received a phone call from one of the big interior magazines, asking if they could do a photo shoot there. She doubted whether Alekto would agree, since she got the idea he was very hot on privacy. Still, she could *always ask* him. And even if he didn't give his permission, she sensed that she had turned a corner—because this was the big break she had been waiting for. *And she had Niccolò to thank for it.*

Security and creative fulfilment were lying within her grasp. So why did it all feel so empty? Why was she having to force herself to look and sound enthusiastic about something she'd always dreamed of?

She sighed. She knew *exactly* why. *Because she'd made the fundamental mistake of falling in love with a man who had never offered her anything but sex.*

'I hope you're coming to my new year's party?' Alekto was saying. 'You really ought to be the guest of honour, after what you've achieved here. Unless, of course, you have already made plans?'

Alannah glanced out at the late afternoon sky, which was now almost dark. The only plans she had made were to buy the TV guide and turn up the central heating, while she waited for Big Ben to chime in a new year she couldn't seem to get worked up about. She thought about getting dressed up for a party attended by Alekto Sarantos and his glamorous friends, and how any sane person would leap at such an opportunity.

But what if Niccolò was there?

Her heart pounded. The possibility was high. It was more than high. They were best mates, weren't they? She shook her head. 'It's very sweet of you—but I think I'll just have a quiet evening in,' she said.

'Up to you.' Alekto shrugged. 'But if you change your mind…'

Alannah went home, bathed and washed her hair—before pulling on her dressing gown and a pair of slouchy socks and switching on the TV. She flicked channels. Crowds of people were already flocking into Trafalgar Square, even though it was still early. People were being interviewed, swigging from beer bottles and giggling—and Alannah suddenly saw herself as a fly on the wall might see her. A woman sitting on her own at nine o'clock on New Year's Eve, wearing a dressing gown and a pair of old socks.

What had she become?

She swallowed. She had become a cliché, that was what. She had fallen in love with someone who had always been out of reach. And yet, instead of accepting that and holding her head up high and just getting on with her life, the way she'd always done, she had caved in. She was like some sort of mole, living in darkness—cowering inside her own safe little habitat, because she was afraid to go out. It was the worst night of the year to be home alone—especially if your stupid heart was heavy and aching—and yet here she was. *Mole.*

What was she so worried about? That she might see Niccolò with another woman? Surely that would be the best of all possible outcomes—it would remind her of how easily he could move on. It would make her accept *reality*, instead of chasing after rainbows.

Tearing off her slouchy socks, she pulled out the gold dress she'd worn at Christmas and slithered into it. Then she slapped on a defiant amount of make-up, her highest heels—and a warm, ankle-length coat. People were milling outside pubs as she made her way to the station and more snow was falling as she caught the underground and got out at Knightsbridge.

It was much quieter in this part of town. There were few revellers out and about around here—this was the world of the private, rather than the street party. But by the time she reached Park View other partygoers were milling around in the foyer and the party atmosphere was contagious. She shared the elevator up to Alekto's apartment with several stunning women and a man who kept surreptitiously glancing at his phone.

The elevator pinged to a halt and the door to the penthouse was opened by a waitress dressed as a flamingo, a tray of exotic-looking cocktails in her hand. Alannah went off to hang up her coat and then wandered along the corridors she knew so well, back towards the sitting room. It was strange seeing the place like this—full of people—when she had only ever seen it empty. Most of the furniture she'd installed had been pushed back against the walls to maximise the space—but the room still looked spectacular. Even she could see that. The colours worked brilliantly—providing the perfect backdrop for Alekto's extensive art collection—and she was particularly proud of the lighting.

In spite of everything, she knew Niccolò would be pleased with her work. He might regret some things, but he would never regret giving her the job and she should take pride in that. A horrible dark pain washed over her, only this time it was underpinned with reproach. She wasn't supposed to be thinking about Niccolò. Wasn't that going to be her one and only new year resolution? That part of her life was over. She had to cut her losses and move on. And it was a waste of time to wonder what it would have been like if she *had* been pregnant. Or to dwell on that irrational and sinking sense of disappointment when she had stared at the test result and it had been negative.

A woman masquerading as a bird of paradise offered her a drink and Alannah took one, but the sweet concoction tasted deceptively powerful and she put the glass down as Alekto Sarantos came over to talk to her.

'You made it, then,' he said, with a smile. '*Thavmassios.* If I had a Euro for every person who has asked me who is responsible for the design of this apartment, then I would be a very rich man.'

'But I thought you *were* a very rich man,' she said, and he laughed, before giving her a thoughtful look. 'I might have some work for you in Greece, if you're interested?'

Alannah didn't even need to think about it. 'I'd be very interested,' she said immediately, because a different country might be just what she needed. What was it they said? A new year and a new start.

'Why don't you call my office on Monday?' he suggested, pulling out a business card and handing it to her.

'I will,' she said, putting it into her handbag as he walked away.

'Alannah?'

A familiar voice curled over her skin like dark velvet and she turned to see Niccolò standing there. His hair and shoulders were wet with melting snow and he was wearing a dark cashmere coat, which made him stand out from all the other guests. Alannah stiffened as his shadow fell over her and her heart began to hammer as she looked up into his shuttered features.

The knot of tension in her stomach grew tighter. But she had come here tonight to hold her head high, hadn't she? Not to hang it in shame. Nor to waste time wishing for something which could never be.

'Niccolò,' she said coolly. 'Fancy seeing you here.'

'What were you saying to Alekto?'

'That's really none of your business.'

'You do know he is world-famous for breaking women's hearts?'

'Why, has he lifted the crown from you?' she questioned acidly. 'And what are you doing still wearing your overcoat?'

'Because I have driven halfway across London looking for you,' he growled.

She frowned. 'Why?'

'Why do you think?' he exploded. 'I went round to your apartment, only you weren't there.' He had spent the afternoon psyching himself up, making careful plans about what he was going to say to her. He had decided to surprise her, because he...well, because he wanted to—and that in itself was uncharacteristic. He had naturally made the assumption that she would have been home alone, only when he'd got there Alannah's apartment had been shrouded in darkness and his heart had sunk. The sight of all those empty windows had suddenly seemed like a metaphor for his life and they had confirmed the certainty which had been growing inside him for days.

Instinct had made him pull out his telephone to speak to Alekto and his hunch was proved right. His friend had coolly informed him that, yes, Alannah *had* been invited to the party and although she'd told him she wasn't coming, she seemed to have changed her mind. In fact, she had just walked in, looking like a goddess in a spectacular golden dress.

Niccolò had turned his car around and driven from Acton, getting snarled up in the new-year traffic—his nerves becoming more and more frayed as an unfamiliar sense of agitation nagged away at him. And now he was here standing in front of her and nothing was as he thought it would be. He had not intended to launch into a jealous tirade because he'd seen her being chatted up by one of the world's biggest players.

Wasn't he supposed to be a 'player' himself?

His mouth hardened.

Not any more.

He was in a roomful of some of the most beautiful

women in the world and yet he could see only one. One who was staring at him with hostility and suspicion and, in his heart, he knew he couldn't blame her.

So why the hell was he demonstrating an arrogance which might cause her magnificent pride to assert itself, and tell him to take a running jump? He needed to keep her onside. To placate her. To make her realise why he had come here. *And to make her realise that it was the only possible solution.*

'I need to talk to you,' he said.

'Talk away.' She gave a careless shrug. 'I'm not stopping you.'

'In private.'

'I'd prefer to stay here, if you don't mind.'

'Unfortunately, *tentatrice*, I do mind.'

Without warning, he caught hold of her hand, his fingers enclosing her hammering pulse as he led her through the throng of partygoers until they had reached one of the bedrooms. He shut the door, just as she shook her hand free and glared at him.

'What do you think you're doing?' she demanded. 'You can't just waltz up to someone in the middle of a party and *manhandle* them like that! You can't just drag a woman from a room because you've decided you want a private word with her. Oh, sorry—I'd forgotten.' She slapped her palm against her brow. 'You can—and you do. Well, you might be Tarzan but I am not your Jane. I don't *do* Neanderthal and I don't *do* arrogant men who think they can just blaze into other people's lives doing exactly what they want. So will you please step aside and let me pass?'

'Not until you've heard me out,' he said, as a strange sense of calm washed over him. 'Please.'

She looked at him for a moment before pointedly glancing at her watch. 'You've got five minutes.'

Niccolò sucked in a breath but for a moment he couldn't speak. His calmness seemed to be deserting him as he realised that this wasn't going to be easy. He was going to have to do something unheard of— something he had instinctively always shied away from. He was going to have to pull out his feelings from the dark place where he'd buried them and he was going to have to admit them. To her. And even when he did, there was no guarantee that it might not be too late.

He looked into the wary blue of her eyes and his heart pounded. 'I need to ask your forgiveness,' he said. 'For all the unjust accusations I hurled at you. For my bull-headedness and my lack of compassion. For taking so long to realise the kind of woman you really are. Strong and proud and passionate and loyal. I've missed you, Alannah, and I want you back. Nobody talks to me the way you do, or makes me feel the way you do. Nobody else makes my heart skip a beat whenever I see her. I want to spend the rest of my life with you. To one day make the baby we didn't have this time. I want to make a real home—with you. Only with you.'

She took a step back, as if she'd just seen a ghost, and she started shaking her head. 'You don't want me,' she said in a hoarse voice. 'You only think you do, because I'm the one who walked away and that's probably never happened to you before. You want someone respectable, who is as pure as the driven snow—because that's the sort of thing you care about. Someone *suitable*. You didn't want me as bridesmaid because you were worried about what other people would think. Because you're hung up on appearances and how things look from the outside, no matter what you say.'

'I used to be,' he said savagely. 'But you have made me realise that appearances and social position don't matter. It's what's underneath which counts. And you have everything that counts. You are soft and smart and funny. You are kind and caring and talented. You didn't even smoke dope at school, did you— even though you were accused of it?'

Startled by this sudden conversational twist, Alannah narrowed her eyes suspiciously. 'Did Michela tell you that?'

He shook his head. 'She didn't have to. I worked it out for myself. I think you may just have covered up for my sister all this time.'

'Because that's what friends do,' she said fiercely. 'That's called loyalty.'

'I realise that now,' he said. 'It's just taken me a long and very circuitous route to get here. But I don't want to talk about the past any more... I want to concentrate on the future.'

He reached within the pocket of his snow-covered overcoat and pulled out a little box. 'This is for you,' he said, and his voice was slightly unsteady.

Alannah watched as he opened it and she was shamefully aware of a sinking sense of disappointment as she looked inside. Had she really thought it was an engagement ring? Was she really that fickle? Because glittering against the background of dark velvet was a brooch shaped like a little honey-bee. Its back was covered with yellow, black and white stones and she found herself thinking that she'd never seen anything so sparkly. She looked up at him, still disorientated.

'What's this?' she said.

'You collect insect brooches, don't you? They're diamonds. The black ones are quite rare. It's for you,' he said again. 'Because I didn't buy you a Christmas present.'

But Alannah felt a terrible lump in her throat as she began to blink her eyes rapidly. 'You just don't get it, do you?' she whispered. 'The brooches I have are all worth peanuts. I wear them because my mother gave them to me—because they *mean* something to me. I don't care if they're diamonds or paste, Niccolò. I don't care how much something is *worth*.'

'Then what if I tell you this is worth what I feel for you, and that is everything. *Everything*.' He moved closer. 'Unless you want me to go to a flea-market to find you something cheaper? Tell me, Alannah—are you going to set me a series of challenges before you will accept me?'

She almost laughed, except that now hot tears were springing to her eyes and she couldn't seem to stop them. 'I don't know what I'm going to do,' she whispered. 'Because I'm scared. Scared because I keep thinking this is all a dream and that I'm going to wake up in a minute.'

'No, not a dream,' he said, taking the brooch from the box and pinning it next to the little grasshopper which already adorned her golden dress. 'I bought you this because I love you. This is the reality.'

Her lips parted. 'Niccolò,' she said again, and now her voice was shaking. 'If this isn't true—'

He halted her protest by placing his finger over her lips. 'It *is* true. It has always been true. The first time I set eyes on you, I was hit by a thunderbolt so powerful that I felt as if you'd cast some kind of spell on me. And that spell never really faded. I love you, Alannah—even though I've been running away from the idea of love all my life. I saw what it did to my mother. I saw it as a weakness which sucked the life from everything in its path. Which blinded her even to the needs of her children.'

She bit her lip. 'I can understand that.'

He sensed her absolution, but he was not finished. 'But what I feel for you does not feel like weakness. I feel strong when I am with you, Alannah. As strong as a mountain lion. As if I could conquer the world.'

She let him put his arms around her and her head rested against his chest. 'That's funny, because right now I feel as weak as a kitten.'

His black eyes burned into her as he gently levered her face up so that she was looking directly at him. 'The only thing I need to know is whether you love me?'

'Of course I love you.' The words came tumbling out as if she'd been waiting all her life to say them. She thought about the first time she'd seen him, when they'd just clicked. It had been a thunderbolt for her, too, and she had never been able to forget him. She thought about how empty her life seemed when he wasn't there. He wasn't the man she'd thought him to be—he was so much more. 'I think I've always loved you.'

'Then kiss me, my beautiful Alannah,' he said softly. 'And let me show you my love.'

Slowly and tenderly, he traced his fingertip along the edges of her lips before lowering his head towards hers and Alannah's heart filled up with so much happiness that she felt as if she might burst with it.

EPILOGUE

'I USED TO think you hated weddings.'

Niccolò looked down into Alannah's face as he closed the door to their honeymoon suite, and smiled at her. 'I did. But that was before I found the woman I wanted to marry. Now it seems that I'm their biggest fan.'

'Mmm. Me, too.' She looped her arms around his neck. 'You did like the dress?'

'You looked beautiful. The most beautiful bride in the world. But then, you could wear a piece of sacking and I still wouldn't be able to tear my eyes away from you.'

'Oh, Niccolò.' She slanted him a look from between her lashes. 'Whoever would have guessed that beneath that cynical exterior beat the heart of a true poet?'

'It's true,' he said, mock-seriously. 'Though I must be careful not to lose my edge. If my competitors find out how much I'm softening, then I will soon be toast in the world of finance.'

'You?' She laughed easily. 'Yeah, sure. Like *that's* ever going to happen!'

He began to unzip her dress. 'Are you tired?'

'Not a bit. Even though it's been a very long day.'

She closed her eyes as the costly gown pooled to the ground around her feet. She had thought he would want a quiet wedding—something discreet, even a little hushed-up. Hadn't she thought he'd want to keep the risk of press interest to a minimum, despite his protestations that her past no longer bothered him? Probably. But once again he had surprised her. It was funny how love had the power to change people and to alter their views on what was important. He had told her that he was going to announce their engagement to the world's press and then he had gone out and bought her an enormous sapphire ring, which he said was the closest colour he could get to the denim-blue of her eyes.

Predictably, some of the old photos from *Stacked* magazine had made an appearance in the papers—but suddenly, they didn't seem to matter. It was slightly surreal to hear Niccolò echoing his sister's words—*and believing them*—by saying really they were very tame in comparison to a lot of the stuff you saw in contemporary music videos.

'I am proud of you, *tentatrice*,' he had murmured, crumpling the newspaper into a ball and hurling it into the bin. 'Proud of all you have achieved and how you have kept your dignity intact. Most of all, I am proud that you have consented to be my wife.'

And she had smiled. 'Oh, darling.'

The wedding was held in London's oldest Italian church, in Clerkenwell, and there was a stellar number of guests. A fully recovered Luis Martinez was there—as was the Sultan of Qurhah, Murat 'the Magnificent'. And naturally, Alekto Sarantos was at his dazzling best, even though he was barely visible through the sea of eager women who were clamouring round him. Michela was matron of honour—her silk gown cleverly hiding the beginning of a baby bump.

With Alannah's encouragement, Niccolò had told Michela the truth about their parents' death—and the admission had brought brother and sister much closer. Because secrets were always more dangerous than the truth, as he'd learned.

Alannah shivered with pleasure as Niccolò lifted her out of the discarded wedding dress and carried her over to the bed, wearing nothing but her underwear, sheer stockings and a pair of very high, white stilettos. As he undressed her she thought about the inhibitions which had once crippled her and which now seemed like a distant memory.

Tomorrow they were flying to the island of Niccolò's birth. He had only been back to Sicily once, after his mother's death—when he had been full of youthful rage and bitterness about the rejection she had suffered at the hands of her own family. But time had mellowed him and Alannah had helped him get some perspective. His maternal grandparents were dead—but he had cousins and uncles and aunts living there. A whole new family for them to get to know. And she was excited about that, too—looking forward to a big, extended family after so many years on her own.

He moved over her, his face suddenly very serious as he brushed her hair away from her cheek. 'Thank you,' he said softly.

She took his hand and kissed it. 'For?'

'For loving me. For being you.'

For being you. He didn't want anyone else, she had come to realise. He just wanted her exactly as she was, with no changes or modifications. He didn't want to rewrite her past, or pretend it hadn't happened, because her past had made her the woman she was today. And he loved that woman.

Alannah sighed.

Just like she loved her man.

* * * * *

HIS UNTIL MIDNIGHT

NIKKI LOGAN

*For Alex and Trev who let me turn their entirely
platonic annual tradition into something much
more dramatic. Thank you for the inspiration.*

Nikki Logan lives on the edge of a string of
wetlands in Western Australia with her partner
and a menagerie of animals. She writes captivating
nature-based stories full of romance in descriptive
natural environments. She believes the danger
and richness of wild places perfectly mirror the
passion and risk of falling in love.

Nikki loves to hear from readers via
nikkilogan.com.au or through social media.
Find her on Twitter, @ReadNikkiLogan, and
Facebook, NikkiLoganAuthor.

CHAPTER ONE

December 20th, four years ago
Qīngtíng Restaurant, Hong Kong

AUDREY DEVANEY FLOPPED against the back of the curved sofa and studied the pretty, oriental-style cards in her hands. Not the best hand in the world but when you were playing for M&M's and you tended to eat your stake as fast as it accumulated it was hard to take poker too seriously.

Though it was fun to pretend she knew what she was doing. Like some Vegas hotshot. And it wasn't too hard to imagine that the extraordinary view of Hong Kong's Victoria Harbour stretching out behind Oliver Harmer was really out of the window of some casino high-roller's room instead of a darkened, atmospheric restaurant festooned with pretty lanterns and baubles in rich, oriental colours.

Across from her, Oliver's five o'clock shadow was designer perfect and an ever-present, unlit cigar poked out of the corner of his grinning mouth—more gummed than smoked, out of respect for her and for the other patrons in the restaurant. It only *felt* as if he bought the whole place out each Christmas, it wasn't actually true. Though it was nice to imagine that they had the entire restaurant to themselves.

'Thank you, again, for the gift,' she murmured, letting the fringed silk ends of the cobalt scarf run between her fingers. 'It's stunning.'

'You're welcome. You should wear more blue.'

Audrey studied Oliver over her cards, wanting to ask but not entirely sure how to raise it. Maybe the best approach was the direct approach…

'You know, you look pretty good for a man whose wedding just fell through.'

'Good' as in *well*. Not 'good' as in *gorgeous*. Although, as always, the latter would certainly apply. All that dark hair, long lashes and tanned Australian skin…

He took his time considering his hand and then tossed three cards face down onto the ornate carved table. 'Dodged a bullet.'

That stopped her just as she might have discarded her own dud cards. 'Really? Last Christmas it was all about how Tiffany might be "the one".'

Not that she'd actually believed him at the time, but a year was the longest relationship she'd ever known him to have.

Maybe she was just in denial.

'Turns out there was more than one "one" for Tiffany.' The tiniest glimmer of hurt stained his eyes.

Oh, no. 'Who called it off?'

His answer came fast and sure. 'I did.'

Oliver Harmer was a perpetual bachelor. But he was also Shanghai's most prized perpetual bachelor and so she couldn't imagine the average woman he dated being too fast to throw away her luxury future.

But she knew from Blake how seriously Oliver felt about fidelity. Because of his philandering father. 'I'm so sorry.'

He shrugged. 'She was with someone when I met her; I was foolish to think that I'd get treated any different.'

Foolish perhaps, but he was only human to hope that he'd be special enough to change his girlfriend's ways. And if ever there was a man worth changing for… Audrey dropped two cards onto the table and Oliver flicked her two replacements from the top of the pack with confident efficiency before taking three of his own.

'What did she say when you confronted her?' she murmured.

'I didn't see any purpose in having it out,' he squeezed out past the cigar. 'I just cut her loose.'

Without an explanation? 'What if you were mistaken?'

The look he threw her would have withered his corporate opponents. 'I checked. I wasn't.'

'Checking' in Oliver's world probably meant expensive private surveillance. So no, he wouldn't have been wrong. 'Where is she now?'

He shrugged. 'Still on our honeymoon, I guess. I gave her an open credit card and wished her the best.'

'You bought her off?' She gaped.

'I bought her forgiveness.'

'And that worked?'

'Tiffany never was one for labouring under regret for long.'

Lord, he had a talent for ferreting out the worst of women. Always beautiful, of course and—*cough*—agile, but utterly barren on the emotional front. To the point that she'd decided Oliver must prefer them that way. Except for the trace of genuine hurt that had flitted across his expression...

That didn't fit with the man she thought she knew.

She studied the nothing hand in front of her and then tossed all five cards down on the table in an inelegant fold.

'Why can't you just meet a nice, normal woman?' she despaired. 'Shanghai's a big city.'

He scooped the pile of bright M&M's towards him—though not before she snaffled yet another one to eat—and set about reshuffling the cards. 'Nice women tend to give me a wide berth. I can't explain it.'

She snorted. 'It would have nothing to do with your reputation.'

Hazel eyes locked on hers, speculative and challenging. Enough to tighten her chest a hint. 'And what reputation is that?'

Ah...no. 'I'm not going to feed your already massive ego, Oliver.'

Nor go anywhere near the female whispers she'd heard about Oliver *'the Hammer'* Harmer. Dangerous territory.

'I thought we were friends!' he protested.

'You're friends with my husband. I'm just his South-East Asian proxy.'

He grunted. 'You only agree to our ritual Christmas catch-up for the cuisine, I suppose?'

'Actually, no.'

She found his eyes—held them—and two tiny butterflies broke free in her chest. 'I come for the wine, too.'

He snagged a small fistful of M&M's and tossed them across the elegant, carved coffee table at her, heedless of those around them sharing the Christmas-themed menu sixty storeys above Hong Kong.

Audrey scrabbled madly to pick them up. 'Ugh. Isn't that just like a squazillionaire. Throwing your money around like it's chocolate drops.'

'Play your hand,' he griped. But there was a definite smile behind it. As there always was. Christmases between them were always full of humour, fast conversation and camaraderie.

At least on the surface.

Below the surface was a whole bunch of things that she didn't let herself look at too closely. Appreciation. Respect. A great, aching admiration for his life and the choices he'd made and the courage with which he'd made them. Oliver Harmer was the freest human being she knew. And he lived a life most people would hunger for.

She certainly did from within the boundaries of her awkward marriage. It was hard not to esteem his choices.

And then below all of that… The ever-simmering attraction. She'd grown used to it now, because it was always there. And because she only had to deal with it once a year.

He was a good-looking man; charming and affable, easy to talk to, easy to like, well built, well groomed, well mannered, but not up himself or pretentious. Never too cool to toss a handful of chocolates in a fine restaurant.

But he'd also been best man at her wedding.

Blake's oldest friend.

And he was pursued by women day in and day out. She would be two hundred per cent mortified if Oliver ever got so much of a hint of the direction of her runaway thoughts—not the least because it would just inflate his already monumental ego—but also because she knew exactly what he'd do with the information.

Nothing.

Not a damned thing.

He would take it to his grave, and she would never fully know if that was because of his loyalty to Blake, his respect for her, or because something brewing between them was just so totally inconceivable that he'd chalk it up to an aberrant moment best never again spoken of.

Which was pretty much the right advice.

She wasn't like the women he normally chose. Her finest day was the day of her wedding when she'd been called 'striking'—and by Oliver, come to think of it, who always seemed to say the right thing at the right moment when she was on rocky emotional ground. She didn't look as good as his women did in their finery and she didn't move in the same circles and know the same people and laugh overly loud at the same stories. She wasn't unattractive or dull or dim—she'd wager the entire pile of M&M's in front of her on the fact that she could outrank every one of them on a

MENSA test—but she certainly didn't turn heads when she was in the company of the beautiful people. She lacked that…stardust that they had.

That Oliver was coated-to-sparkling in.

And in all the years she'd known him, she'd flat out never seen him with someone less beautiful than he was.

Clearly some scientific principle of balance at work there.

And when even the laws of nature ruled you out…

'All right, Cool Hand Luke,' she said, ripping her thoughts back to safer territory. 'Let's get serious about this game.'

That treacherous snake.

Audrey clearly had no idea whatsoever of Blake's latest conquest. Her face had filled just then with genuine sympathy about Tiffany, but nothing else. No shadows of pain at the mention of someone's infidelity, no blanching. No tears for a betrayal shared. Not that she was the tears-in-public type, but the only moisture in those enormous blue eyes was old-fashioned compassion.

For him.

Which meant that either Blake had lied and Audrey had no idea that her husband considered their marriage open, or she *did* know and Blake had worn her down to the point that she just didn't care any more.

And that awful possibility just didn't fit with the engaged, involved woman in front of him.

Oliver eyed her over his cards, pretending to psych her out and throw her game but really using the opportunity to study the tiniest traces of truth in her oval face. Her life tells. She wasn't flat and lifeless. She was enjoying the cards, the food, the conversation. She always did. He never flattered himself that it was him, particularly, that she hurried to see each year, but she loved the single day of decadence that they always shared on December twentieth. Not the expenditure—she and Blake were both on healthy incomes and she could buy this sort of experience herself if she really wanted to—it was the low-key luxury of this restaurant, this day, that she really got off on.

She was the only woman he'd ever met who got more excited by *not* being flashy with his money. By being as tastefully understated as she always was. It suited her down to the ground. Elegant instead of glitzy, all that dark hair twisted in a lazy knot on top of her head with what looked like bamboo spears holding it all together. The way her hands occasionally ran across the fabric of her tailored skirt told him she enjoyed how the fabric felt against her skin. That was why she wore it; not for him, or any other man. Not because it hugged the intriguing curve of her thighs almost indecently. The money Audrey spent on fashion was about recognising her equal in a quality product.

Whether she knew that or not.

Which was why he struggled so badly with Blake's protestations that Audrey was cool with his marital... excursions. He got that they didn't have the most conventional of marriages—definitely a meeting of minds—but she just didn't strike him as someone who would tolerate the cheapening of her relationship through his playing around. Because, if nothing else, Blake's sleeping around reflected on her.

And Audrey Devaney was anything but cheap.

'Oliver?'

He refocused to find those sapphire eyes locked hard on his. 'Sorry. Raise.'

She smiled at his distraction and then flicked her focus back down to her cards, leaving him staring at those long, down-curved lashes.

Did she know that her husband hooked up with someone else the moment she left town? Did that bother her? Or did she fabricate trips specifically to give Blake the opportunity, to give herself necessary distance from his infidelity, and preserve the amazing dignity that she wore like one of her silk suits. He'd never got the slightest sense that she evened the score while she travelled. Not that he'd necessarily know if she did—she would be as discreet about that as she was about the other details of her life—but her work ethic was nearly as solid as her friendship. And, as the lucky beneficiary of her unwavering loyalty as a friend, he knew that if Audrey was in Asia working then that was exactly what she'd be doing.

Working her silk-covered butt off.

And, if she wasn't, he'd know it. When it came to her, his radar was fine-tuned for the slightest hint that she was operating on the same wavelength as her husband.

Because if Audrey Devaney was *on* the market, then he was *in* the market.

No matter the price. No matter the terms. No matter what he'd believed his whole life about fidelity. He'd had enough hot, restless nights after waking from one of his dreams—riddled with passion and guilt and Audrey up against the cold glass of the window facing out over Victoria Harbour—to know what his body wanted.

'Call.' She tossed a cluster of M&M's onto the pile, interrupting the dangerous direction of his thoughts.

But he also knew himself pretty well. He knew that sex was the great equaliser and that reducing a woman that he admired and liked so much to the subject of one of his cheap fantasies was just his subconscious' way of dealing with the unfamiliar territory.

Territory in which he found himself fixated on the only woman he knew who was *genuinely* too good for him.

'Your game.' Oliver tossed aces and jacks purely for the pleasure of seeing the flush Audrey couldn't contain. The

pleasure that spilled out over the edges of her usual propri-
ety. She loved to win. She loved to beat him, particularly.

And he loved to watch her enjoy it.

She flipped a trio of fours on top of the mound of
M&M's triumphantly and her perfectly made-up skin practically glowed with pleasure. Instantly, he wondered if that
was what she'd look like if he pushed this table aside and
pressed her back into the sofa with his lips against that confident smile and his thigh between hers.

His body cheered the very thought.

'Rematch,' he demanded, forcing his brain clean of smut.
Pretty sad when throwing a card game was about as erotic
as any dream he could conjure up. 'Double or nothing.'

She tipped her head back to laugh and that knot piled
on the top and decorated with a bit of stolen airport tinsel wobbled dangerously. If he kept the humour coming
maybe the whole thing would come tumbling down and
he'd have another keeper memory for his pathetic fantasy-
stalker collection.

'Sure, while you're throwing your chocolates away...'

She slipped off her shoes and pulled slim legs up onto
the sofa as Oliver dealt another hand and, again, he was
struck by how down to earth she was. And how innocent.
This was not the relaxed, easy expression of a woman who
knew her husband was presently shacked up with someone
that wasn't his wife.

No question.

Which meant his best friend was a liar as well as an
adulterer. And a fool, too, for cheating on the most amazing woman either of them had ever known. Just *wasting* the
beautiful soul he'd been gifted by whatever fate sent Audrey
in Blake's direction instead of his own all those years ago.

But where fate was vague and indistinct, that out-of-
place rock weighing down her left hand was very real, and

though her husband was progressively sleeping his way through Sydney, Audrey wasn't following suit.

Because that ring meant something to her.

Just as fidelity meant something to him.

Perhaps that was the great attraction. Audrey was moral and compassionate, and her integrity was rooted as firmly as the mountains that surged up out of the ocean all around them to form the islands of Hong Kong where they both flew to meet each December twentieth. Splitting the difference between Sydney and Shanghai.

And he was enormously drawn to that integrity, even as he cursed it. Would he be as drawn to her if she was playing the field like her selfish husband? Or was he only obsessed with her because he knew he couldn't have her?

That was more his playbook.

Just because he didn't do unfaithful didn't mean he was pro-commitment. The whole Tiffany thing was really a kind of retirement. He'd given up on finding the woman he secretly dreamed was out there for him and settled for one that would let him do whatever he wanted, whenever he wanted and look good doing it.

And clearly even that wasn't meant to be.

'Come on, Harmer. Man up.'

His eyes shot up, fearing for one irrational moment that she'd read the direction of his inappropriate thoughts.

'It's just one game,' she teased. 'I'm sure you'll take me on the next one.'

She was probably right. He'd do what he did every Christmas: give enough to keep her engaged and entertained, and take enough to keep her colour high with indignation. To keep her coming back for more. Coming back to him. In the name of her cheating bastard of a husband who only ever visited him when he was travelling alone— though he'd be sure to put an end to that, now—and who took carnal advantage of every opportunity when Audrey was out of the country.

But, just as he suppressed his natural distaste for Blake's infidelity so that he could maintain the annual Christmas lunch with his best friend's wife, so he would keep Blake's secret.

Not only because he didn't want to hurt gentle Audrey.

And not because he condoned Blake's behaviour in the slightest—though he really, really didn't.

And not because he enjoyed being some kind of confessional for the man he'd stood beside at his wedding.

No, he'd keep Blake's secret because keeping it meant he got to have Audrey in his life. If he shared what he knew she'd leave Blake, and if she left Blake Oliver knew he'd never see her again. And it was only as he saw her friendship potentially slipping away like a landslide that he realised how very much he valued—and needed—it.

And her.

So he did what he did every year. He concentrated on Audrey and on enjoying what little time they had together this one day of the year. He feasted like the glutton he was on her conversation and her presence and he pushed everything else into the background where it belonged.

He had all year to deal with that. And with his conscience.

He stretched his open palm across the table, the shuffled cards upturned on it. As she took the pack, her soft fingers brushed against his palm, birthing a riot of sensation in his nerve endings. And he boxed those sensations up, too, for dealing with later, when he didn't have this amazing woman sitting opposite him with her all-seeing eyes focused squarely on him.

'Your deal.'

CHAPTER TWO

December 20th, three years ago
Qīngtíng Restaurant, Hong Kong

BEHIND HER BACK, Audrey pressed the soft flesh of her wrists to the glassy chill of the elevator's mirrored wall, desperate to cool the blazing blood rushing through her arteries. To quell the excited flush she feared stained her cheeks from standing this close to Oliver Harmer in such a tight space.

You'd think twelve months would be enough time to steel her resolve and prepare herself.

Yet here she was, entirely rattled by the anticipation of a simple farewell kiss. It never was more than a socially appropriate graze. Barely more than an air-kiss. Yet she still felt the burn of his lips on her cheek as though last year's kiss were a moment—and not a full year—ago.

She was a teenager again, around Oliver. All breathless and hot and hormonal. Totally fixated on him for the short while she had his company. It would have been comic if it weren't also so terribly mortifying. And it was way too easy to indulge the feelings this one day of the year. It felt dangerous and illicit to let the emotions even slightly off the leash. Thank goodness she was old enough now to fake it like a seasoned professional.

In public, anyway.

Oliver glanced down and smiled at her in that strange, searching way he had, a half-unwrapped DVD boxed set in his hands. She gave him her most careful smile back, took a deep breath and then refocused on the light descending the crowded panel of elevator buttons.

Fifty-nine, fifty-eight...

She wasn't always so careful. She caught herself two weeks ago wondering what her best man would think of tonight's dress instead of her husband. But she'd rationalised it by saying that Oliver's taste in women—and, by implication, his taste in their wardrobes—was far superior to Blake's and so taking trouble to dress well was important for a man who hosted her in a swanky Hong Kong restaurant each year.

Blake, on the other hand, wouldn't notice if she came to the dinner table dressed in a potato sack.

He used to notice—back in the day, nine years ago—when she'd meet him and Oliver at a restaurant in something flattering. Or sheer-cut. Or reinforcing. Back then, appreciation would colour Blake's skin noticeably. Or maybe it just seemed more pronounced juxtaposed with the blank indifference on Oliver's face. Oliver, who barely even glanced at her until she was seated behind a table and modestly secured behind a menu.

Yet, paradoxically, she had him to thank for the evolution of her fashion sense because his disdain was a clear litmus test if something was *too* flattering, *too* sheer-cut. *Too* reinforcing.

It was all there in the careful nothing of his expression.

People paid top dollar for that kind of fashion advice. Oliver gifted her with it for free.

Yeah…his *gift*. That felt so much better on the soul than his *judgement*. And seasonally appropriate, too.

This year's outfit was a winner. And while she missed the disguised scrutiny of his greenish-brown gaze—the visual caress that usually sustained her all year—the warm wash of his approval was definitely worth it. She glanced at herself in the elevator's mirrored walls and tried to see herself as Oliver might. Slim, professional, well groomed.

Weak at the knees with utterly inappropriate anticipation.

Forty-five, forty-four...

'What time is your flight in the morning?' His deep voice honey-rumbled in the small space.

Her answer was more breath than speech. 'Eight.'

Excellent. Resorting to small talk. But this was always how it went at the end. As though they'd flat run out of other things to talk about. Entirely possible given the gamut of topics they covered during their long, long lunch-that-became-dinner, and because she was usually emotionally and intellectually drained from so many hours sitting across from a man she longed to see but really struggled to be around.

It was only one day.

Twelve hours, really. That was all she had to get through each year and wasn't a big ask of her body. The rest of the year she had no trouble suppressing the emotions. She used the long flight home to marshal all the sensations back into that tightly lidded place she kept them so that she disembarked the plane in Sydney as strong as when she'd left Australia.

She'd invited Blake along this year—pure survival, hoping her husband's presence would force her wayward thoughts back into safer territory—but not only had he declined, he'd looked horrified at the suggestion. Which made no sense because he liked to catch up with Oliver whenever he was travelling in Asia, himself. Least he used to.

In fact, it made about as little sense as the not-so-subtle way Oliver changed the subject every time she mentioned

Blake. As if he was trying to distance himself from the only person they had in common.

And without Blake in common, really what did they have?

Twenty-seven, twenty-six, twenty-five...

Breath hissed out of her in a long, controlled yoga sigh and she willed her fluttering pulse to follow its lead. But that persistent flutter was still entirely fixated on the gorgeous, expensive aftershave Oliver wore and the heat coming off his big body and it seemed to fibrillate faster the closer to the ground floor they got.

And they were so close, now.

Ultimately, it didn't matter what her body did when in Oliver's immediate proximity—how her breath tightened, or her mouth dried or her heart squeezed—that was like Icarus hoping his wings wouldn't melt as he flew towards the sun.

There was nothing she could do about the fundamental rules of biology. All that mattered was that it didn't show on the outside.

On pain of death.

Tonight she'd been the master of her anatomy. Giving nothing away. So she only had to last these final few moments and she'd be away, speeding through the streets of Hong Kong en route to her own hotel room. Her cool, safe, empty bed. The sleepless night that was bound to follow. And the airport bright and early in the morning.

She should really get the red-eye next year.

It was impossible to know whether the lurch in her stomach was due to the arrest of the elevator's rapid descent or because she knew what was coming next. The elegant doors seemed to gather their wits a moment before opening.

Audrey did the same.

They whooshed open and she matched Oliver's footfalls out through the building's plush foyer onto the street, then turned on a smile and extended a hand as a taxi pulled up from the nearby rank to attend them.

'Any message for Blake?'

She always kept something aside for this exact moment. Something strong and obstructive in case her body decided to hurl itself at him and embarrass them all. Invariably Blake-related because that was about the safest territory the two of them had. Blake or work. Not to mention the fact that reference to her husband was usually one of the only things that made a dent in the hormonal surge that swilled around them when they stood this close.

The swampy depths of his eyes darkened for the briefest of moments as he took her hand in his large one. 'No. Thank you.'

Odd. Blake hadn't had one, either. Which was a first…

But her curiosity about that half-hidden flash of anger lasted a mere nanosecond in the face of the heat soaking from his hand into the one he hadn't released anywhere nearly as swiftly as she'd offered it. He held it—no caresses, nothing that would raise an eyebrow for anyone watching—and used it to pull her towards him for their annual Christmas air-kiss.

Her blood surged against its own current; the red cells rushing downstream to pool in fingers that tingled at Oliver's touch stampeding against the foolish ones that surged, upstream, to fill the lips that she knew full well weren't going to get to touch his.

She thrilled for this moment and hated it at the same time because it was never enough. Yet of course it had to be. The sharp, expensive tang of his cologne washed over her catgut-tight senses as he leaned down and brushed his lips against her cheek. A little further back from last year. A little lower, too. Close enough to her pulse to feel it pounding under her skin.

Barely enough to even qualify as a kiss. But ten times as swoon-worthy as any real kiss she'd ever had.

Hormones.

Talk about mind-altering chemicals…

'Until next year,' he breathed against her ear as he withdrew.

'I will.'

Give my regards to Blake. That was what usually came after 'the kiss' and she'd uttered her response before her foggy brain caught up to the fact that he hadn't actually asked it of her this year. Again, odd. So her next words were stammered and awkward. Definitely not the cool, calm and composed Audrey she usually liked to finish her visit on.

'Well, goodbye, then. Thank you for lunch.'

Ugh. Lame.

Calling their annual culinary marathon 'lunch' was like suggesting that the way Oliver made her feel was 'warm'. Right now her body blazed with all the unspent chemistry from twelve hours in his company and her head spun courtesy of the shallow breathing of the past few minutes. Embarrassed heat blazed up the back of her neck and she slipped quickly into the waiting taxi before it bloomed fully in her face.

Oliver stood on the footpath, his hand raised in farewell as she pressed back against the headrest and the cab moved away.

'Wait!'

She lurched against her seat belt and suddenly Oliver was hauling the door open again. For one totally crazy, breathless heartbeat she thought he might have pulled her into his arms. And she would have gone into them. Unflinchingly.

But he didn't.

Of course he didn't.

'Audrey—'

She shoved her ritualistic in-taxi decompression routine down into the gap between the seat back and cushion and presented him with her most neutral, questioning expression.

'I just... I wanted to say...'

A dozen indecipherable expressions flitted across his expression but finally resolved into something that looked like pain. Grief.

'Merry Christmas, Audrey. I'll see you next year.'

The anticlimax was breath-stealing in its severity and so her words were little more than a disenchanted whisper. 'Merry Christmas, Oliver.'

'If you ever need me...need anything. Call me.' His hazel eyes implored. 'Any time, day or night. Don't hesitate.'

'Okay,' she pledged, though had no intention of taking him up on it. Oliver Harmer and The Real World did not mix. They existed comfortably in alternate realities and her flight to and from Hong Kong was the inter-dimensional transport. In this reality he was the first man—the only man—she'd ever call if she were in trouble. But back home...

Back home she knew her life was too beige to need his help and even if she did, she wouldn't let herself call him.

The taxi pulled away again and Audrey resumed decompression. Her breath eased out in increments until her heart settled down to a heavy, regular beat and her skin warmed back up to room temperature.

Done.

Another year survived. Another meeting endured in her husband's name and hopefully with her dignity fully intact.

And only three hundred and sixty-five days until she saw Oliver Harmer again.

Long, confusing days.

CHAPTER THREE

December 20th, two years ago
Qīngtíng Restaurant, Hong Kong

OLIVER STARED OUT at the midnight sky, high enough above the flooding lights of Hong Kong to actually see a few stars, and did his best to ignore the screaming lack of attention being paid to him by Qīngtíng's staff as they closed up the restaurant for the night.

The arms crossed firmly across his chest were the only thing keeping his savaged heart in his chest cavity, and the beautifully wrapped gift crushed in his clenched fist was the only thing stopping him from slamming it into the wall.

She hadn't come.

For the first time in years, Audrey hadn't come.

CHAPTER FOUR

December 20th, last year
*Obsiblue prawn and caviar with Royale Cabanon Oyster
and Yuzu*

'YOU'RE LUCKY I'M even here.'

The rumbled accusation filtered through the murmur of low conversation and the chink of expensive silverware on Qīngtíng's equally expensive porcelain. Audrey turned towards Oliver's neutral displeasure, squared the shoulders of her cream linen jacket and smoothed her hands down her skirt.

'Yet here you are.'

A grunt lurched in Oliver's tanned throat where a business tie should have been holding his navy silk shirt appropriately together. Or at the very least some buttons. Benefit of being such a regular patron—or maybe so rich—niceties like dress code didn't seem to apply to him.

'Guess I'm slow to learn,' he said, still dangerously calm. 'Or just naively optimistic.'

'Not so naive. I'm here, aren't I?'

'You don't look too pleased about it.'

'Your email left me little choice. I didn't realise how proficient you'd become in emotional blackmail.'

'It wasn't blackmail, Audrey. I just wanted to know if

you were coming. To save me wasting another day and the flight from Shanghai.'

Shame battled annoyance. Yes, she'd stood him up last year, but she found it hard to imagine a man like Oliver left alone and dateless in a flash restaurant for very long. Especially at Christmas. Especially in a city full of home-sick expats. She was sure he wouldn't have withered away from lack of company.

'And playing the dead best friend card seemed equal to your curiosity, did it?'

Because that was the only reason she was here at all. The relationship he'd had with her recently passed husband. And she'd struggled to shake the feeling that she needed to provide some closure for Oliver on that friendship.

His hazel eyes narrowed just a hint in that infuriating, corporate, too-cool-for-facial-expression way he had. But he didn't bite. Instead he just stared at her, almost daring her to go on. Daring her, just as much, to hold his glower.

'They got new carpet,' she announced pointlessly, thrilled for an excuse not to let him enslave her gaze. Styl-ised and vibrant dragonflies decorated the floor where once obscure oriental patterns had previously lain. She sank the pointed tip of her cream shoe into the plush opulence and watched it disappear into Weihei Province's best hand-tufted weave. 'Nice.'

'Gerard got another Michelin.' He shrugged. 'New car-pet seemed a reasonable celebration.'

Somehow, Oliver managed to make her failure to know that one of Hong Kong's most elite restaurants had re-carpeted sound like a personal failure on her part.

'Mrs Audrey…'

Audrey suppressed the urge to correct that title as she turned and took the extended hand of the maître d' between her own. 'Ming-húa, lovely to see you again.'

'You look beautiful,' Ming-húa said, raising her hand to his lips. 'We missed you last Christmas.'

Oliver shot her a sideways look as they were shepherded towards their customary part of the restaurant. The end where the Chinese version of Christmas decorations were noticeably denser. They racked up a bill this one day of the year large enough to warrant the laying on of extra festive bling and the discreet removal of several other tables, yet, this year, more tables than ever seemed to have been sacrificed. It left them with complete privacy, ensconced in the western end of the restaurant between the enormous indoor terrarium filled with verdant water-soaked plants and fluorescent dragonflies, and the carpet-to-ceiling reinforced window that served as the restaurant's outer wall.

Beyond the glass, Victoria Harbour and the high-tech sparkle and glint of hundreds more towering giants just like this side of the shore. Behind the glass, the little haven that Audrey had missed so badly last Christmas. Tranquil, private and filled with the kind of gratuitous luxury a girl really should indulge in only once a year.

Emotional sanctuary.

The sanctuary she'd enjoyed for the past five years.

Minus the last one.

And Oliver Harmer was a central part of all that gratuitous luxury. Especially looking like he did today. She didn't like to notice his appearance—he had enough ego all by himself without her appreciation adding to it—but, here, it was hard to escape; wherever she looked, a polished glass surface of one kind or another offered her a convenient reflection of some part of him. Parts that were infinitely safer facing away from her.

Chilled Cristal sat—as it always did—at the centre of the small table between two large, curved sofas. The first and only furniture she'd ever enjoyed that was actually worthy of the name *lounge*. Certainly, by the end of the day they'd both be sprawled across their respective sides, bodies sated with the best food and drink, minds saturated with good conversation, a year's worth of catching up all done and dusted.

At least that was how it normally went.

But things weren't normal any more.

Suddenly the little space she'd craved so much felt claustrophobic and the chilled Cristal looked like something from a cheesy seduction scene. And the very idea that she could do anything other than perch nervously on the edge of her sofa for the next ten or twelve hours…?

Ludicrous.

'So what are you hunting this trip?' Oliver asked, no qualms whatsoever about flopping down into his lounge, snagging up a quarter-filled flute on the way down. So intently casual she wondered if he'd practised the manoeuvre. As he settled back his white shirt stretched tight across his torso and his dark trousers hiked up to reveal ankles the same tanbark colour as his throat. 'Stradivarius? Guarneri?'

'A 1714 Testore cello,' she murmured. 'Believed to now be in South East Asia.'

'Now?'

'It moves around a lot.'

'Do they know you're looking for it?'

'I have to assume so. Hence its air miles.'

'More fool them trying to outrun you. Don't they know you always get your man…or instrument?'

'I doubt they know me at all. You forget, I do all the legwork but someone else busts up the syndicates. My job relies on my contribution being anonymous.'

'Anonymous,' he snorted as he cut the tip off one of the forty-dollar cigars lying on a tray beside the champagne. 'I'd be willing to wager that a specialist with an MA in identification of antique stringed instruments is going to be of much more interest to the bad guys than a bunch of

Interpol thugs with a photograph and a GPS location in their clammy palms.'

'The day my visa gets inexplicably denied then I'll start believing you. Until then…' She helped herself to the Cristal. 'Enough about my work. How is yours going? Still rich?'

'Stinking.'

'Still getting up the noses of your competitors?'

'Right up in their sinuses, in fact.'

Despite everything, it was hard not to respond to the genuine glee Oliver got from irritating his corporate rivals. He wasted a fair bit of money on moves designed to exasperate. Though, not a waste at all if it kept their focus conveniently on what he *wasn't* doing. A reluctant smile broke free.

'I was wondering if I'd be seeing that today.' His eyes flicked to her mouth for the barest of moments. 'I've missed it.'

That was enough to wipe the smile clean from her face. 'Yeah, well, there's been a bit of an amusement drought since Blake's funeral.'

Oliver flinched but buried it behind a healthy draw from his champagne. 'No doubt.'

Well… *Awkward…*

'So how are you doing?' He tried again.

She shrugged. 'Fine.'

'And how are you really doing?'

Seriously? He wanted to do this? Then again, they talked about Blake every year. He was their connection, after all. Their *only* true connection. Which made being here now that Blake was gone even weirder. She should have just stayed home. Maybe they could have just done this by phone.

'The tax stuff was a bit of a nightmare and the house was secured against the business so that wasn't fun to disentangle, but I got there.'

He blinked at her. 'And personally?'

'Personally my husband's dead. What do you want me to say?'

All the champagne chugging in the world wasn't going to disguise the three concerned lines that appeared between his brows. 'Are you...coping?'

'Are you asking me about my finances?'

'Actually no. I'm asking you how you're doing. You, Audrey.'

'And I said *fine*.'

Both hands went up, one half filled with champagne flute. 'Okay. Next subject.'

And what would that be? Their one reason for continuing to see each other had gone trundling down a conveyor belt at the crematorium. Not that he'd remember that.

Why weren't you at your best friend's funeral? How was that for another subject? But she wouldn't give him the satisfaction.

Unfortunately, for them both, Oliver looked as uninspired as she did on the conversation front.

She pushed to her feet. 'Maybe this wasn't such a—'

'Here we go!' Ming-húa appeared flanked by two serving staff carrying the first amuse-bouche of their marine-themed Christmas degustation. 'Obsiblue prawn and caviar with Royale Cabanon Oyster and Yuzu.'

Audrey got 'prawn', 'caviar' and 'oyster' and not much else. But wasn't that kind of the point with degustation—to over-stimulate your senses and not be overly bothered by what things were or used to be?

Culinary adventure.

Pretty much the only place in her life she risked adventure.

She sank politely back onto her sofa. It took the highly trained staff just moments to place their first course *just so* and then they were alone again.

Oliver ignored the food and slid a small gift-wrapped parcel across the table.

Audrey stared at the patched-up wrapping. Best he was prepared to do after she'd stood him up? 'Um…'

'I don't expect anything in return, Audrey.'

Did he read everyone this well? 'I didn't imagine we'd be doing gifts this year.'

'This was from last year.'

She paused a moment longer, then pulled the small parcel towards her. But she didn't open it because opening it meant something. She set it aside, instead, smiling tightly.

Oliver pinned her with his intense gaze. 'We've been friends for years, Audrey. We've done this for years, every Christmas. Are you telling me you were only here for Blake?'

The slightest hint of hurt diluted the hazel of his eyes. One of the vibrant dragonflies flitting around the enormous terrarium matched the colour exactly.

She gifted him with the truth. 'It feels odd to be doing this with him gone.'

She didn't want to say *wrong*. But it had always felt vaguely wrong. Or her own reaction to Oliver certainly had. Wrong and dishonest because she'd kept it so secret and close to her heart.

'Everything is different now. But our friendship doesn't have to change. Spending time with you was never just about courtesy to a mate's wife. As far as I'm concerned we're friends, too.'

Pfff. Meaningless words. 'I missed you at *your mate's* funeral.'

A deep flush filled the hollow where his tie should have been. 'I was sorry not to be there.'

Uh-huh.

'Economic downturn made the flight unaffordable, I guess.' They would spend four times that cost on today's meals. But one of Oliver's strengths had always been courage under fire. He pressed his lips together and remained silent. 'Or was it just a really busy week at the office?'

She'd called. She knew exactly where he was while they'd buried her husband. 'Or did you not get my messages in time?'

All eight of them.

'Audrey…' The word practically hissed out of him.

'Oliver?'

'You know I would have been there if I could. Did you get the flowers I arranged?'

'The half-a-boutique of flowers? Yes. They were crammed in every corner of the chapel. And they were lovely,' honesty compelled her to admit. And also her favourites. 'But they were just flowers.'

'Look, Audrey, I can see you're upset. Can I please just ask you to trust that I had my reasons, good reasons, not to fly back to Sydney and that I had my own private memorial for my old friend back home in Shanghai—' Audrey didn't miss the emphasis on *'old'* friend '—complete with a half-bottle of Chivas. So Blake had two funerals that day.'

Why was this so hard? She shouldn't still care.

She shouldn't still remember so vividly the way she'd craned her neck from inside the funeral car to see if Oliver was walking in the procession of mourners. Or the way she'd only half attended to the raft of well-wishers squeezing her hand after the service because she was too busy wondering how she'd missed him. It was only later as she wrote thank-you cards to the names collected by the funeral attendants that she'd finally accepted the truth.

Oliver hadn't come.

Blake's best friend—their best man—hadn't come to his funeral.

That particular truth had been bitter, but she'd been too swamped in the chaos of new widowhood to be curious as to why it hurt so much. Or to imagine Oliver finding a private way of farewelling his old mate. Like downing a half-bottle of whisky.

'He always did love a good label,' she acknowledged.

A little too fondly as it turned out since Blake's thirst for good liquor was deemed a key contributor to the motor vehicle accident that took his life. But since her husband sitting in his den enjoying a sizeable glass or three with the evening newspaper had given Audrey the space and freedom to pursue things she enjoyed, she really couldn't complain.

The natural pause in the uncomfortable conversation was a cue to both of them to eat, and the tart seafood amuse-bouche was small enough that it was over in just mouthfuls.

Behind her, the gentle buzz of dragonfly wings close to glass drew her focus. She turned to study the collection that gave the restaurant its name. There were over one hundred species in Hong Kong—vibrant and fluorescent, large and small—and Qīngtíng kept an immaculate and stunning community of them in the specially constructed habitat.

She discreetly took several deep breaths to get her wayward feelings under control. 'Every year, I forget how amazing this is.'

And, every year, she envied the insects and pitied them, equally. Their captive life was one of luxury, with every conceivable need met. Their lives were longer and easier than their wild counterparts and neither their wetland nor food source ever dried up. Yet the glass boundaries of their existence was immutable. New arrivals battered softly against it until they eventually stopped trying and they accepted their luxurious fate.

Ultimately, didn't everyone?

'Give him a chance and the dragonfly curator will talk your ear off with the latest developments in invertebrate husbandry.'

His tone drew her eyes back. 'I thought you only flew down for the day? When did you have a chance to meet Qīngtíng's dragonfly guy?'

'Last Christmas. I unexpectedly found myself with time on my hands.'

Because she hadn't come.

The shame washed in again. 'It was…too soon. I couldn't leave Australia. And Blake was gone.'

He stared at her. Contemplating. 'Which one of those do you want to go with?'

Heat rushed up her neck.

'They're all valid.' His silence only underscored her lies. She took a deep breath. 'I'm sorry I didn't come last year, Oliver. I should have had more courage.'

'Courage?'

'To tell you that it was the last time I'd be coming.'

He flopped back in his chair. 'Is that what you've come to say now?'

It was. Although, saying it aloud seemed to be suddenly impossible. She nodded instead.

'We could have done that by phone. It would have been cheaper for you.'

'I had the Testore—'

'You could have come and not told me you were here. Like you did in Shanghai.'

Every muscle tightened up.

Busted.

She generally did her best to deal with Shanghai contacts outside Shanghai for a very specific reason—it was Harmer-country, and going deep into Oliver's own turf wasn't something she'd been willing to risk let alone tell him about. But how could he possibly know the population had swelled to twenty-five-million-and-one just that once? She asked him exactly that.

His eyes held hers. 'I have my sources.'

And why exactly were his sources pointing in her direction?

'Before you get too creeped out,' he went on, 'it was social media. Your status listed your location as the People's Square, so I knew you were in town.'

Ugh. Stupid too-smart phones. 'You didn't message me.'

'I figured if you wanted to see me you would have let me know.'

Oh. Sneaking in and out of China's biggest city like a thief was pathetic enough, but being so stupidly caught out just made her look—and feel—like a child. 'It was a flying visit,' she croaked. 'I was hunting a Paraguayan harp.'

Lord. *Not making it better.*

'It doesn't matter, that's in the past. I want to know why you won't be returning in the future.'

Discomfort gnawed at her intestines. 'I can't keep flying here indefinitely, Oliver. Can't we just say it's been great and let it go?'

He processed that for a moment. 'Do all your friends have best-by dates?'

His perception had her buzzing as furiously as the dragonflies. 'Is that what we are? Friends?'

'I thought so.' His eyes narrowed. 'I never got the sense that you were here under sufferance. You certainly seemed very comfortable helping me spend my money.'

'Oliver—'

'What's really going on, Audrey? What's the problem?'

'Blake's gone,' she pointed out needlessly on a great expulsion of breath. 'Me continuing to come and see you... What would be the point?'

'To catch up. To see each other.'

'Why would we do that?'

'Because friends nurture their relationships.'

'Our relationship was built on someone who's not here any more.'

He blinked at her—twice—and his perfect lips gaped. 'That might be how it started but it's not like that any longer.' An ocean of doubt swilled across the back of his gaze, though. 'I met you about six minutes before Blake did, if you recall. Technically, I think that means our friendship pre-dates Blake.'

That had been an excruciating six minutes, writhing under the intensity of the sexiest man she'd ever met, until his infinitely more ordinary friend had wandered into the Sydney bar. Blake with his narrower shoulders, his harmless smile and his non-challenging conversation. She'd practically swamped the man with her attention purely on reactive grounds, to crawl out from under Oliver's blistering microscope.

She knew when she was batting above her average and thirty seconds in his exclusive company told her Oliver Harmer was major league. Majorly gorgeous, majorly bright and majorly bored if he was entertaining himself by flirting with her.

'That doesn't count. You only spoke to me to pass the time until Blake turned up.'

He weighed something up. 'What makes you think I wasn't laying groundwork?'

'For Blake?'

His snort drew a pair of glances from across the room. 'For me. Blake's always been quite capable of doing his own dirty work…' As if it suddenly occurred to him that they were speaking of the dead, his words petered off. 'Anyway, as soon as he walked in the room you were captivated. I knew when I'd been bested.'

What would Oliver say if he knew she'd clung to Blake's conversation specifically to avoid having to engage with his more handsome friend again? Or if she confessed that she'd been aware of every single move Oliver made until the moment she left her phone number with Blake and fled out into the Australian night.

He'd probably laugh.

'I'm sure it did no permanent damage to your self-esteem,' she gritted.

'I had to endure his gloating for a week. It wasn't every day that he managed to steal out from under me a woman that I—' His teeth snapped shut.

'A woman that what?'

'Any woman at all, really. You were a first.'

She shook her head. 'Always so insufferable. *That's* why I gave my phone number to him and not you.'

That and the fact she always had been a coward.

He settled back into his sofa. 'Imagine how different things would be if you'd given it to me that day.'

'Oh, please. You would have bored of me within hours.'

'Who says?'

'It's just sport for you, Oliver.'

'Again. Who says?'

'Your track record says. And Blake says.'

Said.

He sat forward. 'What did he say?'

Enough to make her wonder if something had gone down between the two friends. She hedged by shrugging. 'He cared about you. He wanted you to have what he had.'

The brown flecks amid the green of his iris seemed to shift amongst themselves. 'What did he have?'

'A stable relationship. Permanency. A life partner.'

Would he notice she didn't say 'love'?

'That's rich, coming from him.'

'What do you mean?'

He glanced around the room and shifted uncomfortably in his seat before bringing his sharp, intent gaze back to her. Colour stained the very edge of his defined jaw. Audrey reached up to press her hand to her topknot to stop the lot falling down with the angle of her head. The pins really weren't doing their job so she pulled them out and the entire arrangement slid free and down to her shoulders.

His expression changed, morphed, as she watched, from something pointed to something intentionally dull. 'Doesn't matter what I mean. Ancient history. I didn't realise old Blake had such passion in him.'

'Excuse me?'

'Such possession. I always got the impression that your marriage was as much a meeting of minds as anything else.'

Heat raced up from under her linen collar. *What's wrong, Oliver, can't imagine me inspiring passion in a man?* 'You hadn't seen us together for years,' she said, tightly.

Why was that?

'My business relies on my ability to read people, Audrey. I hung out with you guys a lot those few years before your wedding. Before I moved to Shanghai. The three amigos, remember? Plenty of opportunity to form an opinion.'

Did she remember…?

She remembered the long dinners, the brilliant, three-way conversations. She remembered Oliver stepping between her and some drunk morons in the street, once, while Blake flanked her on the *protected* side. She remembered how breathless she felt when Oliver would walk towards them out of the twilight shadows and how flat she felt when he walked away.

Yeah. She remembered.

'Then you must recall how partial Blake was to public displays of affection.' Oliver used to get so embarrassed by them, looking away like the fifth wheel that he was. Hard to imagine the confident man that he now was being discomposed by anything. 'Wasn't that sufficient demonstration of his feelings?'

'It was a demonstration all right. I always got the feeling that Blake specially reserved the displays of affection for when you were *in* public.'

Mortification added a few more degrees to the heat that was only just settling back under her jacket. Because that was essentially true. Behind closed doors they lived more like siblings. But what he probably didn't know was that Blake saved the PDAs up most particularly for when Oliver was there. Scent marking like crazy. As though he was subliminally picking up on the interest she was trying so very hard to disguise.

She breathed in past the tightness of her chest. 'Really, Oliver? That's what you want to do today? Take shots at a dead man?'

Anger settled between his brows. 'I want to just enjoy today. Enjoy your company. Like we used to.'

He slid the gift back across in front of her. 'And on that note, open it.'

She sat unmoved for a moment but the steely determination in his gaze told her that was probably entirely pointless. He was just as likely to open it for her.

She tore the wrapping off with more an annoyance she hoped he'd misread as impatience.

'It's a cigar.' And a pack of cards and M&M's. Just like three years ago. Her eyes lifted back to his. Resisted their pull. 'I don't smoke.'

'That's never stopped me.'

She struggled against the warm memory of Oliver letting her beat him at cards and believing she hadn't noticed. 'That was a great day.'

'My favourite Christmas.'

'Nearly Christmas.'

His dark head shook. 'December twenty-fifth has never compared to the twentieth.'

She sat back. 'What do you do on Christmas Day?'

'Work, usually.'

'You don't go home?'

'Do I go to my father's home? No.'

'What about your mum?'

'I fly her to me for Chinese New Year. A less loaded holiday.'

Audrey just stared.

'You're judging me,' he murmured.

'No. I'm trying to picture it.'

'Think about it. I can't go back to Sydney, I can't go to a girlfriend's place on Christmas without setting up the expectations of rings and announcements, and the office is nice and quiet.'

'So you work.'

'It's just another day. What do you do?'

'I do Christmas.' She shrugged.

But it wasn't anywhere near as exciting as flying to see Oliver. Or as tasty as whatever festive treat Qīngtíng had in store for her. And it didn't warm her for the rest of the year. It was roast dinners and eggnog and family and gifts that none of them needed and explaining ad nauseam every year why Blake wasn't there.

Here she'd got to split her focus between the beautiful skyline that was Hong Kong and Oliver. Depending on her mood.

Her eyes fell back on his gift. She picked up the cigar and clamped it between her teeth in a parody of him. Two seconds later she let it fall out again.

'Ugh. That's horrible.'

His laugh could have lit the other end with its warmth. 'You get used to it.'

'I can't imagine how.'

Yet somehow, while it tasted awful on her own lips, she caught herself deciding it might taste better on his. And then she had to fight not to stare there. Oliver made that a whole lot harder by leaning forward, picking up the cigar where she'd dropped it, rolling it under his nose and then sliding the sealed end between his teeth. Pre-loved end first.

Something about the casual intimacy of that act, of him putting her saliva into his mouth so effortlessly—as if they were a long-term couple perfectly used to sharing bodily fluids—sent her heart racing, but she used every ounce of self-control she had to keep it from showing as he mouthed it from the right to the left.

Not the worst way to end your days if you were a cigar—
Stop!

Behind his easy smile his gaze grew unnaturally intent. And she grew inexplicably nervous.

'So,' he started, very much like one of his poker-plays, 'if we're not friends what are we?'

She choked slightly on her Cristal. 'Sorry?'

'I accept your assertion that we're not friends. But I wonder, then, what that means we are.'

Rabbit. Headlights. She knew it wasn't dignified and she knew exactly how that bunny felt, watching its fate careen inevitably closer.

'Because there were two things that defined our relationship for me...' He used the word 'defined' as though it meant 'constrained'. 'One was that you were the wife of a friend. Now—tragically—no longer the case. And the other was that we were friends. Apparently also now no longer the case. So, tell me, Audrey—'

He leaned forward and swilled the liquid in his glass and his eyes locked on hard to hers.

'—where exactly does that leave us?'

CHAPTER FIVE

Lobster calamari tangle in braised southern ocean miniatures

TENSION BALLED IN amongst the food in Audrey's stomach. She should have seen this coming. He wasn't a gazillionaire for nothing; the acute sharpness of his mind was one of the things that she…appreciated most about Oliver.

She flattened her skirt carefully. 'We're…acquaintances.'

Excellent. Yes. A nice neutral word.

He considered, nodded, and she thought she was safe. But then his head changed—mid-nod—into more of a shake. 'No, see that doesn't work for me. I wouldn't normally spend this much time—' or this much money, presumably '—on a mere acquaintance.'

'Associates?' She hid the croak in a swallow of champagne.

'Definitely not. That suggests we do business. And that's the last thing on my mind when we're together. It's why I enjoy our Christmases so much.'

'Then what do you suggest we are?'

He thought about that. 'Confidantes.'

He'd certainly shared a lot of himself with her, but they both knew it didn't go both ways.

'How about cohorts?' she parried.

He scrunched his nose. 'More consorts. In the literal sense.'

No. That just put way too vital an image in her head. 'Sidekicks?'

He laughed, but his eyes didn't. 'What about soulmates?'

The words. The implication. It was too much.

'Why are you doing this?' Audrey whispered, tight and tense.

'Doing what?'

What was it exactly? Flirting? Pressing? She stared at him and hoped her face wasn't as bleak as her voice. 'Stirring.'

He drained the last of the Cristal from his glass. 'I'm just trying to shake you free of the cold, impersonal place you put yourself in order to have this conversation.'

'I don't mean to be impersonal.' Or cold. Though that was a term she'd heard before courtesy of Blake. In his meaner moments.

'I know you don't, Audrey. That's the only reason I'm not mad at you. It's a survival technique.'

'Uh-huh…' She frowned in a way she hoped would cover the fact he was one hundred per cent right. 'And what am I surviving?'

'This day?' He stared, long and hard. 'Maybe me?'

'Don't flatter yourself.'

Four staff with exquisite timing arrived with the second seafood plate of the degustation experiences ahead of them. Two cleared the table and two more lay down matching shards of driftwood, decorated with glistening seaweed, and nested in it were a selection of oceanic morsels. A solitary lobster claw, calamari in a bed of roe, a fan of some kind of braised whitebait and—

Audrey leaned in for a good look. 'Is that krill?'

Oliver chuckled and it eased some of the tension that

hung as thick as the krill between them. 'Don't ask. Just taste.'

Whatever it was, it was magnificent. Weird texture on the tongue but one of the tastiest mouthfuls she'd ever had. Until she got to the lobster claw.

'Oh, my...'

'They've really outdone themselves with this one.'

The whole selection slid down way too easily with the frosty glass of Spanish Verdelho that had appeared in front of each of their dishes. But once there was nothing left on their driftwood but claw-husk and seaweed, conversation had no choice but to resume.

'Ask me how I know,' Oliver urged and then at her carefully blank stare he clarified. 'Ask me how I know what it is that you're doing.'

She took a deep slow breath. 'How do you know what I'm supposedly doing, Oliver?'

'I recognise it. From dealing with you the past five years. Eight if you want to go right back to the beginning.'

Oh, would that she could. The things she would do differently...

'I recognise it from keeping everything so carefully appropriate with you. From knowing exactly where the boundaries are and stopping with the tips of my shoes right on the line. From talking myself repeatedly into the fact that we're only friends.'

Audrey's heart hammered wildly. 'We are.'

He leapt on that. 'So now we *are* friends? Make up your mind.'

She couldn't help responding to the frustration leaching through between his words. 'I don't know what you want from me, Oliver.'

'Yes, you do.' He shifted forward again, every inch the predator. 'But you're in denial.'

'About what?'

'About what we really are.'

They couldn't be anything else. They just couldn't. 'There's no great mystery. You were my best man. You were my husband's closest friend.'

'I stopped being Blake's friend three years ago, Audrey.'

The pronouncement literally stunned her into silence. Her mouth opened and closed silently in protest. She knew something had gone down between them but…that long ago?

She picked up the M&M's. 'This long?'

'Just after that.' He guessed her next question. 'Friendships change. People change.'

'Why didn't you tell me?' she whispered. *And why hadn't Blake?* He knew that she saw Oliver whenever she went to Hong Kong. Why the hell wouldn't her husband tell her not to come?

He took a long breath. 'I didn't tell you because you would have stopped coming.'

Only the gentle murmur of conversation, the clink of silverware on plates and the hum of dragonfly wings interrupted the long, shocking silence. There was so much more in that sentence than the sum of the words. Two staff materialised behind them, unobtrusively cleared away the driftwood and shell remnants and left a small palate cleanser in their place. Then they were alone again.

'So, my comments today can't have been a surprise, then.' She braved her way carefully through the next moments. 'You knew I was going to end it.'

'Doesn't mean I'm going to acquiesce politely and let you walk off into the sunset.'

Frustration strung tight and painful across her sternum. 'Why, Oliver?'

He swapped the cigar from the left side of his mouth to the right. 'Because I don't want to. Because I like what we do and I like how I feel when we do it. And because I think you're kidding yourself if you don't admit you feel the same.'

The challenge—and the truth—hung out there, heavy and unignorable.

A nervous habit from her childhood came screaming back and, even though she knew she was doing it, she was helpless to stop her palms from rubbing back and forth along her thighs.

In desperation, she spooned up the half-melted sorbet and its icy bite shocked the breath right back into her. Oliver waited out her obvious ploy.

'I—'

Lord, was this wise? Couldn't she just lie and be done with it? But this was Oliver staring at her with such intensity and it didn't matter that he only saw her for ten hours a year, he could read her better than she could read herself.

'I enjoy seeing you, too,' she sighed. 'You know I do.'

'So why end it?'

'What will people say?'

Was that the first time she'd ever surprised him? Maybe so, given how unfamiliar that expression seemed on his face. 'What people?'

'Any people.'

'They'll say we're two friends having lunch.'

And dinner and sometimes a late supper to finish up with, but that was besides the point. 'They'll say I'm a widow moving on before her husband's scent has even left the house.'

'It's just lunch, Audrey. Once a year. At *Christmas*.'

'As if the people I'm worried about would give a rat's what season it is.'

'What do you care what they say? You and I will both know the truth.'

She shot a puff of air between her lips. 'Spoken just like

a man with more money than a small nation. You might not care about yours but reputations *mean* something to me.'

He shook his head. 'How is it any different than what we've been doing the past five years? Meeting, spending the day together.'

'The difference is Blake isn't here any more. He was the reason I came.'

He made it legitimate.

Now it was just…dangerous.

'Most women would be worried about *that* getting to the gossips. A married woman flying around the world to see a man that's not her husband. But you didn't care about it before you lost Blake—why do you care now?'

'Because now I'm—'

She floundered and he bent in closer to study her. 'You're what? The only thing that's changed in our relationship is your marital status.'

Her body locked up hard as awareness flooded his eyes.

'Is that it, Audrey? You're worried now because you're single?'

'How will it look?'

'You're a widow. No one will give a toss what you do or who you see. There's no hint of scandal for them to inhale.' But as she stared at him in desperate silence the awareness consolidated down into acute realisation. 'Or are you more concerned about how it will look, *to me*?'

Her pulse pounded against her throat. 'I don't want to give the wrong impression.'

'What impression is that?' Cool and oh, so careful.

'That I'm here because… That we're…'

He flopped back against the plush sofa, the cigar hanging limply from his mouth. 'That you're interested?'

'That I'm offering.'

Expressions chased across his face then like a classic

flicker-show and finally settled on heated disbelief. 'It's lunch, Audrey. Not foreplay.'

That word on *those* lips was all it took; her mind filled then with every carnal thought about him she'd ever suppressed. They burst out just as surely as if someone took the lid off the tank holding all those dragonflies captive, releasing them to fill the room and ricochet off the walls. It took all her concentration to force them back into the lead-lined box where she usually kept them.

'Seriously, what's the worst that could happen? If I made a move on you, you'd only have to say no.'

Her lips tightened even further. 'It would be awkward,' she squeezed out.

His snort drew the glance of the maître d'. 'Whereas this conversation is such a pleasure.'

'I don't think your sarcasm is warranted, Oliver.'

'Really? Your inference is that I would make some kind of fool of myself the very moment you're available.' Disbelief was wiggling itself a stronghold in his features. 'How new do you imagine I am to women, Audrey?'

He was so close to the truth now, she didn't dare speak. But that just gave him an empty stage to continue his monologue. And he was getting right into the part.

'I'm curious. Do you see me as pathetically desperate—' his whisper could have cut glass '—or is it just that you imagine yourself as so intensely desirable?'

Hurt speared straight down into that place where she kept the knowledge that she was the last sort of woman he'd want to be with. 'Stop it—'

But no. He was in flight.

'Maybe it wouldn't be that way at all. I'm considered quite a catch, you know. They even have a nickname for me. Could your crazy view of the world cope with the fact that I could make a move and you wouldn't be *able* to say no? Or want to?'

There was no way on this planet that he wouldn't see the sudden blanche of her face. The blood dropped from it as surely as if the sixty floors below them suddenly vaporised.

And *finally* he fell silent.

Stupid, blind, lug of a man.

Audrey stood and turned to stare at the dragonflies, her miserable arms curled protectively around her midsection where the intense ache was still resident. It was that or fling her hands up to her mortified face. Beyond the glass, the other diners carried on, oblivious to the agony swelling up to press with such intent against her chest wall.

'Is that it?' Oliver murmured behind her after a mute eternity. 'Is that why you don't want to be here?'

Mortification twisted tighter in her throat. She raised a finger to trace the glass-battering of a particularly furious dragonfly wedged in the corner of the tank who hadn't yet given up on its dream of freedom. 'I'm sure you think it's hilarious.'

The carpet was too thick and too new to betray his movement, but she saw his reflection loom up behind her. Over her. He stopped just before they touched.

'I would never laugh at you,' he said, low and earnest. 'And I would never throw your feelings back in your face. No matter what they were.'

She tossed her hair back a little. Straightened a little more. She might be humiliated but she would not crawl. 'No. I'm sure you've had prior experience with the inconvenient attachment of women.'

That was what made the whole thing so intensely humiliating. That she was just one of dozens—maybe hundreds—to fall for the Harmer allure.

'I care for you, Audrey.'

...but...

It had to be only a breath away. 'Oh, please. Save it for someone who doesn't know you so well.'

The soberness in his voice increased. 'I *do* care for you.'

'Not enough to come to my husband's funeral.' She spun. Faced him. 'Not enough to be there for your *friend* in the hardest week of her life when she was lost and overwhelmed and so bloody confused.' She reached for her handbag on the empty seat at the end of the table. 'Forgive me for suspecting that our compassion-meters aren't equally calibrated.'

With a deft swing, she had the handbag and all its contents over her shoulder and she turned toward the restaurant's exit. Remaining courses, be damned.

'Audrey—' His heavy hand curled around her upper arm. 'Stop.'

She did, but only because she'd made quite enough of a scene for one lifetime. And this was going to be the last memory of her he had; she didn't want it to be hysterical.

'I think I should explain—'

'You don't owe me an explanation, Oliver. That's what makes this whole situation so ridiculous. You owe me nothing.'

He wasn't hers to have expectations of. He wasn't even her husband's friend any more. He was just an acquaintance. A circumstantial friend.

At best.

'I wanted to be there, Audrey. For you. But I knew what would have happened if I'd flown in.' He took her hands in his and held them gently between them. 'You and I would have ended up somewhere quiet, nursing a generous drink and a bunch of stories long after everyone else had gone home, and you would have been exhausted and strung out and heartbroken.' She dipped her head and he had to duck his to keep up eye contact. 'And seeing that would have broken my heart. I would have taken you into my arms to give you support and make all the pain just vanish—' he took a deep breath '—and we would have ended up in bed.'

Her eyes shot back up. 'That wouldn't have happened—'

His hands twisted more firmly around hers, but not to hold her close. He used the leverage to push her gently away from him. 'It would have happened because I'm a heartbeat and some sorely tested willpower from doing it right now. I *want* you in my arms, Audrey. I *want* you in my bed. And it has nothing to do with Blake being gone because I've wanted the same thing each Christmas for the last five years.'

Every muscle in her body tensed up and he knew it.

Amazing, excruciating seconds passed.

'But that's not who we are,' he went on. 'I know that. Reducing what we have to the lowest common denominator might be physically rewarding but it's not what our... *thing*...is worth. And so what we're left with is this awkward...awareness.'

Awareness. So he felt it, too. But it wasn't just awkward, it was awful. Because she suddenly got the sense that it made Oliver as uncomfortable as it made her. Not expressing it, just...feeling it.

'I value your friendship, Audrey. I value your opinion and your perception and your judgement. I get excited coming up here in the elevator because I know I'm going to be seeing you and spending a day with you picking through your brilliant mind. The only day I get all year. I'm not about to screw that up by hitting on you.'

Oh. A small part of her sagged. But was it relief or disappointment? 'I'm so sorry.'

'Why?'

The blood must have returned to her face if she could still blush. 'Because it's such a cliché.'

'It's flattering. The fact that a woman I value so highly finds things in me to value in return is...validating. Thank you.'

'Don't thank me.' That was just a little bit too close to patronising.

'Okay. I'll just be silently smug about it instead.'

The fact that she could still laugh, despite everything… Yet, sure enough, the sound chuffed out of her. 'That seems more like you.'

They stood, nothing between them but air. And an emotional gulf as wide as the harbour.

'So now what?'

He considered her and then shook his seriousness free. 'Now we move on to the third course.'

CHAPTER SIX

Pineapple, hops, green tomato served in Brazil-nut-coated clusters

DID THE EARTH lurch on its axis between courses for the rest of Qīngtíng's chic clientele? None of them looked overly perturbed. Maybe this building was constructed to withstand earth tremors.

Because Oliver's entire existence had just shifted.

The two of them retreated to silence and polite smiles as a stack of curious, bite-size parcels were placed before them and the waiter announced in his accented English, 'Pineapple and green tomato clusters coated in Brazil nut.'

The parcels might have been small but he and Audrey each took their time first testing and then consuming the tart morsels. Buying time. Really necessary time. Because the last thing he felt like doing was eating.

He'd come *this* close.

He almost touched her, back then when she'd turned her blanched face away from him with such dismay. He almost pulled her back into his chest and breathed down onto her hair that none of it mattered. Nothing that had gone before had any relevance.

Their slate started today, blank and full of potential.

But that wasn't just embarrassment on her face. That

was dread. She didn't *want* to be feeling any kind of attraction to him.

She didn't deserve his anger. He'd reacted automatically to the suggestion that he *was* as pitiful as he'd secretly feared when it came to her, but it wasn't Audrey's fault she'd pegged him so accurately. His anger was more appropriate directed at himself. *He* was the one who couldn't get another man's wife out of his head. *He* was the one who found himself incapable of being with a beautiful woman, now, and not wanting to peel back the layers to see the person inside. And *he* was the one who was invariably disappointed with what he found there, because they all paled by comparison.

Audrey was the best woman—the best human being—he knew. And he knew some pretty amazing people. But she was the shining star atop his Christmas tree of admired friends, just as glittering and just as out of reach.

And right up until a few minutes ago he'd believed she was safe territory. Because right up until a few minutes ago he had no idea that she was in any way into him. He'd grown so used to not acting on all the inappropriate feelings he harboured.

What the hell did he *do* in a world where Audrey Devaney was both single and into him?

'What happened with you and Blake?' she suddenly asked, cutting straight through his pity party. Her eyes were enormous, shimmering with compassion and curiosity. And something else... An edge of trepidation.

No. Not a conversation he could have with her. What would it achieve now that Blake was dead? 'We just... grew apart.'

Two pretty lines appeared between her brows. 'I don't understand why he didn't say something. Or suggest that I stop coming. For so long. That seems unlike him.'

'You'd expect him to force you to declare your allegiance?'

She picked her way, visibly, through a range of choices. 'He knew why I came here. He would have told me if it was no longer necessary.'

Necessary. The bubble of latent hope lost half of its air. The idea that she'd only been coming each year to please her husband bit deep. Attraction or no attraction.

'There must have been something,' she urged. 'An incident? Angry words?'

'Audrey, leave it alone. What does it matter now that he's gone?'

She leaned forward, over the nutty crumbs of the decimated parcels. 'I never did understand why you were friends in the first place. You're so different from Blake.'

'Opposites attract?' That would certainly explain his still-simmering need to absorb Audrey into his very skin. Too bad that was going to go insatiate. 'We weren't so different.' At least not at the beginning.

But, those all-seeing eyes latched onto the mystery and weren't about to let go. 'He did a lot of things that you generally disagreed with,' she puzzled. 'I'm trying to imagine what it would have taken to drive you away from him.'

Her unconscious solidarity warmed him right down to the place that had just been so cold. 'What makes you think it wasn't something *I* did?'

Her lips twisted, wryly. 'I knew my husband, Oliver. Warts and all.'

And that was about the widest opening he was ever going to get. 'Why did you marry him?'

The curiosity changed focus. 'Why do people usually marry?'

'For love,' he shot back. Not that he'd know what that looked like. 'Did you love him?'

And could she hear how much he was hoping the answer was 'no'?

'Marriage means different things to different people.'

Nice hedge. 'So what does it mean to you?'

She hesitated. 'I don't subscribe to the whole "lightning bolt across the crowded room" thing.'

It was true. There'd been no lightning bolt when she walked into the bar that first day. But when she'd first pinned him with her intellect and locked those big eyes on him just minutes later, he'd had to curl his fingers under the edge of the bar to keep from lurching backwards at the slam of *something* that came off her. Whatever the hell it was.

A big, blazing ball of slow burn.

'You don't aspire to that?' he dug.

'The great romantic passion? No.' A little colour appeared on her jaw. 'It hasn't been my experience. I value compatibility, shared interests, common goals, mutual respect, trust. Those are things that make a marriage.'

A hollow one, surely. Although how would he know? No personal experience to reference and a crap example in his parents' marriage, which barely deserved the title— just a woman living in the purgatory of knowing her husband didn't love her.

He risked a slight probe. 'Did Blake agree with that?'

She brought her focus back to him. 'I... Yes. We were quite sympathetic on a lot of things.'

Well, there was one area in particular that old Blake was definitely *un*sympathetic with Audrey.

Fidelity.

'You never looked at someone else and wondered what it might be like?' He had to know.

Her eyes grew wary. 'What *what* might be like?'

'To be with them. Did you never feel the pull of attraction to someone other than Blake and wonder about a relationship that started with good, old-fashioned lust?'

'You're assuming that *wanting* and *taking* are connected. It comes back to that mutual trust and respect. I just
wouldn't do that to my partner. I couldn't.' Her eyes narrowed. 'I thought you, of all people, would understand that.'

A cold stone formed in his gut. *Of all people...* 'You're
talking about my father?' They'd never discussed his father
and so he knew whatever she knew had come from Blake.
The irony of that...

'Was he very bad?'

He took a deep breath. But if sharing something with
her, especially something this personal, was the only intimacy he was going to get from Audrey Devaney, he'd embrace it. 'Very.'

'How did you know what he was doing?'

'Everyone knew.'

'Including your mother?'

'She pretended not to.' For her son's sake. And maybe
for her own.

'Did she not care?'

His stomach tightened at the memory of the sobbing he
wasn't supposed to have heard when she thought he was
asleep. His jaw tightened. 'She cared.'

'Why did she stay?'

The sigh wracked his body. 'My father was incapable
of fidelity but he didn't drink, he was never violent, he remembered birthdays and he had steady employment. He
was, in all other ways, a pretty reasonable father.'

If you didn't count a little thing called integrity.

Part of Oliver's own attraction to Audrey had always
been her values. This was not a woman who would ever
have knowingly done wrong by the man she shared vows
with. Just a shame Blake hadn't returned the favour.

'So she chose to stay.' And that had been a green light
in his father's eyes. The ultimate hall pass.

'Maybe she didn't think she could do better?'

'Than a man who was ruthlessly unfaithful—surely no one would think that?' It hit him then how freely he was having this discussion. After so many years of bleeding the feelings out in increments.

She shook her head. 'I don't know that you'll ever be able to relate. Because of who you are. Successful and charming and handsome. It's not that easy for everyone else.'

His heart swelled that she thought him handsome enough to say it aloud. 'You think I don't have my demons?'

She stared at him. 'I'm sure you do. But doubting your worth is not one of them.'

She wasn't wrong. His ego had been described by the media as 'robust' and in the boardroom as 'unspeakable'.

'And can you, Audrey? Relate?'

She stared out across the harbour to the towering giants on the other side. But her head nodded, just slightly. 'When I got to upper school I'd gone from being the tubby, smart girl to the plain, smart girl. I didn't mind that so much as long as it also came with "smart" because that was my identity, that was where I got my self-worth from. Academic excellence.'

'I wish I'd known you then.'

Her laugh grated. 'Oh, no… The beautiful people and I didn't move in the same hemisphere. You would never have even seen me then.'

'That's a big assumption to make.' And kind of judgemental. Which wasn't like her at all.

She leaned forwards. 'For the first two years of high school boys didn't want to know me. I was invisible and I just got on with things, under the radar. And then one day I got…discovered. And that was the end of my cruise through school.'

'What do you mean "discovered"?'

'The same way species are discovered even though they've been there for centuries. I didn't change my hair or get a makeover or tutor the captain of the football team. It wasn't like the movies. One day I was invisible and the next—' she shrugged '—there I was.'

'In a good way?'

She took a healthy swallow of her wine. 'No. Not for me.'

The pain at the back of her eyes troubled him. 'What happened?'

'Nothing. At first. They just watched me, wherever I went. Like they weren't sure how to engage with me.'

They...like a pack.

'One of them asked me out to a movie once. Michael Hellier. I didn't know how to say no kindly so I said yes and it was all over the school in minutes. They hunted me down, then, the girls from that group, and they slammed me against the bathroom wall and told me I was fishing outside of my swamp.' She lifted her eyes. 'But he'd asked me, I couldn't just not turn up. So I went. I don't even remember what film we saw because all I could think about the entire time I was with him was those girls. I convinced myself they were spying from the back row. I barely spoke to him and I didn't even take off my coat even though I was sweating like crazy under it, and when he tried to put his arm around me I literally froze. I sat there, totally rigid for the entire movie, and the moment the credits rolled I stammered out my thanks and I ran out of the cinema.'

Oliver sat silently, the whole, miserable story playing out in his mind, his anger bubbling up and up as it proceeded.

She turned more fully towards him, eyes blazing. 'I enjoyed it, Oliver. The attention of those boys. I enjoyed that none of them quite knew how to deal with me. I enjoyed being a puzzle in their eyes and I enjoyed how it made me feel. The shift in power. It felt like vindication for every tease I'd endured as a kid. As if *"See! I am worthy."* I liked being visible. And I liked being sought after. I liked how fast my heart beat when I was near him because he was interested in me. And I totally played up to it.

'But I earned what happened to me.' She sighed. 'And I earned every cruel nickname they gave me after that. I tried to play a game I wasn't equipped for and I lost. I never made that mistake again. I never *reached* like that again. And after a while that starts to feel really normal. And so maybe something like that happened to your mother—'

God, he'd totally forgotten they'd been talking about Marlene Harmer.

'—something that taught her not to overreach.'

Or hope? Or expect more from people?

Or feel, maybe?

He asked the first thing that came to him. The thing he'd always, secretly, wanted to know. 'Is that why you chose Blake that day in the bar? Because some jerks in school taught you not to aim higher?'

The words hung, unanswered, between them. It was the first time either of them had ever acknowledged what had happened that night. How actively she'd focused her attention on Blake rather than on him. Almost to the point of rudeness.

And also hovering out there, in bright neon, was his presumption that Blake was somehow *less*. But deep down he knew that to be true—at least when it came to Audrey.

Audrey was never meant to be Blake's.

Not in a just world.

Indecision swam across her gaze, and he watched her trying to decide what was safe to reveal. When she did speak it was painfully flat and her eyes drifted slightly to his left. 'Blake was within reach.'

Low-hanging fruit.

Oliver flopped back against the rear of his sofa, totally lost for words, understanding, just a little bit, what Audrey had just said about vindication. He'd always wondered what drew Audrey to Blake instead of him that day, but such thoughts were arrogant and unkind given Blake was supposedly his best friend. So he'd swallowed them. Buried the question mark way down deep.

And now he had his answer.

An absurd kind of hope—totally at odds to the conversation they were having—washed through him.

Audrey didn't pick Blake because she deemed him the better man...

He was just the *safer* man.

Just like that, a whole side of her unfolded like spreading petals revealing an aspect to her he'd never suspected.

'It kills me to think that my mother would have harboured those kinds of feelings about herself and that my father would have reinforced them...'

Did she realise that when he said 'my mother' he really meant Audrey? And instead of his father, he meant himself? To imagine this extraordinary woman sitting in that bar all those years ago, smiling and chatting and sipping her drink and all the while going through a mental process that ended in her deciding she wasn't worthy—

She! The finest of women.

It killed him.

'You know her best,' Audrey murmured. 'I'm just hypothesising how she might have allowed that to happen. Everyone has a different story.'

Her furious back-pedalling made sense to him now. She'd exposed herself and so she was retreating to safer ground. But no, he wasn't about to let her do that. Not when he'd finally made some headway into knowing her.

Really knowing her.

He reached forward and took her hand. 'I wish I could impress upon her just how amazing a woman she is.'

She swallowed twice before answering. 'You could just tell her.'

'Do you think she'd believe me?' His thumb traced the shape of her palm. 'Or would she look for the angle?'

Hints of alarm etched across her expression. 'If you say it often enough eventually she'll have to believe you.'

Was it that simple? Could simple reinforcement undo the lessons—the experience—of years?

He released his breath slowly and silently. 'I would have seen you, Audrey. I give you my word.'

Because *she* was special, though, not because he was, particularly.

She tipped her head back towards the sofa-top. 'I could have done with a champion.'

Chivalrous wasn't exactly what he was feeling now, but he absolutely would have defended her against those who would have caused her this hurt. Who would have changed her essence.

He would have taken on half the school for her.

'And I could have done with your strength. And your maturity.'

She smiled, gently slipped her hand out from his and sat back against her seat. 'Really? Were you a wild child?'

Ah. Back to safety. Any topic other than her.

But he let her go, incredibly encouraged now that he'd picked up the key to getting inside her. Because the beautiful thing about keys was that you could use them as and when required. And in between you tucked them away somewhere safe.

This one he tucked away in a pocket deep inside his chest and he let her have the breathing space she obviously needed.

'Oh, the stories I could tell.'

'Go ahead.' She settled into her seat and seemed to have totally forgotten that less than half an hour ago she was heading for the door. 'We've still got five courses.'

Yep. That was what he had. Five courses and the rest of the day to make sure Audrey Devaney didn't disappear from his life forever.

CHAPTER SEVEN

Pomegranate, blood orange and Campari

HOW WAS IT possible that she'd just revealed more about herself in a few minutes to Oliver than she had in her entire marriage to her husband? Blake was all about the now; he lived for the moment, or planned for the future. But he spent no time looking back and he didn't ever show a particular interest in her past beyond what it meant for his present. They talked—a lot—and they shared ideas and grand schemes and they got excited about some and disappointed about others but it was never remotely personal.

She'd certainly never told him about those awful few months at school. He wouldn't have understood.

But if ever there was a man who should have not understood, he was sitting across from her today. Oliver with his comfortable background, his top-end schooling and his voted-most-likely-to-succeed status. Oliver *was* those boys from her past. He would have dated those girls that had slammed her up against the bathroom wall. He probably had!

He shouldn't have been able to empathise at all.

Yet he did. And it was genuine.

'Pomegranate, blood orange and Campari sorbet,' the maître d' announced, appearing at the side of their table with staff wielding another dish. In perfect synch, they positioned a fan of frosted antique tablespoons each packed with crushed ice and a ball of sorbet neatly balanced on the head of the spoon. They looked just like Christmas baubles sitting in snow.

'Thank you,' Audrey murmured, smiling as they left, bowing. After they'd gone, she added, 'They're very deferential to you, Oliver.'

'The quality of service is one of the things Qīngtíng is famous for.'

Mmm, still… 'They bow extra low to you.'

'I spend a fortune with them whenever I'm in Hong Kong.'

Suddenly the thought that he might come here with other people—maybe with other women—grew and flashed green in her mind. This was *their* place. It didn't exist when they weren't here, surely?

'Tell me about your year,' she blurted, to force the uncomfortable idea off her tongue before thought became voice. 'Did you ever hear from Tiffany?'

His lips twisted. 'She married someone else by Valentine's.'

'No! So fast? That's terrible.'

'He adores her and doesn't mind the lack of intelligent conversation. And she has more money than she can spend and a secure future. It was a good match.'

'Better than you?'

'Infinitely.'

'Why were you with her, Oliver? If she wasn't all that bright?'

His eyes shadowed and he busied himself with the sorbet. But he didn't change the subject and eventually he lifted his head to meet her eyes again. The faintest sheen dotted his tan forehead.

'Tiffany was engaging in her own way. I found her complete disregard for social convention refreshing. Besides,

I get my intelligent conversation elsewhere so I didn't feel the lack.'

'You were going to *marry* her, Oliver. Grow old with her, maybe father her children. And you didn't look to her for meaningful conversation?'

His lips thinned. 'Intellect isn't everything.'

No. Everyone had different strengths. She knew that better than most. Yet...

'Oliver. This is *you* we're talking about. You would have wasted away without a mental match in life.'

'What if I couldn't find a match?'

She practically snorted her pomegranate ice. 'That's a big call, isn't it? To assume that no woman could be your intellectual match.'

His eyes blazed. 'Not mine, Audrey. *Yours*.'

Her antique spoon clattered back onto its saucer.

But he didn't shy away from her startled gaze. 'You set a high bar, intellectually. Diversity of knowledge, your wit, your life experience. That's hard to equal.'

'Wh...' What was she supposed to say to that? 'Why would you *try* to match it?'

He leaned forwards, leading with his hazel eyes. 'Because you're the woman against which I measure all others, intellectually. You're my gauge of what's possible.'

'Me?' Her squeak was hardly the poster child for mental brilliance.

'And I haven't found anyone like you, yet.' He studied her as she squirmed. 'That makes you uncomfortable?'

'Yes!'

'Because you don't agree with my assessment of your smarts or because you don't want to be my bar?'

Her heart thundered so hard at the back of her throat she thought he might hear it pulsing below her words. 'Because pedestals are wobbly at the best of times.'

'Or is it just knowing that I consider us a perfect intellectual match that makes you nervous?'

If he said *intellectual* one more time she would scream; it only served to remind her how not matched they were in other ways.

She took a long breath. 'I'm flattered that you think so.' But only because of how highly she esteemed his mind. But then she saw how incredibly *un*-uncomfortable he looked. The devil lurked behind that sparkle in his eyes.

Oh.

'You're teasing me.'

'Hand on heart.' His big fist followed suit and he shook his head. 'But I knew your modesty wouldn't allow you to believe it.'

'You must meet some extraordinary people.'

'None who I'd want to spend an entire day just talking to.'

She stared, crippled by the monument of that. 'No pressure, then.'

Two diners looked around at Oliver's bark of laughter. 'Yeah, the next word out of your mouth better impress.'

She consciously coordinated the muscles necessary to breathe and then used the outward part of the breath to say, 'Euouae.'

Oliver blinked.

'It's a musical mnemonic to denote the sequence of tones in the Seculorum Amen.'

'See what I mean?' His smile broke out on one side of that handsome mouth. 'Who knows that?'

She blew out a long breath. 'It's also the longest word in the English language made up of only vowels.'

'Okay, now you're just showing off. Eat your sorbet.'

'Thank you, Oliver,' she said, as soon as her mind would work properly again. 'That's quite a compliment.'

'No, actually, it's a curse. I can't tell you how many dinners I've sat through waiting for something like Eweyouu—'

'Euouae.'

'—to casually come up.'

'Hopefully none of those meals were as long as this
one, then.'

'I'm serious, Audrey; you've spoiled me for other
women.'

And just like that she was speechless again. And her
blood was back to its thundering.

Intellectually, she reminded herself. *Only in that one
way.* Because the women Oliver Harmer chose had beauty
and grace and breeding and desirability and experience and,
Lord knew, more elasticity than she could ever aspire to.

'So, you just…lowered your bar?'

'I decided that I could get my fix of conversational stim-
ulation every Christmas instead.'

'You're assuming that your wife would be happy for
us still to meet each year. I'm not sure I would be if you
were—' she nearly choked on the word '—mine.'

He shrugged. 'It wouldn't be negotiable.'

'Famous last words. What would happen when you were
completely smitten with her and she turned her big violet
eyes up to you and let them fill with tears and begged you
not to go?'

'Really? Violet.'

'I'm sure she'd be exceptional.'

He gave her that point. 'I'd hand her a Kleenex and tell
her I'd see her later that evening.'

'And if she let her robe fall open and seduced you into
staying?'

His eyes darkened. 'Then I'd cancel the car and take the
chopper to make up the lost time.'

'And if she threatened you with divorce?'

'Then I'd call my lawyer and let him deal with the weeping,' he huffed, eyes rolling. 'Do you imagine I'm so easily manipulated, Audrey?'

No. She couldn't imagine him falling for any of that.

'So what if the woman that loved you sat you down and stoically explained how much it hurt her that you got from someone else something she couldn't give you.'

His pupils enlarged and then the deepest of frowns surrounded them. 'God, Audrey...'

Had he never thought about what it might do to the woman 'lucky' enough to get him? She much preferred to think that a woman he chose would select door number four. The vaguely dignified option. Of course, the alternative would be to say nothing and just *ache* every year as December twentieth approached.

Yeah, that had worked really well for her.

He blew air from between tight lips and forked his fingers through his hair.

'You see my point?' she murmured.

'So you're basically dooming me to a bachelor's life forever, then? Because I've been looking, Audrey, and you're not out there.'

'I'm just saying you can't have Frankenstein's bride.'

He tipped his head.

'You don't want a regular woman with flaws and room for improvement. You want the intelligence of one woman, the courage of another, the serenity of a third. And you want it all wrapped up in a beautiful exterior.'

'She doesn't have to be beautiful.'

Pfff. 'Yes, she does, Oliver. You only date stunning women.' The Internet was full of pictures of him with his latest arm decoration.

'You think I'm that shallow?'

All right then... 'When was the last time you were seen in public with a plain, ordinary woman?' she challenged.

And he shot back, fast and sure. 'I have lunch with one every Christmas.'

The air whooshed out of her, audibly. But it wasn't indignation and she didn't flounce out. She sat as straight and dignified as she could and opened her mouth to say something as witty as he probably expected. But absolutely nothing came to her.

So she just closed it again.

He swore. 'Audrey, I'm sorry. I spoke carelessly. That was supposed to be a compliment.'

Because he deigned to lower himself long enough to eat in public with a less than beautiful woman? 'Your flattery could do with some refinement, then,' she squeezed out.

'You are so much more than the particular arrangement of your features. I see all the things you *are* when I look at you, not the things you *aren't*.'

Clumsy, but at least he wasn't patronising her with claims of inner beauty.

'Please, Audrey. You're the last person on this planet that I would want to hurt. Or that I'm fit to judge. My social circle tends to fill with beautiful stars on the rise. I don't date them for the pleasure of sitting there looking at them. I date them to see what else they have going for them.'

It wasn't all that inconceivable. She could well imagine the facility with which a stunning woman would find herself with access to the kind of people Oliver mixed with. Where else was he going to meet women? And she absolutely couldn't blame them for being drawn to him, once there. He was Oliver Harmer.

He took her hand across the table. 'It's really important to me that you don't think I'm that kind of man.'

And it wasn't as if he were giving her a news flash. She detached her hand from his under the pretence of wiping her mouth with her napkin and sighed. But she wasn't about to be a princess about this. She was a big girl.

'I wake up to myself every day, Oliver. I know where my virtues lie.' Or didn't.

'I would give every cent I have—' The greenish-brown of his eyes focused in hard but as he spoke he turned away, so that the words were an under-breath jumble. And something in his expression made her really want to know what came next.

'Every cent, what?'

'For you to recognise your strengths.'

Had even the kitchen staff stopped to listen? Every sound that wasn't Oliver's low voice seemed to have vanished. But something stopped her from letting his words fill her heart with helium.

'I don't need you to do this, Oliver.' In fact she really would rather he didn't. 'I don't care what you think of my appearance.'

'Of course you do. Because you're human and because I just reinforced all those jerks at your school with my stupid, careless words.' He stood and pulled her to her feet. '*I* care what you think of *my* appearance.'

It was such a ludicrous concept—not that he cared, but that there was any question about how good he looked—she actually laughed. Out loud. 'No, you don't.'

'I changed three times before coming here today.'

She looked him over, some of her pre-shock spirit returning. 'And this was your best effort?'

The lips that gaped at her then were stained slightly red with pomegranate ice and looked more than a little bit like they were flush from kissing. 'This is all brand-new gear!'

'Oh, you shopped too? Wow.' Her umbrage eased a bit more.

'And I didn't shave this morning because you once said you liked stubble. Four years ago.'

A reluctant laugh tumbled out of her. 'Oh, that's just sad, Oliver.' It didn't matter why he was demeaning himself to stave off her further embarrassment, she was just very grateful that he was. She peered up at him. 'I know what you're doing.'

'What am I doing?'

'You're lying. To make me feel better.'

His eyes narrowed as he towered over her. 'Is it working?'

'Yes, actually.' Purely based on the fact he cared enough to try. He'd meant what he said but he hadn't meant it to be hurtful.

He took half a step closer. 'Great then.'

'Besides, you always look good. You don't have to try.'

'Small mercy. There are plenty more ways that I feel deficient around you, Audrey.'

The wealthiest and most successful man she knew? 'Like how?'

Indecision carved that handsome face. 'I live in fear that I'll glance up suddenly and catch you looking at me with the kind of patient, vacant tolerance I give most of my dates.'

'You think I'm humouring you?'

His shrug only lifted one big shoulder. 'You only came here at all because of Blake. Maybe it's all Christmas charity.'

The thought that she'd caused someone to question themselves the way she had—even someone as profusely confident as Oliver—made her squirm. Though she knew the ramifications of correcting him were steep.

'I'm still here, aren't I?'

He knuckled a loose piece of her hair more securely behind her ear. 'Ah, but you came to say goodbye.'

'I did,' she breathed. That was totally her plan when she walked in. Until something had changed without her consent. 'So why haven't I?'

His eyes glittered and his hand turned palm side up and

curled around her cheek. 'Something else I'd give my fortune to know.'

A steam train thundered through her brain. 'You're rapidly running out of fortunes.'

'Benefit of a double-A credit rating.' His thumb crept across to trace the shape of her bottom lip. 'I can get more.'

'What are you doing?' she whispered, and he knew exactly when to drop the game.

'Everything I can before you tell me to stop.'

She absolutely should. They were in a public place and this was *'The Hammer'*, notorious player and corporate scourge of Asia. And more to the point, this was Oliver. She had no business letting him this close, no matter how much the furthest corner of her soul tried to tell her differently.

It didn't matter that she was no longer anyone's wife. It didn't matter that he was the one controlling the lazy drag of his fingers and therefore any resulting public exposure. Those things only made it more dangerous. More ill advised.

But as his hazel eyes blazed down on her and his big, smooth thumb pressed against the flesh of her lips she struggled to remember any of those things.

And her mouth opened.

CHAPTER EIGHT

Baked scallops, smoked eel with capsicum salsa and a Parmesan and dill crust.

'STOP.'

She wasn't inviting him in. She was locking him out. Of course she was. This was Audrey.

Oliver drew his hands back into his own personal space and stepped away from her, more towards the wall-that-would-be-a-window. The soothing, ancient presence of the mountains far behind Victoria Harbour anchored him and stopped his heart from beating clear through his chest and then through all that glass into the open air of the South China Sea.

'Shorter than I'd hoped,' he murmured at the vast open space. Yet so much further than he'd ever imagined he'd get.

'We're in a public restaurant, Oliver.'

'I have a suite just upstairs.' As if that were really what stopped her.

But she ignored the underlying meaning. Again, because she was Audrey. The woman had more class than he could ever hope to aspire to.

'I thought we were on the top floor?' she said, smoothing her skirt and keeping the conversation firmly off what had just happened. All that...touching.

'The top public floor. There's a penthouse.' Technically part of the sixtieth floor but a half-dozen metres higher.

'And you have it?'

He turned and faced her. And the music. 'It came with the restaurant.'

Her brows dipped over slightly glassy eyes. He loved that he'd made them that way. But then they cleared and those fine brows lifted further than he imagined they could go. 'You *bought* the restaurant?'

'I did.'

She shook her head. 'What's the matter? No good restaurants closer to Shanghai?'

'I like this one.'

And Qīngtíng had the added advantage of being saturated in echoes of his time together with Audrey. And when she didn't come last year he began to believe that might be all he'd ever have of her.

Memories.

'Clearly.' And then her innate curiosity got the better of her. 'What did it cost?'

God, he adored her. So classy and yet so inappropriate at the same time. Absolutely no respect for social niceties. But he wasn't ready to put a price tag on his desperation just yet. Bad enough that his accountant knew.

'More than you can imagine. It wasn't on the market.' He'd just kept offering them more until they caved.

Understanding filled her eyes. 'That's why you seemed so familiar with the dragonfly keeper. And why they bow so low for you.' And why he got to call the chef *Gerard*. 'You're their boss.'

'They treat everyone that well,' he defended. Badly.

'Why did you buy it?'

Uh…no. Not something he was going to admit to the woman who'd made it clear she wasn't after anything more with him. In words and, just moments ago, in deed.

He cleared his throat. 'It's a fantastic investment. The return is enormous.' As much an unexpected bonus as the big, luxurious, lonely suite right above their heads. 'Do you want to see it?'

She turned her confusion to him.

'The penthouse. It's pretty spectacular.'

'Is it…? Are you…?' She took a deep breath. 'Will you be sleeping there tonight?'

Was that her subtle way of asking whether there was a bed up there? 'You're safe with me, Audrey.'

Heat flared at her jaw. 'I know.'

Though, hadn't he been the one to instigate the toucha-thon just now? 'It's so much more than a bedroom. It's like a small house perched atop this steel mountain.' She didn't have a prayer of hiding the spark of interest. So he went for the kill shot. 'Every window gives you a different view of Hong Kong.'

She was inordinately fond of this city, he knew. In fact, pretty much anything oriental. It made him wonder what she'd thought of Shanghai; if she'd liked it as much as he did.

And why, exactly, was that important…?

Indecision wracked her face. She wanted to see it, but she didn't want to be alone with him away from the security of a restaurant full of unwitting chaperones. So who did she trust less—him or herself?

Her eyes flicked to her left as two restaurant staff approached from the direction of the beautifully disguised kitchens and placed their next dish on the table.

'Oh, great!'

Audrey hadn't been quite that animated about the arrival of the previous dishes. But she certainly rushed back to her seat with enthusiasm now. Oliver half smiled and followed her.

'Scallops and smoked eel swimming in a sea of capsicum with a Parmesan and dill crust,' Ming-húa announced before departing. Each dish composed of an enormous white shell in which three tender scallop and eel pairs sat, awash, in a red liquid salsa. A two-pronged splade balanced across each one.

'Did Blake burn you financially?' Audrey asked, breathless, as she tucked into her scallops.

It was absolutely the last thing he expected her to say, although retreating behind the memory of her departed husband shouldn't have surprised him.

'No. Why?'

'I figured money would have to be the only thing big enough to drive a wedge between the two of you.'

Oliver moderated a deep breath. She wasn't going to let this go. 'Look, Audrey…Blake and I were friends for a long time and people change in that time. Values change. The more time we spent apart, the less we had in common.'

Except for Audrey. She was their constant.

'I just don't understand why he would have kept it a secret, unless it was a big deal of some kind.'

Even in absentia, he was still lying to cover his old friend's ass. But it was more than that. Hadn't she just shared the misery of her childhood, all those issues with self-worth? What would it do to her to learn her husband was a serial adulterer?

The burning need to protect her surged through him. 'Let it go, Audrey.'

But something was clearly troubling her. She was eating the scallop as though it were toast. Biting, chewing and swallowing with barely any attention on the succulent food. 'What values?'

He faked misunderstanding.

'You said that values changed with time. What values changed between the two of you, if it wasn't about business?'

'Audrey—'

'Please, Oliver. I need to know. Was it your values?'

'Why do you need to know?'

She eyed him as she slipped the last succulent morsel between her lips. 'Because a few years before he died, he changed. And I want to know if it's connected.'

Dread pooled in his belly. 'Changed how?'

'He just…' She frowned, trying to focus what was obviously a lot of thoughts all rushing her at once. 'He became…affectionate.'

The second surprise in his day. 'Affectionate?'

'He grew all touchy-feely. And he'd never done that before.'

'You got worried because he got *more* intimate with you?' Exactly what kind of a marriage had they had?

'It was just notable by its sudden presence.' She cleared her throat. 'And it escalated every November. Like clockwork.'

The weeks leading up to her annual pilgrimage to Hong Kong. Overcompensating for the fact that he was lining up to betray her in the most fundamental way possible, probably.

'So I thought…that is, I wondered…' She closed her eyes and took a long slow breath. 'I thought it might have been related to me coming here. That he was struggling with it.'

'But he was the one who encouraged you.'

'I know, that's the part I don't understand. But I knew he had problems with how I was with you when we were all together and so I thought maybe he believed—'

She snapped her mouth shut.

How I was with you… Oliver filed that one away for later dissection. 'He believed what?'

'That there was something going on.' She flushed. 'With us.'

There were no words. Oliver could only stare. She was

so very far off the mark and yet so excruciatingly close to the truth.

'But there wasn't,' he hedged.

'Blake didn't know that.' She threw her hands up. 'It's the only thing I can think of to explain it.'

Is it really, Audrey?

It wasn't until she spoke that he realised he had—aloud. 'What do you mean?'

Crap. 'I mean there could be dozens of other alternatives. Blake knew he could trust you with his life.'

That was what made his betrayal all the more vile.

'I thought, maybe he confronted you with it and, knowing how you felt about your father, you might have been insulted and the two of you might have fought...?'

Maybe that was what her subconscious wanted her to believe.

'He didn't confront me.' That much he could safely say. Blake was the confront*ee* not the confront*er*.

'Oh.' Those two appealing little forks appeared between her brows again. 'Okay.'

She was out of ideas. Oliver knew he could just change the subject and she'd go with that because that brilliant mind of hers was flirting around the edges but was determined not to see the possibility of truth. And who could blame her?

But would it eat at her forever?

She lifted the half-shell and used the splade to scoop up some of the rich, vibrant sauce. Her frown didn't dissipate even as she sipped at her dish.

No. She wasn't going to let her curiosity die with her husband. She was just going to let it fester and worsen her deeply suppressed self-doubt as only secrets could. But telling her the truth wouldn't achieve much better.

Except maybe bring it all out into the light where she could deal with it. Surely something like that lost some of its power when it was exposed to the light. Rather than poisoning as a fear. If Audrey knew nothing, he'd have been content to leave it that way but she knew enough that she would eventually work her way around to the truth or, if not that, then her subconscious would whisper cruelly in her ears forever. Or she'd hear it from someone else instead of in the protective company of a friend.

He studied her strong face and made his decision.

'It was guilt, Audrey.' The splade froze halfway to her mouth. 'If Blake changed then he was overcompensating because he knew what was going to happen the moment you left the country.'

Those enormous blue eyes grew. 'What do you mean?'

He took a deep breath and trashed the memory of a dead man.

'Your husband had affairs, Audrey. Lots of them. Every year while you were here with me.'

The effusive apologies of the staff for what was essentially her own mistake bought Audrey a few precious moments to get her act together. Immaculate girls in exotic Chinese silk dabbed and pawed at the ruined linen of her outfit where the splade, the shell and its entire remnant contents had tumbled out of her deadened fingers.

Oliver watched her with concern through the chaos and all the bodies.

She'd never had so many hands on her breasts and thighs at one time. How ironic to consider that in the same moment as discovering that her husband—who'd barely troubled himself to pay more than businesslike attention to the private parts of her body—was apparently sleeping all around town the moment she left the country.

Betrayal stung, heated and raw in that place behind her heart she never let anyone go.

And tears stung just as angry in her eyes.

'Ming-húa—' Oliver barked and then spoke quietly to
the maître d', who then rattled a fast command to his staff
who, in turn, scattered on individual errands. One left a
clean towel with Audrey but it wasn't going to do much
against the red stain that spread like a chest-wound down
her cream front.

'Come on,' Oliver said, pulling her to her feet. 'You can
change upstairs.'

Code for *I'm taking you somewhere you can have your
meltdown in private.*

She let him pull her towards the exit, his hand hot and
secure around her ice-cold one. But as they got to the el-
evators he led her, instead, up a carpeted circular staircase, which opened discreetly onto one side of the public
restaurant lobby.

At the top of the stairs, the furnishings changed slightly
to the polished floor and neutral décor so popular in this
part of China. It actually felt quite welcoming since her
home in Australia was much the same. Executive beige.
Blake's taste, not hers. All very stylish but totally without soul.

Like their marriage.

Oliver swiped a keycard through the scanner and swung
open a pair of big, dark doors into an amazing space.

The view shouldn't have stolen her gaze so immediately considering it was only a half-floor higher than the
restaurant they'd spent all afternoon in, but the penthouse
sat squarely on the top of the building and its windows
wrapped around three-hundred-and-sixty degrees of amazing view. Some of it was the much taller buildings around
them and the patches of mountainside in between, but the
majority was the towering chrome and glass forest that
was the buildings of Central Hong Kong and, across the
harbour, Kowloon.

It didn't matter that the living area wasn't large because it had the most spectacular back yard she'd ever seen.

Pity she was in no mood to enjoy it.

'Tell me,' she gritted the moment the door closed behind her.

But Oliver waited until he'd removed her dripping jacket and folded it on the non-porous safety of the slate bench top in the open-plan kitchen. Short of removing her blouse and skirt, too, there wasn't much else he could do to clean her up.

Audrey folded her arms across her damp front and walked to the enormous window to just...stare.

'He called them his Christmas bonus.' Oliver sighed behind her.

Pain lanced through her. That was just crass enough for Blake, too. 'Who were they? Where did he find them?'

'I don't know, Audrey.'

'How long have you known? The whole three years?'

'The first year I thought maybe he'd grow out of it. But when he did it again the following year, I realised it wasn't a one-off. So I confronted him about it.'

She squeezed her hands around her elbows. 'So...five years in total? Also known as *our whole marriage*?'

Her voice shook on that and she saw him behind her, reflected in the glass of the balcony, his head bowed. The most defeated she'd ever seen him.

'I'm so sorry, Audrey. You don't deserve this.'

'Why didn't you tell me sooner?' she whispered.

'Because I knew how much it would hurt you.'

She spun. 'You preferred to leave me in a marriage where I was being made a fool of?'

'I couldn't be sure you didn't know.'

She couldn't prevent the rise in her voice. 'You thought I might *know* and *stay*?'

Like his mother? Was that what his upbringing taught him?

'I couldn't be sure,' he repeated. 'It's not an easy sub-ject to raise.'

Which would explain why half their day had gone by before he elected to mention it.

'Is *this* why you didn't come to his funeral?'

'I've explained why—'

'Right. In case you couldn't keep your hands off me.' She snorted. 'I didn't actually believe you about that.' The hurt she was feeling had to go somewhere, and Oliver was right there.

'Well, you should, because I meant every word. Why do you think I sent your favourite flowers and not his? I wanted to be there for *you*.'

'Just a shame that Blake didn't share your enthusiasm for me or he may not have felt the need to stray.'

Ugh. Even the word sounded so wretched. And even though her head knew that *Blake* was the one who'd been so sad and weak, it didn't stop her from feeling like the pathetic one.

'So you and he…' Oliver risked.

She spun around. 'Did we have a rich and fulfilling sex life? Apparently not. I knew I didn't rock his world but I didn't realise I'd driven him to such desperate lengths.'

'It wasn't you, Audrey.'

'It was at least half me!'

He crossed to her, took her hands from around her ru-ined blouse and cupped them. 'It wasn't you at all.'

'Well, it wasn't Don bloody Juan. He seems to have had no problems in that regard.'

'I swear to you, Audrey, there was nothing you could have done differently.'

'How would you know? Did he—?' *Oh, God.* 'Did he talk to you about our sex life, or lack thereof?'

Yeah, that would be the final humiliation. Oliver could add *dud lay* to her mounting debit column.

'No. He did not. But he did talk quite freely about his other...encounters. Until I shut that down.'

She sunk onto an ottoman and buried her face in her hands. 'I feel like such a fool. How could I not have seen?'

'He didn't want you to see.'

'Then how could I not have guessed?' She shot back up onto her feet. 'We lived such separate lives but I was with him every day—surely I should have at least suspected?'

'Like I said, you look for the best in people.'

'Not any more,' she vowed.

'Don't.' He crossed to stand in front of her. 'Don't let him change you. Your goodness is why people will judge him for this, not you.'

People? Her face came up. 'How many people know?'

He dropped his eyes to the carpet. 'A few. I gather he wasn't all that subtle.'

A sudden image of Blake with a buxom post-adolescent on each arm strolling through inner Sydney filled her mind and thickened her throat. Everything she wasn't. Young, stacked, lithesome and probably the kind of performer in bed that she could never hope to be.

And so public... Maybe he wanted to be caught? Wasn't that what the experts said about men who had affairs? And maybe she would have caught him out if she'd been paying the slightest bit of attention to her marriage.

Reality soaked in as the tears dried up. She'd set herself up for this the day she gave her work and her friends and her hobbies more importance than her marriage.

She straightened on a deep inward breath.

'Audrey...' Oliver warned, his voice low. 'I know what you're doing.'

She tossed back her hair. 'What am I doing?'

'You're tallying up the ways this is your fault.'

He knew her so well. How was that possible?

'Do I need to say it again?' he growled.

'Apparently you do.'

He stared at her, indecision scouring that handsome face. Then he stepped forward and took her hands again, squatting in front of her. 'Audrey Devaney, this was *not* your fault.'

He spoke extra-slowly to get through her hysteria.

'There was nothing in this world that you could have done to change this—' he tightened his hold on her hands so much she actually glanced down at his white knuckles '—short of changing gender.'

Her tear-ravaged eyes shot back up to his one more time. Utterly speechless. But then denial kicked in.

'No—'

'I think he'd known a really long time,' he went on, calmly. 'I think he knew when we were growing up, I think he knew when you guys first started dating and I think he knew when he walked down the aisle with you. But I also think he just couldn't be on the outside what he didn't feel on the inside. Not long term.'

'You're defending him?'

'I'm defending his right to be who he truly was. But, no, I'm not defending his actions. Cheating is cheating and he was hurting someone I care deeply about. That is why I ended my friendship with him.'

'And he knew that?'

'He got a very graphic farewell visit.'

'You were in Sydney? Why didn't you tell me?' Although the answer to that was ridiculously patent. To someone whose brain cells weren't in a jumbled pile. 'Sorry. Don't answer that.'

Just then the tiniest knock came at the big brown doors. Almost like a kitten scratching. Oliver crossed to it and pulled one open and one of the stunning staff from earlier drifted in. She held a neat fold of gorgeous blue silk, threaded through with silver.

'A change of clothes for you,' Oliver explained. 'Your suit will be laundered onsite and returned to you before you leave tonight.'

The girl smiled, revealing flawless, tiny teeth to go with the hourglass figure and hand-span waist, and nudged the clothes towards her. Audrey felt foolish being treated with such kid gloves, so she took the clothes, thanked the girl and turned to go find a bathroom.

'Second on the right,' Oliver called after her.

It was a matter of only minutes for her to strip out of her ruined business suit and into the dress that the girl had clearly picked up in the boutiques on street level. Three-quarter length, with the high collar and short sleeves typical of Chinese fashion and accentuating every curve. The depth of the blue was truly stunning and the threads of silver cast a glow that refracted up to include her face.

Which only served to highlight the tear-struck devastation there. As if things weren't bad enough.

She sagged down onto the broad bath edge and slumped, exhausted, against the cool of the tiled wall.

Blake's secret life certainly explained a lot. His at times enigmatic behaviour, which she'd chalked up to business tensions. His emotional detachment, never rude but always a few degrees…separated. And their lacklustre—and downright perfunctory—sex life.

Technically correct but lacking any real heart.

Turned out there was a very good reason for that.

And *she* wasn't *it*.

Her relief at that far eclipsed the shock of discovering her husband was gay. How sad that Blake hadn't ever managed to reconcile that part of his life. That he felt the need to lie to everyone around him even while it ate him up inside.

And how sad that she couldn't have been there for him in his struggle. Because she would have. Her feelings for him might not have been traditional or immense but they were genuine, even when she didn't always like the things he did. If he'd confided in her, she totally would have supported him. Even as she left him.

Because hiding inside a marriage was no way to be happy.

Audrey looked back up into the mirrors lining the far side of the bathroom and practically heard them whisper…

Hypocrite.

She'd held onto her fair share of secrets, too, within their marriage. Not quite as destructive as Blake's, but then again her secrets weren't quite as colossal as his.

She tilted her head slightly back in the direction of the living room. Towards Oliver.

Not quite.

Thanks to China and its quirks, Audrey knew exactly what she'd find under the bathroom sink. A small refrigerator loaded with bottles of water and, on the left, a stack of dampened, refrigerated towels. Manna during Hong Kong's steamy wet season. Stocked just because during the dry. A lifesaver now.

She pressed the topmost wet towel to her flushed face, trying to restore some semblance of order.

'Audrey?' Oliver murmured through the door.

She opened it just a crack.

'I thought you might want this?' He squeezed her purse through to her.

'Thank you. Um…here…' She bundled up her skirt and blouse and passed the whole wad back through the gap. 'So she doesn't have to wait.'

As his fingers closed around the clothes they brushed against hers, static sparking in their wake. Except it couldn't be static because she was standing on tiles and the corridor was bamboo-floored. She curled her fingers back into her palm as she pulled it back into the bathroom.

Oliver murmured and was gone.

It took two more towels and some hasty repair work with the travel make-up from her purse until she felt vaguely presentable again. She combed through her chaos of hair, pulled the snug blue dress down the few inches it had ridden up with all her fussing and turned to the door.

Ready or not.

CHAPTER NINE

Ginger fingers with lemon spritzer

'How are you doing?'

It took Oliver a moment to speak after she emerged and when he did there was a hint of tightness to his voice. Uncomfortable at the idea of picking up the conversation where they left off, perhaps, given how hysterical she'd been.

Well, that was over.

The beautiful hostess had departed with her things and so they were alone again, but Audrey wasn't about to resume their previous discussion. She ignored his question and wandered straight past him into a kitchen that looked as if it had been shipped direct from a magazine. And also as if it had never made so much as a cup of coffee. And why would it when the residences in this building were fully serviced by maids and room service?

'Why do you suppose they need two sinks?' she mused.

Excellent. Displacement conversation.

There were dual sinks on opposite sides of the kitchen. Neither of them overlooked the magnificent view, so they clearly weren't for standing at doing dishes.

Oliver moved up behind her. 'Maybe the wealthy entertain a lot? Need the catering facility?'

She turned. 'You say that like you're not one of them.'

'Entertaining is really not where I spend my money.'

'You entertain me every Christmas.'

'You're an exception to the rule.' He watched her as she trailed a finger along the granite bench tops, drifting slowly amongst all the polished surfaces. 'That dress looks—'

He struggled for words and she hoped whatever he was trying not to say wasn't *ridiculous*. Or *absurd*. Or *try hard*.

'—like it's part of your skin. It fits you perfectly.'

It shouldn't, given she was taller by a foot than the average Chinese delicacy. She glanced down at her legs where the dress stopped awkwardly halfway up her calves. 'I think it's supposed to be longer.'

'It doesn't matter. It looks right on you.'

She bowed in a parody of the cultural tradition and as she came up she saw the burst of dark intensity in his gaze. She swallowed with some difficulty. 'That's because you haven't seen me try to sit down in it, yet.'

But that wasn't nearly as difficult as she feared. The dress shifted and gave in all the right places as she sank down onto the edge of the expensive nine-seat sofa running around the far edges of the living space.

'Are we going to ignore it, Audrey?' Oliver said, still standing a few feet away.

It. The proverbial elephant in the room. 'I'm not sure there's much more to say.'

His eyes narrowed. 'Just like that? You've filed it away and dealt with it already?'

No, she'd filed it away *un*-dealt with. As was her wont. She smiled breezily. 'I really don't want to have to reapply my make-up a second time.'

Oliver stared down on her. 'It bothers you that little?'

Oh, where to begin answering that question? Her tight smile barely deserved the title. 'Many things about what he did will always bother me. It bothers me that I misread our marriage so much. It bothers me that he respected it little enough to cheat in the first place. It bothers me that he respected *me* little enough to do it and be so public about it.'

'But not that it was with men?'

She stared. 'You said it yourself. It wasn't *me*. It wasn't Audrey Devaney that he felt the need to stray from; it wasn't *his wife* that he couldn't stomach. It was all of us. My whole gender. There's no better or cleverer or funnier or sexier woman that might have been more suitable than me. His choice means my only lack was a Y chromosome.'

'You don't lack anything, Audrey.'

Get real.

She leaned forward. 'You know my school experience. That led me to bury myself in study during university and not long after graduating I met Blake.' And Oliver, but that wasn't going to help make her point. 'So my entire sense of who I am romantically—' she couldn't even bring herself to *say* 'sexually' '—was from him.'

A man who was just going through the motions for appearances' sake.

'I thought it was *me*. I thought I was to blame for the lack of passion in our marriage. That I didn't inspire it, that I wasn't worth it.'

That she couldn't feel it.

She shuddered in a breath. 'All those tears you just witnessed thirty minutes ago, all that devastation…? That was because the only man I've ever been intimate with preferred other women to me. Because that's how much of a dud I was in bed. But here I sit, just twenty minutes later, tearless and comparatively whole. I'm not mourning my marriage, I'm not cursing Blake's cheating, I'm not even cursing him.' She lifted wretched eyes to his. 'What does it say about me that my first reaction on hearing about all those men was *relief*? Vindication. Because that meant it wasn't *me*. That maybe I'm not broken.'

'I think it says you're human, Audrey. Which I know

won't please you. You're a perfectionist and you like things to be orderly.' He peered down on her. 'And you're certainly not broken.'

She shot to her feet. 'Words. How would you know? Maybe a hotter woman might have been able to satisfy him.'

Oliver smiled. 'Pretty sure it doesn't work like that.'

'My point is that Blake is still my only reference point. So, really, we know nothing. I could still be a dud.'

Jeez, with self-belief like that who needed enemies?

Oliver folded his arms and calmly watched her pace. 'You haven't been involved with anyone else since he died? It's been eighteen months.'

'I've been too busy shoring up my life,' she defended, instantly conscious that maybe it was just further evidence of her lameness. Shoring up her life and conveniently returning directly to type. Her barricaded-up, risk-averse type.

'Audrey, think. You're missing something obvious—'

'Apparently I've been missing it for years!' That her husband wasn't into women. She spun on him. 'And why the hell does this amuse you?'

'—*I'm* attracted to you.'

Pfff. 'You just think the dress is hot.'

Yet her pulse definitely spiked at his words. But, once again, words were cheap.

'I do think the dress is hot but she had a similar one on, too—' he nodded to the front door where the beautiful china doll had just departed '—and I wasn't attracted to her. And you weren't wearing it earlier and I was definitely attracted to you then.'

'You're Oliver—*The Hammer*—Harmer. You'd be attracted to anyone.'

His fists curled that little bit tighter. 'You're going to need to find one slur and stick to it, Audrey. Either I'm guilty of swimming too exclusively down the beautiful end of the gene pool or I'll do anything in a skirt. Which is it?'

'I didn't say you couldn't slum it from time to time.'

That actually seemed to make him mad. For the first time today. 'I think you'd say anything to win an argument.'

Yep. He absolutely had her number there.

Well… Whatever. 'You being attracted to me is a comment on your general randyness not on my abilities—' or otherwise, a little, inner voice whispered '—in the sack.'

He laughed but it no longer sounded amused. 'Careful, Audrey. That sounds an awful lot like a challenge.' He stepped closer.

She tossed her head. 'How like you to read it that way.'

'Why are you so angry at me?'

'Because you're here,' she yelled. 'And because you kept this from me for so long. And because you're—'

Part of the bloody problem.

If not for the extraordinary chemistry she'd always felt around Oliver she might never have noticed it missing from her marriage. But she forced those words back into her throat before they spilled out, and let the tension out on a frustrated grunt instead.

'Because I'm what?'

'You're pushing me.'

'I'm trying to support you. I'm listening. And letting you vent. How is that pushing?'

'You're riling me up intentionally.'

'Maybe that's because I know what to do with you when you're angry. I felt powerless when you were so upset. I've never seen you like that before.'

And she'd be damned sure he never would again. Her chest heaved beneath the sensual silk. And some of her confusion billowed out.

'But that fire in your eyes and the sharpness of your words…? *That* I know.' He slid one arm around behind her and pulled her hard up against his chest. 'That and this feeling that I get when you're on fire.'

He took her hand and pressed it over his left pectoral muscle. His heart hammered wildly beneath it. 'Feel that? That's what you do to me. So please don't tell me I'm not attracted to you.'

She bent back as far as she could in his hold. Eyed him warily. Even as her own pulse began to gallop. 'You're just mad,' she muttered.

'Woman, you have no idea.'

He released her then and turned and crossed to the window. 'Audrey. You kill me. You have so much yet you don't value it. You don't see it.' He plunged both hands into his pockets as if to keep himself from reaching for her again. 'And I sit here every damned Christmas, wanting you, and wondering if you'd recognise the signs, if you had even the slightest clue that you were affecting me that way.'

Silence fell heavy and accusatory. But his outburst was enough to finally get the message through.

He was serious. He was actually drawn to her.

What the hell did she do with that?

'I'm sorry, Oliver.'

He turned back, all the anger gone now. 'I wasn't angling for an apology. I'm angry *for* you, not *at* you. That everything in life has led you to have such little faith in yourself despite all the amazing things you are. And I'm mad at myself that—despite everything my head tells me, despite the total lack of signals from you—my body just doesn't get the message.'

Her chest tightened like a fist.

No, he wasn't angry. He was hurting.

A lot.

'You never let on.'

'If there's one thing I'm good at, it's command over my baser instincts.'

She wet her lips and chewed them a little bit. This was Oliver: a man she cared for and respected. A man she'd been harbouring any number of inappropriate thoughts about for years. And he was telling her that the attraction was mutual.

'How could there be signals...?' she started.

He raised a hand to stop her. 'I understand, Audrey—'

'No, you don't. I meant how could I give you signals, when I was married and I knew how strongly you felt about fidelity? Above all else, I didn't want you to think badly of me.'

Not you.

He stared. 'Why would I?'

'You would have. If you could have seen into my head and read my thoughts sometimes when I was with you.'

Or lots of times when she wasn't.

He hadn't been moving before but somehow his body grew more still. Still and dangerously alert. 'What are you saying?'

'I'm saying that the absence of signals is a reflection of my great need for your good opinion.' She took a deep breath. 'Not my actual feelings.'

The shame in his gaze dissipated, heated and evaporated by the desire that took its place. But still he didn't move.

'You're not married now,' he murmured. 'And I'm hardly in a position to judge you given some of the fantasies I had when you were my friend's bride.'

Her breath tightened and ran out.

He was right. There was nothing stopping them. Blake was gone, and any loyalty she'd ever felt for him had dissolved the moment she discovered his serial infidelity. Oliver wasn't seeing anyone. She wasn't seeing anyone. They were both here in this amazing, private place. And she wouldn't see him again for twelve months.

And no one but them would know.

There was no reason in the world that she shouldn't cross

the empty space between them and put her hands on Oliver Harmer as she'd been dreaming of for years.

And that freedom was completely and utterly terrifying.

She crossed to the window, instead, stared out at the view. All those millions of people just going about their business, oblivious to the torment happening at the top of one of the hundreds of buildings lining their harbour.

'Did you just weird yourself out?' he murmured from behind her.

Right behind her.

He read her like a book. There wasn't a person alive who knew her as well as this man she only saw once a year. She smiled. 'Sure did.'

She could feel him there, his heat reaching out for her, but not touching. Just…teasing. Tormenting. Tantalising.

But she couldn't turn around to save her life. She clung to the ant-sized community far below them and used them as her anchor. Before she floated up and away on this bliss.

'It doesn't have to be weird,' he whispered. 'We're still the same people.'

That was exactly what made it weird. But also so very exciting. As her pounding pulse could attest.

'But you have to want it,' he breathed. 'And you have to think about it. I need you to make the conscious decision.'

'You want me to make the first move?' Please, no… surely?

'I want you to be certain.' His words brushed her ear.

She steadied herself with hands on the window, either side of her body, her hot palms instantly making a thermal handprint on the cool glass.

'What if I'm no good?' She hated how tiny her voice sounded.

The chuckle that rumbled in his chest so close behind her was almost close enough to feel. 'Audrey, I'm not even touching you and it's already good.'

He leaned more of his weight into her, pressing her to the window and the hard tension in his body gave his words veracity. The contrast of the cool glass to her front and his big, hot body at her back made her breath shudder in her throat.

'Let me show you.' His knuckle came up to stroke her hair back from her face, back over her shoulder. And it was that—more than anything he could have said or done—that convinced her.

Because those big, tan, confident fingers...?

They were trembling like an autumn leaf.

Her eyes fluttered shut and she forced all the doubts and fears and questions out of her mind and just let herself *feel*. The moment she tipped her head, exposing more of her throat above the delicate collar hem of the dress, Oliver dropped his lips straight onto her skin, hot and self-assured.

Her legs practically gave way. If not for the press of his body sandwiching her to the glass window she would have slid in a heap onto the expensive bamboo parquetry. Air shuddered in and out of her on inelegant gasps as his mouth and chin nuzzled below the blue and silver collar, then around to the front of her throat, lathing her collarbone. His hands covered hers on the glass and twisted them down to trace, with him, the silken length of her body.

His knuckles brushed the sides of her breasts, her waist, the swell of her hips, leaving her trembling and alive. Then he released her hands and one of his slipped around to press against her belly while the other traced down the outer curve of one buttock. Beneath its underside.

Her eyes flew open.

'Just feel it,' he murmured against her skin. 'Just be brave.'

The strange choice of words was lost again in the excruciating sensations of his lips back on her throat. They climbed up behind her ear, lingered there a moment and then drifted forward, across her jaw, along her cheek.

Searching. Seeking. And when they reached what they were seeking Audrey was more than ready for them.

His mouth pressed against hers on a masculine, throaty sigh, and she twisted slightly in his hold to improve her purchase and meet his exploration with her own.

Wave after wave of vertigo washed over her as she stood, pressed against nothing but open sky and man, all the air in her body escaping out to mingle with Oliver's. She clung to his lips as though they were the only thing stopping her from plunging sixty storeys.

He tasted exactly as she'd dreamed—decadent and masculine and delicious.

He felt just as she'd always imagined—hard and hot and in control.

But so, so much better. Like nothing she'd ever experienced in her life.

Be brave, he'd said. This was what he meant. Take a chance.

Embrace the risk.

She twisted fully in his grasp, pressing her back to the glass, and slid her arms up around his bent neck.

And she kissed him back for all she was worth.

Things really took off then. Oliver slid his foot between her feet and nudged them apart, making room for the expensive fabric of his thigh. That pressed against her everywhere she'd started to ache but it also took over the important job of holding her up, which freed his hands to roam the front of her body where they'd been unable to go moments before.

One plunged up into her hair and the other trailed its way up to a breast. And he relieved her of another ache, there, with a gentle squeeze.

He ripped his mouth from hers as fast as his hand snatched away from her breast. 'You're not wearing a bra?'

Confusion dazzled her, but she answered, 'It was in the

pile you sent for cleaning.' Some of the salsa had soaked through onto it. Which was a ridiculous thought to be having just now.

'That's going to make it a bit harder,' he gritted, blazing the words along the neglected side of her throat.

It was all she could do to harness enough air to keep speaking. 'Make what harder?'

'Stopping.'

'Why would you stop?'

Why *in this world*...?

'Because we're about to have company.'

She ripped her ear away from where his hot lips were torturing them. Company wasn't *just the two of them.* Company wasn't *no one will know.* Company was public. And she was standing with her skirt half hiked up sandwiched between Oliver and the window in the direct eyeline of the door.

He stepped back, but not without reluctance.

'What company?'

'I asked for the next dish to be served up here.'

'Why the hell would you do that?'

Well...wasn't she quite the lady when in the throes of carnal disappointment?

Moisture from her swollen lips glinted on his as he smiled. 'I didn't know this was going to happen. I thought you might have appreciated the privacy.'

She tugged her skirt down. He stepped back.

Looks like stopping is all taken care of. 'I would love privacy right now.'

'You don't have to eat it. We can resume the moment they're gone.' His gaze grew keen. 'If that's what you want.'

Was that what she wanted? Yes, right now it really was. Right now, she was numb all over except for some very dissatisfied, very grumpy, very pointed points of focus that couldn't really think of anything other than resuming. But in five minutes...who knew? By then her brain might have kicked back in and reminded her of all the reasons this was a bad, bad idea.

In five minutes this could all be over.

You have to be certain. That was what he'd said, and maybe this was what he'd meant. That she needed to be certain in the cold, hard light of reality, not the hot, fevered place he'd just taken her.

On cue, the door sounded slightly. She spun to face back out of the window, tugging her dress unnecessarily into position and pretending she'd just been admiring the view, not the sensation of Oliver's hand on the screaming flesh of her breast. Behind her, Oliver accepted the meal with thanks and closed the door quietly.

Then there was silence. So much silence that Audrey eventually turned around.

He stood, staring at her silhouette, the loaded tray balanced in his arms, a question on his face.

Giving her the choice.

Another bonus of being rich, he could ignore the just-delivered food, spend the evening trying out every soft surface in the place—and a few of the harder ones—and nothing would ever be said. At least not aloud.

If only the rest of the world worked that way.

Her pulse hadn't even had time to settle, yet. How could she make a good decision with it still screaming around her body with a swag of natural chemicals in tow?

She made her choice, curling one arm across her torso. 'What's under the lid?'

'Fingers of chilled ginger specially prepared.' If he was disappointed, he didn't let it show particularly. He quirked one eyebrow, deliciously, and wet the lips that had just done such gorgeous damage to hers. 'Want a taste, Audrey?'

Okay, so he wasn't going to let her go easily.

She smoothed her dress once again and then crossed

to the oversized dining table and slid into the seat at one corner. With no chair at the end he would either have to sit next to her or across from her. One was too close but she wouldn't have to look into those all-seeing eyes. The other...

Of course he chose that one, sinking into the seat immediately opposite.

'Stop thinking,' he murmured as he lifted the lid off the delivered tray and spread the contents between them on the table.

'I'm not.'

'You are. And you're partitioning. I can see it happening.' He served up the fanned palate cleanser. 'You're separating the parts of what just happened into acceptable and unacceptable and you're locking them in different boxes.'

She kept her eyes averted.

'But I'm curious to know what you put where.'

She lifted her gaze for an answer.

'Where did you file being here, with me, alone in this suite?'

She took a deep, slow breath. 'Being here is necessary. And sensible.' And therefore completely defensible.

'What about being in that dress?'

'The dress is beautiful. It makes me feel beautiful.' The door was wide open for him to say '*you are beautiful*'. But he didn't. Part of her was pleased that he didn't resort to trite niceties. A smaller part cried just a little bit.

He leaned back in the expensive chair and considered her. 'What would you change? If you could? If money was no object.'

She considered. The shape of her eyes wasn't anything to write home about unaided, but they came up pretty well under skilfully applied make-up. And their colour was harmless enough. Her lips were even and inoffensive, not too small, and they sat neatly under a long straight nose. Even that couldn't be called a problem, particularly.

It was just all so…lacklustre.

'My jaw's a bit square.'

He shook his head once. 'It's strong. Defined.'

'You asked me what I'd change. That's something.'

'It gives you character.'

She laughed. 'Yep. Because all women hunger to have a face "with character".'

'You can have character and still be beautiful. But okay, what else?'

She sighed. 'It's not a case of individual flaws. It's not like I could get a brow-lift or have my ears pinned and I'd feel reborn. It's just that I don't have…' She considered her wording options. 'There's no *standout* feature in my appearance.'

'I could name three.'

'Ha ha.'

'I'm serious. Want to hear them?'

She took a deep breath. Part of her wanted to watch him flounder, to make him own his lies. But a deeper part again wondered if he might see her differently from what she saw in the mirror. Curiosity won.

'Sure.'

'Your cheekbones,' he started, immediately, as though he'd been waiting years to say it. 'You don't highlight them, but you don't need to. And when you smile and your muscles contract their angle seems to intensify.'

She lifted one brow. 'Good to know.'

'And that's number two, despite the sarcasm. Your face is rich with…intelligence. You always look so switched on, so intent. That stands out for me, big time.'

'I have a smart face?'

'Anyone can have a garden-variety pretty face…'

She processed that. His body language said he was serious, but she wasn't about to make a fool of herself by getting all hot and bothered by his praise. 'Wow, I'm very curious to know what could possibly top a "smart" face…'

He didn't hesitate. 'Your body.'

Not what she was expecting. And the intent fixation of his gaze was just a little bit disconcerting. 'Please don't call me athletic.'

'No?' Which meant he'd been about to.

'That's code for "shapeless and flat-chested".'

'Only if you're looking for offence.' He considered her and his eyes darkened before he spoke. 'Here's what athletic means to me.'

He leaned slightly forward.

'Malleable. Flexible.' Every word was more of a breath. 'Resilient. Strong. It's a body that won't break easily under duress.'

The air flowing in and out of her lungs seemed to divest itself of oxygen and she had to increase her respiration to compensate. Her undisciplined imagination filled with images of the kind of duress he might be referring to. And ways of applying it.

'I think of endurance and fortitude—'

'Is everything about sex with you?' she breathed.

Pot. Kettle. Black.

'Who says I'm just talking about sex? What about a long, healthy life? What about childbirth? What about long hikes out there—' he indicated the steep slope of Hong Kong's wilderness trails on a distant green mountain '—and stretching out, long and straight on this sofa watching a movie? A man might see the surface details with his eyes, but his biology is naturally drawn to the kind of mate that will live as long as he does.'

The picture he painted was idyllic and she got the sense that that was exactly what he saw when he looked at her.

Potential.

Not flaws.

Awkwardness—and awareness—surged around them. She never was good with compliments, but there was also the sense that maybe he'd given the subject of her figure a whole lot more thought than just a few seconds.

'Although, yeah, it's definitely the kind of body that tends to make a man start thinking about getting sweaty.' Those thoughts reflected darkly in his eyes. 'And that's a whole other body part paying attention.'

Audrey grabbed the levity like a life raft on the sea of unspoken meaning on which she'd suddenly found herself adrift. 'That's what I figured.'

He joined her in that life raft. 'What can I say? I'm a man of very few dimensions.'

Not true. Not at all. And she was just beginning to get a sense of how much she'd yet to learn about him. And about how long that could take.

'I wish you could see yourself as I see you,' he murmured.

She shrugged. 'I don't lose sleep over it or anything.'

'I know. But I'd love to watch you walk into a room, full of knowing self-confidence instead of doubt.'

She knew exactly what he was talking about. Somewhere along the line she learned to downplay her strengths, maybe to fly under the radar. 'Confidence attracts you?'

'Completely.'

'Is that what the beautiful women are all about?'

'It's not their aesthetics I'm drawn to.'

No. She was starting to realise how shallow her accusation that *he* was shallow really was.

'But sadly the confidence doesn't always hold up. Some of them were the most fragile women I've ever met.'

'Maybe you just expect too much?' she risked.

'By knowing what I want?'

'By expecting it all. And maybe they got the sense that

they were failing to measure up to some undefined standard.'

He stared at her. 'Law of averages. If one woman can have everything I want, then there has to be another.'

She had *everything* he wanted? That was a whole lot more than just intellectual compatibility. Her heart thumped madly. 'And yet I lack the confidence you look for. So incomplete, after all.'

'I said you don't see it, not that you don't have it. You could own any room you walked into if you could just tap into your self-belief.'

If only it were *as easy* as turning on a tap. 'A few more conversations like this one and maybe I will.'

He looked inordinately pleased to have pleased her. 'I live to serve.'

The intensity of his gaze reached out and curled around her throat, cutting off most of her air. 'Really? Then how about serving me another finger?'

Oliver finished his dish way ahead of Audrey. She stalled, wiping up every drop, using it as a chance to cool things off as much as the ginger had. One part of her hungered for more of the physical sensation she'd enjoyed before the food came. Exactly as stimulating as the gastronomic marathon they were undertaking. But another part—the sensible, logical part—knew that there was much more going on with her than just Oliver's desire for some activity of the *athletic* kind.

And *more than* was a big mental shift to be making in one day. Particularly when she'd come here today all ready to say goodbye.

To cut off her supply.

'I think maybe we should head back downstairs,' she murmured.

That surprised him. 'Now?'

She folded her napkin neatly and placed it next to her licked-clean plate on the expensive table. 'I think so.'

'Safety in numbers, Audrey?'

'What happened before was—' *amazing, unprecedented, unforgettable* '—compelling, but I don't think we should necessarily pick up where we left off.'

It was too dangerous.

'You seemed as *compelled* as I was. Can you just walk away from it?'

'I… Yes. The timing is all wrong.'

'We're both single. We're alone in an executive suite looking out over one of the world's most beautiful views. We have the whole evening ahead of us. And it's Christmas. How could the timing be better?'

His knowing eyes saw way too much. Like just how much of a liar she was. 'I just learned my husband was cheating on me…' she hedged.

'I assumed you'd slipped into revenge sex mode.'

'You think me that much of a user?'

'Are you still a us*er* if the us*ee* is fully aware of what you're doing? I'd be delighted to be exploited for any revenge activity whatsoever.' He held his hands out to the side. 'Do your worst.'

Impossible man. And impossible to know if he was serious or joking, or some complicated combination of the two. 'That wouldn't be particularly mature, Oliver.'

'Sometimes the body knows better than the brain what it really wants. Or needs.'

'You think I *need* a good roll in the hay?' Did she strike him as that uptight?

'Who says I'm talking about you?'

Oh, please. 'Like you didn't have sex twice this week already.'

'I did not.'

'Then last week.'

He stared at her. Infuriatingly unabashed.

'Earlier in the month, then.'

'Nope.'

The mere concept of a celibate Oliver was fascinating. But she wasn't going to allow even intrigue. 'Well, that explains today's detour from the norm. You're horny.'

'Any detour we take today—' she didn't fail to notice his use of the future tense '—won't be due to lack of self-control on my part.'

'So bloody cocky,' she muttered, pulling the dishes together into an easy-to-collect pile for the hotel staff. 'And presumptuous if you think I lack self-discipline.'

It was another of the virtues she was prepared to own.

'Far from it. The moment I let you shore up your resolve, I'm screwed. You'll set your mind to leaving and I'll never see you again.'

A raw kind of tragedy lurked behind his eyes. 'So... you're keeping me off kilter, just to be safe?'

'Trying to.'

Huh. It was working. 'How is confessing that going to help your cause?'

'I'm trying something new. Something that goes against everything my instincts tell me.'

She narrowed her eyes at him.

'Honesty.'

'You're always honest with me.'

'I don't lie. That's not the same as being honest. There's a lot I don't say, rather than have to lie to you.'

'Like not telling me about Blake?'

'Like not telling you how badly I want you every time I see you.'

Air shot into her lungs in a short, sharp gasp.

'That's right, Audrey. Every single time. And it's not going to go away just because you refuse to think about it.'

Her chest pressed in on itself. 'I assume you don't want to go back downstairs?'

'I do not.' His gaze was resolute. 'We're too close.'

'Close to what?'

'Close to everything I've wanted for years.'

Wanted. Her, on a plate. It was still too inconceivable to trust. 'Regardless of what I want?'

'If I thought you didn't want it I'd be holding the door open for you right now and calling up the elevator.'

A fist squeezed around her larynx.

'But you do. You just need to let yourself have it.' He glowered down on her. 'And believe you deserve it.'

She curled her arms around the sensual silk of her loaned dress and remembered instantly how much better his arms had felt doing the same thing just minutes ago. *Deserve it?* Did he know what he was asking her to set aside? Years of careful, safe emotional shielding?

Of course she wanted to sleep with him. It seemed stupidly evident to her. But *dare* she? Could she do it and not be crippled by old doubts? Could she do it and not want more? Because he wasn't offering *more*. He was offering *now*.

And right now she had allure working very much in her favour.

'The Audrey of your imagination must be spectacular,' she whispered, enjoying the solar flare that erupted in his smouldering gaze. 'But, seriously, what if I'm just ordinary?'

Or worse. Was that something she could bear him knowing?

He stepped closer and slid his big hand around her cheek. 'Honey, I'm that keyed up I may not even notice what you're doing.'

A choked kind of laugh rattled through her. Bless Oliver

Harmer and his gift for putting her at ease. 'You're supposed to say, "You couldn't possibly be, Audrey".'

'You *couldn't* possibly be, Audrey,' he repeated, all seriousness. 'But I'm done enabling you. If you want to know for sure you're going to have to take a step. Take a risk.' He lowered his hand between them and stretched it towards her, his eyes blazing but steady. 'And take my hand.'

She stared at those long, talented, certain fingers. No trembling now.

If she slid her own in between them she was changing her life, going boldly where she'd never gone before.

A one-night stand.

Sex with Oliver.

That couldn't be undone. And it probably wouldn't be repeated; after all, they only saw each other once a year and a lot could change in twelve months.

Revenge sex, he'd joked. But was it so very funny? She certainly had enough to feel vengeful for. She'd wasted years being modest and appropriate and not throwing herself across the table at a scrumptious Oliver every year out of loyalty to a man who was betraying everything she'd ever stood for. Who couldn't wait for her to leave the country so he could express the man he really wanted to be.

Wasn't she due a little bit of payback?

And wouldn't that moment when Oliver strained over her just as he had in her most secret fantasies…wouldn't *that moment* undo everything that had gone before it? Wouldn't she be reborn?

Like a phoenix out of the ashes of her ridiculous, restrained life.

His fingers twitched, just slightly, out there all alone in the gulf of inches between them and the simple movement softened her heart.

This wasn't sleazy. This wasn't some kind of set-up or

test and there wasn't a bunch of schoolgirls waiting to slam her up against the bathroom wall for daring to reach.

This was Oliver.

And *he* was reaching for *her*.

She lifted her eyes, fastened them to his cautious hazel depths and slid her fingers carefully between his.

CHAPTER TEN

*Lavender-cured crocodile, watermelon fennel salad
served with a lime emulsion*

'AGAIN?'

Audrey's beautiful, sweat-slicked chest rose and fell
right in Oliver's peripheral vision as she sprawled, wild
and indelicate, across his bed, eyeing him lasciviously.

His laugh strangled deep in his throat. 'I won't be doing
it again for a little bit, love.'

'Really? You're not a three-times-a-night kind of guy?'

He rolled over and stared at her. 'Have you never heard
of recovery? Any man who can go three times in a row
didn't do it thoroughly the first time.'

And she'd been done *extremely* thoroughly.

The second time, anyway.

Their first time had been hot, and hard and slick and
they didn't even make it off the sumptuous sofa. He'd been
joking about being so keyed up, but it had taken a gargan-
tuan effort on his part to keep things at a pace that wouldn't
scare her off forever.

Or shame him.

The second time they'd turned nomad; roaming from
surface to surface, view to view, stretching out the torture,
exploring and learning the geography of each other's bodies,
knocking vases off tables and sending light fittings swing-

ing. He'd been determined to make a slightly better—and lengthier—showing than the almost adolescent fumblings on the sofa, and Audrey had risen to the challenge like the goddess she was, matching him move for move, touch for touch.

Until they'd finally collapsed in a heap on the penthouse's luxurious master bed where he really got to show her how he'd earned his nickname.

He rolled his exhausted head towards her. 'You were kidding, right?'

'Hell, yes. I'm numb.'

There we go... That was what a man liked to hear. He flipped his arm with the last remnants of energy he had and patted her unceremoniously on her perfect, naked bottom.

'Take that, Blake,' she said, after the giggles had subsided.

Audrey giggling. Wasn't that one of the heralds of the apocalypse?

'Hell hath no fury...' But it wasn't about vengeance, he knew that. This was much more fundamental.

'It wasn't me,' she whispered to the ceiling. And to every demon still haunting her.

He gave her a gentle shove with his own damp shoulder. 'Told you.'

'Yeah, you did.'

'Do you believe me now?'

'Yeah.' She sighed. 'I do.'

Then more silence.

Oliver studied the intricate plasterwork above them and mulled over words he'd never needed—or wanted—to utter. Found himself inexplicably nervous and utterly shamed of his own cowardice.

So...now what happens?

That was what he wanted to know. Half dreading and half breathless with anticipation at the answer. Because this—what they'd just shared—would be a crime to walk away from. He'd just had his deepest desire handed to him on a plate. Writhing under him.

Yet, he didn't do long-term. He didn't dare. Would he even know how? He'd lost years waiting for a woman with the right combination of qualities to come along. Goodness and curiosity and brilliance and elegance and wild, unbridled sensuality all bundled into one goddess.

He just wasn't going to find a woman on the planet better suited to being his.

Which meant he could *have* this remarkable gift that the universe had provided, but he couldn't *keep* it.

Because Audrey was far too precious to risk on someone as damaged as him.

Sex changed people. Women especially. Women like Audrey doubly especially. She wasn't a virgin, but he'd put good money on tonight being the first good sexual experience she'd had—again that sad, needy little troll deep inside him waved its club-fists triumphantly—and transformative experiences tended to make women start thinking of the future. Planning.

And he didn't do futures. He just couldn't.

There was more than one way of cheating in a relationship. He might never have been actually unfaithful to any of the women he'd been involved with, but he'd been false with every single one of them by not telling them they weren't measuring up to the bar set by a woman they'd never meet. By not telling them that what was between them was only ever going to be superficial.

By not telling them he wasn't in it for keeps.

He could dress it up whatever way he wanted—persevering, giving them a chance, getting to know one another—but the reality was from the moment he first realised they weren't the one, the rest of their time together was one big cheat.

As unfaithful and as unkind as his father. To every single one of them.

And so he'd come to specialise in short-term. He reserved his longest relationships for women who didn't change from first date to last. Predictable women who weren't looking for more. They got entire months.

Audrey wasn't the sort of woman you just kissed and farewelled after a few hot weeks. Look at the lengths he'd already gone to not to farewell her *at all*.

Audrey was someone he cared about deeply. And what happened from here was going to be critical to her remaining someone he was allowed to care deeply about. Because not caring for her was simply not an option. He couldn't even imagine it.

But using her—hurting her—wasn't going to work, either. He'd grown up witness to what it did to a woman to be in a relationship with a man incapable of loving just her.

It rotted her slowly from the inside out.

Bad enough imagining Audrey decaying in her sham of a marriage, but to think of himself being responsible for it... Watching her eyes getting dimmer and dimmer as he emotionally checked out of their relationship.

As he always did.

No. That was not something he was prepared to do to a woman he considered perfection. Who he actually cared for. Who he might love if he had any idea what the hell that meant.

And given his genetic make-up, the chances of him finding out any time soon weren't high.

But lying here drowning in *what-ifs* wasn't going to get them anywhere. Better to get it out in the open. Talk it through. Deal with whatever angst came.

Just ask!

'So what happens now?' he ground out. The longest four words of his life.

'Depends on what time it is.'

Okay. Uh, *not* what he was expecting. He craned his neck to check his TAG. 'Coming up to six p.m.'

Which meant she'd been here for eight hours already.

She rolled over, folding her arms under her as she went and boosting her breasts up into tantalising pillows. 'We still have half a degustation to enjoy.'

The little troll's fists fell limply by his side. She was thinking about food? While he was lying here doing a great impersonation of an angsty fourteen-year-old? 'Really? This hasn't been an adequate substitute?'

Her Mona Lisa smile gave nothing away. 'You said yourself we need to recharge. Might as well stretch our legs and eat while we do that.'

Stretch their legs. As if they'd just had a busy afternoon at their desks. He studied her for signs of weirdness—more than the usual amount—but found none. Her eyes were clear and untroubled.

'You're actually hungry?' Oh, my God, she actually was.

Audrey Devaney might just be the perfect woman.

'Ravenous,' she purred. "That was quite a workout.'

No wonder he adored her. 'You want to be served up here?'

A hint of shadow crossed her expression. 'No. Let's go back downstairs.' But then she sagged and her warm lips fell against the cooling sweat of his shoulder. 'In just a minute or two.'

She was pretty hungry but, more than anything, Audrey wanted to walk back into this public restaurant with Oliver.

With Oliver.

Just for the sheer pleasure of doing it. Nothing but her dress had changed for the restaurant patrons or the staff because most of them probably assumed she and Oliver were already sleeping together. But *she'd* changed. *She* would know what it was like to have the best sex of her life with a man like Oliver Harmer, right over their very heads, and then casually stroll back in for the next course.

It was more decadent a sensation than if they'd served her palate cleanser smeared on Oliver's naked torso.

She stumbled over that image slightly and the fingers curled around hers tightened.

'Okay?'

She threw her gratitude sideways on a breathy acknowledgement. Lord, when had she become so...Marilyn Monroe?

She glanced awkwardly to the other tables for a half-heartbeat. Did she look like a woman who was quite accustomed to having exquisite sex between courses? *Could* she look like that? And it was, hands down, the best sex she'd ever had. With her husband. With anyone else. Even on her own. Her body was still swollen and sensitive and really, really pleased with itself.

What if she looked as smug as she felt?

'Are you sure you're okay?'

'I don't know what the etiquette is,' she admitted, dragging her focus back to their private little corner by the dragonflies as they approached. Were the insects this vivid and lively before or was everything just super-sensory right now?

'To what?'

'To walking into a room after our...bonus course.'

His chuckle eased a little of her nerves. 'I don't think there are any rules for that. You're going to have to wing it.'

'I feel—' *transformed* '—conspicuous.'

'If people are looking at you it's because of the dress, Audrey.'

Right. Not some tattoo on her forehead that said, 'Guess where she's just had her mouth.'

She sank, on instinct, towards her comfortable sofa and Oliver tugged on their still-entwined fingers as he kept moving.

Oh. *Together.*

How odd that—despite everything they'd done with each other and been to each other over the past hours—it was *this* that felt taboo. Like crossing over to the dark side. She joined Oliver on his sofa, facing the other way for the first time in five years, while he scanned her for the first sign of trouble.

She must look as if she was ready to bolt from the room.

She stretched, cat-like, back into his sofa. 'This is quite comfortable, too.'

'I've always liked it.'

Her bottom wriggle dug her a little deeper. 'I think you had the better end of the deal, actually.'

'I would definitely say so, today.'

Sweet.

Terrifying…but sweet.

Oliver did little more than flick his chin at a passing server and the man reappeared a moment later with two glasses of chilled white wine. Audrey smiled her thanks before sweeping her glass up and turning her attention again to the busy dragonflies in the tank that usually sat behind her, and, through its glass sides, the bustling kitchen on the far side of the restaurant.

'I always thought you were terribly sophisticated, knowing the timing of everything in a Michelin-starred restaurant,' she murmured. 'But you were cheating. You can see them coming.'

'It seems it's a night for exposing secrets.'

That brought her eyes back to his. 'Yes indeed.'

'Do you want to talk about it?'

It.

'I don't want to ruin it.' Or jinx it. 'But I don't want you to think I'm avoiding conversation, either.'

'Would you like to talk about something else?'

Desperately. 'What?'

He cupped his wine and leaned back into the corner of the sofa more comfortably. 'Tell me about the Testore.'

The instruments she hunted were certainly something she could get excited about. And talk about until his ears bled. 'What would you like to know?'

'How was it stolen?'

'Directly from the cabin of a commercial airline between Helsinki and Madrid, while the owner used the washrooms.'

'In front of a plane full of people?'

'The cabin was darkened. But Testores get their own seat when they fly so it's unusual that no one saw it being removed. Someone would have had to lean right over into the window seat.'

'Wow, it's that valuable? How did they get it off the plane without being seen?'

'No one knows. We have to assume one of the ground crew was paid off. The plane's cabin security picked up a shadow lingering by the seats and taking it but it was too dark to identify even gender. And short of paying for a seat for the instrument *and* one for a bodyguard I'm not sure what the owner could have done differently. She had to pee. They searched the plane top to bottom.'

The public areas, anyway.

'So how did you begin tracking it down?'

This was what she did. This was what she loved. It wasn't hard to relax and bore Oliver senseless with the details of her hunt for the cello.

Except that he didn't bore easily, clearly. Forty minutes later he was still engaged and asking questions. She'd kicked off her shoes again and tucked her feet up under her, feeling very much the Chinese waif in her silken sheath, helping herself to finger-sized portions of the crocodile and watermelon that was course number seven.

'Can you talk about all of this? Legally?' Oliver queried.

'I haven't told you anything confidential. It's all process.' She smiled. 'Plus I think I can trust you.'

His eyes refocused sharply, as if he had something to say about that, but then he released her from his fixed gaze and reached, instead, to trace the line of her arm with a knuckle. 'Your patience amazes me. And that you're so close to finding it when you started with practically nothing.'

Oh, he had no idea how patient she could be. Just look how long she'd endured her feelings for him. Or how long she could endure his tantalising touch before shattering.

Apparently.

'It's taken all year but we're just one step behind them now. The plan is to get ahead and then we have them. The authorities just have to wait for them to deliver it up.'

'Why don't these people just take it and go to ground for a decade? Put it in a basement somewhere? Hoard it?'

'Criminals aren't that patient for their money and, besides, their industry is full of loose lips. You steal something like a Testore and don't keep it moving and one of your colleagues is just as likely to steal it out from under you.'

'I really don't see the point.'

'Neither do I,' she admitted. 'Why have lovely things if you never see them?'

'I'm surprised the bad guys haven't tried to buy you off.'

'Oh, they've tried.' She smiled. 'My sense of natural justice is just too strong. And I view the instruments a bit like children. Innocent victims. Stolen. Abused. All they want to do is go home to the person that loves and values them and keeps them safe and fulfils their potential.'

Because wasn't that what life was all about? Fulfilling your potential.

The brown in his eyes suddenly seemed more prominent. And chocolaty. And much closer. Which one of them had moved so subtly? Or had they both just gravitated naturally together?

'Want to hear something dumb?' he murmured.

'Sure.'

'That's how I feel about the companies I buy.'

She flicked an eyebrow. 'The near-crippled companies you get for a song, you mean?'

He smiled. 'They're innocent victims, too. In the hands of people that don't value them and don't understand how to make them strong.'

'And you do?'

'I'm like you—a facilitator. I have the expertise to recognise the signs of a flailing business and I gather them up, strengthen them and get them to the people who can give them a future.'

'That's a very anthropomorphic belief.'

'Says the woman who thinks of a cello like a trafficked child.'

She smiled. He was right. 'You don't ever break them up?'

'Not unless they're already falling to pieces.'

That was her greatest fear. Finding an instrument that someone took to with a sledgehammer rather than relinquish. Because some people were just like that: if they couldn't have it, no one would.

'I'm guessing that the people you buy them from don't see it that way.'

He shrugged. 'Hey, they're the ones selling. No one's forcing them.'

'I guess I hadn't realised how similar our jobs are.

Though I get the feeling yours has a lot more facets.' Like a diamond. It was certainly worth a whole heap more.

Oliver studied her as he finished the last of the watermelon. 'That wasn't so bad, was it?'

'What?'

'Having a conversation.'

'We've had lots of conversations.'

'Yet somehow that feels like our first.'

It did have that exciting hum about it. 'I miss conversation.'

'Blake's been gone a while.'

'I never really talked with him. Not like this.' Not like Oliver. 'So it's been a couple of years.'

'Did you move to Antarctica when I wasn't looking? What about your friends?'

'Of course I have friends. And we talk a lot, but they've all known me forever and so our conversation tends to be about…you know…stuff. Mutual friends. Work. Dramas. Clothes.'

'That's it?'

'That's a lot!' But those steady hazel eyes filled her with confidence. 'I'm not… I don't share much. Often.' And she could never talk about Oliver. To anyone.

'You share with me.'

'Once a year. Like cramming.' Did that even count?

Nothing changed in his expression yet everything did. He studied her, sideways, and then reached out to drag soft knuckles across the back of her hand. 'You call me up whenever you want. I'd love to talk to you more often. Or email.'

The cold, hard wash of reality welled up around her.

Right. Because she was leaving in the morning. As she always did. Flying seven thousand kilometres in one direction while he flew twelve hundred in the other. Back to their respective lives.

Back to reality. With a phone plan.

'Maybe I will.'

Or maybe she'd chalk tonight up to a fantastic one-night stand and run a million miles from these feelings. That could work.

A murmuring behind them drew Oliver's gaze.

'Hey, it's starting.'

No need to ask what 'it' was. Her favourite part of December twentieth. Her favourite part of Christmas. Oliver pulled her to her feet and she padded, barefoot, on the luxury carpet to the enormous window facing Victoria Harbour. Below them Hong Kong's nightly light show prepared to commence.

Both sides of the harbour lit up like a Christmas tree and pulsed with the commencement of music that the Qīngtíng suddenly piped through their sound system. Massive lighting arrays, specially installed on every building the length of both sides of the waterfront, began to strobe and dance. It wasn't intended to be a Christmas show but, to Audrey, it couldn't be more so if it were set to carols. She couldn't see a light show anywhere without thinking about this city.

This man.

Oliver slipped her in front of him between the window and the warmth of his body and looped his arms across her front, and she knew this was the light show she'd be remembering on her deathbed.

Emotion choked her breathing as she struggled to keep the rise and fall of her chest carefully regulated. Giving nothing away. The beautiful lights, the beautiful night, the beautiful man. All wrapped around her in a sensory overload. Wasn't this what she'd wanted her whole life? Even during her marriage?

Belonging.

Never mind that it was only temporary belonging; she'd take what she could get.

'I missed this so much last year,' she breathed.

His low words rumbled against her back. 'I missed you.'

The press of her cheek into his arm was a silent apology. 'Let's just focus on tonight.'

She wasn't going to waste their precious time dwelling on the past or dreaming of endless combinations of futures. She had Oliver right here, right now; something she never could have imagined.

And she was taking it. While she could.

'What time does Qīngtíng close?'

His body tensed behind her. 'Got a flight to catch?'

She turned her head, just slightly—away from the light show, away from the other patrons, back towards him. 'I want to be alone with you.'

'We can go back upstairs.'

She took a breath. Took a chance. 'No, I want to be alone, here.'

Okay, that was definitely tension radiating on the slow hiss he released as a curse.

Too much? Had she crossed some kind of he-man line? She turned back to the view as though that was all they'd been discussing. As though it were that meaningless. But every cell in her body geared for rejection and made her smile tight. 'Or not.'

Oliver curled forward, lips hard against her ear. 'Don't move.'

And then he was gone, leaving her with only her own, puny arms to curl around her torso.

Ugh. She was so ill equipped for seduction.

And for taking a risk.

It was only moments before he returned, assuming his previous position and tightening his hold as though he'd never been gone. So... Maybe okay, then? It wasn't a total retreat on his part. The show went on, spectacular and epic, but all Audrey could think about was the press of Oliver's hips against her bottom. His hard chest against her back and how that had felt pressing onto her front not too long ago.

Light show? What light show?

At last, she recognised the part of the music that heralded the end of the nightly extravaganza and she tuned in once again to the sounds around her, reluctant to abandon the warm envelope of sensory oblivion she'd shared with Oliver in the dark.

Like insects scuttling away from sudden exposure, a swarm of staff whipped the restaurant's dishes and themselves back behind closed doors as the lights gently rose. The maître d' spoke quietly in turn to the six remaining couples and each of them collected up their things, curious acceptance on their faces, and within moments were gone.

'Oliver—?'

'Apparently your wish is my command.'

Her mouth gaped in a very unladylike fashion. 'Did you throw them out?'

'A sudden and unfortunate failure in the kitchen and a full return voucher for each of them. I'm sure they're thrilled.'

'Considering they were nearly on their last course—' and considering what Qīngtíng's degustation cost '—I'm sure they are, too.'

He led her back to his sofa.

Ming-húa appeared with a full bottle of white wine, an elegant pitcher of iced water and a remote control and placed all three on the table before murmuring, 'Goodnight, Mr Harmer. Mrs Audrey.'

And then he was gone back through the kitchen and out whatever back-of-house door the rest of the staff had discreetly exited through.

She turned her amazement to him in the luminous glow of the dragonfly habitat.

'Just like that?'

'They'll get it all cleaned up before the breakfast opening.'

Uh-huh. Just like that. 'Do you always get what you want?'

'Mostly. I thought you wanted it, too.'

'Wanting and getting aren't usually quite that intrinsically linked in my world.'

'Have you changed your mind?'

'Well…not exactly…' Although her breathless words were easier to own in the dark with the press of his body for motivation.

He leaned back into the luxury sofa and threw her a knowing look. 'You're all talk, Devaney.'

'I am not. I'm just thrown by the expedience with which that was…dealt with.'

'Careful what you wish for, then, because you might get it.'

Alone again.

Audrey glanced around the stylish venue. Then at the door. Then at Oliver.

His eyes narrowed. 'What?'

'I just need a minute…'

She pushed again to her bare feet and strolled casually to the far side of the restaurant, and considered it before turning.

'Lost something?'

'I'm just seeing how the other half live.'

She peered out of the glass. Their view was definitely better in the dragonfly corner. Although it was, of course, exactly the same. Except Oliver was part of her view over there.

He chuckled and settled back to watch her. She hiked the sensuous fabric of her loaned dress up her legs slightly and then *cantered*—there was no other word for it—around the restaurant usually bustling with people.

'You're mad,' he chuckled, struggling to keep his eyes off her bared legs.

'No, I'm snoopy.'

She stuck her head inside the servery window and checked out the glamorous kitchen. No food left out overnight but definitely a clean-up job for someone in the morning. An industrial dishwasher did its thing somewhere in the corner, humming and churning in the silence.

On a final pass by his sofa, Oliver stretched up and snagged her around the waist, dragging her, like the prey of a funnel-web spider, down into the lair of his lap. Her squeal of protest was soaked up by the luxurious carpet and furnishings.

'Do they have security cameras?'

'Do you imagine they're not fully aware of why I sent them home early?'

The idea that they were all stepping out into the street, glancing back up at the top of their building and imagining—

Heat rushed up where Oliver's lazy strokes were already causing a riot. 'There's a big difference between knowing and seeing. Or sharing on YouTube.'

'Relax. Security is only on the access points, fire escape and the safe. The only audience we have are of the invertebrate variety.'

Her eyes went straight to the pretty dragonflies now extra busy in their tank, as though they knew full well when the staff left for the evening and were only just now emerging for their nightly party.

Oliver reached with the hand not doing such a sterling job of feeling her up and pressed the small, dark remote control. The restaurant lights immediately dimmed to the preset from the light show.

'There you go. We'll be as anonymous as your Testore thief on their flight.'

Lying here in the dark, lit only by the dragonflies and the lights of Hong Kong outside, it was easy to imagine they were invisible.

'So—' he settled her more firmly against his body and made sure that they were connecting in dozens of hot, hard places '—you were saying? About being alone?'

'We have such a short time,' she whispered. 'I didn't want to share you with a crowd.'

A shadow ghosted across his eyes before they darkened, warmed and dropped towards her. 'The feeling is entirely mutual.'

His lips on hers were as soft, as pliable as before, but warmer somehow and gentler. As if they had all the time in the world instead of just a few short hours. She kissed him back, savouring the taste and feel of him and taking the time neither of them had taken upstairs. He didn't escalate, apparently as content to enjoy the moment as she was.

She hadn't indulged in a good old-fashioned make-out session since her teens. And even that hadn't been all that good, truth be told.

But neither of them were superheroes. Before long, her breath grew as tight as the skin of her body and a suffusing kind of heat swilled around and between them. Oliver shed his dinner coat and Audrey scrunched the long, silk dress higher up her thighs in a sad attempt at some ventilation where it counted.

'I feel like a kid,' he rasped, 'making out in the back of his parents' car.'

'Except you know you'll be scoring at the end of the night.' And he already had, twice.

He smiled against her skin. 'With you I'm not taking anything for granted.'

She levered herself up for a heartbeat, let some much-needed air flush in between their bodies and then resettled against him. 'Come on. We both know I'm a sure bet.'

His head-back laugh only opened up a whole new bit of flesh for her to explore and so she did, dragging aching lips down his jaw and across his throat and Adam's apple. He tasted of salt and cologne. The best dish yet.

They lay like that—wrapped up in each other, all hands and lips, getting hot and heavy—for the better part of an hour. Long enough for the ice in the wine bucket to mostly melt away and Audrey to drink the entire contents of the still water Ming-húa had delivered.

'I hope you're not going to get too drunk to be any good to me,' she teased, when Oliver reached for the wine bottle. But he just winked, placing it on the table, and then dunked his glass straight into the fresh, melted ice in the bucket.

'Someone's drunk all the water,' he pointed out. 'And you have to stay hydrated in a marathon.'

'Is that what we're doing? An endurance event?'

'Well, I sure am.' He tossed the water back in one long swallow and a rivulet escaped and ran down his jaw. When his mouth returned to hers it was fresh and straight-from-the-ice-bucket cool.

It didn't last ten seconds.

They kissed a while longer but, even with her eyes closed and her mind very much otherwise occupied, she could feel the subtle shift of Oliver's body as he leaned towards the table. A moment later, he pulled his mouth from hers and placed a half-melted ice block on her swollen lips.

Her whole body lurched as he ran the icy surprise over her top lip and then her lower one, and she lapped at the trickle of melted water that ran into her mouth, smiling as he departed for her chin. Then her throat. Then around to the thumping pulse-point at the top of her jaw. His lips trailed a heartbeat behind the melting cube, kissing off the moisture as the ice liquefied against her scorching skin until it was completely gone.

Four cool fingers slid up her thigh and tucked under the

hem of her underwear while his other hand made a complete mess of her hair.

'Those girls at school must have known what they were doing,' he murmured hard against the ear he was lavishing.

'What do you mean?' She could barely remember them, and that was saying something.

'Even as kids, they must have known a threat when they saw one. That you were capable of this.'

His fingers moved further into her underwear. Into her. She arched into his touch. 'Such shamelessness?'

Greenish-brown eyes blazed into hers. 'Such potential passion. And, yeah, a hint of shamelessness. No wonder the boys finally caught on.'

She couldn't tell him she was packing a lifetime into this one night of the year. That she was hanging *way* outside her comfort zone because she knew she'd be spending the rest of her life safely inside it. Because how was she ever going to find something like this again, now that she'd tasted it?

Outside this day—outside this building—the real world ruled. It was a place where the kind of secret emotions she'd always harboured for sexy Oliver Harmer had no place being aired. And definitely not being indulged.

This was a 'what happens at Christmas stays at Christmas' kind of arrangement.

Casual and easy and terribly grown-up.

And the clock was ticking.

She moved against him to give him better access.

She'd grown lazy harbouring the feelings deep inside, exploiting the fact that he was *safe* to have feelings about as long as she was married. Like some kind of Hollywood star that it was okay to pant after because you knew you'd never, ever be acting on it. She held them close to her chest—clutched desperately, really—and enjoyed the sensations they brought. Enjoyed the what-if. Enjoyed the secret fantasy.

Careful what you wish for, he'd said.

But while she didn't dare indulge the emotional part, she was free to feed the physical part. The safe part. And Oliver was clearly very much up for the same with the hours they had left.

Because what happened here, inside the walls of this building, had nothing to do with the real world. And maybe it never had. Perhaps it had always been their weird little Cone-of-alternate-reality-Silence.

Maybe that was what made it so great.

'The synapses in your brain are smouldering,' he breathed, sniffing in amongst her hair. 'Stop overthinking this.'

'I can't help it,' she gasped. 'I'm a thinker.'

'Everyday-Audrey is a thinker. Go back to during-the-light show-Audrey. She was an impulsive and impressive doer.'

There you go. He saw it, too. There was a different set of rules for this day compared to the three hundred and sixty-four around it.

She twisted in his hold and it only pulled her dress up higher. But since both of them would have much preferred her to be out of it, that wasn't really a problem.

'You're right,' she said, settling more fully against him. 'Enough of the thinking. Let's go back to the feeling.'

Oliver pulled her more fully on top of him and studied her flushed face and shambolic hair.

'Best view ever,' he murmured.

'That's a big call given what's outside the window.'

He craned his neck towards the view. 'Good point. Change of plans.' His warm hand slid into hers. 'And change of view.'

She struggled to her feet alongside him, and Oliver led her, hand in hand, to an expensive, stuffed smoking chair by the window. One she'd always imagined him sitting in while he waited for her to arrive.

He twisted it square on to the view and sat before reaching for her.

'Where were we?'

'Here?' From first-sex to chair-sex in just a few hours. Alice was well and truly down the rabbit hole tonight.

'I wanted this upstairs. I've wanted it for years. You against that view. This is close enough.'

Her skin immediately remembered the cold press of glass against her hot breasts as he'd leaned on her from behind, upstairs, and her nipples hardened. There might not be the same drop sensation here on the chair a few feet back from all that glass and sky, but her stomach was doing enough flip-flops to qualify.

He took her hand and pulled her towards his lap. As she had on the sofa, she shimmied her silk dress higher to get her knees either side of his and then braced herself there.

'God, you're beautiful,' he breathed. 'Lit by all the lights of Hong Kong. It's like a halo.'

Was there a smoother-talking man in all this world? But her body totally fell for it, parts of her softening and throbbing an echo to the honey in his voice and the promise in his eyes. She lowered herself onto his lap.

One masculine hand slid, fully spread, up the tight, silk fabric of her stomach and over her breasts while the other followed it on the other side of her body, trailing the line of the dress's zip like someone following a rail line to the nearest town. At its end point he snagged the slider and lowered it and her loaner dress immediately loosened. It was a matter of moments before the hand at her breasts curled in the sensuous fabric and gently pulled it down her arms, revealing her uncovered breasts, and letting the beautiful fabric that he'd heated with his mere touch bunch, forgotten, around her waist.

'Oliver...' she breathed.

Two hands slid up her naked back holding her close as his body closed the gap between theirs and his mouth moved immediately to her breast, dined there, sucking and coiling and working his magic against the sensitive pucker of nipple.

Her skin bloomed with gooseflesh.

She twisted against the excruciating pleasure and indulged herself by doing something she'd always dreamed of—burying her fingers deep in his dark hair. Over and over, curling and tangling and tugging; luxuriating as he tortured the breasts that had barely seen sun with the rasping caress of stubble.

Her legs officially gave out, but the warmth of his lap was waiting to catch her.

As soon as she pressed down into him, his mouth came away, sought hers out and clung there, rediscovering her before dropping again to the other breast.

Behind him, the polished glass of the dragonfly habitat reflected them both against the beauty of the city skyline. She, a half-naked silhouette balanced wantonly on Oliver's lap, and he, pressed powerfully to her chest, with the stunning beauty of the Hong Kong skyline stretching out behind them. She looked wild and provocative and utterly alien to herself.

This is what Oliver sees.

This was how he saw her.

Liberation rushed through her. She didn't look ridiculous. She didn't look all wrong teetering on the expensive chair. Or not enough like the beautiful people he mixed with. She looked *just like* a beautiful person. She looked absolutely, one hundred per cent right bedded within Oliver's embrace.

They fitted together.

Deep in her soul, something cracked and broke away on

a tidal surge of emotion. Part of a levee wall, a giant fragment of whatever powerful thing had been holding back all her feelings all this time.

They *belonged* together.

And finally they were.

Oliver's silhouette hands released her at the back and reached up to pull the struggling pins from her hair, sending it tumbling down over her bare shoulders, tickling the tops of her bared breasts. His hands framed her face and drew her gaze back down to his, hot and blazing and totally focused.

Those eyes that promised her the world. Promised her forever.

And he was the only man she could imagine delivering it.

His lips, when she met them, were as hot and urgent as the touch that skittered over her flesh, and while she was distracted with that he levered them both up long enough to get his wallet out of his trousers pocket, fumbled in it for a moment then threw the whole thing on the floor.

'How many of those do you have?' she breathed, needing the moment of sanity to ground her spinning mind. Nothing like a condom to bring things screaming back to reality.

'Just the one.'

Disappointment warred with pleasure. *One* was a very finite number. The two he'd used upstairs came from a stash in the en suite cabinet, which might as well be back in Shanghai for all the use it was to them at this moment. Upstairs was a whole world away. But *one* also meant he didn't carry a string of *twelve* in case he found himself on a desert island with a life raft full of flight attendants.

Which was strangely reassuring.

As though *one* made tonight somehow less casual, for him.

But clarity streamed in with the fresh air. That was crazy

thinking. The fact he had a condom at all made it casual. The fact she was leaving for another country in a few hours made it casual. The fact Oliver didn't do relationships made it casual.

But whatever it was. She still wanted it. Come what may.

And she was taking it.

She lowered herself to mere millimetres from his lips and breathed against them. 'Don't break it.'

His chuckle was lost in the resumption of their hot kiss and her brain had to let go of such trivialities as what happened with the condom as it focused on the rush of sensation birthed by his talented fingers and lips. The strength with which he pulled her against his hard body. The expediency with which he solved the barriers of fabric between them. She pressed back up onto her knees to give him room to manoeuvre beneath her and then he shifted lower in the chair just slightly—just enough—and used one hand at her coccyx to steady her while another worked at the wet juncture of her thighs to guide her down onto the rigid, strength of him.

'So damned beautiful...'

His choked words only made her hotter. As it had been the first time, and the second, it was again now—like pulling on a custom-made kid glove. They fitted together perfectly. More perfectly than before, if that was possible, because gravity gave her extra fit. She rose up on her knees again, repositioned, and then sank fully down onto him, heavy and certain.

His throaty, appreciative groan rumbled through them both. Had there ever been a more heartening sound? How was it possible to feel so small and feminine and so strong and powerful at the same time? Yet she did, balanced on him like a jockey on a thoroughbred, with just as much control of the powerful beast below her through the subtle movements of her body.

She tipped her pelvis on a series of rocks and let the choked noises coming from his throat set the tempo. Steady, heavy, slow.

His head pressed back against the armchair as she ground against him, and Audrey curled forwards to trail her mouth across the exposed strength of his throat, exploring the hollow below it. Her position meant her breasts hung within easy reach of his taskless hands so he pressed them both against her flesh—as though they were the fulsome mounds he'd always secretly coveted, as though they were all his big hands could manage—circling his palms in big, hard arcs that mirrored the rhythm of her hips.

The desperate roughness of her want.

'Oliver…'

As her speed increased so did their breathing, and she arched back in his hold. In the terrarium glass, dragonflies buzzed around her reflection like fluorescent faeries…or like living sparks generated by the extraordinary friction of their bodies. Oliver's hands tightened and rubbed her straining breasts and every quivering massage told her how much closer to the edge he was getting. His excitement fuelled hers.

She was doing this to him.

Her.

As she watched the lithe undulations of their silhouette, tight heat coiled into an exquisite pain where they fused together and the armchair rocked with the combined momentum of their frantic bodies.

Up…

Up…

She tipped her head back and vocalised—an expressive, inarticulate, erotic kind of gurgle—as the fibres of her muscles bunched and readied themselves deep inside.

'Now, beautiful,' he strained on a grimace, meeting her

with the powerful upwards slam of his own hips. 'Come for me now.'

Her eyes snapped down to his—unguarded and raw—she let her soul pour out of them.

And then her world imploded.

As if the top storeys of their hotel had just *sheared away* in a landslide, and she went careening down to the earth far below on a roller-coaster tide of molten, magnificent mud. Punishing and protective. Weakening and reinforcing. Twitching and spasming. Utterly overwhelming.

She opened her eyes just in time to see them reflected in the tank, as glittering and ancient as the creatures flying around in it, and just in time to see the torsion of Oliver's big body beneath hers as he came right after her.

A pained stream of air, frozen on the prolonged first consonant of an oath and lasting as long as his orgasm, squeezed out between his lips and teeth. She fell forward into him, weakened, and the change of angle where they were still joined—where he was still so sensitive—caused a full-body jerk in his and the oath finally spilled across his talented lips, loud and crude.

And almost holy.

'Potty mouth,' she gasped against his sweat-dampened ear when she could eventually re-coordinate the passage of air in and out of her lungs.

His breath came in heaves and he swallowed several times before finally making words. 'I have no dignity with you.'

A place deep inside her chest squeezed as hard as the muscles between her legs just had.

...with you.

But she'd been protecting herself for too long to indulge the pleasure for more than a moment before she bundled the thought down where all the others milled, unvoiced, and focused instead on the decadent honey slugging through her veins and the punishing tenderness of flesh she'd finally used as nature intended.

'My God.'

Such simple words but there was something in them, something super powerful in the fact that she almost never invoked the 'g' word. But it belonged here with them today. Because what had just happened between them was as reverential as anything she could imagine.

She twisted sideways and squeezed down next to Oliver as he shuffled over in the big chair, both of them taking a moment to right themselves and their underwear.

Undignified, he had said and he wasn't wrong, but, strangely, dignity had no place here tonight. Neither of them required it and neither of them mourned its absence. Audrey curled into his still heaving body.

'Thank you,' she breathed and felt more than saw the questioning tilt of his head. 'You're very good at this.'

Tension drummed its fingers everywhere their bodies met. Odd, considering she'd given him a compliment.

'We're good *together*,' he clarified.

Her own throaty chuckle was positively indecent. 'I could learn so much from you.'

It was hard to know whether his resulting silence was discomfort at the suggestion of a future between them or something else. But his tone, when he eventually spoke, wasn't harsh.

'I'm like a theme-park ride to you, aren't I?'

'Best ever.'

Fastest, highest, most thrilling. And most unforgettable.

His smile was immediate, but there was an indefinably sad quality to the sigh just before he spoke. 'Come on. Let's move back to the lounge. Will your legs work?'

The idea of stretching out with Oliver as they had earlier, of falling asleep in his arms, was too tempting. She practically rolled off the chair. 'If they won't, I'll crawl.'

Nope. Not one shred of dignity. But when they had so little time together, and when she might well not see him again for twelve months—or at all—really what did it matter?

It was his pedestal, not hers.

She might as well throw herself off it before she tumbled off.

CHAPTER ELEVEN

Salted caramel chocolate ice cream topped with gold leaf

'AUDREY DEVANEY, YOU are such a paradox,' Oliver murmured from his position sitting knees up on the floor beside the sofa a deeply unconscious woman was presently stretched out on. He stroked a strand of dark hair away from her sleep-relaxed mouth.

That mouth.

The one he wanted to go on kissing forever. The one he'd pretty much given up hope of ever getting closer than a civil, social air-kiss to.

The one he'd bruised with his epic hours of worship.

She was like a wild creature released from captivity. Joyous and curious and adventurous yet heartbreakingly cautious. Running wild, tonight, in her attempt to experience everything she'd missed in life.

She was gorging on new experience. They both were.

But just for different reasons.

For Audrey…? She *was* on a theme park ride. The sort of thing you only did once a year but you had a blast while you were doing it. Whatever she lacked in experience, she made up double in raw enthusiasm and natural aptitude.

And for him…?

He knew that the moment she walked out of that door, this amazing woman would be lost to him. Away from the hypnotic chemistry that pulsed between them, her clever mind would start rationalising their night together, her doubts would skitter back to the fore, her busy life and her old-school common sense would have her filing their hours together away as some kind of treasure to be brought out and remembered fondly. Hotly, if he was any judge.

But very definitely in the past.

He traced the fine line of her cool arm with a fingertip.

And that was probably all for the better given he had no kind of future to offer her and she was absolutely not the booty-call type. If he were another kind of man he would happily spend eternity sharing her interests, respecting and trusting her. All the things she valued in a relationship.

If he were that man.

But he wasn't. He'd proposed to Tiffany because he was tired and she was there, and because she was the kind of woman who would have cheated on him long before he could ever cheat on her. *When, not if.*

Because genes would out. His inability to find a woman he could stick to was proof positive.

That was the kind of man he was.

He sure as hell wasn't the kind who could be trusted with what he'd seen in Audrey's eyes back on that chair. The look she was too overwhelmed to disguise. Or deny. The unveiled look just before she shattered into a hundred pieces in his lap. That was not the look of a woman for whom this wasn't a big deal. It was not the look that belonged with the words she was saying.

It was a glimpse of the real Audrey.

And of what he really wanted. What he never knew, until tonight, *that* he wanted.

And what he damn well knew he couldn't have.

Tonight, he got a glimpse of something deeper than just sexy or smart or unattainable. Something much more fundamental.

Audrey's soul communicating directly with his.

That moment when it crashed headlong into his and its eyes flared with surprise and it whispered, incredulously, *Oh, that's right. There you are.*

He wasn't prepared to even put a name to the sensation. Not when a candle could burn longer than the time they had left together. Walking away tomorrow—today, really—was going to hurt her. But short-term pain had to be better than a lifetime of it, right?

But he was weak enough and selfish enough that he wanted to be the man against whom *she* measured all others. He wanted a place in her heart that nothing and no one could touch. Not some future man, not some future experience. A place she would smile and ache when she accessed it, the way he did with his memories of her. The smiles and the aches that sustained him through the year between her visits.

The bittersweet memories that would sustain him through his whole damn life.

And so, as ridiculous and pointless as it probably was, he wasn't letting her out of his sight until the law said he had to. He was going to keep her with him until morning, he was going to drive her back to her hotel and then deliver her to the airport and even the flight gate, personally. He was going to pour everything he wanted to say to her but couldn't into their last hours together and he was going to show her the kind of night a woman would find impossible to forget.

Because if he wasn't going to have her in his life he would damn well make sure he endured in her memory. Haunted it like some sad, desperate spectre. Made an impression on her heart.

A dent.

Hell, he'd take a scratch. She'd spent so long protecting it he wouldn't be surprised to find her heart was plated in three-inch steel. That was what would get her through the disappointment of them parting in seven hours.

Audrey murmured and resettled in her sleep, her fingers coming up to brush her lips as if feeling the memory of his kiss. A tiny frown marred her perfect skin.

But he was no masochist. He would take these last hours before Audrey climbed on her plane in the knowledge that, quite possibly, it was all she was ever going to give him. And he'd keep her close and make it special and live off the memories of it forever.

Too many parts of him needed this night too badly not to.

'Wakey-wakey, beautiful.'

Audrey's lashes fluttered open and it took a moment for her to orient herself against the odd sight that filled her field of vision. It looked like a giant tongue, curled back onto itself and with an ornate, gold insect perched on the top.

'Did a dragonfly escape?' Actually, there were two of them. The first one's twin sat on a matching dish across the table. Really, really spectacular escapees.

'Final course,' Oliver murmured from somewhere behind her.

She lifted her head and the world righted. She was stretched out on the sofa where they'd moved, exhausted, with Oliver's coat draped modestly over her bare legs.

She struggled into a sitting position, wriggling her skirt back down. 'I thought everyone had gone?' She hoped to heaven that was true and no one was in the kitchen while they got all Kama Sutra on the armchair.

'Looks like they didn't want us to miss out on the pièce de résistance. I found it in the kitchen cold room with a note on it saying "eat me".'

Well, that was about perfect for this whole Alice in Wonderland evening. If she grew until she banged her head on

Qīngtíng's ornate ceiling she couldn't have felt more transformed than she did by the night's events.

Emotionally, spiritually.

She was leaving Hong Kong a changed woman.

She swung her legs off the sofa and blinked a few times to regain full consciousness. 'What time is it?'

'Half past five.'

A.M.? They'd lost precious hours to sleeping. She twisted to look behind her. Oliver knelt behind the sofa, his chin resting on the beautifully embroidered back. He looked as if he'd been there a while. He also looked extremely content.

And extremely gorgeous.

The cold, hard light of morning sat awkwardly on her, though. Flashes of how she'd behaved over by the window. The Audrey she'd never suspected was in there. The Audrey only Oliver could have freed.

'What have you been doing?'

'Just watching you sleep.'

She frowned and scrubbed at gritty eyes before remembering the face full of make-up she was probably no longer wearing. Her fists dropped. 'Stalker.'

His soft laugh caressed her in places she'd never felt a laugh before. 'I didn't do it the whole time. I've made a few calls, cleaned the kitchen up a bit—'

Presumably how he'd found the ice cream...

'—and sorted us for breakfast.'

He'd made calls? Done business while she was in a sex-induced coma?

Way to strip the special from something there, Oliver. 'Do you not need sleep?'

'I have the rest of the year to sleep.'

Elation tangled in her chest with disappointment. On one hand, that was tantamount to saying he also didn't want to miss a moment of their day. On the other hand, it said she was definitely getting on that flight at ten this morning.

Had she imagined last night would change anything? He'd made her no promises. If anything he'd forced her to verbalise what they both knew. That this was a time-limited, once-in-a-lifetime offer. No coupon required. She'd gone out of her way not to look too closely at *why* it was happening. She'd just thrilled at the fact it was happening and let the fantasy get away with her. Let herself be whoever she wanted to be.

And last night she'd wanted to be *that* woman. The one who could keep up with a man like Oliver and walk away, head high in the morning.

Regardless of how she felt inside.

And if nothing else Audrey Devaney was a woman who always—always—made the beds she'd lain in. And so she did what always worked for her in moments of crisis—especially at five-thirty a.m.

She ignored it.

She picked up one of the plated dark tongues instead. 'What is this?'

'Chocolate caramel ice cream.'

An understatement if the rest of the evening's astonishments were anything to go by. This was bound to be so much more than just ice cream. 'Why is there a dragonfly on it?'

'It's gold leaf. Qīngtíng's signature dish.'

She peered at the extraordinary craftsmanship. An intricate and beautiful dragonfly perfectly rendered in real gold leaf. No wonder the chef hadn't wanted them to miss it.

'I don't know whether to eat it or frame it,' she breathed, after a long study.

'Eat it. I suspect it's too fine to last long.'

Eating gold. That was going to take a little getting used to. Just like the sudden intimacy in Oliver's gravelly voice. He moved across from her, sat on *her* sofa, and watched her as she sliced her splade down across the back of the decorative insect and took a chunk out of the perfect curl of ice cream.

Salty, caramely, chocolaty goodness teased her senses into full consciousness.

'This is sublime.' Then something occurred to her. 'Is this breakfast?'

Why the heck not when the rest of the past twenty-four hours was Lewis Carroll kind of surreal? Ice cream and gold for breakfast fitted right in.

'This is the end of dinner. Breakfast will be in about ninety minutes.'

Breakfast meant sunrise. And sunrise meant it was time to go back to the real world. Audrey was suddenly suffused with a chill that had nothing to do with the delicious creamy dessert. She laid the splade across her barely touched dish.

'How long before dawn?'

His eyes narrowed. 'Sun-up is at six fifty-eight a.m.'

'That's very precise.'

'It's the winter solstice. A big deal in China.'

Right. Not like he'd been counting the minutes. 'What will we do until then?'

'Why, what happens at daybreak? You planning on doing a Cinderella on me?'

Did he know how close he was to the truth?

'As it happens you won't be able to,' he went on. 'We're going to be somewhere special at sunrise. Somewhere you'd struggle to run away from.'

The most special place she could imagine being as the sun crept over Hong Kong's mountains was back upstairs in that big, comfortable bed wrapped in Oliver's arms and both of them sleeping right through breakfast in satiated slumber.

A girl could dream.

'Sounds intriguing,' she said past the ache in her heart.

'I hope so. I had to pull a few strings to make it happen.'

Was he throwing a bunch of people out of another restaurant? 'You're not going to tell me?'

'No. I'd like it to be a surprise. Though I should ask... Can you swim?'

It was a necessary question.

Forty minutes later, Audrey stood on the pier at Tsim Sha Tsui staring at a gracious, fully restored Chinese junk.

'I've seen this at night going up and down the harbour,' she breathed, walking the boat's moored length, running her hand along the one-hundred-and-fifty-year-old dark hull timbers. Its bright-red sails were usually illuminated by uplights and seemed to those on shore to glow red fire as it drifted silently across the water. This morning, though, no glowing sails, just a network of pretty oriental lanterns throwing a gentle light across the deck cluttered with boating business but devoid of any people.

'That's our sunrise ride.'

She was glad she was still in her silk dress for this, but she was also glad for the drape of Oliver's coat around her shoulders. As soon as she'd stepped out of the car he'd arranged for the slow drive to the Kowloon pier, the cool bite of morning had made itself known. But she tried to keep her appreciation purely functional and not fixate on the smell and warmth of gorgeous man as it soaked into her skin.

On board, they passed the first quarter-hour exploring the rigging and construction of the small junk and appreciating the three-hundred-and-sixty-degree views and the sounds of the waking harbour. But as the sky lightened and the vessel swung in a big arc to drift back up the waterfront again Oliver moved them to the upper deck, really the old roof of the covered lower deck, and propped them up against the mast of the fully unfurled centre sail.

A basket appeared courtesy of a fleet-footed, bowing crewman, filled to overflowing with fresh fruits and gorgeous pastries with a thermos of fragrant coffee. Oliver pressed his back to the mast, then pulled Audrey into the V of his legs and, between them, they picked the delicious contents of the basket clean as the sun rose over the mountainous islands of Hong Kong. The fiery orb first turned the harbour and everything around it a shimmering silver and then a rich gold before finally settling on a soft-focus blue.

The sounds of traditional oriental music drifted across the harbour as they passed a group of workers doing dawn t'ai chi by the water.

'What do you think?' he murmured.

The canvas above them issued an almost inaudible hum as it vibrated under the strain of the morning breeze. The same breeze that gave them motion. 'I think it's spectacular. I've always wanted to sail on this boat.' She twisted more towards him. 'Thank you.'

His lips fell on hers so naturally. Lingered. 'You're welcome.'

Yet it wasn't the same as the many—many—kisses they'd shared tonight because it wasn't really *tonight* at all. It was now *today.* And it was daylight and the real world was waking around them—solstice or not—and getting on with their lives.

Which was what they needed to do.

They'd been doing the whole *make-believe* for long enough.

'You've sure raised the bar on first dates,' she breathed without thinking, but then caught herself. 'I mean…any date.'

Discomfort radiated through his body and into hers. 'It's a kind of first date.'

No, it wasn't. The awkward tension in his voice was a dead giveaway.

'First implies there'll be more,' she said, critically light. 'We're more of an *only* date, really.'

And, importantly, it was the *end* of the only date. After breakfast she really needed to be thinking about picking up her stuff from the hotel and getting out to the airport over on Lantau. Before she made more of a fool of herself than she already had.

Before she curled her fingers around his strong arms and refused, point-blank, to let go.

'You don't see there being more?'

It was impossible to know what his casual question was hoping to ferret out. A yes or a no. It was veiled enough to be either.

Every part of her tightened but she kept her voice light. Determined to be modern and grown-up about this. 'We live in different countries, Oliver. That makes future dates a bit hard, doesn't it?'

'What we live in is a technological age. There are dozens of ways for us to stay connected.'

Not physically. And that was what he was talking about, right? Even though she got the sense he was speaking against his own will. 'I'm not sure I'm really the sexting type.'

Huh. She all but felt it in the puff of breath on the back of her neck.

'So…that's it? One night of wild sex and you're done?'

She twisted in his arms and locked her eyes on his. 'What were you hoping for, two nights? Three?' She held his gaze and challenged him. 'More?'

His face grew intensely guarded.

Yeah. Just as she thought.

'We have until ten,' he reminded her.

'What difference will a few more hours make?'

'Look what a difference the first few made.'

True enough. Her life had turned on its head in less than twelve hours. 'But what difference will it *make*? Really?'

Heat blazed down on her. 'I didn't expect you to be scrabbling to get away from me.'

She sat up straighter, pulled away a few precious inches. 'I'm not scrabbling, Oliver. I'm just being realistic.'

'Can't you be realistic on the way to the airport?'

She studied him closely. His face gave nothing away. Again, part of his success in the corporate world. 'Right down to the wire?'

'I just… This haste is unsettling.'

'You've never tiptoed out of a hotel room at dawn before?'

'Yeah I have, and I know what that means. So I don't like you doing it to me.'

'Oh.' She shifted away and curled her legs more under her. 'You don't like being revealed as a hypocrite.'

'Is it hypocrisy to have enjoyed our night together and not want it to end?'

'It has to end,' she pointed out. But then she couldn't help herself. Maybe he knew something she didn't. 'Doesn't it?'

If he clenched his jaw any tighter it was going to fracture. 'Yeah, it does.'

'Yeah,' she repeated. 'It does.' Because they were only ever going to be a one-off thing. A question answered. An itch scratched. 'Sydney's waiting for me. Shanghai's waiting for you.'

Except of course that he was on the phone this morning making up for time lost to their…adventures. So, Shanghai didn't really need to wait all that long at all, did it?

Was the morning after always this awkward? She could totally understand why he might have snuck out in the past to avoid it.

'Did you make plans for the next few hours?' she tested.

'I did.'

'And you didn't want to run them past me, first? What if I had Testore business this morning?'

Okay, now they just sounded like a bickering couple. But the line between generous and controlling wasn't all that thick. And bickering gave all the simmering pain somewhere to go.

He had enough grace to flush. 'Do you?'

She let out a long, slow breath. Maybe it would be smarter to say yes. To get off this boat and hurry off to some imaginary appointment. But he'd done this lovely thing… 'No. I took care of it all earlier in the week.'

He nodded. Then sagged. 'It was supposed to be the perfect end to the—' he bit back his own words and straightened '—to a nice night.'

Nice. Ouch.

'We're on a one-hundred-and-fifty-year-old private junk on Victoria Harbour at sunrise on the winter solstice. You've done well, Oliver.'

He stared out at a ferry that rumbled past them. Its wake slapped against the junk's hull like lame applause. He sighed. 'So, you want to head back in?'

She probably should.

'I don't want this to end any sooner than it has to.' She caught and held his gaze despite the ache deep in her chest. 'But I do respect that it does have to.'

Denial was one thing… Delusion was just foolish.

She settled back against his legs. 'We'll head back when we're due.'

It took him a while to relax behind her, but she felt the moment he accepted her words. His body softened, his hand crept up to gather her wind-whipped hair into a protected ponytail that he gently stroked in time with the sloshing of the waves. She sank back into his caress.

As if she'd been doing it always.

As if she always would.

Her friend. With shiny, new, short-term benefits.

Maybe that was just what they'd be now. Not that he'd

offered anything other than a vague and unplanned cyber 'more'. She tried to imagine dropping into Shanghai for a quickie whenever she was in Asia and just couldn't. That wasn't her. Despite all evidence to the contrary, overnight. Despite the woman she'd seen reflected in the dragonfly terrarium.

Which was not to say her body wasn't *screaming* at her to be that person, but last night was really about years of longing finally being fulfilled. And it was all about fairy tales and chemistry and the loudly ticking approach of dawn. It had nothing to do with reality. Living together day to day, or the occasional fight, or morning breath or blanket hogging, or making the mortgage or any of the many unromantic things that made up a relationship.

It was what it was. A magical storybook ending to an unconventional friendship.

More than magical, really. It was dream-come-true country.

And everyone knew that anything that seemed too good to be true...probably was. But she'd take it while it was on offer—including the next few hours—because she was unlikely to see its equal again in her life.

Ever.

CHAPTER TWELVE

Sulewesi coffee beans with eggnog and nutmeg

COLLECTING AUDREY'S THINGS and checking out of her hotel room while most people were still asleep took an easy fifteen minutes and then they were back in the limo and heading out to Stanley on the southern-most tip of Hong Kong island. Within the half-hour Oliver was pulling back a chair for her on the balcony of a one-hundred-and-seventy-year-old colonial hotel with views of the South China Sea stretching out forever, and with the single morning waiter much relieved they were only there for coffee.

Albeit a pricey coffee from one of the most exclusive plantations on the planet.

Audrey smiled at him—pretty, but each one getting progressively emptier as the morning wore on. As though she were already on that jet flying away from him.

'Eggnog, Oliver? At eight in the morning?'

'Eggnog *coffee*. And it's Christmas.'

And he wanted to spring into her mind whenever she smelled cinnamon. Or a coffee bean. Or the ocean.

'Can I ask you something?' she said after stirring hers for an age.

He lifted his eyes.

'Is this hard for you?'

Her clear, direct eyes said *be honest* and so he was. Or

as honest as he knew how to be, anyway. 'You leaving in a few hours?'

'All of it. Knowing what to do. Knowing how to deal with it. Or is this just par for the course in your life?'

He took a deep breath. Whatever he said now would set the tone for how the rest of the morning went. How they parted. As friends or something less. Carelessness now could really hurt her. 'You think that last night happens for me all the time?'

'It might.'

'It doesn't.'

'What was different?'

He fought to keep his expression more relaxed than the rest of his tight body would allow. 'Fishing for compliments?'

His cowardice caused a flush of heat in her alabaster cheeks. Of course she wasn't. She was Audrey.

'I don't know how to go back from here, Oliver. And I know that we can't go forward.'

'Depends on how you define forward.'

'I define it as progress. Improvement.' She took a breath. 'More.'

A rock the size of his fist pressed against the bottom of his gut. *Forward* just opened up too much opportunity for hurt for her. This was Audrey. With all kinds of strength yet as fragile as the gold leaf they'd eaten back at the restaurant. She deserved much better than a man who had no ability to commit.

He wasn't about to risk her heart on a bad investment. On *more*.

'Then no. We can't go forward.'

Those enormous, all-seeing eyes scrutinised him but gave nothing away. 'Yet we can't go back.'

'We're still friends.'

'With benefits?'

'With or without. I'll always count you as a friend, Audrey. And I don't have many of those.'

'That's because you don't trust anyone.'

'I trust you.'

Her eyes reflected the azure around them. As crisp and sharp as a knife.

'Why do you?'

'Because you've never lied to me. I'd know if you did.'

'You think so? Maybe I'm just really good at it.' Because she'd been lying for eight years denying the attraction she felt for him and he'd missed that. 'So, do I see you more or less in the coming year? What's the plan?'

Less than once? Was she talking about not coming next Christmas? A deep kind of panic took hold of his gut and twisted. The same agony he'd felt last year when she didn't show. He struggled against it.

'What makes you think I have a plan?'

'Because you're you. And because you had hours while I was sleeping to come up with one.'

He shrugged, a postcard for nonchalance. 'You weren't interested in sexting.'

How could she find it in herself to laugh while he was so tight inside? Even if it was the emptiest he'd ever heard from her. 'I'm still not.' She locked eyes with his. 'So am I right to sleep with other men, then?'

The blood decamped from his face so fast it left him dizzy. 'I didn't realise there was a queue.'

She leaned onto her elbows on the table. 'Just trying to get my parameters. Will you be sleeping with anyone?'

'Audrey…'

'Because Christmas is a long time off.'

Wow, he was like a yo-yo around her. Excited now that Christmas—a Christmas that might include both of them—was back on the radar. But the roller coaster only decreased his control of this situation.

'Warming to your newfound sexuality?'

Her eyes finally grew as flat and lifeless as he feared they would around him. 'Yes, Oliver. I want to give it a good workout with anyone I meet. Maybe even the waiter.'

He stared her down. 'Sarcasm does not become you.'

She lifted both brows.

'What the hell do you want from me, Audrey?'

'I want you to say it out loud.'

'Say what?'

'That this is it. That there is no more. I need to hear it in your voice. I need to see the words forming on your lips.'

There wasn't enough air to speak. So he just stared.

'Because otherwise I will wait for you. I'll hold this amazing memory close to my heart and, even though I won't want it to, it will stop me forming new relationships because I'll always be secretly hoping that you're going to change your mind. And call. Or drop by. Or send me air tickets. And I'll want to be free for that.

'So you need to tell me now, Oliver. For real and for certain. So there is no doubt.' She took the deepest breath her twisted chest could manage. 'Should I be planning to spend any more time with you this year?'

'Have I offered you a future?'

A punch below her diaphragm couldn't have been more effective. But it didn't matter that she couldn't answer, because Oliver's question was rhetorical.

They both knew the answer.

'I don't do relationships, Audrey. I do great, short, blazing affairs. Like last night. And I do long hours at the office and constant travel. My driver sees more of me than most of my girlfriends do.'

Did he use the present tense on purpose?

'But I'm the woman against whom you measure others.'

The words that had been so romantic last night sounded ludicrous in the cold, hard light of rejection.

'You are. You always will be.'

'But that's still not enough to pierce your heart?'

'What do hearts have to do with anything? I respect you and I care for you. Too much to risk—'

'To risk what?'

'To risk you. To risk hurting you more than I already have.'

'Shouldn't that have been something you thought of before you let things get hot and heavy between us? Do you imagine this doesn't hurt?'

Shame flitted behind his eyes. 'You knew the score.'

'Yes, I did. And I went ahead anyway.' More fool her. 'But something changed in me in that stupid armchair this morning. I realised that one day every eight years is not enough for me. I realised I *am* good enough for you. I am just as valuable and worthy and beautiful as any of the other women in your life. And most importantly I am not broken.'

He didn't respond, and the old Audrey crept back in for a half-heartbeat. 'Unless you're a much better liar than I believed?'

No. You couldn't fake the facial contortions and guttural declarations Oliver had made. They were real.

A fierce conviction suffused his face. 'You are not broken.'

'So how do you feel that some other man is going to enjoy the benefits of your…training? How will you feel when you imagine me with my thighs wrapped around a stranger instead of you? When I let someone other than you deep inside me? When I choke on someone else's name?'

His nostrils flared and he gritted words out. 'Not great. But you're not mine to keep.'

'I could be.' All he had to say was 'stay'.

'No.'

'Why?'

'Because I don't want you to be mine.'

I don't want you. Something ruptured and flapped wildly deep in her chest. 'You wanted me last night.'

'And now I've had you.'

Her stomach plunged. Was that it? Question answered? Itch scratched? Challenge conquered? 'No. I don't believe you. You respect me too much.'

'You were a goddess, Audrey. Chaste and unattainable.'

And now she was what…? Fallen? But then something sank through the painful misery clogging her sense. One word. A word she'd used herself. On herself.

Unattainable.

And she realised.

'You thought I was safe.'

His eyes shifted out to sea.

'You thought I was someone you could just quietly obsess on without ever having to risk being called on it. Someone to hang this ideal of perfection on and excuse your inability to commit to anyone else, but utterly, utterly safe. First I was married and you could hide behind a ring and your own values. Then you thought I wasn't interested in that kind of relationship with you and so you just got to brood about it like some modern-day Heathcliff, torturing yourself with my presence once a year.'

Something on the distant horizon sure had his focus…

'But what's a man to do when the woman he's been wanting for so long throws herself at you? You broke your own rule.'

His gaze snapped back to hers. 'I should have been stronger. You were vulnerable.'

'Oh, please, I think we've established that there is no pedestal strong enough to take me and all my foibles. I was pissed off but I wasn't vulnerable. I knew exactly what I was putting my hand up for. And you made a move long before you told me about Blake. So it was hardly reactionary.'

'It was weak.'

'Damn straight it was. And it still is if you're unwilling to just say "it's been fun, but it's over".'

'That's what you want?'

'That's what I need if I'm not to spend the next twelve months suffering death by a thousand cuts. Because if you don't say it—*and mean it*—I won't believe it. I know myself too well.'

He marshalled himself visibly. 'It *was* fun, Audrey. And it *is* over. Last night was a one-time thing. And it's not because of any lack on your part or because it didn't measure up compared to anyone else. It's because that's how I roll. I don't do relationships and nothing and no one can really change a man's nature.'

'Not even a paragon?'

He shuddered a deep breath and his voice gentled. 'Not even a paragon.'

'So what will you do for the rest of your life? Be alone?'

'I'll find another Tiffany.'

'Someone to *settle* for?'

'Someone I can't hurt.'

What did that *mean*? 'You think the Tiffanys of this world don't have feelings?'

'She was as hard as I am.'

That stopped her in her tracks. 'Why do you think you're hard?'

'Because I can't—' But he wouldn't let himself finish that sentence.

Love? Was that what he'd refused to say aloud? Well, she wasn't about to be the first. 'You think you *can't* be in a relationship just because you *haven't* been in a successful one?'

'I'm not afraid to acknowledge my weaknesses, Audrey. I just don't do commitment.'

She sat back hard into her bamboo-woven chair. 'What if it's weakness not to even try?'

Two lines cut deep between his eyebrows. 'It's not just about me. It's not some lab experiment or computer formula. There's another person there. A living breathing feeling person existing in a marriage that's not healthy for them.'

Marriage? Wait… How had they got there?

'But it's okay if she's…hard?' she said. Wasn't that the word he'd used?

'If she knows the score. Accepts it.'

'Accepts what?'

'The limitations of the relationship.'

'Oliver, I really don't understand—'

'Do the maths, Audrey,' he grated. 'You're a smart woman.'

She was, but clearly not in this. 'Are you talking about a relationship without commitment?'

'Commitment *traps*.'

She flopped back into her chair. 'Who? You?'

'Her.'

Wait… 'Is this about your mother?'

'She was trapped with a worthless human being because of her feelings for him.'

'She made a conscious choice to stay, Oliver.'

'There was no choice. Not back then.'

Did he fear love because he'd seen his mother suffer at the hands of an unfaithful husband? 'I can't imagine her being a weak woman.'

He blinked at her. 'What? No.'

'Then she made her own choices. Informed choices. She stayed because she wanted to. Or she decided he was worth it.'

'If not for me she could have walked. Should have.'

Did he hear his own Freudian slip? He blamed his mother for toughing it out with a serial cheater. 'It was the eighties, Oliver, not the fifties. She could have left him, even with a child in tow. Plenty of women did.'

'She wanted me to have a father.'

'Then that was her conscious decision. And it was a noble one. She loved him. And you.'

There. She said it aloud. The L word.

'Love trapped her.'

There was that word again. Maybe it wasn't about the love, maybe it was about the trapping.

'So, this is about your father?'

'If she'd cared as little as he obviously did the whole thing wouldn't have hurt her so much.'

Someone I can't hurt.

Oh.

A wash of dreadful awareness pooled in her aching chest and gut. She had to force the words across her lips. 'You don't want to repeat your parents' marriage. Where one person has feelings the other doesn't.'

This was his way of telling her he didn't—couldn't—love her. And this was why another Tiffany was a better bet for him.

'I don't ever want you to feel the way she felt.'

Trapped. In a one-sided relationship.

'You assume it would be that way.'

'I know myself.'

He meant he knew his feelings. But she was desperate enough to push. 'So you just avoid any kind of commitment just in case? What if I'm the exception?'

'You deserve someone who can be everything you are.'

'Yet, apparently, this paragon is still not worthy. Except for a bit of wham-bam-thank-you-ma'am.'

'You're the best person I know,' he muttered.

Oh, please... 'You just defiled the best person you know. I'd hate to see how you treat everyone else.'

She pushed her half-finished coffee away and stumbled to her feet. Correction, half-drunk but most definitely finished.

Like this relationship.

'This is what's going to happen now,' she began, working hard to keep the thick clag of pain from her voice. 'You are going to call your car around and tell him to take me to the airport. We will drop you back at your hotel on the way and all of this will be a surreal memory by morning.'

She omitted the part about her crying all the way back to Australia and never having another relationship again in her life. That didn't seem conducive to a dignified exit.

'I'm coming to the airport...'

She stopped and glared at him. 'Because this isn't hard enough?'

'Because it's over for me, then, too. I need to see you walking away.'

'Why, Oliver? Why not just let me go? Do the right thing.'

'I'm already doing the right thing. One day I hope you'll believe that.'

She knew she could hold it all together back to the harbour, but could she do it all the way over to Lantau? And then waiting for her flight to board?

She turned from him and walked towards the stairs, not even sure she could hold it together as far as the top tread. Behind her, he murmured into his phone, and as her foot touched the last flight, the limo pulled up outside the charming old building.

She crawled in without a word.

Oliver followed.

They sat as far apart as the spacious back seat would allow.

All the way back to Central Hong Kong Audrey peered out of the window at the complicated mix of green, verdant hills and dense, crowded, multicultural residential areas. Chances were good she'd be back in Hong Kong on a future instrument hunt but she knew she'd only ever have flying visits. This was no longer a place of pleasure.

It was now wrecked.

She swallowed past the thick lump resident in her throat.

As they approached the Western Harbour tunnel over to Kowloon and Mainland China she glanced east and saw the same junk they'd breakfasted on puttering between bigger vessels in the busy harbour, her sails ablaze. Filled with other people who would imagine it as *their* special thing. Only to discover it wasn't special at all.

Just like this whole experience.

Perhaps she'd projected too much of her own feelings onto Oliver. Perhaps she'd been foolish to indulge them after they'd come back down to the restaurant. *She'd* reignited things between them then, not him. She had to own that. She'd thought she was capable of handling a one-night stand but that was when it was *circumstance* keeping them apart, not some ill-defined deficiency on her part.

Whatever it was that meant Oliver couldn't imagine himself loving her as much as she—

Across the car, he seemed to flinch as though he could hear her thoughts and knew what was going to come next.

—loved him.

Her stomach plunged and she blamed the tunnel that sank deeper under Victoria Harbour. There really was no question: she'd adored Oliver Harmer for years. The only mystery was when, exactly, it had graduated into love. Her body had recognised it in the wee hours of this morning, when his hands were in her hair and he was buried deep in her and his eyes blazed up at her in a way that was so close to *worship*...

She didn't have any experience in what love looked like but she'd felt so certain that it looked just like that. That moment where her soul and his connected. Her subconscious had named it even if she hadn't.

But what would she know?

Maybe he always looked like that when he came?

What if she was exactly as ill equipped to be with a man like Oliver as she'd always feared? What if the whole night had just been one big try-hard exercise on her part and he was just trying to extract himself from an uncomfortable situation?

What if she'd overreached after all?

The tears she'd done such a good job of holding back refused to let that last thought go unanswered. They spilled silently over her lids, along her lashes and then down her cheeks. She let them run, only the tunnel walls to witness.

But the spill became a river and the river a trembling torrent, and as they surfaced out of the tunnel and merged onto Highway 5 she couldn't disguise what was happening any longer.

'Audrey—'

Her hand shot up in warning to him as her body doubled over at the combined pain of his rejection and the humiliation of this moment. Only the glass of her window stopped her from crumpling right over and she pressed her forehead against its cool reassurance.

The minute strength she had left was in her silence and so she still didn't give the slightest voice to the sorrow.

'Audrey…'

No. Not compassion, not from Oliver. She struggled against him when he moved closer and slid one arm around her shoulders, but her pathetic resistance was no match for his gentle strength.

'Shh…'

He pulled her against his chest, into his arms and just

held her. No platitudes. No promises. No lies. Just silent compassion.

And that made it all so much worse.

She was losing the man she loved and her best friend all at the same time.

The last of her resilience gave way on a hoarse, horrible sob and she buried her shame into his chest. She cried as they passed Stonecutter's Island. She cried as they crossed onto Tsing Yi. She cried as they rose on a suspension bridge high above the water and breached the two-kilometre ocean passage to Lantau. She cried right past the turnoff to the most magical theme park in China and she cried the full length of Highway 8.

And the whole time, Oliver just stroked her hair, fed her tissues and held her.

For the last time, ever.

A voice crackled on the intercom and she recognised the name of Hong Kong's primary airport. That and the interrupting voice was enough to lurch her up out of Oliver's gentle hold and back to her far corner where she pressed a series of fresh, folded tissues to her stinging, swollen eyes.

And still Oliver didn't speak.

What was there to say?

She'd just melted down on him for the second time in twenty-four hours. He'd already said he didn't know what to do with her when she was like this. And Hong Kong's traffic meant it was a long ride with a hysterical woman.

Tough luck, buddy. This one's all on you. This was his decision. This was his issue.

'I don't want you to come in,' she gritted between pats. 'At the airport.'

'I need to see you to your gate.'

To make sure she actually left? She half turned her head to beg him, 'And I'm asking you to do what *I* need, not what *you* need.'

His silent stare bored into the back of her head. 'Okay, Audrey.'

'Thank you.'

The limo negotiated the tangle of taxis, buses and private cars clogging the airport's approach until it began moving up the causeway. That seemed to press Oliver into action at last.

'Don't you think it would be easier for me to just go with the flow,' he bit out. 'To just say "see you in Sydney" and to swing by when I'm in town for a hot hook-up? I didn't want to be that man.'

That brought Audrey's gaze back around to his. 'Should I applaud?'

'I'd like you to understand. My motives if not my reasons.'

'You're avoiding commitment. Seems patently clear.'

He exhaled on a hiss. 'I'm avoiding—' He cut his own words off. 'I didn't want to hurt you, Audrey. I *don't* want to. I'm sorry, but, as bad as we both feel, ultimately it will be better this way.'

'You have nothing to apologise for, Oliver. You've lived up to your reputation and given me a night I will never forget. For so many reasons.' Her smile was tight. 'I get it, I really do.'

'Do you?'

'I'm going to go back to Sydney, throw myself into my work and concentrate on low-hanging fruit from now on.' That was a lie, she wasn't going to be interested in fruit of any kind for a long, long time.

'Audrey, don't do that to yourself. This is about me, not you.'

He seemed to wince at the triteness of his own words.

'You're right. This is about you and your inability to let go of the past. This is about you being so afraid that you'll end up like your father you're avoiding any kind of commitment at all. You dress it up in chivalry and concern for me, but, let's be honest, this is all about you.'

His eyes grew as hard as his clenched jaw.

The limo pulled up to the concourse and Audrey had her door open practically before it had stopped. Oliver leapt out after her as the driver came around to the rear for her case.

'I've held a candle for you since I met you, Oliver. You were everything that I wanted and believed I didn't deserve. You came to be symbolic in my life of my own deficiencies and I wore them like a badge of shame.

'But you know what? I *don't* deserve the man you are. You are the one that doesn't measure up, Oliver Harmer. You are so fixated on not being the serial cheat your father was, you can't see that you've become exactly like him, ravaging from woman to woman spreading the misery around.

'Well, I'm done doubting myself.' She poked his chest. 'I'm awesome. And clever. And pretty. And loyal.' Every poke an accusation. 'And the best friend a person could have. I would have been fierce and proud by your side and someone you could face life with, head-on. But that honour is going to go to someone else and I'm not going to be able to find him while you're still in my life.'

She let her expressive hands drop by her sides. As dead as she felt. 'So this is it, Oliver. After eight years. No more card games, no more conversations, no more long, lazy lunches that you can cling to in lieu of a real relationship with a real woman.' Her shoulders shuddered up and then dropped. 'No more Christmas. If I'm not in your life then I'm out of it. You don't get to have it both ways.' She settled her bag more firmly between them. 'Please don't email me. Or call. Don't send me a birthday card. Don't invite me to your wedding with whichever Tiffany you find next.'

Fortunately, she'd used up all her tears coming across the causeway. Oliver wasn't so lucky and the glitter of those hazel eyes just about broke her heart anew.

Audrey swung her bag around, smiled her thanks to the driver trying so very hard not to listen, and then forced her eyes back onto Oliver before whispering tightly, 'But I *beg* you not to settle for a loveless life. That is not what your mother sacrificed her life to teach you.'

And then she turned and he was gone from her vision.

From her life.

But never, ever, ever from her heart.

CHAPTER THIRTEEN

December 20th, this year

THE PERFECT, PRACTISED English washed over him as Oliver stared out across Victoria Harbour at the building that housed Qīngtíng and the penthouse at its very top, absently rolling an uncut cigar between his fingers. He had no trouble picking the restaurant out; he'd grown proficient at spotting it from any of Kowloon's major business centres courtesy of his hours of distracted staring.

Even with his lawyer and partner here, he should have been attending. This deal was too important to insult with his inattention the very people he wanted to buy out. But the fact they were speaking in English instead of requiring him to negotiate in Mandarin meant they were already deferring. And that meant they had already decided to sell.

The rest was just a dance.

Meaning his attention was that much freer to wander across the harbour and up sixty storeys of steel.

His brain made him schedule a day full of Hong Kong meetings today, the twentieth, but his heart insisted they be here, in Kowloon, in full view of Qīngtíng across the harbour. As if he'd somehow know if a miracle occurred and Audrey turned up. As if his eyes would make her out, standing, arms folded around herself, against that wall of window. A distant speck against a sea of silver and chrome.

A point of business required him to refocus, but the moment it was addressed he let his gaze wander back to the restaurant, let his mind wander back to last Christmas. That extraordinary, dreamlike twenty-four hours.

He'd been as good as his word and never contacted Audrey again. No emails, no phone calls, no letters, no messages. Well, not the sort she'd warned him against, anyway. He always had a talent for loopholes.

But it had been purgatory this past year. What a fool he'd been to imagine he could just go back to his life in Shanghai and work her out of his system and get by on a steady diet of memories. He'd had to work at it—really freaking work—just to get through those first weeks. Then months. Then seasons.

And now the year had passed and the moment he'd dreaded was here.

The moment Audrey *didn't* come to Christmas.

Again.

She'd hit him with some home truths that day at the airport. Hard, overdue, unpleasant words that he'd promptly blocked out. It took him weeks to begin to digest them. First he'd used his anger to justify letting her leave. Then he rationalised and remembered how much pain she'd been in and how much courage it must have taken to stand there and let him have it with both barrels.

And finally he saw the sense of her words and, as if letting the words in made them material, he suddenly saw evidence of her truth everywhere he went. Getting in his face.

Mocking him.

His failure to form successful relationships *was* all about him. And he *had* used his friendship with Blake as a protective screen from behind which he indulged his feelings without having to own them.

And once the denial started to drop he saw more and more. How he'd lied to himself all this time believing it was his high standards that made it impossible for him to connect to just one woman. Hardly surprising he could never find her when that was the last thing his subconscious wanted.

He was no more honest with himself about why it didn't work out than he was with them.

But that was not the sort of epiphany a man could simply *unsee*. So he began dating again, testing the theory, testing himself, hunting for someone who could offer him the same soul-connection that Audrey had offered that night in the chair. That she'd been offering him for years. Hungry to find what he'd had a taste of.

And it just wasn't there.

Even though—this time—he was genuinely open to finding it. And being unable to find someone as good as Audrey didn't get any more comfortable for being in the cold light of reason.

At least, before, he'd had all his denial to keep him company.

And so he'd thrown a lifebuoy out, courtesy of a favour someone owed him, and just hoped to heaven that Audrey was in a perceptive mood when the unsigned Christmas parcel was delivered last week. And receptive. Or even rabidly furious, as long as it was an emotion strong enough to bring her back to Hong Kong.

Back to the restaurant.

Back to him.

Because he had an apology to deliver. And a friendship to try and save. And possibly a fragile, wounded spirit to save, too.

Behind him, the massive boardroom doors snicked softly and opened. Jeannie Ling murmured in the ear of the man closest to the door and he nodded then tapped a few keys into his tablet surreptitiously.

Seconds later Oliver's smartphone vibrated.

He glanced down disinterestedly at the subject line of his partner's email:

Ph. Msg-urgent

But then his body was up and out of his chair even before his mind had fully registered the words and phone number on the next line, and he was halfway to the door before any of the ridiculously wealthy and overly entitled people in the room realised what was happening.

Pls call Ming-húa

He hadn't come.

Audrey stared into the busy, oblivious world of Qīngtíng's dragonflies and cursed herself for the ideological fool she was.

Of course he hadn't come. He'd moved on. The online gossip sheets made that patently clear. In fact he'd probably moved on by last Christmas. Whatever they'd shared here in Hong Kong was ancient history. Solstice fever. Even the restaurant had gone back to being what it was. Just a place you went to eat food.

She glanced over towards the restaurant's festively decorated glass wall. The smoking chair was no longer resident.

Their chair.

Hastily removed as a bad memory, probably. Or quite possibly a hygiene issue.

Heat flooded her cheeks but the dragonflies didn't much care. They went about their business, zipping around, feeding and frolicking and dipping their many feet in the crystalline water that circulated through their beautiful, make-believe world. Only a single individual battered against the corner of the terrarium, repeatedly. Uselessly.

She knew exactly how it felt.

Most of what she'd done this past year was useless battering. Existing, but not really living. Punctuated by insane bouts of emotional self-harm whenever her discipline failed her and she'd do the whole stalker number online and search out any clues about Oliver.

What he was up to. *Who* he was up to. Whether he was okay.

Of course, he always was.

On her weak days, she imagined that Oliver never contacting her again was him honouring her request, respecting her, and she'd get all sore and squishy inside and struggle with the reality that it was over. But on her stronger days she'd accept the reality—that not contacting her was probably a blessed relief for a man like The Hammer and that there was nothing to really *be* over.

Nothing had even started.

If you didn't count the wild sex.

She'd vacillate between bouts of self-judgement for her stupidity, and fierce self-defence that she'd fallen for a man like him, convincing herself that it was possible for someone to be a pretty good *guy* without necessarily managing to always be a good *person*.

Except that, like it or not, he'd been more than pretty good. Oliver was exceptional. In so many ways. And knowing that only made his inability to love her all the more brutal.

What the hell was she thinking coming here? She could have done what she needed to do by email.

Almost as she had the thought, a flurry of low voices drew her focus, through the terrarium, past the dragonflies, over to the restaurant's glamorous entrance.

To the man who'd just burst in.

Oliver.

Her whole body locked up and she mentally scrabbled around for somewhere to hide. Under her sofa. In the lush terrarium planting with the dragonflies. Anywhere other than here, with the terrified-bunny look on her face, peer-

ing at him through the glass like the coward she wanted
so badly not to be.

It took his laser-focus only a heartbeat to find her.

His legs started moving. His eyes remained locked on
hers as he powered around the outside of the terrarium and
stopped just a metre away. His intent gaze whispered her
name even though no air crossed his lips.

'Explain,' she gasped aloud, before she did something
more ill-advised.

Not, *'Hello Oliver,'* not, *'How dare you look so good
after such a crap year?'*; not even, *'Why are you here?'*
All much more pressing issues.

'Explain what?' he said, infuriating in his calmness. As
if this weren't the biggest deal ever.

'Why my Testore trail leads to you.'

His steady eyes didn't waver. 'Does it?'

'Why the instrument I've been slowly working my way
towards for two years suddenly turns up in a luggage locker
at Hongqiao train station.'

He stepped one pace closer. 'Asia's biggest train station.
I imagine that's not the only secret it's harbouring.'

Both arms folded across her chest. 'Shanghai, Oliver.'

'Coincidence.'

'What did you do?' Every word a bullet.

He studied the dragonflies for distracted moments and
when he brought his eyes back to hers they were defiant.
'I made a few phone calls. Called in a few favours.' He
shrugged. 'It's not like I donated a kidney.'

She peered at him through narrowed eyes. 'You just
happened to be owed a favour by the exact someone who
knew where the Testore was?'

He sized her up, as if trying to determine how far he
could take the nonchalance. 'Look...I called in a marker
with a colleague, they called one in from someone else and

it reverse dominoed all the way up to someone who knew the right people to ask.'

'And then what?'

'Then I bought it.'

'A million-dollar instrument?'

'Can you put a price on a trafficked child?'

Ha ha. 'You realise you're an accessory to a crime, now?'

His eyes grew uncertain for the first time since he'd walked in the door and he frowned. 'I hoped I'd get bonus points for repatriating it.'

But she wasn't ready to give him those points yet. 'You perpetuated the problem by rewarding the syndicate for their crime. Now they'll go out and steal another cello.'

'Is that really what's bothering you, Audrey? Wasn't it more important to get the cello back into safe hands than to arrest whatever mid-level thug with a drug-debt they'd have made take the fall?'

Did it matter how the Testore was recovered or what favours were exchanged and promises made? Or did it only matter that its rightful owner literally broke down and sobbed when it was returned to her, triggering Audrey's own tears—tears she'd thought she'd used completely up?

Maybe it only mattered that Oliver had cared enough to try.

'What's bothering me is why you did it.' And by 'bother' she meant 'making my chest ache'.

'Because I could.' He shrugged. 'I have connections that you would never have had access to.'

'A million dollars, Oliver.' Plus some change. 'Excessive, even for you.'

'Not if it helped you out.'

Blinking didn't make the words any easier to comprehend—or believe—but this was not the time to let subtext

get the better of her. 'I'm amazed that you have any fortune at all if you make such emotionally based decisions.'

'I don't, generally. Only with you.'

'Did you think I wouldn't figure it out?' That an anonymous key in a Christmas parcel leading her to a Shanghai
train station wouldn't be clue enough?

'I knew you would.'

'So did you think I'd gush with gratitude?'

'On the contrary. I hoped it might piss you off enough
to get on a plane.'

Manipulated again. By the master. She shook her head.
'Well, here I am. Hope you don't want your million bucks
back.'

'Forget the money, Audrey. I sold one of my company's
nine executive apartments to raise the cash. It had only
been used twice last year.'

The world he lived in.

'What if I'd just taken the cello and run?'

That resulted in insta-frown. 'Then I'd have been no
worse off.'

Ugh. 'This was a mistake.'

'Audrey—' his voice suspended her flight after only
two steps '—wait.'

She ignored his command. 'Thank you for doing my job
for me. I'll put a good word in with the authorities for you.'

'You're leaving?'

'Yes. I shouldn't have come at all.'

What she should do was get back onto her ridiculously
expensive short-notice flight and head back to her ridiculously expensive Sydney house. Blake's house that she'd
not had the courage or energy to move out of. The house
and the life she hated.

He stepped round in front of her. 'Why did you?'

Because she was slowly dying inside knowing she'd
never see him again? Because she'd managed the first six

months on pride and adrenaline but now there was nothing left but sorrow. Because she was addicted.

'No idea,' she gritted. 'Let me rectify that right now.'

He sprinted in front of her again. 'Audrey, wait, please just hear me out.'

'Didn't we say enough at the airport?' she sighed.

'You said quite a lot but I was pretty much speechless.'

Seriously? He got her back here to have the last word?

'Ten minutes, Audrey. That's it.'

It was impossible to be this close to those bottomless hazel eyes and not give him what he was asking. Ten minutes of her time. In return for a million-dollar cello.

She crossed her arms and settled into the carpet more firmly. 'Fine. Clock's ticking.'

'Not here,' he said, sliding his hand to her lower back and directing her towards the door.

She stopped and lurched free of his hot touch. 'No. Not upstairs.' That had way too many memories. Although, reasonably, there were just as many down here.

But at least, here, there was an audience. Chaperones.

What are you afraid of? he'd once challenged her. *Me or yourself?*

He just stared, a stoic plea in his eyes.

'Oh, for God's sake, fine!' She swivelled ahead of him and marched back out into the elevator lobby then up the circular stairs off to the side. The plush carpet disguised his footfalls but she could feel Oliver's closeness, his eyes on her behind.

'You've lost weight,' he announced.

She froze. Turned. Glared.

Yes, she'd bloody well lost weight and she really didn't have much to spare. Now her 'athletic' was more 'catwalk' than she'd have liked. Especially for preservation of dignity. She didn't want him knowing how tough she'd been doing it.

His hands immediately shot up either side of him. 'Right, sorry…keep going. Ten minutes.'

At the top, he passed her and ran his key card through the swipe and the big doors swung open just as they had last year. She followed him into the luxurious penthouse—

—and stopped dead just a few feet in, all the fight sucking clear out of her.

Over by the window, over where he'd first touched her with trembling hands all those long, lonely nights ago, a new piece of furniture had pride of place overlooking the view.

An overstuffed smoking chair.

Their chair.

The sight numbed her—emotionally and literally.

'Why is that here?' she whispered.

He seemed surprised by the direction of her gaze. 'I had it brought up here. I like to sit on it, look out. Think.'

'About what?'

'A lot of things.' He took a breath. 'Us, mostly.'

She turned wide eyes on him 'There is no "us".'

His shoulders sagged. 'There was. For one amazing night. I think about that, and I miss it.'

Every muscle fibre in her body tightened up, ready for the 'but'.

He stepped closer. 'I sit in that chair and I think about you and I miss *you*.'

'Careful,' she squeezed out of an airless chest. 'I might get the wrong idea and let my *feelings* get away with me.'

When had she become so angry?

He took her hand, seemed surprised by its frigidity, and led her to the luxurious sofa circling the raised floor of the formal area. The sofa that they'd made such fast, furious love on that first time. She pulled her fingers free and crossed to the chair, instead, curling her hands around its ornate back, borrowing its strength. Using it as a crutch.

Exactly the way her memories of it had been this past year.

'I need you to know something,' he said. 'Quite a few somethings, actually.'

She straightened, listening, but didn't turn around. The Hong Kong skyline soothed her. Speaking of things missed...

'I started wanting you about ten minutes after you walked into that bar all those years ago.' The greenish-brown of his eyes focused in hard. 'Then in the years that followed, I would have given every cent I had to wake up to you just once instead of clock-watching as midnight approached and waiting for the moment you'd flee down the stairs until the following Christmas.'

Her breath slammed up behind the fist his words caused in her chest until she remembered that 'wanting' was not the same as *'wanting'*.

One was short-term and easily addressed, apparently. Maybe that was why he'd lured her back here. Round two.

'I was captivated from the first time you locked those expressive eyes and that sharp mind on me. You were a challenge because you seemed so disinterested in me and so interested in Blake and that just didn't happen to me. And I'd sit there, enduring Blake's hands all over you—'

'Embarrassed by it.'

'Not embarrassed, Audrey. Pained. I hated watching him touch you. I hated thinking you preferred his company, his touch, to mine. And that was when I realised there was more than just ego going on. That I didn't just *want* you. I had *feelings* for you.'

Her fingers curled into the brocade chair-back and she whispered, 'Why did you send me the key, Oliver?'

'Because you were right and because I wanted to tell you that, face to face, and I thought it would get your attention.'

'Right about what?'

'All of it. The Heathcliff thing. It was so much easier to be consumed with longing and never have to face the reality of what that actually meant. And then to disguise that with work and endless other excuses. You were my best friend's wife. As unattainable as any woman could possibly be. Completely safe to fixate on.

'I convinced myself that my inability to connect to women—just one woman—was about having high standards. It was easy to find them wanting and easier still to disregard them because they failed to measure up to this totally unattainable idyll I had. The idea of you.'

He came around in front of the chair, folded one knee on its thick cushion to level their heights and met her eyes. 'I would find fault with the relationships before they got anywhere near the point of commitment purely to avoid having to face that moment.'

The anguish in his face wheedled its way under her skin and she itched to touch him. But discipline, for once, did not fail her. 'Which moment?'

'The moment where I realised that I wasn't actually capable of committing to them. That I was no more capable of being true to someone than my father. So I'd get out before I had to face that or I chose women who would cheat on me first.'

Oh, Oliver...

'I counted myself so superior to him all this time—me with my rigid values and my high moral ground—but the whole time I was terrified that I had inherited his inability to commit to someone. To love just one someone.' He lifted harrowed eyes to hers. 'And that if ever I let myself, then I'd be exposed as my father's son to someone to whom it would really matter.'

He stroked her cheek.

'But then I had you. In my arms. In my bed. And every single thing I'd ever wanted was being handed to me on a platter. The woman against whom every other woman I'd ever met had paled. It was all so suddenly *real*, and there was no good reason for us not to be together—in this chair, in this room, in this town and beyond it. I panicked.'

'You told me you couldn't see yourself loving me. You were quite clear.' Saying it aloud still hurt, even after all this time.

'Audrey.' He sighed. 'My father took my mother's love for him and used it to bind her in a relationship that he didn't have to work for. He didn't value it. He certainly didn't honour it. What if I did that to you?'

'What if you didn't? You aren't your father, Oliver.' No matter what she'd said in anger.

'What if I am?' Desperation clouded his eyes. 'Your feelings were going to force me into discovering. That's why I pushed you away.'

Just twelve months ago she'd stood here, in this penthouse, terrified that she was somehow deficient. And Oliver had proven her wrong. And in doing so changed her life. Now was her chance to return the favour.

'You are not broken, Oliver Harmer. And you are as much your mother's son as you are your father's. Never forget that.'

He suddenly found something in the giant Christmas tree in the corner enormously fascinating, as if he couldn't quite believe her words were true.

'Could she love?' Audrey pressed.

'Yes.'

'Then why can't you?'

Confusion mixed in with the anguish. 'I never have.'

'Have you not? Truly?' She straightened and locked her eyes. 'Can you think of no one at all?'

He stood frozen.

She kept her courage. 'It can be easy to overlook. I once loved someone for eight years, almost without realising.'

His skin blanched and it was hard to know whether it was because she'd used the L word in connection with him or because she'd used the past tense.

'When did you realise?'

She ran her hands across the back of the chair's fine embroidered fabric. 'Out of the blue, this one time, curled up in a chair.'

He still just stared. Silence ticked on. She forced herself to remain tough.

'So, was that what you wanted to tell me?' she checked. *'It's not you it's me?'*

'It *is* me, Audrey. But no, what I really wanted to do was apologise. I'm sorry I let you leave Hong Kong believing there was anything you could have done differently or anything you could have been that would have made a difference.'

And his guilt was apparently worth a rare cello.

Her lips tightened. 'You know, this seems to be the story of my life. Last time it was my gender, this time there was nothing I could have done differently short of *caring less.*'

'This is nothing like Blake.'

'I'm not ashamed of my feelings. And I'm not afraid of them either. Unlike you.'

His eyes tarnished off as she watched. 'Meaning?'

'Exactly what I said. I think you are afraid of the depth of your feelings. Because feeling makes you vulnerable.'

'What I'm afraid of is hurting you.'

'Isn't that my risk to take? Just as it was your mother's choice to stay with your father.'

Two deep lines cut down between his brows. 'You can't *want* to make that choice.'

'I wouldn't if I believed that you've inherited anything more than eye colour from your father. You dislike him too much. If anything I'd expect you to grow into the complete opposite of him just out of sheer bloody determination.'

'I saw what losing his love did to my mother.' Tense and tight but not angry. 'How vulnerable it made her.'

'Don't you trust me?'

'You know I do.'

'Then why do you think I would hurt you?' she begged. 'I chose to be vulnerable with you last Christmas because I couldn't think of a single person in the world that I trusted more with my unshielded heart.'

'I'm afraid I might hurt *you*.'

'By possibly abandoning me at some point in the future?'

'I saw what it did to my mother.' For the first time, the tension in his face hinted at hostility. Except, now, she knew that was what fear looked like on him. 'And I felt what it did to me.'

She sucked in a breath, loud and punctuated in the frozen moments of silence before he crossed to the edge of the sofa. He pulled a hanging tinsel ball into his hands and punished it with attention.

'You?' she risked.

He spun. 'My father opted out of his *family*, Audrey, not just his marriage. He abandoned me, too.'

'But he didn't abandon you. He's still there now.'

Bleak eyes stared out of the window. 'Yeah, he did. He just couldn't be arsed leaving.'

For a heartbeat, Audrey wondered if she'd pushed him too far, but then that big body slumped down onto the sofa, head bowed.

She crossed to his side, sat next to him, curled her hand over his and said the only thing she could think of. 'I'm sorry.'

He shook his head.

She turned more into him. 'I'm sorry that it happened. And I'm sorry that it has affected you all this time. Love is not supposed to work that way.'

As her arms came up he tipped down into them, into

her hold and slid his own around her middle. She embraced him with everything she had in her. This was Oliver after all, the man she loved.

And the man she loved was hurting.

He buried his face in her neck and she rocked him, gently. One big hand slid up into her hair, keeping her close, and she felt the damp of tears against her neck.

'You can love, Oliver,' she said, after minutes of silent embrace. 'I promise. You just need to let yourself. And trust that it's safe to do it with me.'

His silence reeked of doubt.

She stroked his hair back. 'Maybe your love is just like one of the companies you rescue. Broken down by someone who didn't value it and treat it right. So maybe you just need to get it into the hands of someone who will nurture and protect it. And grow it to its full potential. Because you have so much potential. And so do we.'

His half-smile, when he sat up straighter, told her exactly how lame that analogy was. But too bad, she was committed to it now.

'Someone like who?'

'Someone like me. I'm looking to diversify my portfolio, as it happens.'

'Really?'

She shrugged. 'I had a bad investment myself not so long ago, something that could have been very different if I'd given it the time and focus it deserved. But I've learned from my mistakes and know what to do differently next time.'

His smile twisted. 'Well, no one's perfect.'

'So how about it? Think I might be the sort of person you'd trust a damaged company to? I come highly recommended for my work in the recovery of trafficked stringed instruments.'

He nodded and pressed a grateful kiss to her forehead. 'Very responsible. And honourable.'

'And I have federal security clearance,' she breathed as he pressed another one to her jaw. 'They don't give those to just anyone. At all.'

His nod was serious. 'Hard to argue with Interpol.'

'And…um…' She lost her train of thought as his lips found the hollow between her collarbones. 'I have a blue library card. It means I can take books out of the reference section.'

Kiss. 'Persuasive.'

'And I'm not *him* any more than you are.' The lips stopped dead, pressed into her shoulder. 'So if I'm willing to take a risk on you despite the fact you've already hurt me once, the least you can do is return the favour.'

He pulled away to stare into her eyes for the longest time.

Then, in the space between breaths, the cool damp of his butterfly kisses became the warm damp of his mouth working its way up her throat. Her jaw. Roaming. Exploring. Rediscovering.

'I never should have let you go,' he breathed, hot against her ear, right before tonguing her lobe.

She twisted into him, seeking his lips. 'You had to. So I could come back to you, again.'

And then they were kissing. Hot and hard and frantic. Slow and deep and healing.

'I don't want to love anyone else,' he grated, twisting her under him and pressing her into the sofa with his strength. 'I don't want to trust anyone else. Only you, Audrey. It was only ever you.'

He stroked her hair back and applied kiss after kiss to her eyelids, cheekbones, forehead. Worshipping with his mouth. She reached up and stilled his hands, stilled his lips with her own and caught his eyes and held them.

'I love you, Oliver. I always have. I always will. And

my love makes me stronger and better whether we're together or not.'

He twisted so that they faced each other on the spacious couch. 'I don't ever want to go hours without you, let alone months. Not again.'

'Then that's how we'll do it,' she breathed. 'One day at a time. Until days have become weeks and weeks years, and before you know it we'll have been together, in love, as long as we were apart, in love.'

'I can't imagine what it would have been like being alone without loving you all those years. How desolate it would have been.'

Loving you...

There was such veracity in the way it just slipped out in the middle of that sentence. As though it had always been a part of his subconscious and they weren't the most important words she'd ever heard.

Her laugh was five-eighths sob.

Something occurred to him then. 'Imagine if we'd never met. If you'd gone to the bar next door that day. I wouldn't have had you to keep me sane all this time.'

'Imagine if I'd been braver that first day and actually managed a proper conversation with you.'

'I never would have let you go,' he vowed.

'We'd be an old married couple by now.'

His smile bit into her ear. 'We'd be the horniest married couple Hong Kong had ever seen.'

She lifted her head. 'Hong Kong?'

'We'd have lived here, wouldn't we?'

Audrey considered that. 'Yeah, I think we would. Maybe you would have bought this penthouse anyway.'

'I bought the restaurant for you, after you didn't come, so I would always have you.'

'A little excessive, really.'

He huffed. 'A little desperate.'

She traced his lip with her tongue tip. 'I love you, desperate.'

'I love you, period.'

Okay, so she didn't mind hearing it formally, too. She would never, ever tire of hearing it.

They studied each other, drowning in each other's depths and tangling their fingers.

'I have a gift for you,' he said almost sheepishly as he crossed to the expensive tree in the corner.

'The cello wasn't enough?'

He handed her the parcel, small and suspiciously square and faultlessly gift-wrapped. 'I would have sent it to you if you hadn't come.'

'The paper is too perfect to ruin—'

He took the parcel from her and tore the beautiful bow off the top, then handed it back. Problem solved.

Inside a distinctive jeweller's box taunted her. 'Oliver...'

'Don't panic. It's not a ring,' he assured. 'Not this time.'

Not this time...

A tiny leather tie lifted off the clasp and let her open the box. She couldn't help the soft gasp. Inside, resting as though it had just alighted on the black silk pillow, was an exquisite stylised dragonfly necklace, its tiny white-gold body encrusted with gemstones and its fine wings a mix of aquamarine and laser-cut sapphire. At its head, a woman's torso carved from jade, bare-breasted and beautiful.

'That reminded me of you,' he murmured, almost apologetic. 'Wild and stylish and natural all at once. I had to have it.'

Tears welled so violently it was almost impossible to appreciate the handcrafted beauty. 'It's...'

Were there enough words to sum up what this meant to her? Such a personal and special gift. More meaningful than any cello. Or restaurant. Or penthouse.

This was up there with the chair for things she'd run

back into a burning high-rise for. She pressed herself into his arms, the jeweller's box curled into one of the fists she snaked around his neck.

'It's perfect,' she breathed against his ear. 'Thank you.'

Her teary kiss was more eloquent than she could ever be and so she buried herself in his chest, crawling onto the sofa with him and letting the thrum of her heartbeat against his communicate for her. He draped the dragonfly around her neck and it nestled down between her breasts. Over her heart.

Oliver busied himself playing with it, alternating between stroking it and the breasts either side of it. Slowly the dragonfly heated with the warmth coming off her.

'Do you think Blake sensed it?' she said, after some time, to distract herself from his talented fingers. 'How drawn to each other we were?'

'What makes you ask that?'

'He was always so uptight when I was around you. I figured maybe he could sense my attraction.'

'Are you kidding? You have the best poker face in the world. I had no clue and I was perpetually on alert for the slightest sign.' She frowned and he kissed it away. 'I think it's more likely he could sense my attraction. I'm a mere grasshopper to your sensei of emotional discipline.'

'But why would he care if you were attracted to me, given what we now know?'

'Dog in a manger?' Oliver nibbled his way up her shoulder blades. 'Maybe he resented my attention to his property.'

As tempting as it was to drop the conversation and find out where all that nibbling would lead to, something in her just wouldn't let it go. 'It wasn't resentment. It was envy.'

He grinned and it just needed an unlit cigar to be perfect. 'Maybe it wasn't about you? I *am* pretty sexy…'

He laughed but Audrey sat up on her elbow, considered him. 'And Blake *was* pretty gay.'

'No, Audrey. I was kidding.'

Her whole body tingled with revelation. 'He was jealous *for* you, not *of* you. That makes so much more sense.'

Something final clicked into place. How flustered Blake used to get if she came to dinner looking hot. It wasn't attraction, it was anger—that Oliver might grow interested. And all the random, unprovoked touching…that must have been designed to get a reaction out of Oliver, not her.

Maybe Blake had loved his best friend for more years than she had.

'He wanted you,' she said. 'And you wanted me. And he saw that every single time we were all together.'

There was a weird kind of certainty in the thought. No wonder he thought there was something going on in Hong Kong. He knew the truth. He just knew it much earlier than either of them.

'Poor Blake,' she whispered. 'Trapped behind so many masks. And you and I were supposed to be together all along.'

There was just no question. Again, that strange cosmic rightness.

'We may be slow,' he said, burrowing into the place below her ear, 'but we got there.'

'Promise me no masks between us, Oliver. Ever. Promise me we'll go back to Audrey and Oliver who can talk about anything, who will share anything. Even the tough stuff.'

He kissed his way to her lips, then, seeing how very serious she was about that, he rested his chin on her forehead and placed his hand on her heart. 'I give you my solemn oath, Audrey. Whenever we have something tough to discuss we'll curl up in that chair and talk it out and we won't leave it until we're done. No matter what.'

Her eyes shifted right. 'Our chair?'

'Our chair.' He lifted his chin to stare into her eyes. 'Why?'

'I was hoping it could be used more for evil than for good,' she breathed. 'And it has been a very, very long time between chairs.'

Desire flooded Oliver's gorgeous gaze. 'Fortunately, it's a multipurpose chair. But, come on.' He pulled her to her feet and towards the window. 'Let's make sure it's *fit* for purpose.'

* * * * *

THE MOST
EXPENSIVE NIGHT
OF HER LIFE

AMY ANDREWS

*To the Kohli family, our lovely UK friends –
Amanda, Nick, Lauren and Matthew.*

*Even though we live on opposite sides of the
world, your friendship warms our hearts.*

Amy Andrews is a multi-award-winning, *USA TODAY* bestselling Aussie author who has written over fifty contemporary romances in both the traditional and digital markets. She loves good books, fab food, great wine and frequent travel – preferably all four together. To keep up with her latest releases, news, competitions and giveaways sign up for her newsletter – amyandrews.com.au/ newsletter.html.

CHAPTER ONE

A ROADSIDE EXPLOSION in the darkest depths of a war zone three years ago had left Blake Walker with a finely honed sense of doom. Today that doom stormed towards him on a pair of legs that wouldn't quit and a ball-breaking attitude that was guaranteed to ruin his last day on the job.

Ava Kelly might be one of the world's most beautiful women but she redefined the term *diva*.

Doing this job for her had been a freaking nightmare.

'Blake!'

Her classy Oxford accent grated and Blake took a deep breath. He went to the happy place the army shrink had insisted he find—which at the moment was anywhere but here.

Last day, man, keep yourself together.

'Ava,' he greeted as she stopped on the opposite side of the beautiful maple-wood island bench in the kitchen where he was poring over some paperwork. He'd polished the top to glass-like perfection with his own two hands. 'Problem?'

'You could say that,' she said, folding her arms and glaring at him.

Blake did not drop his gaze and admire how the arm-crossing emphasised the tanned perfection of her cleavage. Even if it was on open display in her loosely tied gossamer gown that reeked of a designer label and through which her itty-bitty, red bikini could also be clearly seen.

He did not think about how wet she was underneath it.

About the water droplets that dripped off the ends of her slicked-back hair or trekked down the elegant line of her throat to cling precariously to her prominent collarbones before heading further south.

Blake did not look.

Blake was in a good place in his life. He was fit and healthy after a long period of being neither. He was financially secure. He had direction and purpose.

He could get laid any night of the week with just one phone call placed to any of half a dozen women. He didn't need to ogle the one in front of him.

She was trouble and he'd already had too much of that.

Instead he thought about the month-long holiday he started tomorrow—no braving a clutch of paparazzi every morning, no twelve-hour days and, most importantly, no divas.

'Something I can help with?' he asked.

'Yes,' she said, raising her chin to peer down her nose at him in that way he'd got used to the last few months. 'You can ask your salivating apprentice—' she jerked her thumb in the direction of the male in question '—to put his eyes back in his head and keep his mind on the job. My friends aren't here to be gawked at. They come into the privacy of *my* home to get away from objectification.'

Blake glanced over at the three women frolicking in the fully glassed indoor pool that ran alongside the magnificent internal open-air courtyard. They were all tall, tanned and gorgeous and if they were friends of Ava's then they were no doubt models too. Between them there were only twelve triangles of fabric keeping them from being totally naked.

He glanced at Dougy, who was installing some sophisticated strip lighting down the outside of the glass and steel staircase that led from the courtyard to a mezzanine level for sunbathing. Ava was right: he was barely keeping his tongue inside his head. Not that Blake could really blame him. This had to be every young apprentice's wet dream. And he was like a kid in a candy shop.

Sunlight flooded the courtyard through the open glass roof above reflecting off the stark white décor, dazzling his eyes. For a moment Blake tuned out Ava's disapproval and admired what they'd achieved—outside a semi-detached, early-nineteenth-century terraced house, inside a vibrant contemporary home full of light and flair.

'Well?' Ava's huffy demand yanked him back to the conversation.

'Dougy,' Blake said, in no mood to humour her as her gown slipped off her right shoulder exposing more of her to his view. He kept his gaze firmly fixed on the smattering of freckles across the bridge of her perfect little snub nose placed perfectly in the middle of her delicate kitten-like face.

'His name's Dougy.'

'Well, do you think you could rein *Dougy* in? He's acting like some horny teenager.'

Blake sighed. Why was it he liked project management again? He made a note to tell Charlie no more divas. Their business was going gangbusters—they could afford to be choosey.

'Ava,' he said patiently, 'he's nineteen. He *is* a horny teenager.'

'Well, he can be that on his own time,' she snapped. 'When he's on my time, I expect him to have his head down and do the job I'm paying him for. And so should you.'

Blake contemplated telling Ava Kelly to quit her bitching and let him worry about his employees. Dougy was a good apprentice—keen and a hard worker—and Blake wasn't about to make an issue out of what was, to him, a non-issue. But he figured no one had ever used the B word around Ms Kelly—*not to her face anyway*—and he wasn't going to be the first.

Hell, what she needed was a damn good spanking. But he wasn't about to do that either.

The job was over at the end of the day, they were just putting the finishing touches to the reno, and he could suck up her diva-ness for a few more hours.

Blake unclenched his jaw. 'I'll talk to him,' he said through stiff lips.

Ava looked down her nose at him again and sniffed. 'See that you do.'

Then she spun on her heel and marched away. He watched as the edges of her gown flowed behind her like tails, her lovely ankles exposed with every footfall. Higher up his gaze snagged on the enticing sway of one teeny-tiny red triangle.

The end of the day couldn't come soon enough.

A couple of hours later Blake answered the phone to his brother. Blake rarely answered the phone while at a job site but he always picked up for Charlie. His brother might have been younger but he'd been the driving force behind their design business and behind dragging Blake out of the maudlin pit of despair he'd almost totally disappeared into a few years back.

Blake owed Charlie big time.

'What's up?' he asked.

'Joanna rang. She's really upset. One of their biggest supporters is pulling out due to financial issues and she's freaking out they won't be able to continue to run their programmes.'

Joanna was their sister. She'd been widowed three years ago when her husband, Colin, a lieutenant in the British army and a close friend of Blake's, was killed in the same explosion that had injured him. They'd been in the same unit and he'd been Col's captain. And he'd promised his sister he'd look out for her husband.

That he'd bring him home alive.

Not a promise he'd been able to keep as it turned out.

She and three other army wives had started a charity soon after, which supported the wives, girlfriends and families of British servicemen. They'd done very well in almost two years but fighting for any charity backing in the global financial situation was hard—losing the support of a major contributor was a real blow.

And losing Col had been blow enough.

Blake understood that it was through the charity that Joanna kept him alive. It kept her going. It was her crutch.

And Blake understood crutches better than anyone.

'I guess we're in a position with the business now to become patrons ourselves,' Blake said.

'Blake!'

The muscles in Blake's neck tensed at the imperious voice. He took a deep breath as he turned around, his brother still speaking in his ear.

'We can't afford the one million quid that's been yanked from their coffers,' Charlie said.

Ava went to open her mouth but Blake was so shocked by the amount he held his finger up to indicate that she wait without realising what he was doing. 'Joanna needs a *million* pounds?'

He watched Ava absently as Charlie rattled off the intricacies. By the look on her face and the miffed little armfold, she wasn't accustomed to being told to wait. But *holy cow*—one million pounds?

'I need you to move your car,' Ava said, tapping her fingers on her arm, obviously waiting as long as she was going to despite Charlie still yakking in his ear. 'I'm expecting a photographer from a magazine and your beat-up piece of junk spoils the ambience a little.'

Blake blinked at Ava's request. She'd never seemed more frivolous or more diva-ish to him and he was exceptionally pleased this was the last time he'd ever have to see her.

Yes, she was sexy, and in a parallel universe where she

wasn't an elite supermodel and he *wasn't* a glorified construction worker he might have even gone there—given it a shot.

But skin-deep beauty left him cold.

He quirked a you-have-to-be-kidding-me eyebrow but didn't say a word to her as he spoke to Charlie. 'I've got to go and shift my *piece of junk car.*' He kept his gaze fixed to her face. 'We'll think of something for Joanna. I'll call you when I've finished tonight.'

'Who's Joanna?' Ava asked as Charlie hit the end button.

Blake stiffened. He didn't want to tell Little-Miss-I've-got-a-photographer-coming Ava anything about his private life. But *mind your own business* probably wasn't the best response either. 'Our sister,' he said, his lips tight.

'Is she okay?'

Blake recoiled in surprise. Not just that she'd enquired about somebody else's welfare but at the genuine note of concern in her voice. 'She's fine,' he said. 'The charity she runs has hit a bit of a snag, that's all. She'll bounce back.'

And he went and shifted his car so he wouldn't besmirch her Hampstead Village ambience, the paparazzi blinding him with their flashes for the thousandth time.

It was close to nine that night when Blake—and *the diva*—were satisfied that the job was finally complete. The evening was still and warm. Tangerine fingers of daylight could be seen streaking the sky through the open glass panels over the courtyard. Blake was heartened that the long-range weather forecast for September was largely for more of the same.

Perfect boating weather.

Dougy and the other two workers had gone home; the photographer had departed, as had the paparazzi. It was just him and Ava signing off on the reno. Dotting all the i's and crossing all the t's.

They were, once again, at the kitchen island bench—

him on one side, her on the other. Ava was sipping a glass of white wine while something delicious cooked on the state-of-the-art cooktop behind him. She'd offered him a beer but he'd declined. She'd offered to feed him but he'd declined that also.

No way was he spending a second longer with Ava than he absolutely had to.

Although the aromas of garlic and basil swirling around him were making him very aware of his empty stomach and his even more empty fridge.

He was also very aware of her. She'd pulled on some raggedy-arsed shorts and a thin, short-sleeved, zip-up hoodie thing over her bikini. The zip was low enough to catch a glimpse of cleavage and a hint of red material as she leaned slightly forward when she asked a question. But that wasn't what was making him aware of her.

God knew she'd swanned around the house in varying states of undress for the last three months.

No. It was the way she was caressing the bench-top that drew his eye. As he walked her through the paperwork the palm of her hand absently stroked back and forth along the glassy maple-wood. He'd learned she was a tactile person and, despite his animosity towards her, he liked that.

She'd handed the décor decisions over to a high-priced consultant who had gone for the typical home-and-garden, money-to-burn classy minimalist. But it was the accessories that *Ava* had chosen that showed her hedonistic bent. Shaggy rugs, chunky art, the softest mohair throws in vibrant greens and reds and purples for the lounges, beaded wall hangings, a collection of art deco lamps, layers and layers of colourful gauzy fabric falling from the ceiling in her bedroom to form a dazzling canopy over her girly four-poster bed.

Even the fact that she'd chosen a wooden kitchen amidst all the glass and metal told him something about her. He'd have thought for sure she'd have chosen black marble and acres of stainless steel. But clearly, from the smell of dinner, Ava loved to cook and spent a lot of time in the kitchen.

Blake wasn't much of a cook but he loved wood. The family business, until recent times, had been a saw mill and his earliest memories revolved around the fresh earthy smell of cut timber. His grandfather, who had founded the mill fifty year prior, had taught both him and Charlie how to use a lathe from a very early age and Blake had been hooked. He'd worked in the mill weekends and every school holidays until he'd joined up.

He'd personally designed, built and installed the kitchen where they were sitting and something grabbed at his gut to see her hand caressing his creation as she might caress a lover.

'So,' he said as their business concluded, and he got his head back in the game, 'if you're happy that everything has been done to your satisfaction, just sign here and here.'

Blake held out a pen and indicated the lines requiring her signature. Then held his breath. Tactile or not, Ava Kelly had also been demanding, difficult and fickle.

He wasn't counting his chickens until she'd signed on the dotted lines!

Ava glanced at the enigmatic Blake Walker through her fringe. She'd never met a man who wasn't at least a little in awe of her. Who didn't flirt a little or at least try it on.

But not Blake.

He'd been polite and unflappable even when she'd been at her most unreasonable. And she knew she'd been unreasonable on more than one occasion. *Just a little.* Just to see if he'd react like a human being for once instead of the face of the business—composed, courteous, respectful.

She'd almost got her reaction this afternoon when he'd been on the phone and she'd asked him to shift his car. The tightening of his mouth, that eyebrow raise had spoken volumes. But he'd retreated from the flash of fire she'd seen in his indigo eyes and a part of her had been supremely disappointed.

Something told her that Blake Walker would be quite magnificent all riled up.

Charlie, the more easy-going of the brothers, had said that Blake had been in the army so maybe he was used to following orders, sucking things up?

Ava reluctantly withdrew her hand from the cool smoothness of the bench-top to take the pen. She loved the seductive feel of the beautiful wood and, with Blake's deep voice washing over her and the pasta sauce bubbling away in the background, a feeling of contentment descended. It would be so nice to drop her guard for once, to surrender to the cosy domesticity.

To the intimacy.

Did he feel it too or was it just her overactive imagination after months of building little fantasies about him? Fantasies that had been getting a lot more complex as he had steadily ignored her.

Like doing him on this magnificent bench-top. A bench-top she'd watched him hone day after day. Sanding, lacquering. Sanding, lacquering. Sanding, lacquering. Layer upon layer until it shone like the finest crystal in the discreet down lights.

Watching him so obviously absorbed by the task. Loving the wood with his touch. Inhaling its earthy essence with each flare of his nostrils. Caressing it with his lingering gaze.

She could have stripped stark naked in front of him as he'd worked the wood and she doubted he would have noticed.

And for a woman used to being adored, being ignored had been challenging.

Ava dragged her mind off the bench-top and what she was doing to an unknowing Blake on top of it. 'I'm absolutely...positively...one hundred per cent...' she punctuated each affirmation with firm strokes of the pen across the indicated lines '…happy with the job. It's *totally fab.* I'm going to tell all my friends to use you guys.'

Blake blinked. That he hadn't been expecting. A polite, understated thank-you was the best he'd been hoping for. The very last thing he'd expected was effusive praise and promised recommendations to what he could only imagine would be a fairly extensive A list.

He supposed she expected him to be grateful for that but the thought of dealing with any more Ava Kellys was enough to bring him out in hives.

'Thank you,' he said non-comittally.

She smiled at him as she pushed the papers and the pen back across the bench-top. Like her concern earlier it seemed genuine, unlike the haughty *can't-touch-this* smile she was known for in the modelling world, and he lost his breath a little.

The down lights shone off her now dry caramel-blonde hair pulled into some kind of a messy knot at her nape, the fringe occasionally brushing eyelashes that cast long shadows on her cheekbones. Her eyes were cat-like in their quality, both in the yellow-green of the irises and in the way they tapered down as if they were concealing a bunch of secrets.

Yeh, Ava Kelly was a *very* attractive woman.

But he'd spent over a decade in service to his country having his balls busted by the best and he wasn't about to line up for another stint.

Blake gathered the paperwork and shoved it in his satchel, conscious of her watching him all the time. His leg ached and he couldn't wait to get off it.

He was almost free. She was almost out of his life for good.

He picked up the satchel and rounded the bench-top, his limp a little more pronounced now as stiffness through his hip hindered his movement. He pulled up in front of her when she was an arm's length away. He held out his hand and gave her one of his smiles that Joanna called barely there.

'We'll invoice you with the final payment,' he said as she took his hand and they shook.

She was as tall as him—six foot—and it was rare to be able to look a woman directly in the eye. Disconcerting too as those eyes stared back at him with something between bold sexual interest and hesitant mystique. It was intriguing. Tempting…

He withdrew his hand. *So not going there.* 'Okay. I'll be off. I'm away for a month so if you have any issues contact Charlie.'

Ava quirked an eyebrow. 'Going on a holiday?'

Blake nodded curtly. The delicate arch of her eyebrow only drew his attention back to the frankness in her eyes. She sounded surprised. Why, he had no idea. After three months of her quibbles and foibles even a saint would need some time off. 'Yes.'

Ava sighed at his monosyllabic replies. 'Look, I'm sorry,' she said, picking up her glass of wine and taking a fortifying sip. Something had passed between them just now and suddenly she knew he wasn't as immune to her as she'd thought.

'I know I haven't exactly been easy on you and I *know* I can be a pain in the butt sometimes. I can't help it. I like to be in control.' She shrugged. 'It's the business I'm in… people demand perfection from me and they get it but I demand it back.'

Ava paused for a moment. She wasn't sure why she was telling him this stuff. Why it was important he understand she wasn't some prima donna A-lister. She was twenty-seven years old—had been at the top of her game since she was fourteen—and had never cared who thought what.

Maybe it was the gorgeous wooden bench-top he'd created just for her? The perfection of it. How he'd worked at it and worked at it and worked at it until it was flawless.

Maybe a man who clearly appreciated perfection would understand?

'I learned early…very early, not to trust easily. And I'm afraid it spills over into all aspects of my life. I know people think I'm a bitch and I'm okay with that. People think twice about crossing me. But…it's not who I really am.'

Blake was taken aback by the surprise admission. Surprised at her insight. Surprised that she'd gone through life wary of everyone. Surprised at the cut-throat world she existed in—and he'd thought life in a warzone had been treacherous.

In the army, on deployment—trust was paramount. You trusted your mates, you stuck together, or you could die.

'Of course,' he said, determined not to feel sorry for this very well-off, very capable woman. She wanted to play the poor-little-rich-girl card, fine. But he wasn't buying. 'Don't worry about it. That's what you pay us for.'

Ava nodded, knowing that whatever it was that had passed between them before was going to go undiscovered. Clearly, Blake Walker was made of sterner stuff than even she'd credited him with. And she had to admire that. A man who could say no to her was a rare thing.

'Thanks. Have a good holiday.'

Blake nodded and turned to go and that was when it happened. He'd barely lifted his foot off the ground when the first gunshot registered. A volley of gunshots followed, slamming into the outside façade of Ava's house, smashing the high windows that faced the street, spraying glass everywhere. But that barely even registered with Blake. Nor did Ava's look of confusion or her panicked scream.

He was too busy moving.

He didn't think—he just reacted.

Let his training take over.

He dived for her, tackling her to the ground, landing

heavily on the unforgiving marble tiles. Her wine glass smashed, the liquid puddling around them. His bad leg landed hard against the ground sucking his breath away, his other cushioned by her body as he lay half sprawled on top of her.

'Keep your head down, keep your head down,' he yelled over the noise as he tucked her head into the protective hollow just below his shoulder, his heart beating like the rotor blades of a chopper, his eyes squeezed shut as the world seemed to explode around him.

Who in the hell had she pissed off now?

CHAPTER TWO

Everything slowed down around her as Ava clung to Blake for dear life. Her pulse wooshed louder than Niagara Falls through her ears, the blood flowing through her veins became thick and sludgy, the breath in her lungs felt heavy and oppressive, like stubborn London fog.

And as the gunfire continued she realised she couldn't breathe.

She couldn't breathe.

Her pulse leapt as she tried to drag in air, tried to heave in much-needed oxygen. She tried to move her head from his chest, seek cleaner air, but he held her firm and panic spiralled through her system. Her nostrils flared, her hands shook where she clutched his shirt, her stomach roiled and pitched.

Then suddenly there was silence and she stopped breathing altogether, holding her breath, straining to hear. A harsh squeal of screeching tyres rent the pregnant silence, a noisy engine roared then faded.

Neither of them moved for a moment.

Blake recovered first, grabbing his leg briefly, checking it had survived the fall okay before easing off her slightly. 'Are you okay?'

She blinked up at him, dazed. 'Wha…?'

Without conscious thought Blake undertook a rapid assessment. She had a small scratch on her left cheekbone with a smudge of dried blood but that wasn't what caused his stomach to bottom out. A bloom of dark red stained her top and his pulse accelerated even further.

'Oh, God, are you hit?' he demanded, pushing himself up into a crouch. He didn't think, he just reached for her hoodie zipper and yanked it down. Just reacting, letting his training taking over. The bullets had hit the building high but they'd penetrated the windows and in this glass and steel interior they could have ricocheted anywhere.

'Did you get hit?' he asked again as her torso lay exposed to him. He didn't see her red bikini top or the body men the world over lusted after; he was too busy running his hands over her chest and her ribs and her belly, clinically assessing, searching for a wound.

Ava couldn't think properly. Her head hurt, her hand hurt, she was trembling, her heart rate was still off the scale.

'Ava!' he barked.

Ava jumped as his voice sliced with surgical precision right through her confusion. 'I think it's…my hand,' she said, holding it up as blood oozed and dripped from a deep gash in her palm, already drying in sludgy rivulets down her wrist and arm. 'I think I…cut it on the wine glass when it smashed.'

Blake allowed himself a brief moment of relief, his body flooding with euphoria as the endorphins kicked in—*she wasn't hit*. But then the rest of his training took over. He reached for her injured palm with one hand and pulled his mobile out of his back pocket with the other, quickly dialling 999.

An emergency call taker asked him which service he wanted and Blake asked for the police and an ambulance. 'Don't move,' he told her as he awkwardly got to his feet, grabbing the bench and pushing up through his good leg to lever himself into a standing position. He could feel the strain in his hip as he dragged his injured leg in line with the other and gritted his teeth at the extra exertion.

'I'll get a cloth for it.'

Ava couldn't have moved even if her life depended on it. She just kept looking at the blood as it slowly trickled out of the wound, trying to wrap her throbbing head around what had just happened. She could hear Blake's deep voice, so calm in the middle of the chaos, and wished he were holding her again.

He returned with a clean cloth that had been hanging on her oven door. He hung up the phone and she watched absently as he crouched beside her again and reached for her hand.

'Police are on their way,' he said as he wrapped the cloth around her hand, 'So's the ambulance.' He tied it roughly to apply some pressure. 'Can you sit up? If you can make it to the sink I can clean the wound before the paramedics get here.'

'Ah, yeh…I guess,' Ava said, flailing like a stranded beetle for a moment before levering herself up onto her elbows, then curling slowly up into a sitting position. Her head spun and nausea threatened again as she swayed.

'Whoa,' Blake said, reaching for her, his big hand covering most of her forearm. 'Easy there.'

Ava shut her eyes for a moment concentrating on the grounding effect of his hand, and the dizziness passed. 'I'm fine now,' she said, shaking off his hand, reaching automatically for the back of her head where a decent lump could already be felt. She prodded it gently and winced.

'Got a bit of an egg happening there?' Blake enquired. 'Sorry about that,' he apologised gruffly. 'I just kind of reacted.'

Ava blinked. Blake Walker had been magnificent. 'I'm pleased you did. I didn't know what was happening for a moment or two. Was that really gunfire?'

Blake stood, using the bench and his good leg again.

'Yep,' he said grimly. A sound all too familiar to him but not one he'd thought he'd ever hear again. Certainly not in trendy Hampstead Village. He held his hand out to her. 'Here, grab hold.'

Ava didn't argue, just took the proffered help. When she was standing upright again, another wave of nausea and dizziness assailed her and she grabbed him with one hand and the bench with the other. She was grateful for his presence, absorbing his solidness and his calmness as reaction set in and the trembling intensified. His arm slid around her back and she leaned into him, inhaling the maleness of him—cut timber and a hint of spice.

She felt stupidly safe here.

'Sorry,' she murmured against his shoulder as she battled an absurd urge to cry. 'I don't usually fall apart so easily.'

Blake shut his eyes as she settled against him. Her chest against his, their hips perfectly aligned. She smelled like wine and the faint trace of coconut based sunscreen. He turned his head slightly until his lips were almost brushing her temple. 'I'm guessing this hasn't been a very usual day.'

Her low shaky laugh slid straight into his ear and his hand at the small of her back pressed her trembling body a little closer.

'You could say that,' she admitted, her voice husky.

And they stood like that for long moments, Blake instinctively knowing she needed the comfort. Knowing how such a random act of violence could unsettle even battle-hardened men.

The first distant wail of a siren invaded the bubble and he pulled back. 'The cavalry are here,' he murmured.

Blake stuck close to Ava's side, his hand at her elbow. 'Watch the glass,' he said as a stray piece crunched under his sturdy boots. Her feet were bare, her toenail polish the same red as her bikini.

He could hear the sirens almost on top of them now,

loud and urgent, obviously in the street. He flicked on the tap and removed the cloth. 'Put it under,' he instructed. 'I'll go get the door.'

An hour later Ava's house was like Grand Central Station—people coming and going, crossing paths, stepping around each other. Uniformed and plain-clothed police went about their jobs, gathering evidence. Yellow crime-scene tape had been rolled out along the wrought-iron palings of her front fence and there were enough flashing lights in her street to outdo Piccadilly Circus in December. They reflected in the glass that had sprayed out onto the street like a glitter ball at some gruesome discotheque.

And then there was the gaggle of salivating paparazzi and the regular press who'd been cordoned off further down and none too happy about it either. Shouting questions at whoever happened to walk out of the house, demanding answers, calling for an immediate statement.

Safely inside, Ava felt her head truly thumping now. They'd been over what had happened several times with several different police officers and her patience was just about out. Her agent, Reggie Pitt, was there—a pap had rung him—to *protect her interests*, but it was Blake she looked to, who she was most grateful to have by her side.

'Is there anyone you know who'd do this to you or has reason to do this to you?' Detective Sergeant Ken Biddle asked.

Blake frowned at the question. The police officer looked old as dirt and as if nothing would surprise him—like one or two sergeant majors he'd known. But Blake had felt Ava's fear, felt the frantic beat of her heart under his and didn't like the implication.

'You think there's *any* reason to shoot up somebody's house and scare the bejesus out of them?' he growled.

The police officer shot him an unimpressed look before returning his attention to Ava. 'I mean anyone with a grudge? Get any strange letters lately?'

Ava shrugged. 'No more than usual. All my fan mail goes to Reggie and he hands anything suss on to you guys.' Reggie nodded in confirmation of the process.

Blake stared at her. '*You* get hate mail?'

Ava nodded. 'Every now and then. Pissed-off wives, guys who think I've slighted them because I didn't sign their autograph at a rope line, the odd jealous colleague. Just the usual.'

'But no one in particular recently?' Ken pressed.

Reggie shook his head. 'No.'

'We'll need to see them all.'

Reggie nodded. 'You guys have got a whole file of them somewhere.'

Ken made a note. 'I'll look into it.'

'Excuse me,' a hovering paramedic interrupted. 'We'd really like to get Ms Kelly to the hospital to X-ray her head and get her hand stitched up.'

The police officer nodded, snapping his notebook shut. 'Do you have somewhere you can stay for a while? I would advise you not to return here while the investigation is being carried out and the culprits are still at large. Hopefully we can close the case quickly but until then lying low is the best thing that you can do.'

Reggie shook his head. 'Impossible. She's up for a new commercial—she has a call back in LA in two days. And she's booked on half a dozen talk shows in the US next week to promote her new perfume.'

Blake bristled at the agent's obvious disregard for his client's safety—wasn't he supposed to put Ava first? But the police veteran was already on it.

'Cancel them.'

Reggie, who was a tall, thin streak with grey frizzy hair and round wire glasses sitting on the end of his nose, gawped like a landed fish. 'You don't just cancel, Detective Sergeant' he said, scandalised.

'Look, Mr Pitt, in my *very* long experience in the London Metropolitan Police force I can tell you that the best way to avoid trouble is to not go looking for it. Your client enjoys a high public profile, which, unfortunately, makes her *very* easy to find. Every pap in London knows where she lives, for example.'

'I'll get her a private security detail,' Reggie blustered.

'That is of course your prerogative,' the policeman conceded. 'But my advice would still be to lie low, which, by the way, would also be the advice any security person worth their salt would give you.'

Blake decided he liked Ken Biddle after all. He seemed solid. He obviously knew his stuff and didn't suffer fools gladly. And he clearly thought Reggie was an A-grade fool.

Reggie shot the police officer an annoyed look before turning to Ava. 'I'll get you booked into a hotel, darling. Get some security organised first thing in the morning.'

Blake also decided Reggie was an A-grade fool. 'I don't think you're listening, *mate*,' Blake said. 'I think the detective sergeant knows what he's on about. It sounds like it might be best for her to go dark for a while.'

'Ava, darling,' Reggie appealed to her. 'I think they're making a mountain out of a molehill.'

'Someone freaking shot up her house,' Blake snapped. 'Aren't you supposed to have her best interests at heart?'

'It's in Ava's best interests to keep working,' Reggie said through gritted teeth.

Ava's head was about to explode as they discussed her life as if she weren't there. Her hand throbbed too and she felt incredibly weary all of a sudden. She just wanted to lie down somewhere dark and sleep for a week and forget that somebody had shot up her house. Her beautiful, beautiful house.

'Do you think I could just go to the hospital and get seen to first?' she interrupted them.

It was all the encouragement the paramedic needed. 'Right. Question time is over,' he said, stepping in front of them all, and Ava could have kissed him as he took over as efficiently as he'd bandaged her hand earlier. 'We're taking her to the nearest hospital.'

Reggie shook his head. 'No. Ms Kelly sees a private physician on Harley Street.'

The paramedic bristled. 'It's nine o'clock at night. Ms Kelly needs an X-ray, possibly a CT scan. She needs a hospital.'

'The nearest hospital is fine,' Ava assured the paramedic, before Reggie could say any more.

'Are you okay to walk to the ambulance?' the paramedic asked her.

Ava nodded. 'I can walk.'

Blake checked his watch. He could be home and officially on holidays within half an hour. He could almost taste the cold beer he had waiting in his fridge to celebrate the end of having to deal with Little-Ms-Red-Bikini.

Except Ava Kelly looked far from the diva he'd pegged her as right now.

She looked pale and shaken, her freckles more pronounced. The small cut on her cheekbone was a stark reminder of what had happened to her tonight and part of him felt wrong walking away. Leaving her in the clutches of her shark-like agent. He hesitated. She wasn't his responsibility; he knew that. He'd simply been in the wrong place at the wrong time and she was a big girl—what she chose to do next was none of his business.

But he didn't feel she was going to get the wisest counsel from good old Reggie.

'You need me for anything else, Detective Sergeant?' he asked.

Ken shook his head. 'I have your details here if I need to contact you.'

Blake nodded. That was that, then. Duty discharged. But before he could say goodbye her hand reached out and clutched at his forearm. 'Can you come with me?'

Blake looked at her, startled. *What the?*

Sure, he'd felt wrong about leaving her but he hadn't expected her to give him a second thought now she was surrounded by people to look out for her. And even though the same part of him—the honourable part—that had urged him to join the army all those years ago somehow felt obligated to see she was okay, the rest of him wanted nothing to do with Ava Kelly and her crazy celebrity life.

They were done and dusted. He was free.

He was on holiday, for crying out loud.

Not to mention he'd had enough of hospitals to last him a lifetime.

But her yellow-green eyes implored him and the doom he'd felt earlier today pounced. He sighed. 'Sure.'

Blake strode into the hospital half an hour later. He'd waited for the mass exodus of press chasing the blue lights of the ambulance at breakneck speed before he followed at a more sedate pace. Then he'd parked his car well away from the main entrance on one of the back streets. He wasn't sure why but when he spotted the bright lights of cameras flashing into the night as he got closer he was pleased he had.

Being photographed nearly every day on his arrival at Ava's and questioned *every freaking day* as to their relationship when clearly he was just the guy running the reno had been bad enough. He didn't need them spotting his car then adding two and two together and coming up with five.

He entered the hospital and enquired at the front desk and a security guard ushered him along the corridors to Ava. He clenched his hands by his side as he followed. Hospitals weren't exactly his favourite places and the antiseptic smell was bringing back a lot of unpleasant memories.

They stopped at a closed door where two other hospital security personnel stood, feet apart, alert, scanning the activity at both ends of the corridor. They opened the door for him and the first person he saw was Reggie speaking to a fresh-faced guy, clearly younger than his own thirty-three years, wearing a white coat and a harried expression. Reggie was insisting that a plastic surgeon be made available to suture his esteemed client's hand.

'That hand,' he said, pointing at the appendage in question, 'is worth a lot of money. I am not going to allow some *junior* doctor to butcher it any further than it already is.'

The doctor put up his hands in surrender. 'I'll page the on-call plastics team.'

'I need a *consultant*,' Reggie insisted. 'Someone who knows what they're doing.'

Blake caught a glimpse of the doctor's face as he backed out of the room. He looked as if he truly regretted coming to work today.

Blake knew exactly how he felt.

He was beginning to think Reggie was actually the bigger diva out of the two of them. He was surprised Ava put up with it. In three months he'd seen her fire an interior decorator, a PA and a personal trainer because they'd all tried to manage her. But she just lay docilely on the hospital trolley and let Reggie run the show.

He wasn't used to seeing her meek and mild.

But he supposed having your house shot at while you were inside it was probably enough to give anyone pause.

At least there was some colour in her cheeks now.

Ava looked up from her hand to discover Blake was in the room. 'Oh, hi,' she said, levering herself up into a sitting position.

The last half an hour had passed in a blur and she'd been unaccountably anxious lying in the CT scanner. The doctor had assured her it was clear but it wasn't until right now she felt as if it was going to be okay. She hadn't been able to stop thinking about the way Blake had pushed her to the ground. It played over and over in her head.

He'd just reacted. In a split second. While she'd been confused about what was happening he was diving for her, pulling her down. She was on the ground before the noise had even registered as gunfire.

'I thought you'd skipped out on me.'

He returned her smile with a fleeting one of his own. It barely made a dent in the firm line of his mouth. Ava wondered how good he would look with a real smile. Would it go all the way to his dark blue eyes? Would it light up his rather austere features? Would it flatten out the lines on his forehead where he frowned a lot? Puff up the sparseness of his cheekbones? Would it break the harsh set of his very square jaw?

'I said I'd be here.'

Ava blinked at his defensive tone, his dialogue as sparse as his features. A man of few words.

'Everything check out okay?' he asked after a moment or two.

This time he sounded gruff and he glanced at Reggie, who was talking on his mobile, as if he was uncomfortable engaging in small talk in front of an audience. Ava was so used to Reggie being around, she barely noticed him any more.

'CT scan is fine,' she said. 'Just waiting for a plastic surgeon for the hand.'

He nodded and she waited for him to say something else but he looked as if he was done. Then Reggie finished his call and started talking anyway. 'I've booked you into your usual suite,' he said. 'We'll organise for a suitcase to be brought to you tomorrow.'

Ava watched the angle of Blake's jaw tighten at the announcement. 'I thought the point of lying low was to *not* go to any of her usual places?' Blake enquired.

The hardness in his tone made Ava shiver. *And not in a bad way.* Blake Walker was a good looking man. Not in the cut, ripped, metrosexual way she was used to. More in a rugged, capable, tool-belt-wearing kind of way. The fact that Blake Walker either didn't know it or didn't care about it only added to his allure.

The fact that Mr-Rugged-And-Capable was looking out for *her* was utterly seductive.

It had been a long time since someone had made her feel as if *she* mattered more than her brand. Her mother had cut and run when she'd been seventeen, leaving her to fend for herself in a very adult world, and Ava had never felt so alone or vulnerable.

Sure, she'd coped and it had made her strong and re-silient—two things you had to be to survive in her world. But tonight, she didn't have to be any of those things because Blake was here.

'They have very strict security,' Reggie bristled. 'Ava will be perfectly safe there.'

Blake snorted in obvious disbelief. 'Have you cancelled her commitments yet?'

Reggie took his glasses off. 'I'm playing that by ear.'

'You know, in the army you learn that you don't secure an object by flaunting it in front of the enemy. I think you need to take the advice of the police and have her lie low.'

'If Ava put her career on hold for every whack job that ever wrote her a threatening letter she wouldn't have had much of a career.'

'Well, this whack job just signed his name in automatic gunfire all along the front of her house. I think her safety has to take precedence over her career for the moment.'

Ava had to agree. Frankly she'd been scared witless to-night. She took Reggie's advice on everything—he'd been with her a long time—but in this she needed to listen to the guy who had crash tackled her to the ground to keep her safe.

Who believed her safety was a priority.

Reggie hadn't been there. He couldn't understand how frightening it had been.

'I've known Ava a long time, Mr Walker,' Reggie said. 'A lot longer than you. And she's stronger than you'll ever know. She'll get through this just fine.'

'He's right, Reggie,' she said as the silence grew.

Just because she was strong, it didn't mean she was going to go down into the basement while she was home alone to investigate the thing that had gone bump in the middle of the night.

Because that was plain stupid.

And she hadn't had longevity in a career that wasn't known for it by being stupid. Strength also lay in knowing your limitations and accepting help.

After a solid sleep she might be able to think a little straighter, be a little braver, but tonight she just needed to feel safe.

'I'm pretty freaked out,' Ava continued. 'I think listening to the advice of the police is the best thing. At least for tonight anyway.'

'So where are you going to go, Ava?' Reggie demanded. 'You can't go back to your home and everyone else you know in London is as famous as you.'

Ava didn't even have to think to know the answer to that question. She just reacted—as Blake had done earlier tonight. 'I can go to Blake's.'

CHAPTER THREE

BLAKE GAPED AT Ava as her yellowy-green gaze settled on his face. '*What?* No.' He would rather amputate his other leg than have Ava Kelly as a house guest.

'Just for the night,' she said.

Blake shook his head. 'No.' She sounded so reasonable but he had to wonder if the bang to her head had sent her a little crazy.

He was on holiday, for crying out loud.

Reggie—bless him—looked at his client askance. 'Absolutely not!' he blustered. 'You don't know this man from a bar of soap.'

Blake watched as Ava pursed her perfect lips and shot her agent an impatient look. 'I have seen this man—' she pointed at Blake '—almost every day for the last three months. That's the longest relationship I've had with *any* man other than you, Reggie. This man—' she jabbed a finger in his direction again '—pulled me down to the ground and *shielded me with his body* while some nutcase fired bullets at my house.'

'And thanks to him you have a cut face, a gash in your hand that requires stitching and an egg on the back of your head the size of a grapefruit.'

Blake bit off the bitter *you're welcome* that rose to his lips. He didn't expect thanks or praise for yanking her to the ground. His military training had taken over and he'd done what had to be done. What anyone with his background would have done. But he didn't expect to be accused of trying to maim her either.

Ava reached her hand out to Reggie and he took it. 'I was frightened, Reggie. Petrified. I couldn't...*breathe* I was so scared.' She'd been like that after her mother left—terrified for days. Then she'd hired Reggie. 'He makes me feel safe. And it's just for tonight.'

Reggie looked as if he was considering it and Blake began to wonder if he was invisible. 'Er, excuse me...' he interrupted. 'I don't know if either of you are interested but I said no.'

'You were the one who said she should lie low,' Reggie said, looking at him speculatively, clearly coming around to his client's way of thinking. 'You said the point was for her not to go to any of her usual places.'

Blake could not believe what he was hearing. They were both looking at him as if it were a done deal. As if his objections didn't matter in the face of the fabulous Ms Kelly's needs.

'I meant wear a wig, don some dark sunnies, throw on some baggy clothes and book herself into some low-rent hotel somewhere under a different name.'

'Please,' Ava said, the plea in her gaze finding its way directly to the part of him that was one hundred per cent soldier. 'I feel safe with you.'

'She feels safe with you,' Reggie reiterated, also looking at Blake, his hands in his pockets.

Blake shut his eyes and shook his head. 'No.' He opened his eyes again to find them both looking at him as if he'd just refused shelter to a pregnant woman on a donkey. 'For God's sake,' he said. 'I could live in a dive for all you know.'

Ava shrugged. 'I don't care.'

Blake snorted. 'Right. A world-famous supermodel who insisted on four thousand quid apiece tap fittings is happy to slum it?'

She shrugged again, looking down her nose at him this time, her famed haughtiness returning. 'I can slum it for a night.'

Blake's gaze was drawn to her mouth and the way it clearly enunciated each word. Her lips, like the words, were just…perfect. Like two little pillows, soft and pink with a perfectly defined bow shape. But somehow even they managed to look haughty—cool and mysterious. As if they'd never been touched. Never been kissed.

Not properly, anyway.

Kissed in a way that would get that mouth all bent out of shape.

If she really wanted to slum it—he could bend her perfect mouth well and truly out of shape.

A flicker of heat fizzed in his blood but he doused it instantly. Women like Ava Kelly didn't *really* want to slum it—no matter how much they thought they might. And he wasn't here for that. He'd entered into a contract with Ava to do the renos on her home. Nothing more.

Certainly not open up *his* home—*his* sanctuary—to her. And he'd held up his end of the bargain.

Duty discharged.

'I'm on holiday,' he said, his voice firm.

But Ava did not seem deterred. She just looked at him as if she was trying to figure out his price—and he didn't like it. Not one little bit.

'One million pounds,' she said.

Blake blinked, not quite computing what she'd just said. She actually *had* been figuring out his price? 'I'm sorry?'

'I'll give you that million pounds your sister needs.'

'Ava!' Reggie spluttered.

Blake gave an incredulous half-laugh, a half-snort. *'What?'*

Ava rolled her eyes. 'It's simple. I've had a very traumatic evening and I don't feel safe. I don't like not feeling safe.' It reminded her too much of when her mother left and she was supposed to be past that now. 'But you made me feel safe. And my gut tells me that means something. I've survived a long time in a cut-throat industry by going with my gut. So what's it going to be? You want the money or not?'

'Ava,' Reggie warned.

'Relax,' Ava told him. 'It's for a charity. It's all tax deductible.'

'Oh…well, that's okay, then.'

Blake shook his head as the heat that fizzed earlier flared again, morphing into white-hot fury. 'No,' he said through gritted teeth, 'it's not okay. You think you can just buy people? Just throw some cash around and get what you want?'

She shrugged that haughty little shrug again and he wanted to shake her. 'Everyone has a price, Blake. There's nothing wrong with that. This way we both get something we want.'

Blake ran a hand through his close-cropped hair. Joanna called it dirty blond and was forever trying to get him to grow it longer now he was out of the army. But old habits died hard.

Joanna.

Who he'd already failed once.

He'd told Charlie he'd think of a way to help their sister and the charity that meant so much to her—to all of them. And it was being presented to him on a platter.

By the devil himself. In the guise of a leggy supermodel.

A very bratty supermodel.

'You don't even know what the charity is,' Blake snapped, trying to hold onto his anger as his practical side urged him to take what was on offer.

'Yes, I do,' she said. 'I looked it up after we spoke earlier. A charity that supports our soldiers and their families. Very good for my profile, right, Reggie?'

Reggie nodded. 'Perfect.'

Blake had been in enough war zones to know when he was fighting a losing battle. He also knew he should do the honourable thing and offer her safe haven for free. But he resented how she'd manipulated him and if she could drop a cool mil without even raising a sweat then, clearly, she was good for it.

Still…it all sounded too good to be true.

'It's as simple as that?' he clarified. 'One night at my place and you'll give Joanna a million quid for her charity?'

Could he put up with a pain-in-the-butt prima donna for one night for a million quid?

'As simple as that.'

Blake regarded her. His practical side was screaming at him to take the cash but the other side of him, the one attuned to doom in all its forms, was wary as hell.

'You know there are thousands of men out there who would give anything to have me for a sleepover?'

She shot him a coy look from under her fringe and Blake glanced at her mouth. It had kicked up at one side as her voice had gone all light and teasy.

He didn't want that mouth *slumming* it at his place.

But one million quid was hard to turn down.

'Fine,' he sighed. 'But I leave in the morning for my holiday and you have to be gone.'

'Absolutely.' She grinned. 'I promise you won't even know I'm there.'

Blake grunted as his doom-o-meter hit a new high. *He sincerely doubted that.*

'*This* is where you live?'

Ava stared down at Blake's apparent abode floating in the crowded canal. They'd slipped out of a private exit at the back of the hospital into a waiting taxi after her hand had been sewn up with four neat little sutures and she'd been discharged. Blake had refused to tell even Reggie where he lived and she'd been too overwrought to care but even so *this* was a surprise. If someone had told her this morning she'd be spending the night on the Regent's Canal in Little Venice she'd have laughed them out of her house.

'You wanted to slum it.'

Ava took in the dark mysterious shape. 'People *actually* live on these things?'

'They do.'

Ava realised she couldn't have picked a better place to hide away—no one she knew would *ever* think to look for her here. But still…

She *was* used to five-star luxuries and, while she could forgo four-thousand-pound taps, basic plumbing was an absolute must. 'Please tell me there's a flushing toilet and a shower with hot water?'

'Your fancy suite looking better and better?'

Ava was weary. It was past midnight. She'd been shot at, grilled by the police as if she were somehow at fault, then poked and prodded by every person wearing a white coat or a shiny buckle at the hospital.

She didn't need his taunts or his judgement.

Yes, she'd bribed him. Yes, she'd told him she could handle it. Yes, she was used to her luxuries. But, come on, she just needed to stand under a hot shower and wash away the fright and the shock of the day.

Why couldn't he be like any other salivating idiot who was tripping over himself to accommodate her? But, oh, no, her knight in shining armour had to be the only man on the planet who didn't seem to care that she was, according to one of the top celebrity magazines, one of the most beautiful women of the decade.

And she was just about done with his put-upon attitude. He was getting a million bucks and bragging rights at the pub to the story—embellished as much as he liked because she was beyond caring—of the night Ava Kelly slept over.

She felt as if she was about to crumple in a heap as the

massive dose of adrenaline left her feeling strung out. All she wanted was a little safe harbour.

So, he didn't like her. She couldn't exactly say he was her favourite person at the moment either, despite his heroics.

Life was like that sometimes.

'Look, you're angry, I appreciate that. I railroaded you. But you have the distinct advantage of having being shot at before. I'm sure you're used to it. I'm sure it's *just another day to you.* Me, on the other hand…the only shooting I'm used to is from a camera lens. I promise I'll be out of your hair in the morning, but do you think in the interim you could just lose the attitude and point me in the direction of the hot shower?'

He didn't say anything for a moment but she could see the clenching and unclenching of his jaw as a streetlight slanted across his profile. 'You never get used to being shot at,' he said.

Ava blinked. His words slipped into the night around them with surprising ease considering the tautness behind them. It was a startling admission from a man who looked as if he could catch bullets with his teeth.

It struck her for the first time that he might have been more deeply affected by the incident than she'd realised. But his jaw was locked and serious. He didn't look as if he wanted to talk about it.

She did though—she really did. Suddenly she needed to talk about it as if her life depended on it.

Debrief—wasn't that what they called it in the army?

'Were you scared?' she asked tentatively, aware of her voice going all low and husky.

She was greeted with silence and she nodded slowly when he didn't answer, feeling foolish for even thinking that a brief burst of gunfire would rattle him. Charlie had told her Blake had been to war zones. He'd no doubt faced gunfire every day.

'Sorry, dumb question…'

The silence stretched and she was just about to say something else when he said, 'No, it's not.' Ava blinked at his quiet but emphatic denial.

'Any man who tells you that gunfire doesn't scare him is lying to you.'

Ava stared for a moment. If that had been Blake's impression of scared she had to wonder what level of danger would be required to actually make him look it.

Or maybe he just wasn't capable of strong emotion? *And wasn't that a big flashing neon warning sign?*

'But…you were so…' she cast around for an appropriate word '…calm.'

He gave a short laugh. She'd have to have been deaf not to hear the bitter edge. 'I'm sure my sergeant major, who chewed my arse off every day when I was a green recruit, would be more than pleased to hear that.'

He was being flippant now but she wasn't in the mood—she was deadly serious. 'I thought I was going to die,' she whispered.

His eyes were hooded as he stared at her and she wished she could see them, to connect with him. 'But you didn't,' he said.

His reminder was surprisingly gentle—not facetious like his last remark. 'Thanks to you,' she murmured.

Their gazes held for the longest time. It was quiet canal side and she realised they were standing close—close enough to feel as if they were the only two people in the world after what they'd been through together. To feel united. She waited for him to make some throwaway comment about the house saving her butt or the gunman being a lousy shot. He looked as if he was gearing up to say something.

But he seemed to think better of it, dragging his attention back to the longboat. She watched him step into the bow of the boat, then make a production of unlocking the door before he finally looked at her.

'You want that shower or not?'

The fridge was empty bar a six-pack of beer and Blake gratefully freed one of the bottles as the dull noise of shower spray floated towards him through the distant wall. He sat heavily on the nearby leather armchair, easing his leg out in front of him as he swivelled the chair from side to side. He was not going to think about Ava Kelly naked in his shower.

He was going to drink his beer, mentally plot his course for tomorrow, then crawl into bed.

Or the *couch* as the case might be.

Not his big comfortable king-sized sleigh bed he'd crafted with his own two hands—helping him forget the sand and the heat and the pain and the memories—specially customised for the specs of the wide beam canal boat he'd restored. He could hardly make a guest—a female guest—sleep on the couch. Even if it was large and long and comfortable.

Especially considering Ava was shelling out one million pounds for the dubious *privilege*.

He could certainly hack it for one night. For one million quid he could hack just about anything.

Dear God—he was prostituting himself. A leggy blonde with killer eyes, money to burn and someone wanting her dead had made him an offer he couldn't refuse and he'd rolled over quicker than a puppy with a tummy scratch on offer.

He took a swig of his beer as he dialled his brother's number. 'It's after midnight.' Charlie yawned as he picked up after what seemed for ever. 'Someone better be dying.'

'Only me,' Blake snorted. Then he proceeded to fill his brother in on the events of the evening including the details of the company car Charlie was going to need to pick up from the backstreets near the hospital.

Charlie seemed to come awake rapidly and found Blake's predicament hilarious after ascertaining everyone was okay. 'What is it about you that makes people want to shoot you? I swear to God, only you, brother dearest, could land yourself in such a situation.'

'Oh, it gets worse,' Blake informed his brother as he filled him in on the facts that had resulted in him cohabiting with one of the world's most beautiful women.

'Okay, let me get this straight. *She's* giving *you,* giving Joanna, a million quid to sleep at *yours* for the night.'

Blake shrugged. 'Essentially.' Charlie laughed and Blake frowned, suddenly angry with the world. 'What's so bloody funny?'

'Sounds like a movie an old girlfriend dragged me to once a lo-o-ong time ago. That one with Robert Redford and Demi Moore.'

Blake rolled his eyes. 'She's not asking for sexual favours, you depraved bastard. She's *scared*. She just needs to feel safe for the night. To hide away for a bit.'

'So you're not going to end up in bed together?'

The vehement denial was on Blake's lips before he was even conscious of it. 'I wouldn't sleep with her if we were the only two people left on earth.'

Blake could feel his brother's eyebrow rise without having to see it. 'Why not? I would and I've been happily married for a decade.'

Blake knew his brother would no sooner sleep with Ava Kelly than he would. He was as besotted with Trudy now as he had been ten years ago. 'Sure you would.'

'Okay,' his brother conceded. 'Hypothetically. You gotta admit, she looks pretty fine in a bikini.'

'She's a snooty, heinous prima donna who caused us endless trouble with all her first-world crap,' Blake said, lowering his voice. 'I don't care how good she looks in a bikini.'

'Maybe you should.' Suddenly Charlie's voice was dead serious. 'It's okay to let yourself go every now and then, Blake. Being beautiful and rich and opinionated isn't a crime. That's our demographic, don't forget.'

Blake shifted uncomfortably in his seat. He'd seen so much poverty and desperation in his ten years serving his country. It felt as if he was selling out to admit his attraction to a woman who represented everything frivolous and shiny in a society that didn't have a clue how the other half lived. But he was too tired to get into all of that now.

'She's here for one night and, in case you've forgotten, she's a client.'

His brother snorted. 'Not any more, she's not. Which makes it perfectly okay to…take one for the team, so to speak. How long has it been since you got laid?'

Blake shook his head, not even willing to go there. Just because he chose *not* to spend every night with a willing woman didn't mean he was about to die from massive sperm build-up as his brother predicted. He worked hard every day and came home every night to a place that he'd created that was far removed from the hell he'd known in foreign countries.

That meant something these days. More than some cheap sexual thrill.

Besides, Ava Kelly was so off-limits she might as well be sitting on the moon. If he wanted to get laid, he could get laid. He didn't need to do it with a woman who'd bugged him almost from the first day of their acquaintance.

No matter what vibe he suspected ran between them.

'Is Trudy awake?' Blake tisked. 'You know, your raging feminist wife who I happen to like much more than you? She'd be disgusted by your attitude.'

'She thinks you need to find a woman too. One who can tie you in knots and leave you panting for more.'

Blake didn't say anything for a long time. 'She's in *trouble*, Charlie,' he said as he contemplated the neck of his beer. 'She just needs to feel safe.'

Charlie was silent for long moments too. 'Then just as well she chose one of Her Majesty's best.'

'No,' Blake said. 'I'm just a builder, remember? *And* I'm on holiday. If she didn't come with a million-dollar price-tag attached I'd have walked away.'

Charlie laughed and Blake felt his irritation crank up another notch. 'Whatever helps you get through the night with Ava *freaking* Kelly in the next room.'

Blake snorted at the undiluted smugness in his brother's voice. 'I hate you.'

'Uh-huh. Ring me in the morning before you set out. I want details.'

Blake grimaced. 'Right, that's it, I'm telling Trudy, you grubby bastard.'

Charlie laughed. 'Are you kidding? She's going to want to know every minute detail. She has a huge girl crush on Ava Kelly.'

Blake sighed, briefly envying his brother's easy, loving relationship. 'Maybe she can come here for the night and they can play house together.'

Charlie laughed. 'Only if I can watch.'

Blake shook his head. 'Goodnight.'

'Night,' Charlie said and Blake could hear the laughter in his voice. 'Don't do anything I wouldn't do.'

Blake hung up the phone, not bothering to answer. There was no risk of that. He was tired. *And* annoyed. He wanted this night over and done with. He wanted her gone.

He did not want to *do* anything with Ava Kelly.

Blake lifted the bottle to his mouth and threw his head back, drinking the last mouthfuls in one guzzle. He contemplated getting another one but the shower spray cut out, spurring him into action.

He needed to change the sheets on the bed. And he needed to be out of his bedroom before she was done.

Five minutes later he'd just pulled the coverlet up over the fresh sheets and was reaching for a pillow to change the case when he sensed Ava watching him. He glanced behind him where she leaned heavily against the doorway as if it was the only thing keeping her up.

'You don't have to give me your bed,' she said, the world's weariest smile touching the corners of her mouth. 'Really. Any horizontal surface will be fine.'

He'd loaned her an old shirt and some loose cotton boxers and his clothes had never looked so good. The shirt slipped off one shoulder, outlined her small perky breasts and fell to just below her waist. The band of his obviously too big boxers was drawn by the string to its limits then turned over a couple of times, anchoring low on her hips. A strip of flat tanned belly was bare to his gaze.

And a lot of leg.

Not chicken legs like those he sometimes caught on the telly when shots of skinny models walking up and down catwalks came on the news. They were lithe and shapely. And a perfect golden brown—like the rest of her. He'd avoided looking at them the last three months but it was kind of difficult now they were standing inside his bedroom.

And he'd always been a leg man.

Oh, the irony.

He dragged his gaze up. Her hair was damp and looked as if it had been finger-combed back off her forehead, her face was scrubbed clean, her freckles standing out, her cheeks a little pink from the hot water, the tiny nick a stark reminder of why she was here.

She could have been the girl next door except somehow, even in a scruffy T-shirt, baggy boxers and her eyelids fluttering in long sleepy blinks, she managed to look haughty.

To exude a you-can't-touch-this air.

Should have had that second beer.

'How's the head?' he asked, ignoring her protest, returning his mind and his eyes to the job at hand, stripping the case off the pillow.

'Sore,' Ava said, pushing off the door frame to the opposite side of the bed, grabbing the other pillow and stripping it, managing it quite well despite the handicap of her bandaged hand.

Blake quelled the urge to tell her to leave it. He didn't want her here in his bedroom. Not while he was in it too. It all seemed too domesticated—*too normal*—especially after being shot at only a few hours ago. The bed was big and empty. Big enough for the two of them. And the night had been bizarre enough without him wondering how many times he could roll Ava Kelly over on it.

Or how good those legs would feel wrapped around his waist.

'Did you take those tablets the doc gave you?'

She nodded. 'Just now.' Then she yawned and the shirt rode up a little more. He kept his gaze firmly trained on her face. 'Sorry. I'm so tired I can barely keep my eyes open.'

Blake knew intimately how shock and the effects of adrenaline could leave you sapped to the bone. He threw the pillow on the bed, then peeled back the covers. 'Get in. Go to sleep.' *Soon it will be morning and you'll be gone.* 'You'll feel better tomorrow.'

She smiled at him again as she threw her pillow on the bed. 'I couldn't feel any worse,' she said, crawling onto the bed, making her way to the middle on her hands and knees. Blake did not check out how his shirt fell forward revealing a view right down to her navel.

He just pulled up the covers as Ava collapsed on her side, her sore hand tucked under her cheek, eyes closing on a blissful sigh, her bow mouth finally relaxing. 'Night,' he said.

She didn't answer and for a moment he was struck by

how young she looked. For the first time she didn't look haughty and untouchable—she looked humble and exhausted.

Vulnerable.

And utterly touchable.

Who in the hell would want to kill her? Or had they just been trying to scare her? In which case it had worked brilliantly. Something stirred in his chest but he didn't stay long enough to analyse it.

Ava *freaking* Kelly was lying right smack in the middle of his bed—no way was he sticking around to fathom weird chest stirrings. Or give his traitorous body any ideas.

He stalked towards the door, an image of her long legs keeping him company.

Don't look back. Don't look back.

'Blake.'

Crap. He halted as her soft voice drifted towards him. *Don't look back. Don't look back.*

'Thank you,' she said, her voice low and drowsy.

Blake locked tight every muscle he owned to stop from turning around. He didn't need a vision of her looking at him with sleepy eyes from his bed. Instead he nodded and said, 'See you in the morning.'

Then continued on his way out of the room.

He did not look back.

CHAPTER FOUR

AVA'S PHONE WOKE her the next morning and for a moment she was utterly confused by her surroundings. What was the time? What day was it? Where the hell was she?

Where the hell was her phone, for that matter?

Her head felt fuzzy and her eyes felt as if they'd been rolled in shell grit. If this was a hangover then it was a doozy. The distant trilling of her musical ringtone didn't help. Inside her woolly head, her brain knew that it needed answering but her body didn't seem to be responding to the command to do something about it.

Then a shirtless Blake walked into the room and it all came crashing back to her. The gunshots, the police, the hospital.

Little Venice. Canal boat. Big, big bed.

His hair was damp as if he'd just had a shower, she noted absently as he strode towards her. And he had a hairy chest. Not gorilla hairy, just a fine dusting of light brown hair over meaty pecs and continuing down his middle covering a belly that wasn't ripped but was still, nonetheless, firm and solid. The kind of belly a man didn't get from the gym.

She stared at his chest as it came closer. The men in the circles she moved in were *all* ripped and smooth—every muscle defined, all hair plucked or waxed into submission. It took a lot of upkeep. Whereas Blake didn't look as if he'd ever seen the inside of a salon.

She'd bet her last penny Blake was the kind of guy who thought grooming belonged in the domain of people who owned horses.

'Yours, I believe,' he said, striding towards her and passing it over.

Ava took it with her good hand, ignoring its ringing for a moment. 'What time is it?' she asked.

'Time to go.' His voice was low and serious—brooking no argument. 'I'll make you a coffee.'

And then he turned on his heel and left her staring after him. *Obviously not a morning person.*

Ten minutes later, with Detective Sergeant Biddle's caution weighing on her mind, Ava followed her nose and her growling stomach in the direction of the wild earthy aroma of freshly ground coffee beans. With nothing as basic as a mirror in his room she'd pulled her messy bed-hair back into an equally messy ponytail and hoped Blake didn't have any wild expectations of what a supermodel should look like first thing in the morning.

She needn't have worried—he barely acknowledged her, instead enquiring how she drank her coffee, then handing her a mug. 'Thank you,' she said automatically, wrapping her bandaged hand around it even though the morning already held the hint of another warm day.

He didn't acknowledge that either so she wandered over to one of the two cosy-looking, dark-leather armchairs and sank into its glorious depths. She watched his back as he stared out of the large rectangular picture window above the sink in the kitchen area.

She could just make out the bustle of London traffic over his shoulder—could just hear it too. The sights and the sounds of the city gearing up for another work day. She soaked it in for a moment, preferring the low hum to the ever-expanding quiet inside the boat.

Her gaze fell to his broad shoulders.

She'd never really speculated about what lay beneath

his clothes before—she'd been too busy wondering why he seemed completely immune to her. *Off the market? Playing hard to get? Gay?* But there'd been something about his naked, work-honed chest this morning that was more than a little fascinating.

With his back stubbornly turned, Ava had no choice but to look around her. She sat forward as she did, inspecting the luxurious interior. It was nothing like the old cheap and cheerful clunker she'd been on as a teenager with a friend's family—wider too if her memory served her correctly.

Everything about the interior screamed class. High quality.

Money.

The three stairs down which she'd trudged last night as she'd entered the boat opened into a very large, open-plan saloon dominated by two classy leather armchairs and gorgeous wide floorboards. It was the floors that drew her eye now—a gorgeous blonde wood polished to a honey sheen. In contrast the walls were dark-grain wood panelling until halfway up, then painted an elegant shade of champagne.

A massive flat-screen television sat in a narrow , built-in smoky glass and curved chrome cabinet on the wall opposite her along with a bunch of other expensive-looking gadgetry. On the other side of it, and sitting out from the wall slightly, was an old-fashioned pot-belly stove that no doubt heated the entire boat in winter.

The saloon flowed into a galley-style kitchen, all granite and chrome with no expense spared on the high-end appliances from the full-sized fridge to the expensive Italian coffee machine. They gleamed in all their pristine glamour.

Opposite the kitchen, on her side of the boat, was a booth-style table, with red leather bench seats.

Beyond the dining and kitchen area was a smaller saloon. A dark-leather sofa, looking well worn and comfy, dominated the space. A pillow and some bedding were folded at one end, reminding Ava that Blake had given up his bed for her last night.

Another coffee table with a massive laptop and piles of paper appeared to act as a work space. At right angles to the couch, on the wall that divided off the living area from the rest of the boat, stood a chunky wooden bar. The bottom boasted ten, mostly full, rows of wine and above that was a shelf crammed full of every alcoholic spirit known to man.

Beyond the wall she knew was the bathroom, and beyond that his bedroom. What was beyond that, she didn't know. The back of the boat, she guessed. What was that called? The stern?

Ava dragged her wandering mind back to the interior. All the dark leather, chrome and granite gave it such a masculine feel, like a den or a cave, yet the use of blonde wood and large windows gave it light and space. It was hard to believe that such a small area could feel so big.

Blake had done a fantastic job.

For she had absolutely no doubt that Blake had been responsible for the gorgeous interior—it had his signature all over it. She only had to look at the nearby coffee table to know that. It had been constructed out of a thick slab of dark timber complete with knots. It reminded her of the craftsmanship of her kitchen bench and she placed her coffee mug on it, then ran the flats of her palms across the polished surface.

It was absolutely stunning. She couldn't not touch it.

She glanced up at Blake—still contemplating the London traffic. Clearly he wasn't going to make conversation.

'I'm sorry I barely noticed the boat last night. It's… gorgeous.'

Blake should have known it was too much for her to just drink her coffee and let him call her a cab. He hadn't slept very well last night, which had done nothing for his mood. He took a calming breath and turned round to face her.

She was sitting in the lounge chair cross-legged. His

shirt was still falling off one shoulder and acres of golden leg were on display.

She really needed to go.

Ignoring Ava's considerable charms when she'd been a picky, exacting client had been easy enough. Ignoring them when she was a damsel in distress and in the confines of his boat—not so easy.

'Thank you,' he said.

Ava waited for him to elaborate some more but nothing was forthcoming. 'I'm assuming it's all your own work?' she prodded.

Blake nodded. 'Yes.'

'Hobby, passion or business?'

Blake wondered if she'd shut up if he told her the truth. 'Therapy.'

Ava blinked. That she hadn't expected. She wanted to know more but, as Blake checked his watch, she doubted he was a man who elaborated. 'Is it a narrow boat? I went on one when I was thirteen. It seems wider than what I remember?'

Blake stifled a sigh. 'It's a wide beam,' he said. 'It's twelve foot across. Most narrow boats are about half that.'

'Yes…I remember there wasn't a lot of space…a wide beam seems like a much more liveable option?'

He shrugged and her eyes tracked the movement of his very nice broad shoulders. He'd tucked her head right in under them last night and they'd felt so solid around her— as if they really could stop bullets. She could still remember how safe she'd felt under their protection.

'It depends what you want. Wide beams can restrict your travel options. Not all canals are made for wider boats.'

Ava was about to ask more but Blake drained the rest of his coffee, placed the mug on the sink, then turned to her and said, 'You done?'

Ava, whose mug was almost empty, understood the implied message. *Time to go.* Her night was up. She too drained the contents of her drink, then held the mug out towards him. 'That was delicious. Do you think I could possibly have another? I'm not really a morning person. Coffee helps.'

Blake contemplated telling her no. Something he doubted Ava Kelly had ever heard. But his innate manners won out. He strode towards her and took the mug, turning away from her and her temptingly bare shoulder instantly. He set about making her another cup, conscious of her gaze on his back the entire time.

It unsettled him. *Blake didn't like being unsettled.*

'That was Ken Biddle on the phone.'

Blake, who had been trying to tune her out, turned at the news. 'They got him?' he asked hopefully.

'No.' She shook her head and the ponytail swung perkily.

Blake had a thing for ponytails.

'But they have some promising leads,' she said. 'They're confident they're closing in.'

'That's good, then,' Blake said, turning back to the coffee machine, away from ponytails.

'He thinks I'll only need to lie low for a few more days.'

A presentiment of doom settled around him at the casual note in her voice. 'What are your plans?' he asked, stirring in her three sugars.

Ava watched as Blake's shoulders straightened a little more. She took a calming breath. The second Ken had asked her to keep her head down for a little longer there'd only been one option for her. 'Well, actually...I was hoping I could...stay here.'

Blake dropped the teaspoon and it clattered against the stainless-steel sink. *No. Freaking. Way.* He turned slowly around, careful to couch his distaste at the idea in neutrality. 'But I'm going on holiday,' he said, determined to be firm but reasonable.

'Exactly,' Ava nodded. 'That's why it's perfect—don't

you see? I could boat sit for you, at least until they find the person who shot up my home anyway. I can be anonymous here—certainly no one's going to be looking for me on the Regent's Canal and it'll look like someone's still home here, for a little while anyway. It's win-win.'

'The boat *is* my holiday,' he said, trying to stay calm in the face of her barefaced cheek. 'I'm going up the Kennet and Avon to Bath, giving the boat her first decent run since I finished the fit-out.'

Ava was only temporarily discouraged as the appeal of spending some time afloat, traversing the English countryside on Blake's gorgeous boat, took hold.

If she had to lie low, she might as well do it in style, right?

'Even more perfect. I can come with you.'

This time Blake didn't even bother to act as he stared at her as if she'd lost her mind. Had she seriously just invited herself along on his holiday? 'No.'

'Oh, come on, Blake, please?' Ava climbed out of the chair, feeling at a distinct disadvantage with him glowering down at her. 'It'll just be for a few days and you won't even know I'm here, I promise.'

Blake folded his arms as she neared. He hadn't believed that statement last night and, after a horrible sleep on his couch, he believed it even less this morning. 'No.'

'Look, I'll pull my weight. Seriously, I can help with locks and things. They're much easier with an extra set of hands. And I can…I can cook,' she said, desperately hoping that the way to this man's heart—or his empathy at least—was through his stomach. 'I am an *excellent* cook.' She marched over to his fridge. 'I can keep you well fed,' she said as she opened it, 'while you—'

Ava blinked. The fridge was bare save for a mauled six-pack of beer and a carton of milk.

'Good luck with that,' he said dryly.

Ava turned to face him as the door closed. 'You have no food?'

'I'm expecting a delivery in the next hour or so. It'll stock me up for the trip.'

'Yes, but…what do you normally eat?'

Blake shrugged. 'I have coffee. And there's plenty of places to eat on the riverside.'

Ava shook her head. Oh, man, he was going to want to marry her after a few days of her cooking. 'In that case,' she tisked, 'you definitely need me along for the ride.'

Blake could not believe what he was hearing. 'So, Ava Kelly supermodel, darling of the paparazzi, is going to be content to act like some anonymous little hausfrau-cum-first-mate, cooking and cleaning and being a general dogsbody?'

Blake refused to think what other services she might be able to render.

Ava folded her arms too. 'I think I could manage it for a few days.' She wasn't going to be swayed by his taunts. She'd been called worse things and had worked incredibly hard since she was fourteen. Getting away with him for a few days was the perfect solution.

'Reggie won't like it,' Blake warned.

She gave him one of her haughty, down-the-nose looks. 'You leave Reggie to me.'

Blake rubbed a hand through his hair at her persistence. Just his luck to be saddled with a woman who wasn't used to hearing no. 'Look,' he said, changing tack. 'You want to lie low on a canal boat for a few days? I think that's a great idea. Knock yourself out. There's plenty along here for hire.'

Ava was starting to get ticked off. People didn't usually argue with her so much. They were generally falling over themselves to agree with her. But not Blake. Oh, no.

And she didn't understand why. She knew, in the way that women did, that he found her attractive. And it hadn't been in the way he checked her out, rather in the way he'd *avoided* checking her out. Which was just as telling.

And, *when she hadn't been miffed by it*, she'd admired him for it.

He'd been the consummate professional and that had been a nice change. A man talking to her as if she had a brain and an opinion that mattered and who dealt with all her little niggles and foibles with patience and efficiency was a rare find. He hadn't been condescending. He hadn't humoured her. He'd been straight up. Yes or no or I'll get back to you.

But, sheesh, would it seriously be that repugnant to spend a few days in her company?

'Yes, but *you're* on *this* boat,' she said. Ava walked slowly towards him. She had to make him understand just how last night had shaken her. 'I feel safe with you, Blake.' She pulled up in front of him, standing close enough to reach out and touch him, far enough away not to freak him out. 'If this guy…this person…does happen to find me… if he tried to harm me…or snatch me…'

Ava shuddered just thinking about it. She didn't like knowing there was someone out there who wanted to hurt her. And she was more than happy to lie low until they were caught.

'Don't get me wrong, I wouldn't go down without a fight. I'd kick and scream like a madwoman. But a little extra protection never goes astray, right?'

Blake gaped at the fairy dust she was snorting. *The woman didn't have a clue.* 'Are you crazy? I only have *one* leg. If he *snatches* you, I'm going to be next to useless. My days of running fast are long gone.'

Ava blinked at him and looked at his legs. She'd noticed him limping occasionally but had just figured he'd injured himself somehow. 'You…do?'

'You didn't *know*?' He lifted the jeans on his left leg to

reveal the titanium skeleton of his artificial limb. 'Why do you think I limp?' he demanded.

She looked at it askance, as if it were some unsightly blemish. He supposed someone who made a living out of defining physical beauty would be uncomfortable when confronted with physical imperfection. And then she looked at him with something akin to pity in her eyes and ice froze in his veins.

'Not so pretty, huh?' he taunted as he let the fabric drop back down.

Ava felt awful. She hadn't realised. Her cheeks pinked up—he must think her terribly self-involved. Not only had he pulled her to the ground last night, but he'd also given up his bed for her. Both actions completely without regard for his own safety or needs.

'How'd it happen?' she asked, searching his face.

'It doesn't matter,' he growled.

It *mattered* to her. 'Did it happen when you were deployed?'

Blake glared at her for a moment before answering. 'Yes.'

Ava didn't know what to say without sounding trite or macabre. She settled for, 'I'm sorry,' but even that sounded inadequate. 'I had no idea.'

Blake dismissed her apology with an annoyed wave of his hand. 'It's not your fault,' he said.

'That doesn't mean I can't be sorry it happened.'

Blake was taken aback by the quiet conviction in her voice. So many people said sorry as if it was the standard platitude expected of them. Ava sounded as if she really meant it. 'Thank you,' he said. 'But clearly, I'm not the type of protection you need.'

Ava frowned. 'Are you kidding? You're a war hero.'

He snorted. 'I'm not a hero.' He was so sick of the way that was bandied around. 'I was just in the wrong place at the wrong time.'

'You get blown up and live to tell the tale? That's pretty heroic if you ask me.'

'Nah. That just makes me lucky.' *Unlike his brother-in-law.*

Ava didn't believe that for a moment. She couldn't even begin to imagine the resilience it must have taken to recover from something so life-altering. 'Well, it'll do me,' she said.

Blake was just about over her stubborn insistence. Time to stop being Mr Nice Guy. 'No,' he said, turning away from her to stare out of the window above the sink. *Case closed.*

Ava was even more convinced now that Blake Walker was her man. But how did she get through to him when his resistance seemed impenetrable? She stared at the set of his shoulders casting around for something…anything.

In desperation an idea came to her and she threw it down like the last card she knew it was. 'I noticed yesterday when I was researching your sister's charity that they don't have a high-profile patron?'

His back stiffened noticeably and Ava felt a moment of triumph. Ah, *that* got his attention. *Joanna.* He'd reacted the same way yesterday when she'd asked who Joanna was.

His *sister* was the chink in Blake's armour.

Blake turned around slowly and glared at her and she was even more convinced.

'So?' he said, his voice dropping dangerously low.

She shrugged. 'Every successful charity needs a patron. A big name. Take me with you until the police give me the all-clear and I'll do it. I'll become their patron. I'll attend every event and fund-raiser, I'll represent their interests, speak on their behalf, I'll work tirelessly.'

Blake was once again left speechless by Ava's impulsive offer. Joanna would be over the moon to have a woman of Ava's stature on board. 'Let me get this straight,' he clarified. 'For a few nights on *this* boat you're going to not only give a million pounds to my sister's charity but commit to being its patron?'

Ava nodded. 'Yes.'

Blake shook his head incredulously. 'Why? If you're really concerned about your safety, it'd be much cheaper and a lot less work for you to hire a professional bodyguard.'

'I'm not afraid of hard work, particularly in the name of a good cause,' she said, stepping in a little closer to him, to try and convey how strongly she felt. 'And I can afford it. As for the professional, I don't need one. I just need to lie low. But I also need to feel safe while I'm doing it and *you,* as we've already established, make me feel safe. I can't put a price on that.'

Blake still couldn't wrap his head around it all. 'I think you have more money than brains.'

Ava smiled at him then as she sensed him weakening. 'Please, Blake. If not for me, then do it for Joanna.'

Blake shook his head at her as soft lips curved up in perfect unison, nothing haughty about them now. Clearly she thought she had him all figured out. And certainly she'd found his soft underbelly. She'd made him an offer he couldn't refuse—and she knew it.

But if she thought she could just crook her finger at him and he'd come running, then she could think again. 'Does anyone ever say no to you, Ava?'

Ava let herself smile a little bigger. Was that resignation? 'I do believe you've said no to me several times this morning already.'

CHAPTER FIVE

BLAKE OPENED HIS mouth to tell her *no* one more time—Joanna or no Joanna—but her phone interrupted them and she turned away, heading back to the lounge chair where she'd left it.

'Crap,' she muttered as she recognised her mother's number on the screen. She did not want to have to deal with her now but, she knew from experience, her mother was best kept on a tight leash. 'I'm sorry, it's my mother,' she apologised to Blake.

Blake gestured with his hands for her to take it then turned back to the sink and his contemplation of London to give them some privacy. Except that was kind of hard in the confines of the boat with her standing just a couple of metres away.

To say Ava sounded strained was an understatement. Even with his back to her he could pick up the tension laced through her words. He hadn't realised how much he'd learned about the subtleties of her voice in three months, which was surprising considering Ava's mother seemed to be doing most of the talking.

He didn't hear Ava say once she was okay or retell the events of last night so from that he had to assume her mother hadn't asked. Ava seemed to be asking her not to do something, her request becoming less and less polite.

Then he heard, 'I'm with…a friend.' And, 'I can't say.'

Then finally, 'I'll fill you in when I get back—just don't give any interviews in the meantime.'

Her mother was going to the press?

There didn't even seem to be a goodbye; he just heard Ava's phone clatter onto the dining table.

When he turned around she was staring out of the window currently flooding in sunlight, her back erect, her messy ponytail even now begging him to pull it out.

'You okay?' he asked.

She turned around slowly and the look on her face was in stark contrast to her self-assurance just prior to the phone call. She looked a lot like she had last night—vulnerable.

'I'm fine,' she dismissed, her voice weary. She lifted a hand and absently rubbed the muscles in her neck. The action caused all sorts of interesting movement inside her shirt. *His* shirt.

Blake kept his gaze firmly trained on her face—he was used to doing that. 'You know, you could have told your mother where you were.'

Ava gave a soft snort. 'Ah…no. She's the last person I would tell.'

Hmm. *Interesting.* 'I take it you two don't get along?'

'You could say that,' Ava said dryly.

'Doesn't she approve of you being a model?'

Ava gave a harsh laugh. 'Oh, no, she approves, all right. She's one of the original pageant queens. The same old story, never quite made it herself so lived out her glory through me. Put me in my first baby competition when I was a month old.'

Blake blinked at the bitterness in her tone. 'Let me guess—you won?'

Ava smiled despite the slight derision in his voice. 'I won every one I ever entered until I was two and my father put his foot down and insisted that I have a *normal* life.'

'But you got back into it later?'

'After Dad died, we were in a lot of debt. Mum worked

really hard doing two jobs to keep the house payments going and then I won a nationwide search for the newest young model and…'

Blake nodded. 'You hit the big time.'

'Yes.'

He frowned. 'So…you two disagreed about the direction of your career?'

'No. Mum hired an agent for me. An old school friend of hers…Paul. He managed every aspect of my career, for those first three years. My jobs, my money, my image. I depended on him for everything—it was him, me and Mum against the world.'

Blake still wasn't sure what the issue was. 'That's… bad?'

'It is when he's embezzling your money behind your back and sleeping with your mother, screwing with her head so even when his treachery was discovered she stood by him, defending him in court, imploring me to give him a second chance, then leaving the country with him *and my money*, marrying him and leaving me, at seventeen, to fend for myself.'

A cold fist pushed up under Blake's diaphragm and he took two steps towards her. How could a mother abandon her teenage daughter like that? 'She chose him over you?'

Ava's lips twisted. It had been a long time since she'd let herself revisit how betrayed, how vulnerable, she'd felt. Dwelling on the past wasn't her thing. But it *had* been a most unusual twelve hours.

'Yes. She did. "You're going to be all right, darling," she said. "You're young and beautiful with contracts lined up out the door thanks to Paul," she said. "I need to be loved too," she said.'

Blake rocked his head from side to side as tension crept into his traps. He finally understood what Ava had meant last night when she'd said she'd learned early not to trust.

She'd been betrayed by two people closest to her—no wonder she was a control freak.

'What happened?'

'They were divorced four years later. Mum came home trying to ingratiate herself but I'd already hired Reggie, who taught me three very important things—trust nobody, *always* control your own money and your agent is *not* your friend.'

Blake made a mental note to apologise to Reggie if they ever met again. He'd obviously armed Ava well in the years since her betrayal. *Maybe a little too well.*

It was a difficult concept for him to wrap his head around. Blake's family were big and loud and intrusive and totally in each other's business and that had been hard to take when all he'd wanted to do was hide away and lick his wounds.

But he'd *never* doubted for a minute that they had his back.

'Our relationship is…strained,' Ava said, her hand dropping from her neck.

'I'm sorry,' he said. 'You should be able to trust family.'

Ava couldn't agree more but sadly, for some people, that wasn't possible. 'Don't be sorry,' she said. 'Just take me with you.'

She sounded so utterly defeated and Blake knew there was no way he could deny her when clearly, despite being surrounded by people, she was pretty much alone in the world. She didn't even have family to lean on, for crying out loud. Her father dead. Her mother abandoning her in favour of her agent.

Her d*on't screw with me* act was just that—an act.

She needed someone she could trust and it looked as if it was going to be him.

A decision that would no doubt come back and bite him hard on the arse.

'Patron, huh?'

It took a second for the meaning of Blake's words to sink in. A spark of hope spluttered to life inside Ava's chest. 'Is that…a yes?'

Blake nodded, her caution so uncharacteristic it only added to his conviction. 'That's a yes.'

Ava felt a rush of relief flow through her veins so hot and hard it was dizzying. She smiled as tension leached from her muscles. Then suddenly, feeling light, feeling that everything was going to be all right, she laughed. Then she gave into temptation, crossing the short distance between them and throwing herself against his chest, her arms around his neck.

'Thank you, thank you,' she said, hugging him hard.

Blake sucked in a breath as the full length of her pressed into the full length of him and he liked how she fitted perfectly. Her ponytail swung a little in his direct vision and he wasn't sure he could survive a few days with it screaming *pull me out, pull me out.*

He shut his eyes. *Safe haven, man.* You're her safe haven.

'Okay, okay. No touchy-feely stuff,' he said, prising her off him, setting her back, but then somewhere out on the street a loud bang cracked the air and she practically leapt back into his arms.

Blake's hands automatically slid onto her waist. 'Hey, it's okay,' he said after a moment or two, the frantic beat of her heart thudding against the wall of his chest as her hands clasped his T-shirt. 'It's just a car backfiring.'

Ava barely heard him over the whoosh of her pulse through her ears but she understood from his non-verbals-his calm, solid presence-that there was no imminent threat. 'Sorry.' She grimaced as she pulled away shakily. 'I'm going to be jumpy for a while.'

Her freckles were standing out again amidst the sudden pallor of her face, the tiny graze on her cheek looking more macabre as Blake's hands slid to her elbows. 'It's fine,' he said, squeezing her gently.

'Thank you,' she murmured, her voice thready.

Blake nodded, his gaze drifting to her mouth before pulling back again. *Not going there.* He took two steps away, putting some distance between them.

'I have conditions,' he said.

It took Ava a few seconds to shake the feeling that the boat had rocked beneath her. And as her mouth tingled she knew it wasn't just from the fright. She cleared her throat.

'Conditions?'

Blake nodded. 'Yes. Two.'

Ava regarded him steadily for a moment. 'Okay then, let's hear them.'

He held up one finger. 'No one knows our location. Not Reggie. Not your PA. Not any of your gal pals. You're supposed to be totally incognito and I'm supposed to be having a peaceful holiday. I don't want it turned into a three-ring circus when someone lets it leak to the paparazzi.'

Ava nodded. She was happy with that—she didn't want her location broadcast either, which was why she hadn't told her mother. 'Fine. I'll let Reggie know we're going away for a few days and—'

'No,' Blake interrupted. 'He knows how to get hold of you. He doesn't need to know you're leaving town.'

'I suppose not.' Ava frowned at him; his indigo eyes were shuttered. 'You don't like him much, do you?'

Blake gave a dismissive shrug of his shoulders. He liked him a lot better now he knew some more about the man. 'The question is do I trust him? And I don't.'

Anyone who was willing to put Ava's career ahead of her protection didn't have her best interests at heart as far as he was concerned. It might make him a great agent but it didn't say a lot for him as a human being.

Ava gave Blake a half-smile. She knew that Reggie came across as utterly money-grubbing but that was why she'd hired him. Her career was the most important thing to

Reggie and he was *exactly* who she'd needed in her corner after sleazoid Paul.

Reggie was all about the business. 'He's the only person I *do* trust.'

In this industry where she trusted no one—she put her faith in Reggie's instincts and his ball-breaking rep. He wouldn't rat her out because he took his client confidentiality seriously—it was his calling card.

Blake thought it was sad that the only person Ava trusted had perpetuated her mistrust of others. 'Well, let's agree to differ on that one,' Blake said.

Ava allowed her smile to become full blown. 'I have a feeling that's going to happen a bit,' she murmured.

Blake grunted. *So did he.* Her smile reached out between them, making her mouth even more appealing, and for a moment he forgot that she'd bribed her way into his life—into his much coveted peaceful holiday. When she looked down her nose at him all haughty it was easy to remember that she was a spoiled prima donna who liked getting her way.

But when she smiled at him like a woman smiling at a man, things got a little hazy.

'Two,' he continued, dragging his mind off her mouth and taking another step back for good measure. 'You have to be in some kind of disguise. There's no point in you coming with me to lie low when you look like—'

Blake paused as his gaze skittered down her body and back up again. His boxers and T-shirt did nothing to disguise her body. Not with her bare shoulder, her hair swinging in a ponytail and legs that went on for ever.

He waved his hand in her general direction. 'That.'

A few months ago Ava would have been insulted at the brief survey of her body and his apparent dismissal. But she knew him well enough now to know that he was just too disciplined to give too much away.

She guessed that was the soldier in him.

She looked down at her body, smoothing her hands down the front to the exposed slice of her belly, which, thanks to a hundred crunches a day and regular visits to the tanning salon, she knew to be flat and toned and tanned and pretty irresistible to most people with a y chromosome and a pulse.

'Like what?' she enquired, looking at him innocently.

Blake gritted his teeth, not fooled by her little performance one iota. 'Like Ava *freaking* Kelly,' he said.

She quirked an eyebrow. 'Should I shave my head?'

Blake gave her a sardonic smile. 'I don't think we need to go quite that extreme. Would hate to incur the wrath of Reggie any more than I have. But maybe a wig? Or definitely hats, something to tuck your hair into. And big dark sunglasses.'

His gaze drifted to those legs again. 'And baggy clothes. No itty-bitty shorts and tiny little T-shirts. *No* red bikinis.' For his own sanity if nothing else. 'No make-up. Nothing that draws attention to you.'

Although he had the feeling she could be wearing a sack and men would still look.

'I don't want some yobo at a pub along the canal recognising you and deciding he can make a quid or two ratting you out to the media. Plain is what we're after,' he said. 'Baggy, too big, shapeless—they are your friends.'

Ava blinked. None of those things had *ever* been her friends. Camouflage wasn't what she did. She spent all her working hours flaunting and flattering her body. 'Well, *gee whiz*, that sounds like fun,' she said, her voice heavy with derision.

But still, she could see his point. People had made a lot of money out of her in the past by tipping off the press. And with the furore that was bound to have been whipped up by last night's incident and her going underground— she'd have a pretty price on her head.

And she couldn't help but wonder what it would be like

to be utterly anonymous, even for a short while. *Not* famous for a few days? She'd been on magazine covers and in the public eye since she was fourteen years old and sometimes she was just so tired of the constant attention and scrutiny.

'They're my conditions.' Blake shrugged. 'Take it or leave it.'

'Take it.' She nodded. She could put up with any fashion sin for a few days. 'Not exactly clothes I have in my closet though.'

Blake shook his head. 'Too unsafe to go there, anyway.' He strode over to the dining table where his mobile was on charge, pleased to be out of range of her in his clothes. 'I'll ring Joanna,' he said. 'We can break the news to her about her windfall, then you can tell her what you need and she can buy it for you then bring it here.'

Ava blinked. 'I can't expect your sister to just drop everything and go clothes shopping for me.'

'Trust me—' he grimaced as the dialling tone sounded in his ear '—when she learns about your generosity, she's going to want to have your babies.'

Finally, almost three hours later, they were under way. The groceries had been delivered and put away. So had the second lot that Ava had ordered when she'd realised how basic the first lot were. And an excitable, starry-eyed Joanna had come and gone. The only people who knew that Ava Kelly was on the boat with Blake were Joanna and Charlie.

And Blake trusted them with his life.

God knew between the two of them they'd practically brought him back from the brink with sheer will power alone. All those days and nights when life hadn't seemed worth living, they'd been there getting him through. Loving him, fighting with him, crying with him, getting drunk with him. Whatever it had taken, they'd done it.

It was slow going through the busy London canal system as he headed west along the Paddington arm of the Grand

Union Canal. Tourists were out enjoying the narrow-boat lifestyle either through private hire or with the many companies that ran canal transport services. The weather was glorious—the sky blue and cloudless, the sun warm, a light breeze ruffling his shirt—and had it not been for his unwanted passenger, it would have been perfect.

Although, to be fair, Ava was exceedingly easy company—so far anyway. Dressed in a pair of baggy shorts that came past her knees and a loose T-shirt with her hair tucked into a cap and dark, saucer-like sunglasses completely obscuring her eyes, she looked like any other tourist standing at the helm. Watching the world go by as she soaked up some rays and intermittently answering half a dozen calls, all from Reggie.

Sure, if someone looked hard enough they'd be able to make out the slenderness of her legs, the erect, model-like way she held herself, the superb bone structure of her heart-shaped face. But at a quick glance she looked as far removed from a supermodel as was possible and no one gawked at her, nudged each other and whispered or pointed their fingers.

She was just another one of them.

Mission: Disguise Ava Kelly, accomplished.

But what surprised him was how much she didn't seem to care. Having braved a rabble of paparazzi most mornings for three months, who she kept sweet with the occasional gourmet snacks and frequent photo opportunities, he'd have thought she'd be missing the limelight already. But she seemed content to rub shoulders with him and make occasional conversation.

Not long after they'd cast off she'd disappeared for a while then reappeared twenty minutes later with two crunchy bread rolls stuffed with ham off the bone, crisp lettuce, a slice of sweet pineapple, seeded mustard and rich mayonnaise. Blake had been hungry but hadn't wanted to waste any more time getting away to stop and eat something, so the food had hit the spot.

'Thanks,' he'd said as he'd licked mayonnaise off his fingers and tried not to notice her doing the same.

'The least I can do is feed you,' she'd said.

And feed him she did. Popping down below every now and then, bringing back blueberry muffins warm from the oven one time and a bowl full of cut fresh strawberries another.

By the time they reached Bulls Bridge it was six in the evening, but with the days still staying light until nine they descended into Brentford via the Hanwell locks.

And Ava proved herself even handier with a windlass. Blake knew that the trip he'd planned out would be slow and physically demanding for one person and he'd been looking forward to the challenge. But having Ava operate the locks while he drove the boat did speed things up considerably.

He held his breath as she chatted with people from other boats at each lock, waiting for the moment of recognition. But it never came and they were mooring along a towpath in Brentford just before eight.

The smell of cooking meat hit Blake twenty minutes later as he stepped inside from making sure the boat was secure and helping the novice narrow-boaters who had pulled their boat up in front of them. His stomach growled at him.

But it was nothing to the growl his libido gave as his eyes fell on a scantily clad Ava shaking her very delectable booty to the music that was obviously filling her ear buds.

The baggy was gone.

She was in a short flimsy gown that fell to mid-thigh and seemed to cling to every line and curve of her body from the hem north—it certainly clung lovingly to every contour of her butt. It was tied firmly at the waist, which was just as well as she sang along, in a truly terrible falsetto, and stirred something in a bowl.

Ava Kelly might have excelled at a lot of things but singing was not one of them.

Her hair was wet and down. Her feet were bare.

The supermodel was back.

After standing gawping like an idiot for a moment or two he moved closer and cleared his throat to get her attention.

Ava looked up from the dressing she was mixing. 'Oh, sorry.' She grinned, pulling the ear buds out. 'This song always gets me going. Are you hungry? I'm cooking steak. Plus I think this is probably *the* most divine salad dressing—' she dipped her finger in and rolled her eyes in obvious pleasure '—I've ever made.'

A dark drop of the balsamic-looking liquid landed on her chest, just above the criss-cross of her gown at her cleavage and, God help him, Blake's gaze followed it down. She scooped it up quickly but not before he'd taken note of unfettered breasts. Not a line or a strap mark visible through the clinging fabric of the gown.

He looked back at her face. Hell yeh. He was hungry all right.

Freaking starving.

'I thought we'd eat at the pub up the tow path,' he said.

'Tomorrow,' she dismissed, waving her hand and turning back to the job at hand. 'If you want to have a shower, you have six minutes until these babies are ready.'

Blake shook his head. He was going to need much more than six minutes to calm himself down—even in a cold shower. He'd settle for alcoholic fortification instead.

'Drink?' he asked as he opened the fridge and grabbed the long neck of a boutique beer, twisted the lid off and took a long deep pull.

Ava looked up, watching the movement of his throat as he swallowed. There was something very primal about a man guzzling beer. She wondered what he'd do if she sauntered over and slicked her tongue up the hard ridge of his trachea.

She looked back at the steaks cooking in the pan. 'I'll have one of those, thanks.'

Blake cocked an eyebrow. 'Beer. *You* drink beer?' he said as he pulled one out for her and cracked the lid.

Ava heard the surprise bordering on derision in his voice and looked at him. 'Yes. Why? What do you think I drink?'

'Wheatgrass smoothies,' he said, remembering how she often came home from somewhere in her shrink-wrapped gym gear slurping on something disgustingly green.

She took the beer from him. 'Not when I'm relaxing.'

Blake leaned against the fridge. 'Champagne? Fruity cocktails? Dirty cowboys…or whatever the hell those shots are called that women seem to like to knock back in bars these days.'

Ava laughed. He didn't sound as if he approved. 'I like champagne and fruity cocktails, sure. But underneath it all, I'm just a pint-of-beer girl.'

Blake snorted in disbelief.

But, just to prove him wrong, she tipped back her head and took three very long, somehow very erotic, swallows. His gaze drifted down her undulating neck, to her breasts again—not too big, not too small and extremely perky—then back up. She was smiling at him with that knowing little half-smile of hers, her eyelids shuttered, when his gaze returned to her face.

Ava's pulse skipped a beat as their gazes locked for long moments. Heat bloomed to her belly and breasts, making them feel heavy and tight. She toyed with the neck of the bottle, running her fingers up and down the frosty glass as their stare continued.

After three months of scrupulous politeness, he was finally looking at her. Really looking at her.

And there was a *very* definite vibe between them.

'You shouldn't judge a book by its cover, Blake,' she murmured.

Blake sucked in a breath as her voice broke the connection between them. Her cover had sure fallen away fast these last twenty-four hours since being shot at. And he wasn't sure he liked the unpredictable woman in front of him. At least he knew who the other Ava was.

'I'll set the table,' he said, turning away, grateful for something to occupy his mind and his hands.

Other than putting them all over her.

CHAPTER SIX

AVA WAS STARVING by the time they sat down to juicy steaks, a fresh green salad and warm rolls from the oven complete with garlic butter she'd whipped up.

'Where'd you learn to cook?' Blake asked as he bit into his steak. His groan of satisfaction caused a spike in her pulse and a pull in her belly that was entirely sexual.

She shrugged. 'My dad. He was a chef. My earliest memories were being in the kitchen cooking with him. It was our thing we did together. I think I learned through osmosis.'

Blake quirked an eyebrow. 'You said he died?'

Ava nodded. 'When I was twelve. Heart attack.'

Blake watched as the drying strands of her hair glided over each other, the caramel burnished to toffee beneath the expensive down lights. 'That must have been hard.'

Ava nodded. He didn't know the half of it. 'Emotionally and financially. He had his own restaurant, which was almost bankrupt. It was a tough time...'

Blake could tell she didn't want to elaborate on the subject of her father any more and he didn't push as he shifted the conversation to their route tomorrow. He understood. He was a private person too, he wouldn't want a virtual stranger prying into his personal business either.

The army shrink had been bad enough.

But it wasn't what he'd expected from her. From what

he'd witnessed these last few months she seemed to live so much of her life as an open book. In a goldfish bowl. It had been easy—and far preferable—to think of her as a *brand*, a *product*. As *Ava Kelly, Inc.* instead of a flesh and blood woman.

Except for the last twenty-four hours. Sleeping in his bed, cooking in his kitchen, dancing at his sink.

In her gown.

Her very short, very clingy gown.

Ava slid out of the booth and picked up their plates after they'd finished eating.

'Leave them,' Blake said, also standing. 'I'll do them.'

'I don't mind,' Ava said. She was very aware that she'd hijacked his holiday, completely disregarding his plans and inserting herself into the middle of them. The least she could do was make herself useful. She didn't want Blake to think that her jet-set lifestyle had made her too big for her boots—she didn't expect to be waited on.

He grabbed the plates. 'You cook, I clean. House rules.'

Ava resisted for a moment, holding onto the edges as he pulled them towards him, dragging her in close to him, just two dinner plates separating them. She became aware again of *the vibe*. It hummed between them, filling each breath with his essence, enervating each heartbeat with anticipation. What would he do if she just leaned in and kissed him? That was the beauty of being tall—she didn't even have to go up on tippy-toes. His mouth was right there, level with hers.

'*Boat* rules,' she murmured.

Blake swallowed as she looked down her nose to his mouth, lingering there for a moment before returning to his eyes. He had no doubt she was thinking about kissing him and he quelled a sudden urge to lick his lips for fear of what it might give away.

Or encourage.

She seemed to sway a little closer and he quelled his next urge—to do a little kissing himself—too. Instead he gave a brief smile and took a step back, the plates transferring easily to his hands. 'Boat rules,' he agreed briskly.

Ava blinked as he turned away from her and headed to the sink, gathering wits that had taken up residence somewhere south of her belly button. She'd been sure he'd been about to kiss her.

So why hadn't he?

Was he one of those guys who got a little stage fright when it came to kissing her? Intimidated by her being a *supermodel*? Performance anxiety? Funny, he hadn't struck her as the type. She'd have thought the whole good-with-his-hands thing would translate to the bedroom.

'Okay, fine,' she said, finally finding her voice. 'Your boat, your rules. Knock yourself out.' She looked around the saloon, for a distraction, her gaze falling on the television. 'Would you think me terribly vain if I turned the news on and see what they're saying about me?'

Blake shook his head—anything was preferable to her standing there, her gaze boring into the back of his head. 'Nope. Remote on top of the telly,' he said. 'I'll make us a coffee.'

Because staying awake all night on a caffeine high thinking about nearly kissing her in a gown that should have come with a highly flammable label was just what he needed.

Not.

Ava tucked her legs up underneath her as she flipped through the channels till she found some news. Apart from updates from Reggie concerning her situation, she'd been out of touch with the big wide world for twenty-four hours. And it was good to get engrossed in something other than Blake's big brooding presence.

By the time he joined her fifteen minutes later she was

reasonably absorbed in the news. He passed her a mug and was just settling himself into the other chair when a segment on her was introduced. There was nothing new—no arrests, no suspects, just speculation as the events were recounted. And a little air of mystery as the anchor woman speculated as to Ava's whereabouts now that the famous model had *gone underground*.

There was footage of her house and brief glimpses of her last night in the back of an ambulance as well as loads of file footage of her strutting catwalks, shooting a commercial and her smiling at the gaggle of paparazzi as she left her house, patiently moving through them as they surrounded her.

Blake shook his head at the rabble, half of the photographers walking backwards—completely hazardous—to ring every last photo op out of her. 'I don't know how you do that every day,' he said.

Ava shrugged. 'You get used to it.'

Blake shuddered. 'I couldn't live like that, with every minute of my life on show, a camera in my face.'

'It's okay,' Ava said, swivelling the chair to face him as the segment finished and the anchor starting talking about a string of break and enters. 'I've had a camera in my face since I was fourteen so...' She took a sip of her coffee. 'You just make boundaries,' she said. 'Outside I'm public property, inside I'm off-limits.'

Blake thought that sounded like a fairly limited right to privacy. 'But aren't there days you just want to tell them to—?' He stopped himself short of the phrase he would have used had it been him and Charlie talking.

'Do something anatomically impossible to themselves?' she suggested.

Blake chuckled. 'Yes.'

Ava sighed. The sort of life she led was hard for everyday people to understand. 'I *have* to court them, Blake. I'm twenty-seven years old. That's bloody *ancient* in the circles I move in. *And* I'm getting older every day. The paparazzi, the press…they keep me current, keep me in the hearts and minds of people. Good press, good image equals strong interest. One day soon the interest, the jobs, will dry up but until then Reggie says the paps can make you or break you.'

Blake snorted. 'Your agent is a shark.'

'Yeh.' She grinned. 'That's why I hire him. Someone who's sole job it is in life to look after my career. He does it well. I wouldn't be where I am today without him.'

Blake rolled his eyes. 'Oh, please, you make him sound like he's some saint doing it out of the goodness of his heart. I'm sure he's being more than adequately compensated.'

'Absolutely,' she confirmed as she absently traced the hem of her gown where it draped against her thigh with her index finger. 'He's doing it for his fifteen per cent. But at least *that's* an honest business transaction. Telling the difference was a very hard-earned lesson for me.'

Blake heard the sudden steel in her voice and was reminded again that for all her privilege Ava hadn't exactly had it easy. His gaze dropped to where her finger was doodling patterns on her hemline. With her legs tucked up under her, the gown had ridden up some more until it was sitting high on her thighs. It covered what it needed with a little to spare but that still left a whole lot of long, golden leg on display.

Legs he'd managed not to look at or think about for three months. Legs that he was fast developing a fascination with.

She looked at him then and he dragged his gaze back to her face with difficulty. 'Have you thought about what you're going to do after?' It was the first thing that came into his head that didn't involve her legs. 'When the jobs dry up?'

She shook her head as her finger stroked and swirled.

'Not really. I won't *have* to do anything. I'm financially secure. I have the perfume line I'm launching and Reggie's always fielding offers from media and fashion to keep me busy. But I don't know,' she said, shaking her head. 'I've been modelling since I was fourteen…I *honestly* don't really know anything else.'

Her finger stopped tracing as she looked at him speculatively. 'What about you? Did you have some exit strategy for leaving the army?' Her gaze dropped to his leg then back to his face again. 'Were you…prepared?'

Blake grunted. 'No.' Certainly not prepared for the way he'd left. 'I was a career soldier. Never thought about getting out.'

Something shimmered in her eyes that looked a lot like connection as she lazily swivelled the chair back and forth. He couldn't remember ever having a conversation with a woman like this—apart from his shrink. Ever really wanting to—*including his shrink*.

He hated those conversations.

But, for some reason, it felt as if Ava was in a unique position to truly understand—looking down the barrel of shortened career prospects.

'What *did* you do?' she asked.

Blake looked down at his left leg. 'Spent a load of time in hospitals of one description or another.' High-dependency wards, surgical wards, rehab wards. Surgeon's offices, prosthetic offices, shrink's offices.

He could feel the intensity of her gaze on his face as he stared at his leg. Feel it like an invisible bloom of heat swelling in his peripheral vision.

'I meant after that…?'

She said it so softly, Blake had to turn his head to catch it. *A mistake.* Her finger had stopped its hypnotic path but her gown clung, her hair was now dry, her mouth was soft and, for some inexplicable reason—maybe it was sharing last night's frightening episode—he felt he could talk to her. He'd spent three months avoiding it. Avoiding talking to her about anything other than the reno and her haughty demands.

But she seemed different now. Vulnerable, stripped back, human. Like a woman. Not a brand.

'Well, let me see…I spent the first six months with my head up my arse feeling sorry for myself, consuming large amounts of alcohol and pissing off just about everybody who knew and loved me.' He grimaced. 'I wouldn't recommend you do that.'

Ava smiled. 'Check.'

'Then I got a phone call—' He stopped himself before he went any further.

He'd only ever told the shrink this stuff. And while he felt some weird kind of kinship with her he just couldn't go there. Prior to last night he'd been hard put sharing with her something as basic as his relationship with Joanna. Now, twenty-four hours later he was ready to spill his guts?

It was confusing and he didn't like it.

He raked a hand through his hair. 'Let's just say I got some…news—' news that had shocked him to the core '—and I realised that there *were* worse things than having one leg and that it was time to stop acting like the only person in the world who'd ever had something bad happen to them and get on with it.'

'And that's when you and Charlie formed the company?'

'No.' Blake shook his head. 'That's when I bought this boat.' He looked around the interior. 'I spent a year fixing her up. Stripping her right back and rebuilding her from the hull up.'

He gave a self-deprecating smile. 'Manual work can be quite therapeutic.'

'I can imagine.' An image of Blake in a tool belt as he'd worked on her kitchen bench rose in her mind. Would he have taken his shirt off when he'd been working in the hull of the boat?

He nodded. 'Lots of things to tear down and rip out. Lots of pounding and hammering and loud noisy power tools.'

Ava laughed at the note of relish in his voice. 'Be still my beating heart.'

Blake found himself laughing too. 'It's a guy thing.'

'I'm guessing.' She grinned. 'So…your brother saw what a great job you'd done here and you decided to start the company?'

'No. It evolved out of another company, that Charlie had started five years before that. I was doing some labouring for him in between doing up the boat.' He paused. 'Charlie and Joanna were determined to keep me busy…' He grimaced. 'And then, because I have an engineering background, I helped out with some design things and the company was really starting to take off, but it needed a cash injection to get across the line so he offered me a partnership.'

Ava let it all sink in. So not only was he a war hero but he was an engineer who could design stuff and was so good with his hands he could make his own designs too.

Clearly, he had plenty to fall back on.

'Wow.' She blinked. 'Somehow, despite what most would call an *exceedingly* successful life, you've just made me feel completely inadequate. All I know how to do is wear clothes.'

Blake chuckled at her blatant self-deprecation. 'Hey.' He smiled. 'People need clothes.'

She shot him a quelling look. They both knew people didn't need clothes a person had to earn six figures to afford. 'I'm going to be totally screwed when the next big thing pushes me off my pedestal.'

Blake laughed again. There was something very sexy about profanity coming from her posh mouth. 'Don't be discouraged. I hear they love ex-celebrities for those reality television shows the world can't seem to get enough of.'

Ava shuddered. 'No, thanks. I'm not going on any bug-infested island where I have to pee in a hole in the ground and build my own shelter.' She took in his big broad shoulders and those capable hands. 'Not without you anyway.' Although now the idea was out there it might be worth it to watch Blake in his natural element. Maybe with his shirt off?

A soft fizz warmed her belly as her gaze made it back to his face. 'Sorry.' She lifted and dropped a shoulder in a half-shrug. 'I just can't imagine me there, can you?'

Blake sobered as he followed the movement and the ripple effect it had across her chest. Her breasts jiggled slightly, the fabric clinging to them moulded the movement to perfection. He tore his gaze away, met her knowing eyes.

Crap.

'Before today, no,' he said, ploughing on, determined not to acknowledge either his perving or her awareness of it. 'But I've been impressed with how very unpretentious you've been today. There's been no hissy fit over the cut on your face or hand. No hysteria about career-ending scars. No sitting on your butt expecting to be waited on. You got in and helped *and*—' his gaze flicked briefly to her legs then back again '—current attire excepted, you disguised yourself just as I asked. I know bagging up couldn't have been easy for you, but you did *and* you were very generous about it.'

Pleasure at his praise flooded warmth through her system and heat to areas where pleasure meant an entirely different thing. She wasn't sure why *his* praise meant anything to her. She lived in a world that sung her praises daily—and she pretty much took that for granted. She certainly wasn't looking for more. Certainly not from him.

Maybe it was because he'd been so hard to engage during those three months he'd spent at her house? Ava was used to male attention, hell, she *loved* male attention and generally took it as her due. But there'd been a very definite line between them that *he'd* drawn in thick black marker.

Nothing personal had crossed between them.

He'd been polite and respectful, prompt with her queries and had kept his eyes firmly trained on her face. He'd been one hundred per cent professional, resisting slipping into an easier, more casual relationship she'd tried to establish.

Always holding himself back.

She hadn't been able to break through his reserve. And that had been frustrating, galling and intriguing all at once.

But these last twenty-four hours had seen that line disappear. And here he was actually praising her.

Even checking her out.

She wondered how much further she could take it. It could be fun to find out, to push him a little. Discover his buttons. They were both adults and the night was theirs. She smiled at him as she stroked her palm down her neck to her chest, three fingers finding their way under the lapel of the gown.

'It's a lot easier to be baggy on the outside when you're spoiling yourself underneath it all and there's nothing quite like sexy underwear to make you feel sexy all over no matter what you're wearing,' she said.

Blake frowned. Was she saying what he thought she was saying?

'Joanna agreed,' Ava added. 'She didn't think I should have to let myself go altogether.'

'I bet she did,' he said. His sister was always on some mission to set him up. *But Ava freaking Kelly was way out of his league.*

She ought to know he'd had enough drama in his life without inviting a diva in.

'And,' Ava continued, 'I have to say, she has a real eye for classy lingerie. Not that I have any of it on right now.'

Blake tried and failed not to follow the stroke of her fingers as they played with the lapel. Her fingers rubbed along the edge of the fabric, lifting it slightly, exposing a little more flesh to his view.

The air grew thick between them and Ava sensed that the time was ripe to make a move. It didn't faze her. She knew what she wanted and she had the confidence to go after it.

Some people called that bold. She called it decisive.

'I've been thinking,' she said, her gaze firmly trained on his face, 'about the sleeping arrangements tonight.'

She stopped. Waited. He wasn't objecting. Wasn't bolting. He was watching, intently, his eyes on her hand.

'I don't think it's fair that you should give up your bed for me again and so I thought…maybe we could…share…?'

Those words finally did the trick, dragging Blake's head back from the edge and his eyes back from her cleavage.

Was she…propositioning him?

'You mean…you lie on one side with your head at the top and I lie on the other with my head at the bottom and we both get a good night's sleep?'

Ava shook her head. 'Nope.'

The secret little smile playing at the edges of her mouth, the way she looked down her nose at him with blatant sexual interest, did strange things to Blake's equilibrium. It was just as well he was sitting down.

She *was* propositioning him.

There was nothing touch-me-not about this Ava. This Ava was very, very touchable.

Blake's heart rate slowed right down in his chest as blood rushed south. His brain might be saying no but other parts of him weren't listening. Ava Kelly was trouble with a capital T. And he'd had more than enough trouble to last him a lifetime. Being a supermodel's plaything for a night or two might be every man's wet dream but his doom receptors were working overtime.

'I…don't think that would be such a good idea,' he said.

Ava blinked. Not the response she was used to. *Frankly she thought it was the best idea she'd had in a long time.*

But Blake *had* spent three months keeping his distance and she already knew he was the strong, serious, cautious type.

Well, she didn't get to the top of her game by taking no for an answer and she sure as hell wasn't going to tonight either.

'Okay.' She placed her coffee mug on the coffee table and stood. She walked the three paces that separated their chairs until the outside of her right thigh was brushing the outside of his. She looked down at him.

'I know this isn't what we planned. And I know this isn't the kind of relationship you and I have had to this point. But I'm just going to put this out there.'

Ava's pulse fluttered madly and her breathing sped up as she lifted her right leg to step over his thighs, placing them between her legs. He shifted in his chair and she shut her eyes briefly as the denim scraped erotically against the sensitive inner flesh of her bare thighs.

When she opened them again his indigo gaze was staring straight at the knot of her belt as if he was trying to undo it through mind power alone. Heat flared behind her belly button and tingled at the juncture of her thighs.

'I'm attracted to you, Blake,' she said. 'I think you're attracted to me. We have tonight…maybe a few nights on this boat together and we're both adults. I'm just saying… we could have some fun. That wouldn't be such a bad thing, right?'

Right. Blake knew she was right. He had no problems with two consenting adults having a little fun together. He used to indulge in quite a lot of *fun* before the explosion. But since…

Sure, there'd been women but *fun* didn't really fit into his vocabulary these days. Sex was a lot of things—communication, connection, stress relief. An activity engaged in to relieve a build-up of testosterone.

Pleasurable. Enjoyable. Necessary. But not fun.

Because having fun felt wrong.

'Blake?'

He was still staring at that knot and she could tell he was teetering on the edge. She reached for it then, slowly worked at it with fingers that shook just a little until it slid loose and the belt fell to her sides. The two front edges of the gown slid over each other parting slightly.

She was still covered—barely.

Blake swallowed against a throat that felt as dry as the desert. His erection surged against his jeans and the urge to open her gown, to see more than a glimpse of cleavage, thrummed through his system like the steady backbeat of a tropical downpour. He glanced up at her to tell her to step away but her cat eyes looked back at him, her mouth parted.

He sucked in a breath and curled his fingers into the lounge beside him. 'Hell, Ava.'

Ava felt dizzy from the longing in his low husky growl and she squeezed her legs hard against his to stay grounded.

'I've shocked you, haven't I? I'm sorry. Not very lady-like I guess. I've always been a little too forthright for my own good.'

Blake snorted as her posh ladylike voice made excuses for her brazen proposal. In the grand scheme of shocking, it barely rated as a blip. 'I don't give a rat's arse for lady-like,' he growled.

He liked a *woman* between the sheets, not some snooty *lady* who was worried about getting her hair messed up.

Ava might talk a little on the posh side and have that haughty little look of hers well rehearsed but her frank proposition, the way she'd thrown her leg over him just now, the sureness of her fingers as she'd undone her belt, told him she was no *lady* in the bedroom.

'Well, okay then,' Ava said, smiling down at him. Their gazes locked and she waited for him to reach for her, to make the first move. *Or the next one, anyway.* But she could still see a glimmer of that famous reserve, that wariness in his eyes.

Surely he wasn't…intimidated? Blake didn't strike her as the kind of guy that needed his hand held, but if that was what was required…

CHAPTER SEVEN

AVA SMILED AT him encouragingly. 'It's okay, you know,' she said, 'to be a little…daunted. It's really quite common. Some guys are a little freaked out at first because of who I am… They don't want to screw it up and it makes them… nervous…reticent. But really, I'm just a woman.'

She leaned forward, conscious of her gown gaping a little more and the lowering of his gaze. She picked up his hand, and placed it halfway up her thigh.

'A flesh and blood woman,' she continued. 'Don't think of me as a…celebrity. I'm just Ava…a woman just like any other.'

Blake's gaze stayed fixed on where his hand met her flesh as Ava straightened. Her thigh was warm beneath his palm. And very, very female. Something his erection appreciated with gusto. So much that it almost made him forget her ridiculous statement.

Lord. Her ego sure as hell hadn't been scared into submission last night.

She didn't *intimidate* him.

But she definitely got under his skin.

He dropped his hand from her thigh before he did something completely contradictory like smoothing it up. All the way up. He looked up instead—a much safer alternative—as he mentally thrust the temptation aside.

'No, Ava.'

Ava heard the roughness of longing in his voice despite his denial. What *was* his problem? And then suddenly something else occurred to her and she felt both stupid and insensitive. Throwing herself at him—an *injured* war veteran.

'Oh, God, I'm so sorry,' she whispered. 'Your injuries...' She shook her head. 'I should have thought. I didn't realise you couldn't...that you can't...that you're...impotent... I'm so sorry...'

Blake almost choked at her wild assumption. Right at this second he'd never been more bloody potent in his life.

Or more goaded into proving it.

'Screw it,' he growled, forgetting all the reasons he shouldn't as he grabbed her hand and yanked.

Ava barely had a chance to catch her breath before she landed hard in his lap, looming over him, her thighs straddling his. Her gown had flown open and her bare breasts grazed the neckline of his shirt. Her hands clutched for purchase, finding the hard wall of muscle that constituted his chest.

But she didn't protest or stop to clarify. She just followed her instincts. And her instincts led her to his mouth. A mouth that was seeking hers, his fingers spearing into her hair, his hands dragging her head down to his.

Her mouth down to his.

And when his lips touched hers, full and firm and open, she opened to him too, parting instantly, her nostrils full of the intoxicating scent of him, her tongue savouring the hint of beer and the fuller, earthier taste of aroused man.

His hand slid over her hip to the small of her back, his palm pressing hard against her, and her belly contracted. He slid it up, following the furrow of her spine, and she shivered. He trekked it around to her front, filling his palm with the soft flesh of her breast, squeezing and rubbing his finger across the turgid peak of her nipple, and she arched her back and moaned, 'Blake,' against his mouth.

His other hand slid to her butt cheek and squeezed and she couldn't think for the bombardment of sensations. For the smell of him filling her head. The taste of him consuming her senses. She just needed more.

To be closer, nearer. To imprint herself. To feel him around her.

To feel him inside her.

She couldn't remember ever wanting a man as desperately as she wanted Blake. Men and sex came easy to her and Blake's resistance had been a challenge. But this wasn't triumph she was feeling. This was purely sexual. Blake gave and gave and gave—plundering, stroking, kneading, touching—and she wanted everything he had to offer.

She squirmed against him, signalling a need she was too far gone to ask for. And that was when she became aware of it. A hardness beneath her right thigh. A flatness. Not like his other thigh that had the flexibility of hot flesh over steely muscle. There was no give there. Just rigidity. And a very definite edge. *His prosthesis.*

But then he was yanking her hips forward, bringing her in contact with more flesh on steel. Something hard and long and very, very potent. Making her forget everything else. She tried to move, to obey the dictates of her body, to grind down on him, to feel every inch of his erection, but he held her there, both hands clamped on her butt now, kissing her deeper, wilder, wetter.

'Blake,' she muttered against his mouth as she tried to squirm, to rub herself shamelessly along the length of him.

Blake groaned as he held her fast. He'd only meant this as a demonstration of his capabilities but it was careening out of his control. Her mouth tasted like beer and sin and he wanted to taste her all over. He hadn't bargained for how perfect she'd feel in his hands. How she'd melt into him, all her can't-touch-this veneer evaporating.

Or how very much he'd been denying himself.

Ava Kelly was one hell of a woman and telling himself she was technically still a client and a pain-in-the-butt one to boot just wasn't going to cut it now his erection had taken control.

He wanted to get her naked, he wanted to get her horizontal; he wanted to get her under him. His head was full of her throaty whimpers, his hands were full of her flesh, his mouth was full of her taste but it still wasn't enough.

Her hand found his erection then and he moaned as she palmed it, pressing himself into her hand. His zip fell away beneath her questing fingers and then she was reaching inside his underwear, freeing him, her palm hot against him as she squeezed his girth.

Blake broke off the kiss on a guttural groan, his eyes practically rolling back in his head as he dragged in much-needed air. Her forehead pressed against his and he opened his eyes to the delectable sight of her breasts swaying hypnotically, the light pink nipples darker now as they formed two hard points.

With her hair falling around them in a curtain and the only sound between them the thick rasp of their breath, it was as if they were the only two people in the world. Far away from the world of Ava Kelly and her entourage. Which was just as well with her hand getting so intimately acquainted with his freed erection.

He shut his eyes as she wrapped her hand around him and started to smooth it up and down the length of him.

'God, you're so *freaking* hard,' she whispered into the space between them. 'I knew there was a reason I'd put my trust in you.'

The words were like a bucket of cold water and Blake froze, his eyes snapping open.

Trust.

She had to use *that* word?

He looked down at himself, at her hand on him. *What the hell was he doing?*

God, how had this got so out of hand? He was only supposed to be proving he could get it up, not demonstrating its full working capabilities. Having sex with Ava was a bad idea and her being practically naked with a hand full of his erection didn't make it any less so.

Every instinct he owned—prior to five minutes ago— had told him to stay away, and he would do well to remember that.

She *trusted* him, for God's sake.

The woman had so few people in the world to put her faith in and he was taking advantage of her sucky situation.

'Stop…wait,' he said, shifting in the chair, covering her hand with his, grateful when she stopped the mindlessly good stroking.

Ava frowned, her hand stilling. Her head spun from the sexual buzz, her brain already someplace else where he felt good and hard inside her. 'Wha…?' she said, pulling away slightly.

'Just…no…hop up…' he said. 'Let me up.'

Blake struggled to get up, trying to displace her safely and stand himself without falling in a heap. Ava stood there looking confused, her gown open, her body flushed and lovely, and he turned away to dispel the image, to block it from his sight.

'Blake?'

He felt a hundred kinds of idiot at her plaintive query as he tucked his protesting erection in and zipped himself up. His breathing was still all bent out of shape and he raked a hand through his hair as he took a moment to gather himself.

When he turned back he was grateful she'd done up her gown. But she'd gone from looking confused and unsure to pretty pissed off.

Not that he could blame her. His erection knew exactly how she felt.

'I'm sorry,' he said. 'I shouldn't have started that… I

was trying to prove that everything was in full working order. I just got a little…carried away.'

Ava glared at him. 'You think?'

'I'm sorry,' he repeated. Because what else could he say?

Ava tried to wrap her head around what had just transpired. 'I don't understand,' she said. 'What happened?'

Blake took a steadying breath. 'I don't want to do this.'

Ava snorted. 'You wanted it all right. You wanted it when you kissed me, you wanted it when you touched me and you sure as hell wanted it when I had my hand in your pants.'

Blake had to concede she made some very good points. 'Of course my *body* wants you,' he said. 'I'm a man and you're one of the most beautiful women on the planet and, as you pointed out before, we're attracted to each other. But I'm thirty-three years old, Ava, not some horny teenager who can't control himself. My brain's telling me this is a stupid thing to do.'

Ava gave another snort. 'That's not what your erection was telling me.'

'Yeh, well…' he raked a hand through his hair '…erections tend to be fairly unreliable indicators of what a man should and shouldn't do.'

'Well, at least they're honest,' she said vehemently. 'At least they tell it like it is. I know you wanted me right now, Blake, and I don't know why you're pretending you don't, why you're pretending it's a bad thing. We're just two human beings coming together, finding a little pleasure together. It's really not that complicated.'

Blake was struck suddenly by how spoiled she was sounding. He'd forgotten how irritating that was in the last twenty-four hours. Obviously she'd pegged him as a sure thing and she wasn't impressed with being knocked back. Clearly she was used to getting her way sexually too.

He half expected to see her stamp her foot.

'Is it *so* hard to believe that someone doesn't want to have sex with you?'

Ava heard the underlying disbelief in his question and it made her crankier. 'Frankly, yes.' Men wanted her—always had. And she'd taken her pick.

Blake almost laughed as her haughty look came back and, even barely dressed in a clingy gown, she managed to look imperious. 'Oh, my God, you've never been knocked back, have you?'

Ava gave a very definitive shake of her head. 'Nope.'

Blake did laugh this time. He'd always had a fairly high success rate with women, even since the explosion. But part of becoming a man, in his opinion, was realising that not every woman was going to think you were sex on a stick.

And it was how a guy took that news that separated the boys from the men.

'Well, welcome to the *real* world,' he said.

Ava *did not* think any of this was funny. She still felt jittery as her cells came down from their sexual high without the satisfaction they craved. 'Oh, I see,' she said, putting her hand on her hip. 'This is some kind of life lesson for me, is it?'

Blake should have been astounded by her egocentricity but nothing about her surprised him any more. 'You know, Ava, this may come as a surprise, but not everything is about you.'

Ava ignored his derisive put down in favour of getting to the bottom of a situation she'd never been in before. 'So... let me get this straight. You're attracted to me but you don't want to have sex with me?'

Blake smiled at her obvious confusion. 'Oh, I want to, all right. I'm just not going to.'

Ava stared at him. Well, now she was totally lost. Why not take what you wanted, especially when it was on offer? 'But...why not?'

Blake shook his head. She really had no clue about the

real world. She was so used to getting her way and taking what she wanted from life, because she could, that she never stopped to think that some things were better off left alone.

'Because it's a whole lot of complicated for a few lousy nights, Ava.'

Ava folded her arms. 'There would be *nothing* lousy about them.'

Blake smiled at her snooty self-assurance. 'I'm sure you're right,' he conceded. If she did other things even half as well as she kissed he was doomed.

'So what's the problem?'

He sighed. Obviously she needed it spelled out. 'I'm supposed to be offering you safe harbour, Ava, not taking advantage of you.'

As a British soldier his uniform had been a symbol of security and he'd always taken that seriously. It just didn't feel right somehow to violate the trust she'd put in him. Just because he hadn't asked for it, didn't mean he was going to mess with it.

'And that would make perfect sense if I was here rocking in a corner and jumping at shadows like some little scared mouse. But *I'm* coming on to *you*. I think consent to take advantage of me is implied. So what else have you got?'

Blake pushed a hand through his hair at her casual dismissal of values he held dear.

God, she was irritating.

'How about, I don't like women who are spoiled and self-centred no matter how beautiful they are or how good they look naked. It's not an attractive quality and I'm not some guy who'll turn a blind eye to that just to get laid. I don't want to be your distraction of choice while you're *slumming it* on a canal boat. I'm not some plaything for a rich woman to amuse herself with.'

Ava blinked at his unflattering appraisal of her. Okay, she might be used to getting her own way but she wasn't a complete egomaniac either. She didn't regard him as a *plaything*. She just saw a situation they could both have a little fun with.

'I don't see you like that,' she said, dropping her arms until they wrapped around her waist. 'This isn't me being bored or spoiled either. I just don't see why we should deny ourselves when we both want this.'

'Well, I guess in your hedonistic world you wouldn't,' he said. 'But I learned a few years ago to stay away from things that can blow up in your face and, lady, you have highly explosive written all over you.'

Ava knew that he hadn't meant to flatter her but she was anyway. She was so used to being described as cool and snooty. The media had dubbed her *Keep-Away Kelly* when she'd really hit the big time because of the aloofness she'd worked so hard to cultivate.

It was her point of difference and she'd worked it.

To be told she was the opposite was strangely thrilling. 'Thank you.'

Blake rolled his eyes. 'It wasn't a compliment.'

Ava grinned at his terse exasperation. 'I know. Which strangely only makes me want you more.'

Blake shook his head. There wasn't much else that could be said here. He was determined to keep things between them strictly platonic. She seemed determined to do the opposite.

Ken Biddle had better catch his man quick. *Before Ava caught hers.*

'I'm going to bed,' he said.

Ava watched him turn away, admiring the back view of him as he veered to the left and headed down the corridor, presumably for the bathroom. His limp was barely discernible. 'You should know I don't give up so easily,' she called.

Blake felt her silky threat—or was that a promise?—land on target right between his shoulder blades. 'I'll consider myself warned,' he said, without turning around, then stepped gratefully into the bathroom and shut the door.

He leaned against it heavily, gripping the door handle hard, trying to get control of a groin that had leaped to life again at her sexy warning. His hand brushed something and he looked down to find a scrap of black lace in the shape of a bra.

He groaned as he pulled it off, and held it up in front of him, letting it dangle from his index finger. Pink ribbon weaved along the cup edges delineated them and a little pink bow at the cleavage, complete with diamanté, winked out at him. His groin went from aching to throbbing.

This was the sort of stuff she was going to be wearing under her clothes?

Fabulous.

He hung it back where he found it then pulled out his mobile from his pocket, scrolling to Joanna's number and hitting 'message'.

Thx heaps 4 the lingerie you meddler.

He hit send and waited where he was for the few seconds it took to get a reply. The phone vibrated in his hand and he read the screen. *Thought you might like.*

Blake tapped a reply. *I don't.*

A few more seconds. *OK. Sure. Keep forgetting you are the *only* man on earth not born with the lingerie gene.*

Blake shook his head. *Don't Joanna. Not going there.*

Joanna's *Uh-huh* reply rankled.

I'm not.

The reply came swiftly. *Uh-huh.*

He grimaced as his fingers flew across the touch pad. *God you're irritating. I should have let Charlie strap you to the front of his bike when you were 2.*

Blake waited for the reply. And waited. He was about to give up and get into the shower when his phone vibrated in his hand again. Four words that hit like a sledgehammer.

What would Colin say???

Blake bumped his head back against the door. Low blow. His mate would think he'd lost his mind for just having turned down an invitation to heaven with one of the world's most nicely put-together women.

Another vibration. *He's dead. You're alive. So live.*

Blake hated it when Joanna played on his guilt over Colin. And she knew it. *I definitely should have let Charlie use u as a human bumper bar.*

A smiley face appeared on the screen. *Love you 2. Night xxx.*

Blake shoved his phone back in his pocket, pushing aside the unsettled feelings that both Ava and Joanna had roused. He shucked off his clothes and moved into the large glass shower recess. One of the beauties of a wide beam was all the extra space. It meant you could have more rooms. Or, as he had chosen, *bigger* rooms and he loved the decadence of his spacious bathroom.

On autopilot he went through the now almost second-nature process of taking off his prosthesis and placing it outside the glass area. Still on autopilot he reached for the gleaming metallic railing that was attached to the tiles at waist height the entire way. He barely registered the gritty, high-grip tiles beneath his foot.

He flicked the taps and the water rained down on him nice and hot within seconds. He shut his eyes, forcing himself to relax. To clear his head of his sister's unhelpful suggestions. And Ava's unhelpful seduction.

And the unhelpful build of sexual frustration.

Just because he was horny didn't mean he should act on it. *Not with her anyway.*

He turned, letting the water sluice over his neck, flopping his head first forward then back, enjoying the heat on traps he'd had no idea were so tense. His eyes fluttered open. And that was when he saw it.

A lacy black thong hanging over the shower screen.

Pink ribbon weaved along the waistband and a little pink bow sat dead centre, another diamanté winking down at him.

She'd been wearing that get up under her clothes all day? His traps tensed again.

Crap.

Blake woke the next morning after another fitful sleep to dreadful off-key singing and the smell of frying bacon. His stomach growled and his mouth watered despite the assault to his ears.

He hadn't been sure what to expect this morning after their…disagreement last night and he'd lain awake wondering what kind of a post-spat personality she was.

Was she a flouncer, a sulker, a brooder?

It certainly didn't sound as if she was any of the above if her peppy singing was anything to go by. He reached for his leg and put it on, then reached for his T-shirt and pulled it down over his head. He'd taken it off during the night as replays of Ava straddling him had made the warm night quite a few degrees hotter.

He rubbed a hand through his hair, taking a moment before standing and facing her. Ava's singing stopped momentarily and he could hear the lower murmur of a breakfast news programme on the television. Blake hoped that Ken had some *news* for them this morning. Like they'd found the person or persons responsible for shooting up Ava's house.

She started *singing* again and he made his way to the kitchen and just stood and watched her for a moment as she boogied in front of the cooktop. The gown from last night was on again but was floating loosely by her sides and he felt a sudden kick in his groin at the thought that she might just be naked under there and if she turned around then—

She turned around.

Everything leapt to attention for a brief second and

not even the evidence of his own eyes—that she was indeed wearing something under that gown—could stop the rapid swelling of his erection. Because a spaghetti-strapped, clingy, not-quite-meeting-in-the-middle vest top and matching boy-leg undies on a tall, bronzed supermodel was something to behold.

Her face lit up. 'Ah.' She smiled at him. 'You're up. I'm making bacon butties.'

Blake swallowed. Up? *In more ways than one.* Was there anything more sexy than a woman in skimpy lingerie? Except maybe for a woman in skimpy lingerie cooking bacon?

Ava smiled as Blake's gaze roved all over her. *Yeh, buddy, this is what you're missing out on.* 'How'd you'd sleep last night?' she enquired sweetly.

Blake's eyes narrowed at the suspiciously smug question. So this was the kind of post-spat personality she was—a fighter.

Who liked to play dirty.

Well, he wasn't one of her entourage of men who fluttered around her and kissed her butt. 'Like a log,' he said.

Wrong choice of words as her gaze dropped to the area between his hips with its suspicious bulge.

Which *did not* help the suspicious bulge.

But then her smile slipped a little and a tiny frown knitted her brows together. He looked down at what she'd found so disagreeable and realised, unlike every other time she'd seen him, his prosthesis was on full display.

He supposed a woman as physically perfect as Ava would find his leg rather confronting. He felt absurdly like covering it up. And then he felt really freaking cranky.

Blake's teeth ached from clenching his jaw hard as he waited for her to say something. Something trite or clueless, something about how at least he still had one leg or how *marvellous* prosthetics were these days.

Instead she just dragged her gaze back up to look into his eyes. 'Take a seat. Eggs are just about done.'

CHAPTER EIGHT

THERE WAS NO news from Ken, although Ava Kelly was still the talk of the tabloids and breakfast shows. Speculation as to where she'd disappeared was rife and one talk-back radio station had even offered money to anyone who could produce pictorial evidence of her whereabouts.

Ken was far from impressed with that.

Blake was downright annoyed. He suggested Ava put Reggie to good use and sue their arses off for endangerment. She'd just shrugged, clearly so desensitised to press intrusion that the invasion of her human rights didn't even register.

They got under way again as soon as breakfast was done. They were travelling along a stretch of the tidal Thames and they had to fit into lock times that were mandated by the tide. His plan was to moor somewhere around Windsor overnight then on to Reading the next day where the Kennet and Avon canal began. Once they'd turned into it, they could putt along more lazily, but for now it was full steam ahead.

Or as full steam as possible when the speed limit was four miles per hour!

And Ava Kelly was your very distracting travelling companion.

Blake didn't think she was being deliberately distracting. She was fully bagged up again. Baggy shorts and shirt, her hair all tucked up in a cap, sunglasses firmly in place. She looked as anonymous as the next woman riding the canals.

But he knew what she had on under all those layers.

And that was pretty much all he could think about—every time she moved or talked or offered him something to eat. *Like freaking Eve with the apple.* In fact, even when she wasn't anywhere near him, he was thinking about her and what she might be wearing against her skin.

Did she have on the same spaghetti-strapped vest and matching boy-legs that had been under her gown this morning—the ones that displayed the most perfect belly-button probably ever created? Or had she changed into some other frothy, lacy, silky, maybe be-ribboned scraps of fabric when she'd changed into her outside clothes?

It was annoying how much brain space the speculation was taking up. He should be enjoying the gorgeous sunshine on his face, the breeze in his hair, the spectacular beauty of the English countryside. And while Ava had raved over the magnificence of Hampton Court, he'd barely registered it.

It wasn't good for his mood or his sanity, and it was the last straw when he caught himself trying to look down her top from his vantage point standing at the helm as she asked him a question from the bottom of the three stairs that led to the back of the boat.

'What?' he asked, when he realised he hadn't heard a word she'd said because he swore he caught a glimpse of red satin.

Ava, who'd deliberately leaned forward a little, gave him an innocent smile. 'I said are you ready for some lunch now?'

'Yep. But not here.'

Blake knew he had to get off the boat. Get away from the lure of her and red satin. Put himself amongst people, where he had to behave rationally. *And not tear her clothes off with his teeth.*

'There's a pub just up ahead,' he said. 'About five minutes away. We'll moor and eat there.'

'Fab,' she said and smiled up at him.

Blake pushed the boat a little harder.

Ava was enjoying watching the array of boats go by and the sun on her face as they sat in the reasonably full beer garden that fronted the river. They were sitting at one end of a bench—the other end a family group were chatting away oblivious to who was sharing their table with them.

By tacit agreement, Blake had gone inside and ordered for them while Ava stayed out. Being incognito worked best when she exposed herself to scrutiny as little as possible. Sitting in a riverside beer garden just like any ordinary girl was clearly possible, but the more people she spoke to, the more she risked exposure.

She was pleased when Blake came back with two pints of cold beer. It was warm in the sunshine and she felt hot in her baggy attire. What she wouldn't give to be in her bikini now, or at least in clothes that didn't cover her from neck to knee.

'You remembered,' she said, smiling at him as she lifted her glass and tapped it against the rim of his larger one. 'Cheers.'

Blake watched her guzzle it like a pro then lick the froth from her mouth. *Sexiest thing he'd ever seen.*

'Mmm,' she murmured after taking several deep swallows, quenching the thirst the hot sun had roused. 'That hit the spot. It's warm, isn't it?'

Ava put the beer down and pulled on the neckline of her shirt, fanning it back and forth rapidly to try and cool the sweat she could feel forming between her breasts. She hadn't done it to provoke Blake but it was pleasing when his eyes narrowed and followed the movement.

She was glad his sunglasses didn't obscure his eyes as hers did. She liked knowing exactly where he was looking.

He looked kind of hot and bothered himself and she smiled. 'Aren't you roasting in those jeans?' she asked.

Blake shrugged. 'I'm okay.'

Ava regarded him. Did he always cover up his prosthesis? She'd been surprised when she'd seen it this morning. Not because she thought it was grotesque but because Blake always seemed so sure of himself, so confident, so...able. Seeing his leg had been a reminder that he wasn't, or at least that it wasn't so effortless for him.

'Do you never wear shorts?' she asked.

He dropped his gaze to his beer and took another sip and she could tell he was uncomfortable with the subject.

'Perfect weather for them,' she pushed as he turned his head to take in the activity on the busy river. 'You don't like people knowing?' Ava guessed tentatively.

Blake sighed as he turned back to face her, putting his beer down. 'I don't care who knows or doesn't know. Jeans...avoid conversations I *don't* want to have.'

Ava got the message loud and clear. But she wanted to have the conversation anyway. 'Like how it happened?'

'Yes.'

'What a hero you must be?' she guessed again.

Blake rolled his eyes. 'Yes.'

'How brave you are?'

He nodded. 'Yes.'

The level of chatter around them was sufficiently high that they could talk without fear of being overheard and Ava really wanted to know more about the circumstances of his amputation. The man had pushed her to the ground as someone shot up her house, purely out of instincts that had obviously been honed during his time in war zones.

As far as she was concerned he *was* a hero.

'How *did* it happen?'

Blake didn't really fancy talking about it with her, but at least talking was keeping his mind off her red bra. In fact maybe he could use it to his advantage. 'If I tell you, will you promise to not hang your underwear in my shower?'

Ava was momentarily surprised by his blatant blackmail. But it was satisfying to know that her *under*wear was getting *under* his skin. 'Deal.'

Blake took another sip of his beer. 'It happened the usual way,' he said dismissively. 'On patrol in the middle of nowhere. A roadside bomb. An IED. All over red rover.'

Ava should have expected the abridged version. 'Did anyone die?'

Blake steeled himself not to flinch at the question. 'Yes. One.'

Ava nodded slowly at another abridged version that told her nothing of the emotional carnage he must have borne. 'And the leg? Did you lose it straight away or after?'

'It was pretty mangled. They amputated it as soon as I hit the hospital.'

His words were flat, his answers matter-of-fact but Ava could see the tension in his muscle, the tightness of his jaw.

'That must have been…incredibly painful,' she murmured.

Blake gripped his glass as the sounds of his screams flashbacked to fill his head all over again. He wondered if people—if Ava—would think him so heroic if they knew how loudly he'd screamed. Lying in agony in the dirt, his eardrums blown out, the warm ooze of his own blood welling over the hand he'd reached down to try and stop the pain.

If they knew his brother-in-law lay dead beside him and Blake hadn't even given him a single thought.

'It was.'

Ava was about to say more. To push more. To ask more. But the waiter arrived, placing their ploughman's lunches in front of them and an extra bowl of hot chips for Ava, and Blake's white-knuckled grip on his glass eased as he picked up his knife and fork.

'Let's eat,' he said.

Ava sighed. *Conversation over.*

They didn't talk much over lunch, for which Blake was grateful. Ava seemed happy enough to drop her line of questioning and just eat and enjoy the sunshine, with occasional questions about their route for the afternoon.

He didn't really talk about what had happened to him—not with civilians anyway. His family knew the most of it. The army shrink knew more. Joanna at one stage had wanted to know every detail and had wanted to go over and over it ad nauseam and, even though it had been horrible and he'd dreaded seeing her number flash on his phone screen or hearing her wobbly, strung-out voice in his ear, he'd done it because he'd owed her.

The only people he could really talk to about it with any level of comfort were the guys he'd served with because they were the only ones who could *truly* understand any of it. But he rarely saw any of them and when he did, contrary to popular perception, none of them were particularly keen to rehash old war stories.

Talking about it with Ava wasn't his definition of fun but at least he'd won a concession from her so maybe it had been worth it.

He watched her as she laid her cutlery on her empty plate then reached for the tomato sauce bottle and squirted great dollops all over her hot chips, then sprinkled a heart-attack quota of salt over the top. She picked one up in her fingers, and ate with gusto, sighing a little sigh. She added two more to her mouth, then, before they were fully swallowed, another two.

A dollop of sauce smeared at the corner of her mouth and Blake's gaze was drawn to it—he couldn't help himself.

'What?' she asked around her mouthful of hot chips. Then she picked up the remnant of her beer and washed them down, licking her lips free of sauce and beer residue.

The woman made the simple act of eating into a sexual enterprise.

'Isn't your body supposed to be a temple or something?' he asked. 'Aren't supermodels supposed to always be on some kind of diet that involves no carbs and lots of egg-white omelettes and running on a treadmill for six hours a day?'

'Ugh, no thanks.' Ava shuddered as she picked up another chip and popped it in her mouth. 'My mother used to be strict about that stuff as I was growing up and—'

Ava stopped. She didn't want to think about her pageant-queen mother. It was a long time ago and it always put her in a bad mood and the sunshine and company were just too good.

'Anyway…I do exercise…mostly…but…' She sighed. 'I have to admit, I'm not a fan and it's hard to see the point when I'm one of those people who have good genetics with a great metabolism and can pretty much eat whatever without putting on weight. I've been really blessed like that.' She grimaced. 'I'm one of those women other women hate.'

Blake could see that. Most women he knew had some kind of body hang-up or other trying to keep up with impossible images in women's magazines. Images that she perpetrated.

'The thing is,' she said as she chomped on another chip, 'I just freaking love food. I don't know if that's because of Dad's influence or not but it's just…I don't know, like… air to me. I *need* it.'

'And,' she said, picking up another two chips and dipping them in a puddle of sauce on the bottom of the bowl, 'I'm starving all the time, which is why I cook a lot at home and wanted an amazing kitchen, which you—' she jabbed another chip in his general direction before popping it in her mouth '—gave me in spades. No pics of me at restaurants stuffing a three-course meal down then asking for seconds of dessert. I eat like a supermodel when I'm in public and then come home and cook up something amazing in my beautiful kitchen because by then I'm so freaking hungry I'm almost faint with it.'

Blake knew it shouldn't, but her appreciation of both his kitchen and for food in general turned him on. Just talking about how much she loved food had clearly got her all enthused and excited. She was using the chips to emphasise her points and her cheeks were all flushed and her freckles were standing out. He wanted to whisk her glasses off and see if the yellow highlights in her eyes were glittering fit to match the sun on the Thames.

There was nothing haughty or spoiled about *this* Ava, who was chowing down on hot chips and cold beer.

Ava chose another chip, realising there were only five left and she hadn't offered him any. 'Oh, God, sorry,' she said, picking up the bowl and pushing it towards him. 'Do you want any? They were so good I got carried away.'

Blake chuckled at her half-hearted offer. He couldn't see her eyes but he'd have been deaf not to have heard the reluctance in her voice. 'They're all yours,' he said, waving them back.

'Good answer.' She grinned as she dived for the remaining chips.

Blake's breath caught in his lungs. If *this* Ava straddled him right now his powers of resistance would be totally useless.

By six o'clock that evening they'd moored just upstream from Windsor Castle. The unparalleled views of the extensive grounds surrounding the castle as they had floated past had been amazing and Ava, who had apparently *met* the queen, had been excited to see the royal standard flying high from the round tower indicating Her Majesty was in residence.

After last night, Blake hadn't expected to enjoy the day as much as he had. He'd expected Ava to be petulant and difficult—like a spoiled child who hadn't got her way—but she'd been perfectly well behaved and he was smiling to himself as he came in from outside, pulling a beer bottle from the fridge and cracking the lid.

If Ava could keep up her ordinary-girl act and give the sex-kitten/prima-donna a rest, it could be an enjoyable time, while it lasted. Of course, it could be even more enjoyable if he allowed himself to be seduced. But he was determined to show her he was one of the good guys. That she *could* trust him.

A cutting board with chopped tomatoes and onions sat waiting on the kitchen bench and fresh basil spiced the air. Ava wasn't dancing around his kitchen and, as he'd heard the pump kick in while he'd been checking the ropes, he assumed she was showering.

His brain wandered to that delightful prospect before he pulled himself back from the image. *Do not think about her showering.* What he needed to do was go and grab some supplies out of his room while she wasn't in it. Some clothes and toiletries etc.

Except when he stepped into his bedroom he discovered she wasn't in the shower. He pulled up short just inside the doorway as his gaze fell on bare golden shoulders.

Ava looked up as Blake entered the room. Their eyes met and there was a world of surprise in those few seconds. But there were other things as well, especially when his gaze dropped and lingered at the point where her damp hair brushed her collarbones.

There was a hell of a lot of want in that lingering contact.

They'd had a good time today. Blake had seemed to relax more as the day had worn on and she was even left with the impression that he might actually *like* her. Certainly not how she'd felt after last night's debacle.

And there'd been something so sexy about the way he handled the boat. Maybe it was the whole *Captain Capa-*

ble thing he had going on or maybe it was just the way his T-shirt had fitted snugly across solid biceps.

Either way, his attraction had cranked up several notches since last night and her belly tightened at the thought of just how capable he might be on the big beautiful bed right in front of her.

'Hi,' she said, breaking the silence that stretched between them.

'Oh, sorry,' Blake said, dragging his eyes back to hers—no easy feat considering she was dressed in nothing but a towel. 'I thought you were still in the shower.'

Ava shrugged and watched as his gaze followed the motion. She raised her hand to where the towel was firmly tucked into itself between her breasts and was satisfied when his gaze took the trip with her.

'Nope. Not any more,' she murmured. 'All fresh and clean.'

Blake took an absent sip of his beer that he'd forgotten he was even carrying. 'Yes.'

A small smile played on Ava's lips at his obvious distraction. Blake could deny himself as much as he liked in the name of honour but it was pretty obvious what he really wanted. 'Did you want something?' she asked. 'Or were you secretly hoping to catch me getting dressed?'

Blake frowned as the words yanked him out of his stupor. He really hoped she didn't seriously think he'd come into the room to cop a perve. He wasn't some horny bloke who let the content of his underpants dictate his actions. He'd proved himself to be pretty honourable under circumstances where most men would have cracked and she could take a flying leap into the canal if she thought otherwise.

But then he noticed that predatory gleam from last night in her eyes again, which suited all her languid feline grace, and he knew what this was.

Goodbye, ordinary girl. Hello, sex kitten.

Ava watched Blake transition from annoyed to wary

but she wasn't about to let it stop her. 'It's okay, you know, to admit there's something between us, Blake,' she said, gliding forward. 'To want to do something about it. I know that you feel you're in a position of trust but I'm not going to think any less of you.'

Even in a towel, with acres of tanned, toned flesh on display, she still pulled off a superior look better than anyone he knew. Maybe he should have let her off at the castle for the night with the Queen.

At least she wouldn't be here, naked but for a towel, tempting him to forget what was right, forget that every instinct he possessed warned him to stay way away from her.

Her shoulders were, oh, so bare, oh, so lovely as she pulled up in front of him. Right in front of him. He doubted he'd even have to extend his arm its full length to brush fingers along her collarbones. To yank her body flush with his.

Blake pulled his gaze up, meeting her frank, knowing eyes. A whole world of temptation stared back at him. 'Yes, but *I'll* think less of me,' he said.

She looked at him through half-closed lashes like some silver-screen goddess, one of her snooty little half-smiles playing on her mouth. 'I promise you won't have to *think* at all.'

She seemed to have shifted tack from last night—from brash self-assurance to coquettish flirtation and Blake decided he liked this Ava better. Almost as much as he liked the possibility of a little mindless sex despite the faint echo of warning bells clanging somewhere. He'd spent a lot of the last few years inside his head, thinking. Just like now. Letting that all go while he lost himself in Ava for a while was an attractive proposition.

He looked at her mouth, which was dead ahead. Right there, ready to claim, her lips two perfect arcs aside from the tiny dip in the middle of the top one that was incredibly fascinating. He'd really like to lick her just there.

And along those lovely collarbones.

It would be so easy. He leaned his shoulder into the door frame. 'Just leave my brain on the table by the bed, huh?'

Ava, encouraged by the way he appeared to be considering her words instead of rejecting them outright, broadened her smile. 'Well not entirely. Don't forget what they say about the body's largest sexual organ being the brain.'

Blake gave a soft snort. 'Only men with small penises say that.'

Ava was momentarily surprised by his quick, disdainful comeback and then she laughed. He was so serious and yet the quip had been fast and witty. If he'd just put a smile on that marvellous mouth it could even be classed as banter.

It definitely made him seem more approachable and her hopes soared. 'Well, that…' she let her gaze travel down to the area between his hips, then back up again '…counts you out.'

Blake's groin leapt to life at her blatant reminder. He could still feel the warm clamp of her hand around him. How right it had felt when she'd stroked him last night good and firm, *just the way he liked it.*

His fingers itched to touch her. To stroke along her shoulders, up her throat, along her mouth. But being dressed in only a towel was a double-edged sword. Sure, she might look sexy and gorgeous and utterly accessible, but it also reminded him of how vulnerable she was and he was reminded of her pallor and fright straight after the shooting.

He was reminded that she was under his protection. 'I was never in,' he said and hoped it sounded definite.

Ava sensed he was wavering. She smiled at him, not convinced that *he* was convinced. Still *convinced s*he could talk him round if she trod carefully. God knew, her abdominals were scrunched so tight in anticipation she'd never need do another sit-up again.

She sighed as she took a half-step closer. 'You're hard on a girl's ego, Blake Walker.'

Blake didn't trust her easy-going reply, not when she

was somehow closer than she'd been a moment ago. Somehow more enticing.

Okay, this was getting dangerous. *Time to step away from the sex kitten.*

He took a mental pace backwards. 'I'm sure your ego can take it,' he said dryly.

Ava sensed his withdrawal but tried not to panic. She could still reel him in; she was sure of it. 'You know us supermodels.' She shrugged again for good effect, satisfied when his gaze locked on her shoulders. 'Always needing someone around assuring us we're beautiful.'

Blake battled the urge to assure Ava with his tongue down her throat, or in her ear or licking all the way down her body. Instead, he straightened in the doorway. 'Oh, you're beautiful, Ava Kelly,' he said. 'But I'm going to take a shower.'

A cold one.

Ava raised an eyebrow. 'Is that an invitation?'

Blake's groin roused further as a bunch of possibilities played through his head. *A very cold one.* 'No. It is not,' he said, then turned away.

No, no, no. Ava knew she'd lost him. Stubborn man. But she refused to give up. 'Blake.' She slipped a hand on his retreating shoulder.

Blake tensed. He wished she wouldn't touch him. He didn't want her to touch him. It made him want to touch her right back. And a bunch of other things too. He turned.

'What?' he asked impatiently. 'Time to offer me some more money?'

Ava gasped as if he had slapped her. It stung that he was throwing her bribery back in her face. But most of all it stung because he made it sound so cheap.

'Go to hell,' she snapped. 'You think you're such a goody bloody two shoes? You think self-denial is so freaking honourable? Go right on ahead, you believe it, whatever helps you get through the night, *buddy.* But you and I *both* know how badly you want this, how much you want to succumb and how it's only a matter of time before you give into temptation.'

Blake was taken aback by the ferocious yellow glitter in her eyes as all Ava's fierce feline juju leapt out at him. She was pretty angry at him and yes, he conceded, maybe that *had* been a low blow.

But she was hitting pretty low too and her accuracy was startling. Still, no way was he going to let her know that. 'Ava, I wouldn't succumb to temptation if you were lying naked on my bed,' he said, jabbing a finger towards it, 'with beer poured all over you.'

Ava knew there were only two possible comebacks to that. One was to slam the door in his face. Choosing the other, she reached over and plucked the beer out of his hands. 'Wanna bet?'

CHAPTER NINE

ANY ISSUES AVA might have once had with taking her clothes off in front of strangers had died very quickly when she'd hit the big time. Over a decade in front of one camera or another she could very definitely look at her body with objectivity—the way the people who paid her did. For them she was just a canvas for an artist aka fashion designer to decorate in whatever way he/she wanted.

Years on catwalks where quick crowded changes were paramount and modesty something that nobody worried about had taught her that nudity was passé and certainly nothing to be ashamed of or worried about. Parading around in clothes that often left little to the imagination—be it on the catwalk, or for a magazine shoot or a television commercial—had compounded this view.

So lying on her back on Blake's bed, wriggling to the very centre, then peeling her towel away was no biggie for her. Even if he'd never seen her in a single magazine, he'd been given a pretty good preview last night.

Except, at the last moment, as the towel fell away, she raised the leg closest to him, bending it at the knee and placing the foot flat on the bedspread, shielding the full view of her lower half from his eyes, providing a modicum of decency. She wasn't sure why she did it but she felt suddenly reluctant to strip off all the way.

Aware Blake was watching every single move, she raised

herself up on one elbow and, facing the ceiling, she tipped her head back, her hair brushing the coverlet, and took a long deep swallow of his beer. Then she held it just above the hollow at the base of her throat.

Blake could *not* tear his eyes away from a butt-naked Ava sprawled in the middle of his bed. An erection big enough to cause cerebral infarction from lack of blood flow to his brain pressed painfully against the zip of his jeans.

Her breasts were firm, the slight side swell utterly tempting, her nipples enticingly lickable. Her belly dipped down from her ribs and the play of muscles there as she held her torso semi-upright was fascinating, drawing his attention to the inward swirl of her perfect belly button.

He swallowed. 'Ava.'

She looked at him for long moments, her gaze knowing, and he wished he could turn away from the delectable sight of her, but he was powerless to resist. She gave him a slow sexy smile as if she knew he was waiting for the show, then she slowly tipped the bottle up.

Blake felt her gasp hit him square in the groin as cold beer spilled down her naked skin. He watched as it flowed down her sternum, branching out as it ran down her body, sending rivulets across the swell of her breasts, her nipples ruching at the contact of the cold liquid. It dipped into the valleys of her ribs and washed down the centre of her abs, spilling down her sides and pooling in her belly button.

Her leg hid how much lower it might have flowed, which was just as well. He did not want to think about *that* combination of beer and woman.

It wasn't conducive to clear thinking.

He shut his eyes, thinking about all the reasons why this was a bad idea. Damsel in distress. Knight in shining armour. Protector. Defender.

Honour.

Trust.

He opened his eyes in time to see her collapsing back

against the bed. She held her hand out to him and said, 'Please,' like freaking Eve lying down on a bed of apples. *Really red, really juicy apples.*

And something snapped inside him then. There was only so much provocation he could stand and what the hell he was holding out for when she was a grown woman who clearly knew her own mind was a mystery not even he could fathom any more.

He strode into the room until he was standing beside the bed, looking directly down at her. *At all of her.* Every last inch. A beautiful contradiction in femininity. Smooth and firm. Soft and supple—interesting curves and sculpted muscles.

And very, very sticky.

His gaze tracked the path of the beer from her throat to where it had pooled in her belly button and then lower. Yes, it had run lower, drenching the trimmed strip of hair at the apex of her thighs.

And he was suddenly very, very thirsty!

Her foot dangling over the edge of the mattress rubbed against his leg and streaked heat up his thigh, urging him on. And he wanted to. A part of him wanted to join her on the bed immediately and lick every last trace of sticky, beery residue off her until she was begging him to stop.

And then do it all again.

She lay looking up at him with lust in her eyes and a knowing little smile, as if she'd ghost-written the Kama Sutra, but part of him could see past her brash outer confidence now to the vulnerable woman beneath, and that was who he wanted to touch.

Ava suppressed the growing need to squirm under his scrutiny. Her nipples got harder. Her breath grew shorter as his gaze lowered and lingered between her legs, streaking heat *everywhere*. She could feel the trickle of moisture where he stared and she wasn't entirely sure it was all beer.

His gaze pulled away again and fanned up and over

her. He was looking at her as if he wanted to eat her up but wasn't sure where to start. Other men looked at her as if she had a staple through her navel. As if she were some prize they'd won.

As if they'd scored with a supermodel and they were looking at her to perform like one.

Blake was looking as if he was trying to map her entire body. Locate all her hotspots. Work out what he was going to do to them. And how long he was going to spend doing it.

Like a recon mission.

Like a soldier.

Either that or he was committing her to memory before he did a bolt. Something she doubted she'd survive now he'd brought her right to the brink of arousal. *Without so much as touching her!* Because she was very, very aroused.

'Blake?'

Her voice was husky and she dragged in some quick breaths to dispel the annoying weakness. But she was pleased when it seemed to bring him out of his intense study.

Not that he answered her or even said a word. He just locked gazes, put a knee on the bed beside her leg, leaned onto his hands and lowered himself slowly down, his head level with her belly. When he was a whisper away from the puddle of beer in her belly button, he broke eye contact and touched his mouth to her abdomen, his tongue swiping at the now warm liquid.

Ava gasped, her back arching, her hand reaching down, ploughing through Blake's dirty-blond hair. She held him against her, afraid he was going to stop or that she was going to float right off the bed.

Don't stop, she wanted to say, but there was no need as the hot flat of his tongue swiped and swiped in ever-widening circles around and around her belly until she was whimpering and calling his name.

'Blake.'

Blake looked up from his ministrations—all the way up. Over her belly and up her ribs, skimming her breasts, fanning up her throat to her mouth, opening and shutting, silently begging him for more. 'Yes?'

She raised her head and looked at him with eyes that weren't quite focused. 'I...I...'

I...what? *What?* Ava couldn't speak. All the man had done was lick her belly—after making her wait for two days *and several minutes*—and she was putty in his hands. But it didn't matter because he was lifting his head, travelling up, up, up and before she could protest the lack of him down there he was up top, his mouth on hers, his hands in her hair, his body pressing her into the mattress.

And he felt so good all she could do was hold onto him and follow where he led.

And he led with spectacular commitment. His mouth opening wide, demanding hers do the same, kissing and licking and sucking, dragging every morsel of lust and need and want from her lips. Groaning against her mouth, absorbing the husky timbre of her noises that alternated from strong and strident to weak and whimpery and desperate. Joining the shuddery husk of his breath with hers.

And all the time his hands stroked and caressed, from her neck down, flowing everywhere, whispering heat and seduction wherever they touched. Promising lust and good times and secrets she never knew existed.

Eventually, the drugging lash of his mouth left hers and she protested. 'No, no,' she moaned, grabbing for him, reaching for his head, for his face, to bring him back where she needed him, to her mouth, where he'd poured all the lust and desire she'd never have known was even there but for this bubble of time.

But then he was kissing her again, saying, 'Shh, shh,' against her mouth, hushing her with his kisses and the magic of his hands as they stroked over her belly. And then, pushing her arms up above her head, restraining her there saying, 'I want to lick beer off you,' as he licked lower, down her jaw, her neck, her chest.

And it might have been weak of her but Ava, under the influence of his very clever tongue, let him.

Blake knew the moment she let go. The moment she stopped wanting it to be about them and let him make it all about her. It was the second his mouth opened over her nipple and, even though every muscle in her body tensed, her back arching up, pushing more of the gloriously hard tip against his palate, she clearly surrendered to him.

Her hands stopped questing, stopped pushing against the bond of his, trying to move, trying to reach for him. Her body melted into the mattress. Her head fell back, her mouth open wide as if breathing was all she could manage.

He liked that.

He liked that he'd made her incapable of anything but the very basics of life.

It allowed him free rein and he took it mercilessly, tasting her everywhere. Ravaging her nipples to hard peaks over and over until she begged him for release. Leaving there to head south, laving her belly with his tongue again, skating around the juncture of her thighs despite the desperate lifting of her hips, using his tongue to devastating effect on the sensitive skin of her inner thigh, her legs wide open, the intoxicating mix of beer and woman ratcheting up his heart rate, making his mouth water.

Making him want to bury his head there and taunt her with his tongue until she came long and hard. But he was determined to have all of her as he licked down to her bikini-red toenails.

Ava was lost in a world where she floated somewhere off the ground in a place full of sensations that swirled and skipped in a kaleidoscope of pleasure, drenching her in sweet, sticky rain. And she surrendered to it—lolled in it. Twirling and sliding, getting absolutely soaking wet.

There was something missing; she knew that. It nagged

at the back of her mind but she couldn't quite pinpoint it. Then his fingers brushed up her thighs then teased against the core of her and she cried out at the intensity of it, wanting it to end, urging him to get her there.

But knowing somewhere inside her she *never* wanted it to end.

His fingers stroked and swirled, round and round, going hard, then backing off, going hard again until she was begging him to end it. But he didn't. Instead the hard probe of one finger slipping inside her had her crying out, then another as his wicked tongue laved the flesh of her inner thighs.

And just when she thought she couldn't take any more his mouth was on her, tasting her, his tongue circling hard around the sensitive bud, and she bucked against him, crying out.

That was what was missing. She wanted to taste him too. Wanted to put him in her mouth and know the contours of him.

The velvet and the steel, the sweet and the salt of him.

She didn't want to just lie here and be serviced.

'Blake…' she panted trying to sit up, trying to reach him. 'Blake…please…let me taste you too…'

'No,' came the muffled reply, his hand clamping down hard on her abdomen, the vibrations of his voice exquisite torture against her ravaged flesh. 'You. Just you.'

Ava fell back against the bed. She should have said no. *No, no no.* Insisted they be equal partners in this. She should have been worried that his honourable streak was going to see her fulfilled while leaving him wanting but she'd just used up her one last rational thought.

So she surrendered to him and this time he didn't back off with fingers or tongue, he just drove her higher and higher until Ava could feel herself drawing tight, so tight she didn't think she'd be able to breathe, and for a moment as everything coalesced into one powerful pinpoint of time her lungs seized and she swore for a second or two she did actually stop breathing altogether.

Then air came rushing into her lungs and she grabbed it, sucking in and out as ecstasy slammed into her. She grabbed Blake's head, holding him where he was as it undulated through her body, bowing her back off the bed, forcing a primal cry from the deepest part of her soul.

And she rode it all the way to the end.

Blake's heart rate was still unsteady as he lazily kissed and sucked his way back up Ava's body. She was still away in the land of sexual limbo and he was taking full advantage of her inebriated state to touch her some more, to make sure he'd lapped up every last trace of beer from her very delectable body.

He hadn't known what to expect from this—sex with Ava. Frankly he'd spent most of his time trying *not* to think about it. But he'd never thought it would be so fulfilling just to get her off. For someone as sexually confident as Ava she'd given him control so easily—as if her control freak was a mask she wore but was only too happy to lose. And her complete immersion in what was happening to her body had been heady stuff.

He swirled a nipple in his mouth and she moaned long and low as he felt it grow hard against his tongue.

He released his mouthful to look up at her. 'You're back,' he murmured.

Ava smiled at him. She twined her fingers in his hair, as best as she was able amidst the short strands 'Barely. I think I died for a short while.'

Blake chuckled, stroking his fingers up her arm. 'It's okay. I would have given you the kiss of life.'

Ava rolled her eyes. 'That's what got me into this mess.'

Blake raised an eyebrow as he stroked lazy fingers over the rise of her right breast. 'Would we call this a mess?' Of course the situation had mess written all over it but enjoying Ava's body had been divine.

Ava shut her eyes as the caress hummed right through her still-buzzing middle. 'No,' she said, opening her eyes. 'We would not.'

Blake dropped a kiss on her shoulder and nuzzled her there. 'Good.'

Ava stroked his hair, her mouth brushing against the ends, absently noticing the way it just brushed his nape, falling far short of the neckline of his shirt.

'You still have all your clothes on,' she said.

Blake lifted his head. 'What can I say? You were insatiable.'

'I think we need to do something about that, don't you?' she asked, reaching down to the small of his back, and grabbing a handful of his shirt.

Blake considered her for a moment. He wanted to get naked and do the wild thing with her. God knew his erection was still a living, breathing mammoth inside his underwear and he wanted to feel it buried deep inside her. But it wasn't simply a matter of just taking his clothes off.

'Duck,' she said to him as she ruched his shirt up his back, pulling it up to his shoulders. 'I want to even the playing field.'

Blake looked down at her body, his gaze lingering in all the places he'd been. 'I like uneven playing fields.'

Ava rolled her eyes. 'I bet you do.' She tugged on his shirt again but he resisted. 'Blake?'

Blake sighed. 'There's not exactly a sexy way to remove a prosthetic leg,' he said.

Ava blinked. She'd forgotten about his leg. Hadn't thought about the…logistics of sex with a prosthesis. Or how it made Blake feel. 'Does it…embarrass you…to take it off in front of someone…in front of a woman?'

'No,' he said. Not that he'd ever taken it off in front of a woman who personified human beauty. 'But it's a bit like stopping to put a condom on…it's a big dose of reality, which can be a bit of a passion killer.'

Ava regarded him for a moment or two. 'Well, we can't have that, can we?' she murmured.

Then she pushed against his shoulders and, as he fell back on the bed, she followed him over, rolling up until she was straddling his hips. The juncture of her thighs aligned perfectly with the bulge in his jeans and she pressed herself against him, revelling in the hard ridge. It was satisfying to hear the suck of his breath and watch his eyes shut as his big hands came up to bracket her hips.

'Feels like the passion's very much alive to me,' she murmured.

Blake opened his eyes. She was a sight to behold. Her drying caramel hair fell in fluffy waves against lovely shoulders thrust proudly back. It emphasised the firmness of her high breasts boasting erect, perfectly centred nipples. Her stomach muscles undulated and her belly button winked as her hips rocked back and forth along the length of him.

Each pass rippled urgent pleasure through the deep muscle fibres of his belly. It also caused a fascinating little jiggle through her breasts and Blake couldn't drag his eyes off them.

'I don't know,' he muttered. 'I think I've died and gone to heaven.' Then he curled up and claimed a nipple.

Ava gasped as Blake's hot mouth sucked her deep inside. She raked her fingers into his hair, capturing his head to her chest, and holding him fast. His teeth grazed the tip and her head dropped back. He switched sides, grazing the other nipple as he sucked it hard and deep, and when his fingers toyed with the other one her lips parted on a moan as she dragged in much-needed air.

Blake revelled in the moan. But he wanted more. He wanted to taste her. To swallow her moan as it vibrated against his tongue. He broke away, sought her mouth, found it as she protested his absence.

'Shh,' he said against her mouth, his hands stroking down her naked back. 'I've got you.' And when she moaned again and opened wide to the invasion of his tongue he kissed her deep and wet.

Released from the intimate torture of her nipples, Ava was able to think a little clearer—even though all he'd done was switch from one form of havoc to another. The man could kiss for England! But she needed more than that now. He was thick and hard between her thighs and *that* was what she needed.

Ava grabbed for his shirt and pulled it up his back. Then she broke off the kiss and hauled it the rest of the way off, tossing it behind her. And then her hands were on his smooth, naked shoulders and she sighed and pressed a kiss to them, they felt so good.

His hands slid to her breasts and she shut her eyes for a moment as his thumbs stroked across her nipples and he started kissing her neck.

Then she shoved his chest hard and watched him fall back against the mattress. 'Hey,' he protested, reaching out for her.

But she just shook her head and said, 'My turn.'

And if Blake thought she looked amazing before it was nothing to how she was looking now, astride him buck naked staring down at him as if he were the main course and she were *starving*.

Ava gazed down at all his broad magnificence. The dusting of hair over his meaty pecs, the solid firmness of his abdominals. A work-honed chest. A *real* man's chest. She stroked a finger right down the centre, from the hollow at the base of his throat to where the waistband of his jeans stopped her journey. Muscles contracted beneath her finger and his breathing became more ragged.

And then she just had to taste him.

Blake groaned as her mouth tentatively touched the spot where her finger had started its journey. Her hair fell forward, brushing his chest, and he slid his hand to her shoulder and stroked down her back, revelling in the feel of her skin beneath his palm as he revelled in the feel of his skin beneath her tongue.

By the time she got to his nipples there was nothing tentative about her touch. They circled and circled as he had done to her. Sucking and licking. Flicking her tongue back and forth over them and he shut his eyes and let the sensations wash over him.

Then she headed lower. Exploring his ribs, his stomach, his belly button.

And then lower.

His zip came down, his underwear was peeled back and at the first touch of her tongue to his screamingly taut erection he bucked and cried out. And then she was relentless. Swiping her tongue up and down the length of him, filling her hot, hot mouth with him, sucking him in deep and hard, feeling so good, so right.

He buried one hand in her hair and the other one in the coverlet, gripping the sheets as she drove him out of his mind.

It wasn't long before the tug of an orgasm made its presence known. Under her ministrations it was inevitable that he would build quickly but he didn't want it to be like this.

Not the first time.

'Ava,' he said on an outward breath. 'Stop.' She didn't stop. If anything she sucked harder. 'Ava,' he said again, curling half up, pulling at her shoulder, pulling her up.

'Wha…?' she asked, looking at him, a frown on her face.

Blake almost gave in. Her mouth was moist and swollen and she had a glazed look in her eyes that almost undid him.

'If you don't stop that now it's going to be all over and I want to be inside you when I come,' he said.

Ava's brain took a second to power up again but quickly

got up to speed. She smiled at him. She'd been wondering what it would feel like to have him hot and hard inside her for the last few months. 'Condoms?'

Blake smiled back and nodded towards the bedside table. 'In the drawer.'

She was off the bed and back at his side again in fifteen seconds, tearing at the condom with shaking fingers. And then she was sheathing him, and then straddling him and leaning over him, easing herself into position, kissing him as she slowly aligned herself.

He gripped her hips hard as she slid home and her gasp and his groan mingled as they both just stilled for a moment and enjoyed the feel of their joining. And then she was pushing up and away from him, sitting proudly, her breasts bouncing as her hips undulated, finding a perfect rhythm.

Her hair was wild, and her yellow-green eyes were even wilder, all feline and primal. And she didn't look haughty now, riding atop him. Actually, no, she did. She looked like a madam on her steed and he bucked hard into her as she picked up the pace.

'God, you're magnificent,' he groaned, holding out his hands to her.

'You're pretty magnificent yourself,' she gasped as she intertwined her fingers with his.

And then neither of them talked. They just moved. Up and down. In and out. Harder. Faster. Building, building, building. Using their joined hands to lever their actions, pushing hard against each other's palms, finding every inch and every bit of depth they could.

And then she was gasping, her eyes opening wide, and she was crying out, 'Blake! Blake!' and the urgency of it all slammed into his belly and he felt himself coming apart too, joining her, calling out her name too, 'Ava!' as he came and came and came, his heart rate off the scale, bucking and thrusting like a machine, determined to give her every last bit of him, their hips slamming together as he drove and drove and drove up into her.

And he didn't stop, not even after they were both spent, not until she collapsed on top of him.

CHAPTER TEN

IT WAS AFTER eight the next morning when Blake finally stirred. He'd always been an early riser but, given that he and Ava had spent a lot of the night burning up the sheets, it was hardly surprising that he'd slept in.

She felt good spooned against his chest. As did his erection, cushioned against the cheeks of her bottom, and the handful of her hip beneath his palm. He stroked his hand down her thigh and was rewarded with an enticing little wiggle.

'Morning,' he murmured as he nuzzled her neck.

Ava smiled sleepily as the prickles of Blake's whiskers beaded her nipples. She deliberately pressed her bottom back into him as she stretched. 'What time is it?'

Blake shut his eyes as her moving weakened his resolve to get going. 'Time to get up.' They should have been under way by now.

'Really?' she asked, slipping her hand behind her and between their bodies, finding him big and hard and ready. And not for a day on the water. 'I think,' she said, giving him a squeeze and smiling when he sucked in a breath, 'you're already there.'

Blake kept his eyes shut as her hand moved up and down the length of him. 'I am,' he said, his own hand dipping down her belly and disappearing between her legs.

Ava gasped as his fingers brushed against the thoroughly abused nub, already begging for more. She let him go, slipping her arm up behind his neck, anchoring herself as she angled her hips to accommodate the slide of his erection between her thighs and the glide and rub of it along the seam of her sex.

'Man-oh-man,' she moaned. 'That feels so good.'

Blake, getting under way completely forgotten, whispered, 'You ain't seen nothing yet,' in her ear and proceeded to rub and glide from one side while his fingers worked her from the other and it wasn't until she was begging him for completion that he whispered, 'Condom.'

And Ava didn't need to be told twice.

A couple of hours later they stirred again. Blake dropped a kiss on her neck. 'We really do have to get going at some stage today,' he murmured.

Ava's eyes fluttered open. 'Why?' she asked as she turned in his arms, one arm sliding over his waist, her head resting against the soft pillow of a pectoral muscle.

Blake propped his chin on top of her head. 'Because I'm on a schedule, here. I can't stay on holiday for ever.'

Ava smiled. 'You're a schedule kind of a guy, aren't you?'

He nodded. 'And proud of it. That's what over a decade in the military does for you. That's what got you your reno on time,' Blake reminded her. He looked down at her head. 'I've seen those behind-the-scenes-at-a-fashion-show docos on the telly—those things run to tight schedules too.'

'They do,' Ava conceded. 'And I can run to a schedule as professionally as the next model. But when I'm on *holiday*…' she glanced up at him '…schedules go out the window. That's *the point* of a holiday. It's all about being flexible.'

Blake smiled down at her. 'Oh, you're *very* flexible.'

Ava rolled her eyes. 'Why can men never resist an opening?' But she kissed him anyway because he was right there and he looked even more tempting this morning than he had last night.

'My point is,' she said, pulling back from the kiss, 'you're on holiday. You don't really have to *do* anything or *be* anywhere. For instance, we could stay here in bed all day together. We could kiss and cuddle, have lots more sex, doze off, wake up, watch some telly, eat gourmet snacks I can prepare. You know…just have some fun?'

Blake felt the usual clench of his gut at the word *fun*. He knew it shouldn't affect him, that he had as much right to a full happy life, *to fun*, as the next person, but it still felt wrong to be enjoying himself when so many guys he knew couldn't.

'We can do whatever we want,' Ava continued, oblivious to Blake's consternation, 'because *we're on holiday.*'

Blake forced himself to smile and push the downer thoughts away. *He was allowed to have fun.* His shrink had told him that over and over.

'Ah, but *you're* not on holiday,' he reminded her, injecting a deliberately teasing tone into his voice. 'You've just hijacked mine. *Bribed* your way in if my memory serves me correctly.'

The thought was sobering but Ava refused to let it get her down. 'Well, it feels like it. I haven't had a lot of idle days since turning fourteen.'

Blake heard the pensive note in her voice and stroked his finger down her face. The last thing he wanted was to drag her down too. 'Okay, then, you win. A rest day.'

Ava laughed. 'In that case I better get us something to eat. Cos I don't think either of us are going to be getting much rest.'

Blake smiled. 'No,' he said. 'Allow me.'

Ava quirked an eyebrow. 'You? You can cook? You who only had a six-pack of beer in the fridge two days ago?'

'I can manage coffee, toast and fruit,' he said indignantly as he rolled onto his back, then swung into a sitting position and flicked the wall-mounted telly on with the remote, handing it to her. 'See what the media is saying about your situation and then check in with Ken.' He reached for his leg propped against the wall. 'I'll get us some breakfast or brunch or lunch...or whatever it is.'

He went through the motions of getting into his prosthesis as Ava flicked through the news channels. He could have had crutches just to get around the boat, a lot of amputees used them for domestic purposes, but he hadn't wanted to become reliant on them, preferring to always use his leg.

Blake looked around for his clothes but as he had no idea where they'd ended up last night he figured he might as well just throw on some new ones.

Ava's gaze was drawn to him as he skirted around the bed, briefly interrupting her view of the telly as he strode to his wardrobe. His brawny masculinity wasn't diminished by the prosthesis, if anything it emphasised it—a silent testament to his heroism. But there was just something kind of surreal about it and she couldn't help but laugh.

He turned and quirked an eyebrow at her and she clamped a hand over her mouth. *Way to be sensitive, Ava.* 'I'm sorry,' she said, embarrassed by her behaviour. 'I'm not...I don't—'

'What's the matter?' he interrupted and she could see the teasing light in his indigo eyes. 'Never seen a naked man with a fake leg?'

'You look like Bionic Man,' she blurted out, still clearly suffering from foot in mouth. But he did. His broad chest and shoulders and his narrow hips were perfectly proportioned. The hard, powerful quads and calves of his good leg balanced out the hard moulded plastic and titanium lines of the prosthetic. He looked half man, half machine.

Strong. Super strong.

Ava kicked the sheets off and swung her legs over the side of the bed. 'It's kind of a turn-on actually.'

He watched her walk towards, him, one hundred per

cent naked, one hundred per cent up to no good, staring at his body as if she wanted to eat him. His groin fired to life.

'You're not going to be one of those chicks who has a thing for amputees, are you? Hangs out on all the forums and dating sites?'

Ava shook her head as she sank to her haunches in front of him. 'No,' she said, looking up at him, past the rapid thickening happening before her eyes. 'Just for you.'

Blake's heartbeat pounded through his ears as her gaze feasted on the jut of his now fully fledged erection. 'Ava,' he warned as the muscle fibres in his belly and his buttocks turned to liquid. 'Food…Ken…'

'Later,' she dismissed as she raised herself up, her hands gliding up his legs and anchoring at the backs of his thighs, her mouth opening around him.

Blake's groan came from somewhere primitive inside him as hot, wet, delicious suction scrambled his brain of any rational thought. He reached for the cupboard and held on for dear life.

Later that afternoon, Blake was sitting propped against the headboard of his sleigh bed, idly flicking through channels as Ava dozed by his side. It was another warm day and they'd kicked off the sheets a long time ago so she was lying on her back stark naked, completely comfortable with her nudity.

His phone vibrated on the bedside table and he checked it. Charlie. *Still hanging with the supermodel?*

Blake smiled. *Yes.*

The reply was fast. *Slept with her yet?*

Blake's gaze wandered to her naked body, his chest filling with something akin to contentment. His fingers slid across the touchpad. *You are a pervert.*

Another fast reply. *So that's a yes?*

Blake gave a soft snort as he typed his reply. *Goodbye.*

A little yellow face with a dripping tongue hanging out

its mouth appeared on the screen and Blake shook his head at his brother's juvenile wit as he returned the phone to the bedside table.

He flicked his gaze back to the telly just as an ad break came on. He was about to change the channel when Ava came on the screen. 'Hey,' he said, giving her a gentle nudge. 'Wake up, you're on the telly.'

He couldn't believe he was in bed with a woman whose face was on the telly. Her celebrity had been easier to wrap his head around when he'd just been the guy renovating her house.

Ava stirred, opening her eyes to see the cologne commercial she'd shot last year. 'Oh, yeah.' She smiled, half sitting, wriggling back, insinuating herself between Blake's thighs, snuggling her bottom in and draping her back to his stomach, her head under his chin. His arms encircled her waist and they watched it together.

Ava was proud of the commercial and had had a lot of fun filming it with one of England's most dashing young actors. It was moody, edgy, very dark and sexy, suiting the bouquet of the cologne.

Blake wasn't so enamoured as Ava, showing almost as much flesh as she was now beneath a transparent white hooded gown, was chased and then caught, her dress ripped open down the front and her neck *and parts distinctly lower* thoroughly ravaged by a dark, brooding, shirtless man.

The voice-over said, 'Beast. For the animal in us all.'

Okay, no actual prohibited-for-PG-viewing bits could be seen, but it was a very fine line and the subliminal messages were heavily sexual.

'What do you think?' she asked, turning her neck to look at him as the commercial ended.

Blake cast around for something to say that wouldn't annoy her when clearly she was pleased with the results. 'I think if I owned these,' he said, his hands sliding up her belly to her breasts, 'I wouldn't want anyone else touching them.'

Ava smiled. She wasn't surprised by his reaction. People outside the industry didn't understand how it worked. She glanced back at the telly. '*I* own these,' she said, sliding her hands up under his, cupping her own breasts, his hands falling away.

She looked down at herself, at her hands, aware he was looking too before letting go.

'Anyway…it's all just make-believe. We did that shot about a hundred times, there's a full set of people watching you, a director telling you a bit to the right, a bit to the left, hot lights, make-up people, a ticking clock. It's not as sexy as it looks.'

'So how do your boyfriends cope with that? Because, frankly, I'd want to punch that guy in the head.'

Ava laughed. 'Well, that's very Neanderthal of you.' She knew she shouldn't find that attractive but somehow it fitted with his whole ex-soldier, Bionic Man persona and she was secretly thrilled.

Blake guessed he should apologise for his prehistoric possessive streak but he didn't. 'I just don't get how it works.'

'Which is precisely why I don't have *boyfriends*. Lovers, yes, boyfriends, no. Lovers are disposable, boyfriends tend to get jealous. And only from within the circles I move in because you have to be in the biz to understand how very little all that—' she waved her hands at the screen '—means. Models, actors…they know how it works.'

'Wow,' he said derisively. 'You really are slumming it with me.'

She glanced up at him but he was smiling down at her and didn't seem to be too insulted. She ran her hand down his thigh. 'I'm making a special exception for you.'

'So, you don't have…relationships?' Didn't all women crave relationships? Connections?

Hell, didn't all human beings?

Ava looked down, following her hand as it absently caressed his thigh. 'No. Best not to. Relationships require trust. I've had some major disappointments in that sector earlier in my career, a couple of guys talking to the press and with Mum and Paul…let's just say I wised up pretty quickly.'

'That sounds kind of lonely though…'

Okay, he wasn't exactly King of relationships either, but not because he didn't believe in them. He just wasn't sure if damaged goods made very good partners.

Ava traced the outline of Blake's quad with her index finger as she shrugged. 'I don't have time for men who want to hold me down…hold me back. I don't have time for their petty jealousies. I have a finite amount of years I can do what I do and I'll worry about relationships after. For now dating and the occasional spot of casual sex with a guy in a similar situation to me suits just fine.'

Blake absently rubbed his chin against the fineness of her hair as he absorbed her very definitive views.

Ava turned her neck to face him, unnerved by his silence. She'd come to her relationship conclusions a long time ago the hard way and it had never mattered to her before what anyone thought.

But somehow it did right now.

'You think that makes me cold and unfeeling?'

'No,' Blake said and meant it.

Ava had to be the least cold and unfeeling person he knew. Sure, her snooty *touch-me-not* public image was meant to convey that, but if he'd learned anything about her at all these past three days it was that she was a strange mix of hot and cold. Strong and vulnerable. Public and private.

And he felt privileged to know the real woman beneath the distant haughty smile.

'I think you've taken control of your life and you know what you want. A lot of people never do that.'

'Damn right,' she said as she looked back at her hand on his thigh, his chuckle vibrating against her back. 'What about you and relationships?' she asked. 'You're still single.'

Ava stopped tracing the quad on his good leg and drew a line with her finger down the thigh of his amputated leg, which seemed almost the same length as its opposite number. The quad almost as meaty. 'Has this stopped you?'

Blake looked down at her hand. 'No. But there's a lot of…baggage attached to me…and I'm not much of a talker. So…that makes it hard to see past the outside to what's underneath.'

Except Ava had. Ava had known him for three months before she'd even been aware he *had* a prosthesis. She hadn't treated him differently—no pity for the cripple or reverence for the returned war hero. She'd been demanding and snooty and utterly self-absorbed. As testy with him as everyone else around her.

And despite what a pain in the butt she'd been, he suddenly realised how refreshing it had been. How deep down he'd looked forward to going to her place for a slice of equity in a world where everyone in his orbit treated him just a little bit differently than they had before he'd lost his leg. He knew they didn't mean to or even realise that they were, but he was sensitive to the subtleties.

Would Ava have been so demanding and critical if she'd known he was an amputee? Or would she have *made allowances*?

'Yep,' Ava said. 'I hear ya.' She totally understood where he was coming from with that—people never looked past her outside package.

Her palm skated to the end of his thigh and tentatively cupped his stump. His quad tensed and for a moment she thought he was going to pull it away. But he slowly relaxed into her hand and she became aware of its rounded contours.

It felt so…smooth. So…healed. So…innocuous.

Nothing liked the jagged, shredded mess it must have been to have lost it. She shut her eyes against a hundred television images she'd seen over the last decade. She couldn't even begin to imagine what he'd been through. The trauma. The pain. The loss.

'Does it hurt?' she asked after a moment.

Her hand felt cool against the stump and so pretty against the blunt ugliness of it, it took all Blake's will power not to pull away. 'No.'

'Did it?' she asked. 'Sorry, of course it did… It's just that I saw this documentary once, interviewing returned soldiers, and there was this one guy who'd lost a leg and he said he was in so much shock at the time he didn't feel anything, no pain…nothing. He didn't even realise his leg had been blown off until he woke up in hospital. He doesn't have any memory of losing it at all.'

Blake's screams, never far away, echoed in his head. Unfortunately for him, his memory had perfect recall. 'It hurt,' he said grimly. 'A lot. I screamed like a baby.'

Ava turned at the blatant contempt in his voice. 'Your leg was blown off,' she said, frowning at him. 'That must have been *incredibly* painful… I can't even begin to imagine…did you think you didn't have the right to express that pain?' She lifted her hand off his leg to his face. 'Do you think *anyone's* going to judge you for that?'

Blake saw compassion and pity in her eyes. Just as he'd seen in countless people over the last three years. And, thanks to his shrink, he'd learned that it was a natural human reaction to a sad and shocking situation. But he still had problems accepting it at face value because the truth was he judged himself more harshly than anyone else could have.

'There were other men injured in the blast, Ava. Men who were *my* responsibility.'

Ava didn't need to be a psychiatrist to tell Blake was

judging himself plenty. 'Blake…are you telling me you still have to be a leader when you're bleeding in the dirt somewhere with a severed leg?'

He stared at her. 'They were my men. They looked to me.'

Ava's skin broke out in goose bumps at the utter desolation in his voice and the bleakness in his eyes. 'Even when you're injured?' she asked gently. 'Wasn't there some kind of second in command?'

Blake nodded. 'Yes. He was dead.' Colin, dead in the dirt beside him.

Ava shut her eyes. *Not helping, Ava.* 'I'm sorry,' she said, twisting in his arms, moving, straddling him, settling her butt on the tops of his thighs until they were face to face. 'I'm so sorry,' she repeated.

Then she lowered her head and kissed him—slow and sweet. 'So sorry,' she whispered against his mouth as she pulled away, hugging him close.

It felt good to have his arms circle her body, bringing her in closer until they were flush, his head nestled against her neck, her chin on top of his head.

'What was his name? Was he married?'

Blake shut his eyes, dragging in big lungfuls of her sweet-smelling skin, trying to block out the image. 'Colin,' he said. 'And yes, he was married.'

Ava could hear the roughness in his voice and she held him closer for long moments. 'Do you blame yourself?' She pulled back to look at him. 'For him dying?'

Blake looked up into her earnest gaze. That wasn't an easy question to answer. There was the logical answer. And the emotional one. And they both blurred into each other.

Ava didn't wait for him to reply. 'Would *he* blame you? This…Colin?'

Blake shook his head. It was a complicated situation but he didn't have to think about it to know the answer to that one. 'No.'

'Well, isn't that your answer?' she asked.

Blake shook his head. *If only it were that simple.* '*I* was supposed to look out for him,' he said.

'Because he was one of your men?'

Blake shook his head. 'No. Well...yes, but...' Blake paused, the desire for her to understand pushing hard at his chest. 'Because he was one of my closest friends and... my brother-in-law.' He placed his forehead against her collarbone, his lips brushing her chest. 'Colin was Joanna's husband.'

Ava shut her eyes as his heavy words felt oppressive against her chest. The guilt in his voice was undeniable. Oh, *dear God*—how had Blake survived that? She tightened her arms around him.

'I'm *so* sorry,' she said.

Having to face his amputated leg every day must be a constant physical reminder of what he'd lost. Having to face Joanna, *his sister,* must be a constant *emotional* reminder. She was surprised he'd ever got his life together again.

That must have taken real strength.

Her breath stirred the hair at his temple and Blake held her tighter too. He was used to superficial sympathy from people but with Ava wrapped around him like this it felt real.

'Have you talked to anybody about any of this?' she asked after a few moments.

Blake gave a soft snort, pulling back from her neck. 'Ad nauseam,' he said. 'The army supplies a shrink.'

'So they should,' she muttered. 'Has he helped?'

'*She,*' Blake supplied and smiled to try and soften the topic and erase the anguish from her gaze. 'And yes, actually. I was kind of resistant but, yeh...I'm in a much better place after talking to her than I had been.'

'Well, that's...good,' Ava said, feeling slightly mollified.

Blake smiled and made a concerted effort to drag himself out of the funk they'd descended into. Even he knew this was a far cry from the *fun* she'd prescribed earlier.

'It is,' he murmured, dropping a kiss on the fluttering pulse at the base of her throat. 'Although I prefer other forms of therapy.'

Ava shut her eyes as his tongue traced wet circles up the hard ridge of her throat, sinking into the heat and the thrill of it. 'Like what?'

Blake smiled as her reply buzzed against his lips and she dropped her head back to give him better access.

She might not be able to do anything about the demons in his head or erase all the bad stuff that had happened to him, but she could definitely give him her body. Maybe that was wrong, maybe she should be trying to get him to talk and open up, but she couldn't help but think that a man who'd been through what Blake had been through deserved to choose his own path to wellness.

And right now, in this moment, there was something she *could* do to help him forget for a little while.

She was definitely up for a little sexual healing.

CHAPTER ELEVEN

THE NEXT THREE days drifted by in a perfect little bubble. A bubble where she wasn't a supermodel and he wasn't a one-legged pleb totally out of her league. No lady and the carpenter thing. Just good company and great food and amazing weather.

Laughter and sunshine.

Long days of lazily navigating the waterways of southern England. Waving to fellow boaters. Operating locks. Eating at pubs.

And the nights? Long, hot, sweaty nights of a more frantic persuasion. Eager to be naked and explore. Being bold and forthright. Pushing each other to the limits of their sexuality.

Never quite getting enough.

It was as if they both knew deep down it could never last and therefore the everyday masks they wore to face the world were stripped away. Pretence was shed and there was only room for the real and the raw.

The investigation was progressing according to Ken. They were tracking down leads, leaving no stone unturned. But no arrests had been made and his advice to keep lying low remained the same.

Ava should have been getting antsy. Ordinarily she would have been going out of her mind, not doing anything, worrying about her time out of the limelight and how that might impact her career. Reggie certainly was. Fretting about it day and night with his increasingly desperate calls and texts. Pleading with her to allow him to feed the press something…anything…any morsel to keep them fed and watered and interested.

But after a decade of unfettered availability, anonymity was seductive. A simple life on the water with a simple man was even more seductive.

And while the British press and the paparazzi were in a feeding frenzy over *Ava Watch,* obsessing over her whereabouts, reporting any faux sighting as if she were Elvis, Ava was revelling in her new-found freedom to just…be.

To not put on make-up.

To not go to the gym every day.

To stuff her face with banoffee pie at a pub and not have to watch for a telephoto lens.

To kiss Blake publicly and not worry that she was going to read about her engagement or possible pregnancy in some tabloid the next day.

But the bubble burst late on day six with a very sombre intrusion. And it was the beginning of the end.

Blake's phone rang while they were having dinner at a pub in Devizes. They were talking about the Caen Hill staircase lock they were going to tackle the next day. A good six hours of lock after lock, twenty-nine in total.

Ava watched him frown at his screen and push the answer button. He didn't say much, just, 'Right…right,' and 'When?' and 'Where?' but his face got grimmer and grimmer and she could feel a cold hand slowly closing around her heart.

'What's wrong?' she asked as he pushed the end button.

'Change of plans. I have to go to a funeral tomorrow.'

Ava blinked. No more information appeared to be forthcoming. 'Oh. Okay…who?'

'A guy I served with.'

His reply was clipped and his face, which had been

animated about the adventure ahead just a few minutes ago, was suddenly as bleak and forbidding as a thunder-clap. 'Where?'

'A little village outside Salisbury. I'll hire a car in the morning. I can be back by nightfall.'

Ava nodded. She wasn't sure what she should do, or say. Should she push him for more—did he want that? Or should she take him back to the boat and distract him? She looked down at their half-eaten meal, suddenly not remotely hungry. She looked around at the cheery pub crowd enjoying the late evening warmth in the beer garden.

'You want to go back to the boat?'

Blake nodded. 'Yup.'

They walked along the towpath in silence. Blake was tight-lipped and she didn't even attempt to hold his hand as she had on their way to the pub. Once they were inside the boat and Blake had locked the door behind them she turned to him and said, 'Do you want to talk about it?'

Blake shook his head, grabbing her arm and yanking her flush with his body. 'No,' he said and slammed his mouth down onto hers as he swept her off her feet and carried her into the bedroom.

Distraction it was.

The next morning dawned cool and miserable. They woke to rain patting lightly on the roof and a grey light barely making it through the curtains.

The symbolism was not lost on Ava.

'I can come with you,' she said, snuggling her back into his front, her bottom into his groin, reaching for the bone-deep warmth that seemed to have evaporated in the cold grey light.

She felt him tense and hastened to assure him. 'Not to the funeral,' she clarified. 'But for the trip. For...company.'

She expected him to say no. And for a long time he didn't say anything at all, his warm hand firm and unmov-

ing on her belly. 'Sure,' he said. 'Company would be...
good.'

And then he was kissing her neck and his hand was sliding between her legs and Ava opened to him, welcoming
another session of feverish sex, knowing instinctively that
Blake needed a physical outlet for the grief he couldn't express any other way.

A few hours later they'd been driving for an hour in virtual
silence when Ava couldn't bear it any more. The landscape
was as bleak as the mood in the car and her indecision was
driving her nuts.

Say something, don't say something.

But in the end, she couldn't pretend they were just going
for a Sunday drive in the countryside.

'What's his name?' she asked.

Blake's knuckles tightened on the steering wheel. 'Isaac
Wipani.'

Ava frowned. 'That's an unusual surname.'

'He's a Kiwi. His father was a Maori. Died when he
was a boy.'

'Didn't you say you served with him?'

Blake nodded. 'He joined us from the New Zealand
Defence Force after he met and married an English girl.'

'How old was he?'

'Twenty-nine.'

Ava almost asked him how it happened. But really, did
it matter? A man was dead. A young man. A soldier. 'Did
they have children?'

'Two.'

If anything, Blake's face got grimmer and any other
questions died on her lips. She wished they had the kind of
relationship where she could slip her hand onto his thigh,
to loan him some comfort. She knew they'd shared something special the last few days but what were four days and
nights of sex compared to a lost comrade?

And he looked so incredibly unreachable in his dark suit and even darker mood she was too paralysed to try.

They made it just in time for the funeral. Blake deposited her in a pub opposite the churchyard where the service was taking place and she sat at a cosy booth cradling a coffee, looking out of the rain-spattered window at the bleak day.

Lucky for her, Joanna had thought to include clothes for when the Indian summer came to an abrupt end, which it was always bound to. The black jeans and duffel coat were baggy but the tie at the waist helped and a slouchy knitted beanie even looked quite funky and fashionable when she tucked her hair up inside it and let it pouch to one side like a beret.

It was too dark inside to wear her sunglasses but Ava still felt utterly incognito.

Half an hour later and on to her second coffee, Ava noticed movement across the road and watched as six uniformed soldiers hefted a coffin draped with the Union Jack high on their shoulders through the churchyard towards the headstones. A woman in black and two little children holding her hand came next. Then other people, silent mourners, followed at a respectable distance. A lot in uniform. A lot of civilians too.

Ava could see what was happening very clearly from her seat as the procession stopped at a clearing on the outer edge of the headstones, fresh earth piled nearby. She knew she shouldn't watch. That it was a private affair, not some spectacle to gawk at. But the sight of those two little kids broke her heart. Her breath was heavy in her lungs and she couldn't seem to look away.

Her eyes sought Blake through the crowd. Needing to find him, to see him, to know he was okay. She started to panic when she couldn't locate him, her eyes darting around more desperately. And suddenly he was there— one grim-faced man amongst a group of grim-faced men, mainly uniformed standing to one side—and she breathed again.

A loud cry cracked the laden air like a whip and Ava startled at the unexpectedness. It had come from the direction of the gravesite and her eyes scanned for the source.

It was a man's cry. A warrior's cry. A call to arms. It had easily penetrated the four-hundred-year-old stone walls of the pub and no doubt was even now echoing right down the high street if the heads poking out of windows were any indication.

She looked back towards the church in time to see movement down the far end of the gathering, about a dozen khaki-uniformed men, in two lines, one behind the other.

The men were bouncing on the balls of their feet, their knees slightly bent, their arms folded out in front of them. They advanced towards the coffin sitting at the end of the waiting hole in the ground, calling out and grunting, their faces fierce. Then it became more organised, with the men all chanting in unison, stamping their feet in time as they slowly closed in on the coffin, slapping their hands against their chests.

Ava recognised it as the special dance she'd seen the New Zealand rugby team do at the World Cup a few years back. As the men surrounded the coffin, their forceful rhythmic chants echoing through the entire village, she felt tears well in her eyes and goose bumps prick at her skin.

It was raw and primitive and so achingly mournful she couldn't remember ever seeing anything so…savage be so utterly beautiful.

As suddenly as it started, it stopped, the angry chants falling silent, and there were long moments where nothing but the light patter of rain could be heard. Then, one by one the group of soldiers straightened, tall and strong, and slowly walked backwards from where they'd come, their solemn gazes locked on the coffin, their moving tribute to a brother-in-arms complete.

'Such a shame, isn't it?'

Ava dragged her gaze away from the window at the sudden intrusion. She looked up to find the woman from behind the bar, who collected her empty coffee mug. She held out a box of tissues and Ava realised her face was wet.

'Thanks,' she said, taking a couple and dabbing at the tears.

'Such a lovely family. Jenny, the widow, she grew up just outside here, went to school just down the road,' the older woman continued as she wiped Ava's table down. 'They got married in that church.' She shook her head, tucking her dishcloth in her front apron pocket. 'Offered him a full military funeral, you know, but he never wanted that. He was coming home in three weeks…'

Ava nodded even though she didn't know. Didn't understand. Probably never would. All she could think about was Blake and what had happened to him. What if he'd died? What if she'd never known him?

The thought was so awful she could barely breathe.

'Another coffee, luv?'

She nodded. 'Yes, please.'

Ava had almost finished the third cup when the pub door opened, letting in a blast of cold, miserable air and a rowdy bunch of uniformed men and a smiling Blake. She waved at him as he looked around for her and he headed towards her.

'Hi,' Blake said as he reached the booth. He smiled at her and then frowned as she barely managed one in return. She looked as if she'd been crying. 'Are you okay?'

Ava shrugged. 'I saw that…dance.'

'Ah.' He nodded. 'The haka.'

'Yes, that's it.'

'It was a funeral haka,' he said. 'Some of the guys Isaac served with in New Zealand were over here.'

'It was…' Ava rubbed her hands up and down her arms. Even though the duffel coat was thick she still felt chilled.

'Blake, you dirty dog!'

Ava was kind of pleased for the booming interruption. She wasn't ready to articulate how deeply the funeral haka had affected her.

'You never told us you had a bird waiting for you,' a strapping great blond guy said, slapping Blake on the back. 'And a very nice-looking one at that. How are you, darlin'?' he said, holding out his hand, which Ava duly shook. 'I'm James but they just call me Jimbo.'

'Ava,' she said after a slight hesitation and a quick glance at Blake. It might not have been a common name but it was hardly unusual.

Jimbo certainly didn't bat an eyelid over it. 'Hey, guys,' he called over his shoulder. 'Come check out Blake's bird. Bring those beers over here and a champagne for the lady.'

'Sorry.' Blake grimaced. 'I hope you don't mind?'

Mind? Blake was actually smiling, which, considering his recent grimness, was a miracle. It was the most comfortable she'd seen him apart from when he was sanding wood or steering the boat.

Ava quirked an eyebrow at the man who had interrupted them. 'Make it a beer, Jimbo.'

'Oh, mate.' Jimbo laughed. 'You're on a winner there.'

Blake smiled down at her and said, 'Yeh. I think you're right,' and Ava smiled back, suddenly warm all over.

The next several hours, squashed into a booth with five strapping men, were the most educational of Ava's life. She'd have thought the mood would be sombre, and certainly there was talk about Isaac and toasts drunk to him, but mainly they just talked guy stuff and joked around with each other.

Ava was good at talking to men and fitted into the easy banter as if she'd been born to it. Jimbo, who was drinking steadily, would look at her every now and then with narrowed eyes then look at Blake and say, 'She looks really familiar.'

But she'd just shrug and tell him she had one of those faces and change the subject, getting him to tell her another story about what Blake was like during basic training, which Blake weathered like a trouper.

In fact all four of the guys who'd joined them seemed to have great stories about Blake and she encouraged them outrageously. Clearly he was well liked and respected and she was enjoying hearing about that part of his life—before he'd become so serious.

She also listened to Jimbo's female woes. The only single man at the table besides Blake, clearly he found women puzzling. She dished out some sensible advice about what women wanted and explained why infidelity was generally a deal breaker for women.

'You're lucky to have her.' Blake rolled his eyes as Jimbo repeated the decree for the tenth time.

'I don't know,' Ava said. 'Maybe I'm lucky to have him.'

'Oh, you are, you are,' Jimbo agreed. 'Good. Honourable. And brave. The man was awarded the second highest decoration for bravery you can get for what he did.'

Ava stilled. This from a man who had rejected the term hero over and over? 'What did you do?' she asked, turning to Blake.

Blake shook his head. 'It was nothing,' he dismissed. 'I was just in the right place at the right time.'

'Pulled a wounded soldier and four kids from a house fire while some bastards shot at him,' Jimbo supplied.

Ava stared at him as silence descended around the table. 'You did?'

Blake sighed. She was looking at him differently. He hated that. 'Anyone would have done it,' he said.

Jimbo burped loudly. 'Nah,' he said belligerently. 'I don't think I would have.'

A murmur of *me neither* rattled around the table and Ava

quirked an eyebrow at him. 'They're lying,' Blake said. He knew these guys inside out and back to front. 'Every one of them would have.'

'Yeh, but it was you,' Ava persisted. 'You who ran into a burning building, *under fire*, and pulled a wounded man and a bunch of kids out.'

'Because I was *there*,' Blake said, exasperation straining his voice. 'It's not like you think about it—you just react. I went in to get Pete and there were a bunch of kids in there too. What was I going to do, leave them?'

Ava shook her head. 'Of course not.' Blake would no sooner turn his back on them than he had on her in her hour of need. 'Sounds like hero material to me,' she said.

'Cheers to that,' Jimbo said, raising his glass, oblivious to the undercurrent between Blake and Ava. 'Captain Blake Walker, my hero.'

Blake opened his mouth to object. He wasn't going to have a bunch of guys still serving their country while he *sanded wood* toasting him as a hero.

'And Ava, his good looking bird. Never was there a man with such great taste in women.'

Blake didn't have a comeback for that. Neither did his good-looking bird. So they laughed along with the rest of the table until someone changed the subject.

'Stop looking at me like that.'

It was after five and they'd been driving for ten minutes. Blake could feel Ava's sideways glances like prickles beneath his ribs. He didn't want to have a conversation with her about the revelations of the day. It was bad enough she knew—he could do without the analysis.

Seeing the guys he'd served with again was always a bittersweet experience. But today had been a sombre day, a day where they'd laid a mate to rest. It wasn't the time or place to be talking about an event that happened eight years ago during his first tour of duty. Some ancient history *glory* that the brass had deemed worthy of recognition.

'So...you don't think you deserve the medal, is that it?'

Blake sighed. 'I don't think they should give out bravery medals for an act of common human decency. Servicemen do stuff like that every day in war zones,' he dismissed. 'I was just doing my job.'

Ava couldn't believe how blasé Blake was being. 'You saved the life of four kids and a soldier.'

'No, Ava, I didn't,' he said wearily. 'Pete died.'

A cold hand squeezed Ava's gut. 'He didn't make it?'

'No. He did not. Between the bullet to his gut and his burns, he passed away en route to hospital.'

Some of his bleakness leached across the space between them and settled over her like a heavy skin. How had that made Blake feel?

'I'm so sorry,' she murmured. 'That's...awful.'

'Yeh, well...that's war for you.'

Ava didn't know what to say to that. How could she even begin to imagine the things he must have seen? She looked out of the window at the grey day, misty rain forming streaky rivulets of water as it hit the glass. She'd been given a unique insight into him today, seeing him through the eyes of a group of men who clearly liked and respected him.

Ava wished she knew that man. Or had known him, anyway. She had a feeling he didn't exist any more.

Blake brooded for the next hour as they drove in silence. He hadn't meant to be so harsh with her, but he'd been to one too many funerals over the last decade and they had a tendency to mess with his head. Their closeness of the last few days seemed a distant memory now and he was sorry he'd been the one to destroy it, especially when all he really wanted was to get lost in her for a while and forget about the world and how insane it could be.

Her phone rang, the sound of rock music shattering

the oppressive silence. She pulled it out of her pocket and looked down at the screen before looking at him.

'It's Ken,' she said as she quickly answered it.

Blake assumed from the one-sided conversation and Ava's palpable relief that the police had finally caught the culprit, a fact she confirmed when she hung up a few minutes later.

'They made an arrest,' Ava said, smiling at him.

A heaviness descended upon Blake's chest. 'Who?'

'Grady Hamm.'

Blake frowned at the cartoonesque name. 'There's somebody in this world called Grady Hamm?'

Ava laughed. 'Yes. There is. He's an agent. Isobella Wentworth's agent.'

'Okay...and she is?'

Ava rolled her eyes at him. Hadn't everybody in the world heard about the seventeen-year-old catwalk débutante? 'An up-and-coming model. Britain's next big thing? And up for the same advertising campaign I am.'

'Ah.' The penny dropped. 'And he shot up your house to keep you out of the picture for a bit?'

She nodded. 'Well, he didn't shoot it up. He paid someone else to do it but, yes...it was just a scare tactic, apparently.'

A surge of anger jettisoned into Blake's system and he gripped the steering wheel as he remembered how frightened Ava had been. There was nothing *just* about it. 'A scare tactic that worked.'

'Yes. Until Isobella found out and dobbed him in.'

Blake whistled. 'That must have taken some balls for a teenage wannabe to turn in her agent.'

Ava nodded in agreement. It did. She knew the kind of fortitude that took intimately. 'I owe her, definitely.'

Blake contemplated the road for a few seconds as the full implications of the arrest sank in. 'So, you're free to go back home,' he said, injecting a cheeriness that felt one hundred per cent false after such a sombre day.

'Yes.' That should have been exciting but Ava felt as if they had unfinished business between them.

'It's time for your stitches to come out anyway,' he said, trying to be practical.

Ava looked down at the sticking plaster on her palm. 'Yes,' she said again.

'You should take the car as soon as we get back to the boat. You could be in London by nine.'

Ava knew that not only sounded feasible but sensible. But there was no way she was leaving Blake tonight.

Not after today.

'I'll go in the morning,' she said.

Blake opened his mouth to protest. There was no reason for her to stick around—their arrangement had only ever been temporary. But her phone rang again. 'Reggie.' She grimaced as she answered.

'Ava, darling, you have to get back here pronto!'

Reggie's voice was shouting in her ear as he spoke over what could only be a huge gaggle of press all yelling at him in the background. She could picture him now standing on the top of his steps leading into his Notting Hill office.

'Listen to them,' he said over the din. 'Come back, get a picture with Isobella. They're going nutso down here.'

Ava shook her head as she pulled the phone slightly away from her ear. She couldn't. And she couldn't explain why either. She just couldn't. 'I'll be back in the morning.'

'Ava…' Reggie spluttered. 'Don't be ridiculous. This is the kind of publicity you just can't buy.'

Ava was sure it was but that wasn't the point as she glanced at Blake. 'I'll see you tomorrow,' she said and hung up on his continuing protests.

'He's right, Ava.' Blake had heard every shouted word in the whisper-quiet confines of the hire car.

Ava shook her head. 'I'm not leaving tonight.'

'Ava.'

'I'm. Not. Leaving.'

CHAPTER TWELVE

AVA WASN'T SURE how long she'd been asleep when a loud cry woke her from her deep post-coital slumber. Her eyes flicked open and for a few seconds in the dark, her heartbeat thundering in her chest, she grappled to orientate herself. Then the cry came again—anguished, full of pain—and there was movement beside her and she realised Blake had vaulted upright in bed.

She groped through a groggy brain and leadened muscles to make sense of what was happening as he rocked back and forth.

'Blake?' She reached over and flicked on the lamp, her eyes shutting as the light hit them. 'What's wrong?' she asked, her hand sliding up his bare back as her eyes slowly adjusted to the light.

Blake sucked in a breath, biting back the expletive and another bellow of pain. 'It's my leg,' he seethed at the all too familiar sensation of hot jagged metal jabbing into his stump. Like the blast pain all over again. He raised his thigh and slammed it down against the mattress over and over trying to ease the crippling burn.

Ava shook her head as the mattress reverberated with the pounding. His leg? What did he mean? 'What's wrong with it?' she asked over his guttural groaning, looking down at it for signs of redness or bleeding or anything that could be causing him so much pain.

But it looked exactly the same as it always had.

He didn't answer her, just groaned louder as his movement grew more frantic and he became increasingly distressed. He kneaded his fisted hand so hard into his quad all the way down to his stump she winced and then he started pounding it, lifting his fist up then bringing it down hard.

'Don't, stop it,' she said, tears threatening in the face of his inconsolable pain and the brutality of his actions. She felt utterly useless. 'Please,' she said, pulling at his arm. 'Stop…you'll hurt yourself.'

He ignored her, shaking her hand off, his seething breath sucking noisily through clenched teeth as he pounded at his leg.

Ava didn't understand what was happening. Was he having a nightmare? Some kind of a flashback. Was he awake? 'Why are you doing that?' she asked, grabbing for his arm again.

'Because it helps with the phantom pains,' he yelled trying to shrug her restraining hands off.

Ava vaguely recalled having read an article on phantom limb pain a few years back. Something about residual nervous involvement in the amputated limb. Not that she remembered a single skerrick of anything that could be useful right now.

'That helps?' It was hard to believe anything so brutal could be used to treat pain—it seemed counter-intuitive.

'Yes.' Blake could already feel it starting to ease its grip. 'Pressure on the stump helps.'

Ava blinked. *There was pressure and there was pressure*. Surely it was going to be bruised tomorrow? Before she could think about it, she was shifting, moving, kneeling on her haunches between his legs. The fact that they were both naked hadn't even registered.

'Let me try,' she said, placing her hand over his fist, pushing it away, quickly replacing it with her hands, wrapping them around his stump and applying firm even pressure, squeezing rhythmically.

Blake felt himself slowly relax as Ava's hands worked their magic. He doubted they would have had any effect had it not already started to ease up—but they felt cool and heavenly now as the pain proper started to fade.

Ava concentrated on the job at hand, determined to at least try and help him, satisfied as he seemed to be slowly relaxing, his breathing settling, his death grip on the sheet with his other hand easing. 'Does this happen often?' she asked.

Blake shut his eyes and tried to focus on his breath and not the pain as the shrink had counselled. 'In the beginning quite a lot but I was one of the lucky ones able to get on top of it with medication…and time.'

Ava looked up at him. He had his eyes shut and despite his body slowly relaxing he looked haggard and tense in the lamplight. 'But it's obviously not cured.' She couldn't bear the thought of him, here alone, going through this with no one around to comfort him.

'I usually wear a sock-thing to bed over the stump, which is a good maintenance strategy that seems to keep them at bay. But…'

Blake opened his eyes to find her looking at him.

Ava didn't need him to finish. 'I've been here and you haven't been wearing anything to bed.' Guilt washed over her and tears pricked her eyes again—had *she* been responsible for this relapse?

He shrugged. 'It's okay. I doubt the funeral helped, either. I'm sure my shrink would say there's some psychological component as to why this is happening tonight.'

He sighed and rubbed a hand along the back of his neck, shutting his eyes again. 'It's been a hell of a day.'

Ava ducked her head as the tears threatened to become a reality. A hell of a day? It had been a hell of a *life* for him.

Serving his country. Earning a medal for bravery and

just brushing it off as if it were nothing because he truly believed he'd only done what any decent human being would have done. Paying bodily for that belief. Still paying. Still going to funerals. Still waking in the night to excruciating pain from a leg that was no longer there.

The stump was smooth beneath her hand now but the pain… She couldn't bear the thought of the pain he must have endured. If what she'd seen tonight was just a tiny indication of how it must have been in those moments straight after the explosion, she didn't know how he'd got through it.

The haka chants drummed through her head with each knead of her hands—the anger and the anguish washing over her, swelling in her chest, building and building, pressure in her throat and her lungs and pricking at her eyes and nose.

Blake felt something warm and wet on his thigh and looked down to find a single drop of moisture. He glanced up at Ava's downcast head. 'Hey,' he said, trying to look under her curtain of caramel hair.

He slid his hand to her jaw and gently lifted her chin to find tears dampening her cheeks. 'Why are you crying?'

Ava shook her head. She couldn't answer. She knew if she said one thing everything would come tumbling out and that would not be pretty because it churned in a big ugly mass inside her with no real cohesion.

'Ava. It's okay,' he murmured, smearing a newly fallen tear across her cheek with a thumb. 'I'm fine now. The pain's gone. You helped,' he assured her. 'You helped a lot.'

He dragged her closer and she shifted until she was straddling him, her arms around his neck. He looked up at her, kissing her nose and eyelids and her cheeks. Kissing the tears away. 'Shh,' he said. 'Shh.'

The lump in Ava's throat became bigger. She'd never met a man so…good. He reminded her of her father and she clung even harder to his neck

'Talk to me, Ava,' he murmured quietly as he dropped butterfly kisses all over her face. 'Talk to me.'

She shook her head. 'I can't...I can't bear the thought of the...pain you must have been through,' she said, trying to talk past the constriction in her throat. 'You've been through so...much and here's me with my own pathetic little troubles. For crying out loud, you have no leg, you have all this guilt about Colin and get...terrible pain and you have to keep going to funerals all the time and I...and I...'

'Oh, Ava, no...shh,' Blake said, pushing his hands into her hair, cupping her face so she was looking right at him. 'Someone shot at your house—'

Ava could feel more tears clogging in her throat and squeezing out of her eyes. 'But it was just to scare me. It wasn't for real...not like what you've faced.'

'Hey,' he said, pushing her hair back off her face. 'I was there. It was pretty real if you asked me.'

Ava nodded even as her brain dismissed the sentiment. There was real and there was *real*. 'Were you scared...over there?' she asked.

Blake nodded. 'Sometimes...yeh.'

A sob rose in Ava's throat. Blake who was strong and brave had felt fear and pain and been exposed to so much loss because his country had asked it of him. 'Why do we fight each other?' she whispered.

Blake felt helpless in the face of a question he had no clue how to answer. Her yellow-green eyes were two huge pools of compassion and anguish. 'I don't know,' he said.

And then he kissed her because that he did know. He did know how he could make it better. For tonight anyway.

The parting the next morning was a lot harder than Ava ever imagined it would be. They weren't *just* two people who had shared a boat for a week. He'd been more than the safe haven she'd asked of him. They'd shared a bed. Intimacies. They'd opened up their bodies and shared themselves.

More than either of them had ever shared before with someone other than their nearest and dearest.

It was another rainy day and Ava snuggled into her coat as they stood by the hire car saying their goodbyes. 'Maybe we could see each other…when you get back to London,' Ava suggested.

She'd never been with anyone like Blake—for good reason. But maybe it was time to revisit that?

Blake shook his head, remembering the constant presence of media in her life, the way the paps had bayed for a comment at the roped-off area the night of the shooting. And that commercial they'd watched together with the guy ripping off her gown and ravaging her.

He really didn't think he'd be very good with stuff like that.

'I think you and I live in very different worlds,' he said. 'I don't think I could live in yours and—' he glanced over at the boat '—I'm pretty sure you don't want to live in mine. Best to quit while we're ahead.'

Ava nodded. He was right, of course, but there was part of her that didn't want to let go.

'I'll see you around no doubt at the charity functions,' Blake added. 'The Christmas Eve fund-raiser is going to be huge. They've booked out the London Eye and I have a feeling Joanna's going to be working her new patron like a dog.'

Ava smiled. 'I look forward to it.'

Blake opened the door for her. 'Goodbye, Ava,' he said.

He could easily have leaned in and kissed her but, in his experience with Ava Kelly to date, he had trouble stopping at just one.

Ava nodded. 'Thank you for everything,' she murmured.

Blake grinned because the weather and the mood of the last twenty-four hours had been sombre enough without continuing it. 'It was my pleasure.'

She grinned back. 'And mine.'

And then she ducked into the car and he shut the door

after her and she started it up and within a minute she was watching him grow smaller and smaller in the rear-view mirror.

The bubble had well and truly burst.

And for two long months she didn't see him. The frenzy and the endless speculation about Ava and Isobella had died down thanks to an A-list celebrity cheating on his wife, and the whole tawdry affair blew over. Ava went to America for ten days, and scored the new commerical. She did the talk show circuit—now more in demand than ever—and she and Reggie made inroads on her calendar for the next year while cultivating new contacts.

She flew to Milan and then on to Paris. All the designers wanted her because of her rekindled buzz and Reggie made sure they paid. But when she strutted onto the catwalk and caused a mini-sensation thanks to her recent notoriety the cameras popped and people noticed what she was wearing.

September became October back in the UK and all trace of that blissful bubble of sunshine on the English canals had vanished. The weather was bleak and dreary. Cold with endless drizzle that seeped damp into everything including the marrow.

Ava thought about Blake constantly. Wondered what he was doing. Wondered how his holiday had gone. If he was back at work yet. She picked up the phone to call or text him a dozen times a day. But never followed through.

Which was just as well—she was too busy anyway. There weren't too many nights she wasn't out and about on some dashing escort's arm—openings, galas, red-carpet events. If it was on and it was *big*, thanks to Reggie and Grady Hamm, she was there.

Not that she spent the night with any of her escorts. Her intentions were always open but as the night progressed she'd spend more and more time comparing them to Blake and it didn't seem to matter that they'd just been named in the top one hundred beautiful people or had landed a lead role in a Hollywood blockbuster.

None of them measured up.

She knew Blake was just an anomaly and had he been around he'd tell her she was just obsessing about him purely because she couldn't have him.

But that didn't make him, or the lack of him, any less distracting.

And then Remembrance Sunday dawned, another fittingly bleak day, and Ava lay in bed with the covers pulled up to her chin, not even bothering to get up. She wondered if Blake was attending a service somewhere. Maybe hanging out in a pub with some of his army mates?

Maybe getting quietly drunk on his boat?

It was only a knock at her door around ten a.m. that roused her from her lethargy. For a moment she even contemplated not answering it, but hauled herself out of bed, throwing on a polar fleece gown, welcoming any distraction.

Or at least she'd thought so until she opened her door to find her mother, conspicuous by her absence these last couple of months, flirting with the press with all her brash blonde falseness. She'd been on Ibiza when Ava's house had been shot up and, apart from that one phone call, this was the first Ava had seen or heard of her for six months.

Sheila Kelly air-kissed Ava's face for the sake of the cameras and swept inside requesting a tour of the renovations. Ava shut the door on the 'give your mum a kiss, Ava' calls coming from the little clutch of paps and girded her loins.

She complied to her mother's request but was mentally preparing herself for the catch. For the ulterior motive.

Sheila cooed appreciatively at all the big-ticket items—at the roof and the pool and the acres of glass and steel—but sniffed dismissively at the homey wooden kitchen.

'You could pay a personal chef on what you earn,' she tutted.

And there it was, the entrée her mother was clearly looking for. Ava waited patiently for her mother to come out with it. 'Paul rang offering me another book deal,' she announced casually.

Ava barely supressed a snort at the mention of her ex-agent's name, now doing shonky off-shore deals in the literary field. She didn't understand how her mother could still associate with him. Ava reached for her handbag that was on the kitchen bench. 'How much this time?' she asked, pulling out her cheque book.

'A quarter of a million,' Sheila said. 'Since your little… scandal with Isobella, the price for a tell-all memoir has gone up considerably.'

Ava gritted her teeth. She paid her mother a generous allowance every month that kept her in houses and holidays, but she stopped by at least a couple of times a year for a top-up.

'I should just write it, darling,' Sheila said. 'Paul said it could be very lucrative for me. I wouldn't need to depend on you then.'

Ava snorted—she bet he had. 'No,' she said, signing the cheque. 'No tell-all. You write a single word and I will cut you off.' She tore it out of the book as noisily as she could.

Ava didn't care what her mother wrote about her—her twisted version of the truth. Ava knew the real story. But she didn't trust her mother not to tell lies about her father and that she couldn't tolerate. She wouldn't let her father's memory be besmirched.

'There's no need for that,' her mother replied waspishly as she took the cheque.

Ava folded her arms. 'Good.'

They stared at each other for a moment, then Sheila said, 'I'll be off, then.'

Ava nodded. Of course. Her mother had got what she'd

come for. There was no hug or air kisses this time—no cameras inside the house.

She watched as Sheila headed to the door and let herself out, surprised to find her hands were shaking as she put the cheque book back in her bag. A sense of being alone in the world assailed Ava, which, given how many people she had around her, was absurd in the extreme.

But she cursed her mother anyway, stupid tears in her eyes.

And before she knew what she was doing she was tracking back to her bedroom, picking up her phone off the bedside table and scrolling through her contacts.

Blake answered on the second ring. 'Hello?'

Ava shut her eyes, feeling foolish for having even rung him now, but his voice sounded so good.

'Hello?'

'Blake…'

There was a very definite pause at the other end before he said, 'Ava,' in a voice so wary she could practically cut the trepidation with a knife.

The tears built more insistently behind her eyes and she was glad she had them closed.

'Are you okay?'

Ava shook her head. 'No. Can you come over?'

Blake knew it was a bad idea when he left his boat the second her husky request was out. He knew it was a bad idea as he pulled up in front of Ava's house and four different cameras took pictures of him and one of the paps said, 'Hey, aren't you that builder guy?' He knew it was a bad idea when she answered the door in nothing but her dressing gown and a haughty look.

But it didn't stop him stepping inside when she pulled the door open. And it didn't stop him wanting to kiss her. It sure as hell didn't stop him *actually* kissing her when she shut the door, the haughtiness evaporating as she reached for him, and put her mouth to his.

Later he would come to know it as the FFK—the first fatal kiss—but in that moment nothing mattered. Not the two months of separation, not endless footage of her with other guys, not the giant divide in their lives so aptly demonstrated by the cameras on the other side of the door.

He just sucked her in, his senses filling with the smell and the taste of her as he pushed her hard against the nearby wall and devoured her mouth as if it were his last meal.

He groaned as she opened to him, kissed him back with equal vigour. He'd missed her—the feel and the smell and the taste of her. He'd missed her snooty little smile and the way she ate her food and her sexy, frilly lingerie hanging everywhere.

He missed her complete lack of inhibitions.

He missed the way she kissed—wide open and full throttle. The way he didn't have to duck and she didn't have to rise up on tippy-toe to align their mouths. The way her mouth was always just right there level with his and, God help him, always one hundred per cent willing.

Ava clung to Blake as the kiss went on and on. She hadn't realised how much she'd been starving for his mouth until it was on hers again.

And now it was time to feast.

'God, I missed you,' she said, pulling back slightly, their gazes meshing as she tried to catch her heavy breath, each oxygen molecule drowned in lashings of Blake.

Which was true—but not the full truth. She'd *more* than missed him. *She loved him.* As soon as she'd opened the door to him—no, before that—as soon as he'd knocked, she'd known.

Because he'd come.

She'd asked and he'd dropped everything to be here. No questions. Just action.

There'd only been two men in her life who'd done that

for her and she loved both of them too. One was her father. The other was Reggie.

And now there was Blake. Her big, brave, wounded warrior who had come without hesitation when she'd called. Who was looking at her with desire and lust but also with a healthy dose of wariness, his barriers fully up, clearly *not* loving her back.

So there was no way she could tell him—she'd learned a long time ago not to give *any* man that kind of power over you.

But she *could* show him.

She *could* love him with her body. And whisper it in her mind.

Blake sucked in a breath as the noise of his zip coming down sounded loud enough to be heard outside. He bit back a groan as her hand brushed his erection, reaching down to stop her, shutting his eyes as he dragged himself back from the lure of what could be.

His head spun with the effort and the sweet intoxication of her. He hadn't come for this.

No matter how much he wanted it.

Nothing had changed between them. If anything it had reverted to what it had always been. Ava crooking her finger and expecting him to come running.

Which he had.

He'd told her once he wasn't going to be her plaything and he meant it.

He captured her hand and pulled it up, trapping it against his chest as he leaned his forehead on hers and drew in some unsteady breaths. They both did.

When he felt under control again he eased back a little and said, 'What's this about, Ava?'

Ava felt all the desperation leach out of her at his calm enquiry. She let her head flop back against the wall. 'Sorry,' she said, her voice annoyingly husky. 'My mother was here. She always makes me a little crazy.'

'What did she want?'

Ava's gaze met his. 'The same thing she always wants. *Money*. Paul, who's now in publishing, keeps waving a tell-all book deal under her nose and I keep matching his offers.'

Blake's jaw clenched against a wave of disgust. What pieces of work they both were. 'Did you give it to her?'

Ava shrugged, hugging herself against how tawdry it all sounded. 'I've got the money.'

Blake shook his head at her wretchedness, his need to smash things duelling with her need to be comforted. He'd tried to forget in their two months apart how truly alone she was in the world but here it was in full Technicolor.

Sure, she might not have been short for an escort to a film premiere but she had no real family to look out for her.

Except Reggie.

And now him.

He took two calming breaths, then closed the short distance between them, his hands sliding to her hips. He could be outraged later. For now she really did need him.

He stroked a hand down her face. 'I'm sorry,' he said. 'What can I do?'

Ava gave him a half-smile as she slid her hand onto his arm. 'Right now? You can help me forget about my mother.'

Blake dropped his gaze to her mouth then flicked it up again, his resistance completely shot. 'Just once.'

Ava's smile broadened. 'Absolutely. But she's a *very* hard woman to forget. Might take you all day.'

Blake grinned.

CHAPTER THIRTEEN

TWO WEEKS LATER Blake was up late working on a kitchen design for a client when he heard dainty footsteps on the bow and then a familiar little knock and his pulse kicked up in anticipation.

They shouldn't still be doing this.

But they were.

He was *still* helping Ava forget her mother—every single night. All night long. They didn't seem to be able to stop no matter how much they said they were going to as she left each morning.

It was that first fatal kiss that had done it.

He'd been fine resisting the *notion* of her for two months—finishing his holiday, going back to work, getting on with his life. Fine with her image seemingly everywhere. Fine with opening the paper and reading about her. Fine to be the *friend* Ava had referred to in her media statement on her return to London, which hadn't lessened the speculation as to how she'd managed to lay so low for a week.

But then she'd kissed him and a wellspring of craving had erupted inside him and he *could not get enough*.

He certainly couldn't stop.

He'd broken the seal on his resistance and there was no way he was getting that sucker back. It had flown the coop and there was no hope of recapturing it.

But the worst thing was, it was more than sexual—how much more he didn't want to think about. He just knew he actually looked forward to her company—something he'd have never thought possible a few months ago.

It was as if there were two different Avas—the public persona, *Keep-out Kelly*, who left them wanting more with her *touch-me-not* smile and her ball-breaking business sense. And then there was the private persona. The one who let her guard down. The one who tramped onto his boat every night fresh from some red-carpet event schmoozing with the A-list eager to be with *him*. The one who cooked gourmet snacks for him in her underwear, who burped after she skulled half a can of beer, who smiled at him with her *touch-me-everywhere* smile.

Who left the boat every morning looking a hot mess and didn't seem to care.

Maybe that was part of the allure, the continuing of what they'd had for that week out on the canals. Where she could be nobody and they could be lovers and no one was around to care. No paps taking her picture or fans asking for her autograph.

Just him and her and their bubble.

The knock came again just as he'd almost reached the door and a muffled, 'Open up, I want to do unspeakable things to your body,' had him quickening the pace.

'I beg your pardon.' He grinned as he pushed open the door to a freezing London night to find her standing huddled into a long black coat buckled at the waist and her collar up to keep her neck warm. 'I object to being so outrageously objectified.'

'Oh, really?' Ava said, raising an eyebrow, unbuckling her coat and opening the lapels to reveal her nudity.

Blake's eyes widened as he forgot all about the bracing cold pushing icy fingers inside the boat, his gaze fixed on the hard points of her nipples.

'*Now* can I do unspeakable things to you?' she demanded.

Blake grabbed her hand. 'I am all yours,' he said as he pulled her inside.

Half an hour later they were lying in the dark together. Blake was drifting his fingers up and down her arm enhancing Ava's post-coital drowse. The urge to blurt out her feelings was never far away but something always held her back. She thought Blake might feel the same way, or at least feel something more than sex, but things were so perfect—she didn't want to rock the boat.

Literally or figuratively.

'I love this boat,' she said instead, rolling onto her side and snuggling into him. 'It's like my secret hideaway.'

Blake smiled. '*Mi casa es su casa,*' he said and surprised himself by how much he meant it. She *was* welcome here any time.

'It was my hideaway for a long time. It was like a…lifeline or something…somewhere to lick my wounds.'

Ava brushed her lips against his shoulder. If anyone had needed a place to lick his wounds it had been Blake. If she'd gone through what he'd endured, she'd still be holed up in a drunken stupor.

'You mentioned once that you'd received some news that made you realise there were worse things than having one leg. Do you mind me asking what it was?'

Blake stared at the ceiling for long moments.

'One of the guys in my unit…he had the same thing happen to him about six months after me, lost a leg. But…'

Blake hesitated. He'd never told anyone about this. But it felt right unburdening himself to Ava, especially in their private little bubble.

'He also had his genitals blown off.'

Ava gasped, rising up on her elbow to look down at him. 'That's…terrible.'

She felt absurd tears prick the backs of her eyes as she tried to grapple with what that must mean to a person. How would she like to go through her life never being able to be physically intimate?

Blake saw the shine in her eyes as he reached out to tuck a stray strand of caramel hair that had fallen forward behind Ava's ear and he gave her a gentle smile.

His Ava was surprisingly mushy on the inside.

His Ava. The thought was equal parts terrifying and tantalising.

'It made me rethink my attitude, that's for sure. I mean, there I was, essentially fully functional, while some guys… they're never going to be fully functional. At least I could still have sex. Still…' he looked into Ava's yellow-green eyes shining with compassion '…make love to a woman.'

Ava's heart felt like a boulder in her chest. She shifted, moved over him until she was lying on top of him, her forehead pressed into his neck, his heartbeat loud in her ear. His arms wrapped around her body and a tear slid out of her eye.

After a few moments she raised her head to look down at him. 'Make love to me,' she whispered.

Blake lifted his head and kissed her. He should say no. They weren't supposed to be dragging this impossible thing out. But he couldn't. He wanted to do exactly as she'd asked.

So he rolled her over and made love like there was no tomorrow.

Ava felt a lot more sombre the next morning as he saw her off the boat. The plight of the soldier he'd told her about last night had wormed its way under her skin and she held him a little longer, kissed him a little deeper. Usually Blake stayed inside the warmth of the boat as she exited but it was as if he could sense her sadness, and even though he was only in his boxer briefs and T-shirt he climbed out with her and held her for as long as she needed.

'You okay?' he asked as she finally pulled away.

She very nearly confessed then and there, but she felt absurdly close to tears again and she doubted she could get it out without being a big snotty mess and she had a magazine shoot to get to in just over an hour.

She gave him a small smile and a nod. And even though she knew she shouldn't ask she said, 'See you tonight?'

He kissed her. And even though he knew he shouldn't agree, that they should be ending this, he said, 'Tonight.'

But by two o'clock in the afternoon everything had changed.

Blake was at work when he got the first inkling of the storm that was about to take over his life. He was at his desk when he looked up to see Joanna and Charlie approaching and his keen sense of doom kicked into overdrive.

They pulled up in front of his desk looking like they did that day a few years ago they'd called by the boat together—a united front—ready for an intervention. 'What?' he asked warily.

Joanna fiddled with his stapler. 'I've just seen you on the telly.'

Blake frowned. *'What?'*

'On the news. Pictures of you,' she clarified. 'And Ava. On the boat.'

Blake's frown deepened. 'During my holiday?' he asked.

'Umm…no,' Joanna said, putting his stapler down and picking up a ruler, tapping it lightly on his desk. 'Apparently they were…taken this morning.'

Charlie folded his arms across his chest and eyeballed his brother. 'You *are* shagging her.'

Joanna dug Charlie hard in the ribs and he grabbed his side.

Blake stood as his mind went back to this morning. To kissing her goodbye out in the open. Not that he'd been looking, but he certainly hadn't noticed a clutch of paps. Maybe someone on a neighbouring boat recognised her and decided to make a quid or two?

'What kind of pictures?' he asked.

'I'm-shagging-Ava-Kelly pictures,' Charlie said. 'Or at least that's what your hand on her arse and your tongue down her throat says to me.'

'I mean do they look clear? Are they professional or amateur?'

'You can tell it's you and her *very* clearly,' Charlie said. 'But it looks like they were taken from a distance, like you see in all those magazines, with a telephoto lens or something.'

Blake plopped back onto his chair. Photographers had been staking out his boat? Had they followed her or had someone tipped them off?

The very thought gave him the creeps.

'What did they say about the pictures?' he asked.

'They were wondering who you are and if you were Ava's latest,' Joanna said, still tapping the ruler. 'If you were the friend she'd hidden away with for that week she'd dropped out…stuff like that.'

Blake didn't know how to feel about the news except for the fact that it probably made it easier to make the break they should have made a fortnight ago.

Which should have made him relieved.

It didn't.

'Oh, well, I guess it pays to be nobody, huh?' he dismissed absently.

Joanne and Charlie looked at each other and Blake's skin prickled with unease. The tapping of the ruler got louder and Blake snatched it out of Joanna's hand. 'Just say it,' he said.

'They're already speculating about…your leg,' she said.

Blake frowned. *His leg?* Of course…his boxers this morning would have been no match for a telephoto lens.

'Must be a slow news day. I'm sure everyone will move on soon.'

He sure hoped so because the idea of a lens trained on his boat was a little too reminiscent of a rifle sight for his liking.

Joanna shook her head. 'The pictures are practically going viral online and on social media,' she said, her voice doubtful. 'The British press are still all dying to know where Ava went for that week... The whole thing with Grady Hamm has caused a huge stir, Blake. Combine that with the pretty intense interest her love life has always roused and I don't know that this is going to blow over so soon.'

Blake's phone rang. 'It's Ava,' he said as he answered the call.

'There's photos of us on the news.'

Blake almost laughed at her panicked opener. No preamble—just straight to the point. 'Yes. I know.'

'I'm *so, so* sorry. They must have followed me.'

Blake shrugged. 'Yeh, but I'm not anybody so...I'm sure it'll all blow over.'

Her groan was Blake's first indication that he might be underestimating the situation. 'Blake...they're going to know who you are within hours. Their editors are going to want to know every single thing about you and I wouldn't be surprised if it's in all the evening papers. There's probably someone going through your rubbish right now.'

Blake laughed. 'Why would they want to go through *my* rubbish?'

'*Because your hand is on my arse,*' she said testily. 'And they don't know who you are, which is driving them crazy. It's only going to be a matter of time before one of them realises you're the guy who was at my place for three months.'

Blake couldn't believe they'd be interested in a guy like him. 'And when they do they'll find there's nothing very exciting about me at all and they'll move on.'

'Oh, Blake. You don't know how intrusive this is… How could you?'

Her tone was hopeless and he started to worry. For her. 'I'm a big boy, Ava. I'm sure I'll cope.'

'I don't think you should go to the boat tonight.'

'What?'

'I think they'll be waiting for you. They're kind of persistent.'

And then it really dawned on him what she was saying. 'So…you're not coming tonight?'

'No.'

Blake tried to rein in his disappointment. A part of him could see it was a good thing—something they should have done a fortnight ago—but part of him didn't want to let go either.

'You know if you didn't want to come…if you wanted it over, you could just say.'

'Blake…no.' Her voice was instantly dismissive and he believed her. 'Trust me, you're not going to want me where they'll be. Maybe we can meet somewhere else. A hotel, maybe?'

'A hotel?' Blake couldn't believe what she was saying. 'You want a place that charges by the hour or do you prefer your *usual* suite?'

'Blake…please…I'm just trying to save you from this. It's probably going to get ugly.'

Blake snorted. *As if he cared about ugly.* It sounded like she was more interested in saving herself and her rep to him.

Fine by him.

He should never have let it get this far anyway. 'Well, you do what you've got to do,' he said tersely and hung up.

He looked at Joanna and Charlie, who had clearly been listening. 'What are *you* going to do?' Joanna asked.

Blake rolled his eyes. 'I'm going to finish up here for the day, then I'm going to go home.'

Charlie and Joanna exchanged looks and Blake resolutely ignored them.

* * *

By nightfall, Blake had changed his tune. The evening papers were full of his arse grope and when he was heading down the walkway to his boat's permanent mooring it was surrounded by paps. A few months back he wouldn't have known a paparazzo if he'd fallen over one—now he was all too familiar with them.

He'd backed away and ended up at Charlie's place with Joanna flicking between news stations.

Ava rang and texted several times but Blake, feeling grimmer and grimmer as the night progressed, did not feel like talking. By the time he'd bunked down on the couch the press knew his name, rank and serial number. By the time he woke in the morning they knew a lot more than that.

Charlie had got up early to buy all the tabloids and it was clear no part of Blake's life had been considered sacred.

Ava had been right—he'd had *no* idea how voracious the press could be. His army record was there for anyone, anywhere to read. His tours, the units he'd served with, the explosion and his subsequent amputation with a close-up of his prosthesis.

One paper exploited his military record with the headline—*Ava's Crippled War Hero.* Another took a different tack with—*The Carpenter and the Lady.* They'd got comments from his neighbours, people he used to serve with and clients he'd worked with.

But the hardest thing of all was the big splash about his commendation. His *act of heroism* was recounted in all its trumped-up glory. Blake felt ill. The news was making him out to be some kind of Second Coming and all he could see was Pete dying in the back of a military ambulance. Colin, lying dead in the dirt while he cried out in pain.

So many men dead and permanently maimed and this... *crap* was all they cared about?

How would the men he'd served with, *men who were*

still serving, still putting themselves on the line, feel about all this?

He was so angry he wanted to smash things with his bare hands. Angry about frivolous 'news' and first-world privilege, but mostly about confirming something he'd always known deep down—he couldn't live like this. Under constant scrutiny.

Ava and he were worlds apart and they never should have crossed the divide.

This was his worst-case scenario and he was living it.

His life was under the magnifying glass along with the lives of everyone he'd ever touched. People who'd never asked for this.

These last two weeks had been some of the happiest of his life. But this…nightmare was the flipside.

'Blake?' Joanna squeezed his shoulder and handed him a coffee. He took it and scooted over so she could sit beside him. 'They're not lying, Blake. I know you find this hard to take, but what you did *does* make you a hero to a lot of people.'

'Do you think Colin would say that?' he demanded and hated that he'd made her flinch.

Joanna recovered quickly and looked him straight in the eye. 'Colin would say it most of all.' She squeezed his knee. 'You were always his hero. He looked up to you. He was proud to serve with you. But you know what, Blake? He would have done it anyway. With or without you. What happened to him could have happened at *any* time.'

Blake shut his eyes against the way out in words. It could have-but it didn't. It happened on *his* watch.

A knock interrupted them. 'That'll be Ava,' Joanna announced, pushing herself up.

Blake almost choked on his first sip of coffee. 'And how *does* Ava know I'm here?'

'I told her, *stooped.*' Joanna grinned. 'She's my new best friend, didn't you know? Besties tell each other everything.'

'Joanna.' His voice held a warning.

'You have to talk to her, Blake. She's worried about you.'

'It's not going to work out between us, Joanna, so you can just stop planning the hen night.'

Joanna shook her head. 'Well, then, you're an idiot. She's the best thing that ever happened to you, Blake.'

CHAPTER FOURTEEN

BLAKE OPENED HIS mouth to rebuff Joanna but she was already heading towards the door and before he knew it Ava was standing in front of him and he was standing too.

She was wearing what appeared to be a very expensive, very glittery tracksuit, her hair up in a ponytail.

And she looked as if she hadn't slept a wink either.

She took a step towards him but his, 'I hope no paps followed you because I do not want Charlie and Trudy embroiled in this circus,' stopped her in her tracks.

Ava sucked in a breath against the hostility in his tone. It was as if the last five and a half months hadn't happened at all and they were back at square one.

'I know a thing or two about shaking the press,' she said tersely.

Blake snorted. 'Apparently not enough.'

'Look, I'm sorry,' she sighed. 'I never wanted this to happen.'

'And yet here we are.'

Ava shoved her hands into her pockets. Her fingers were freezing and it didn't have much to do with the cold November morning. 'Reggie's working on it,' she said. 'We can fix it. We can salvage it. I'm going to put out a statement.'

'Saying what?' he demanded.

Ava took a deep breath. Time to lay her cards on the table. She hadn't wanted it to be like this but fate had forced her hand. 'Well, we could deny it. Say that we're just friends. Or…we could say that our relationship is new and we'd like privacy while we explore it.'

Blake blinked. *What the*? 'So I can be your bit of rough?' he snapped. 'The *carpenter* to your *lady?* Or some…pity-screw to make the *crippled* war hero feel better about himself?'

Ava shut her eyes against the ugliness of the headlines he'd just thrown in her face and the contempt in his voice. He had every right to be angry. Tears built behind her lids but she forced them back. His life had been turned upside down because of her—it wasn't the time for stupid girly tears.

'I'm sorry about what they're saying,' she said, opening her eyes. 'About what they've revealed. If I could turn back the clock, believe me, Blake, I would. But I'm *not* sorry you're being recognised for what you did. You deserve those accolades.'

Blake shook his head. She didn't get it. She really didn't get it. The men who'd died, who were still fighting—they were the ones who deserved the accolades.

'Pete *died*, Ava. I don't want his family reading all about the *hero* who didn't *quite* manage to save their loved one in the newspapers, dragging up all their grief again. Thinking I'm using his death as some cheap publicity stunt to pull a supermodel.'

Ava felt the cold from outside seep inside her at his suggestion. *Surely no one would think that?*

'Don't you think it's hard *enough* for them this time of year, with Christmas around the corner?'

Ava felt helpless. She was used to this level of intrusion from the press, immune to it in a lot of ways, but she still remembered how shocking it had been in the beginning.

'I'm sorry for them that it's being dragged up,' she murmured. 'But I for one think heroism should be celebrated. Too often we celebrate beauty and money and power and yet there are guys like you, defending the free world. I think we should recognise heroes more often.'

Blake ran a hand through his hair. 'You don't get it,' he said bitterly. 'I don't want to be a hero, Ava. Men are still over there. Others are *dead.*'

Sometimes, when he woke in the middle of night, the guilt over that was more than he could bear. He looked over her shoulder and caught Joanna's eye before returning his gaze to Ava.

'I'm *not* going to cash in on *their* accolades.'

Ava felt almost paralysed by the hard line of rejection running through his voice. He hadn't even been this harsh with her in the beginning and her pulse hammered a frantic beat against her wrist.

She didn't want to lose him. She couldn't.

'Fine. What about just being my hero, then?'

Ava moved in closer until there was just a coffee table separating them. She knew if she didn't say it now she never would. And maybe if she'd said it earlier they wouldn't be where they were. 'I love you.'

It took Blake a few seconds to compute the revelation. And even then it was too hard to wrap his head around. *'What?'* he spluttered. *Love?* That was the most ridiculous thing he'd ever heard. 'I thought this was just…a fling, a… casual thing.'

Ava put her hand on her hip, her fingers digging in hard at his rejection, at his trivialisation of her love. She'd never told any man she loved him before and it felt like a knife to the heart to be so summarily dismissed.

'Really? Is that what you thought?' she asked scathingly.

This was a lot more than a casual fling between them and they both knew it.

'Really?' she repeated. 'All those things we've been through, all those nights lying in bed talking and talking and talking? That was just casual?'

Blake didn't even try to pretend she wasn't right. Ava

had been a bright spot in what had become a pretty beige life. A life he'd thought was fine. But never would be again.

He folded his arms as he cut right to the crux. 'I can't live in a goldfish bowl.'

Ava bit her lip. His words sounded so final and she swore she could hear her heart breaking over the silence in the room. 'I'm not *just* a girl on a boat, Blake. I *never* was. That goldfish bowl is my life for the conceivable future.'

Blake nodded. 'I know. But I don't want any part of it.'

She put her hand on one folded forearm feeling suddenly desperate, tears threatening again. 'So that's it?' she asked, her voice wobbling. 'You're not even going to fight for us? You can fight for this country but not for me?'

Blake hardened himself to the injury in her voice. Only Ava could be so dramatic. 'There isn't an us,' he said testily.

'Please,' Ava whispered, her hand tightening around his arm. There *was* something between them. She knew it. And she knew it could be good. 'We could make it work. We just have to want it bad enough.'

Her plea cut right to his heart but Blake shut it down. He'd had enough of complicated in his life. He'd sensed right from the beginning that she was going to be trouble and he'd been right.

Now his face was splashed all over the national newspapers. *Pete's* life and death splashed about too. Blake's grief and his guilt staring back at him in black and white for the entire nation to share.

All he'd wanted when he'd got things back on track was to have a quiet conflict-free life.

A life with Ava would be *neither* of those things.

Blake dropped his arms and her hand fell away. 'I don't want it bad enough,' he said and turned away.

And this time Ava did hear the crack as her heart split wide open.

The following wintery weeks were the perfect foil for Ava's mood. Christmas in London was always beautiful as decorative lights went up everywhere and the Christmas tree arrived in Trafalgar Square, but Ava didn't really notice. She didn't notice the roasting chestnuts vendors or the ice skaters at Hyde Park or the elaborately dressed windows in the department stores.

It was all too bright and sparkly for her when inside she identified more with the barren trees than the gay lights of Oxford Street.

She was merely going through the motions. Smiling and talking when she needed to and just trying to get through the rest. The media, as always, nipped at her heels but it was pleasing to note they'd stopped camping out regularly at Blake's boat since she'd denied their relationship in a press release, citing him as a friend only.

It didn't mean she stopped thinking about him. Stopped wishing in her darkest hours that she *were* that girl on the boat. It just made it easier to bear not to have to see his face next to hers on the news or in the papers every day.

But Christmas Eve came around quicker than she'd hoped and she knew she was going to have to face him again. The charity gala was the event of the year and, as the new patron, Ava was expected not only to attend but to shine.

And that was exactly what she told herself as she dressed to the nines. She had a certain image to project—glamour and sophistication—and she had every intention of wowing Joanna and all the others who had paid five thousand quid a head to ride the London Eye with her for a couple of hours.

Including Blake.

She wore a plush crimson, long-sleeved velvet gown that clung to her body and swept to the floor in a short train. A fur-trimmed hoodie attached to the back set it off and loaned her a touch of the regal when she smiled for the cameras with her famous haughty smile in front of an illuminated Eye.

And she spent the next three hours in a glass bubble, sipping champagne, laughing and chatting with people, new ones with each revolution. Smiling until her face ached, forcing herself not to search the bubbles above and around her for the one person she wanted to see the most.

Maybe he hadn't come?

On her second-last revolution for the night, Joanna and her founding partners along with some of the charity workers joined her and Ava relaxed a little. They talked about the success of the night and the upcoming events for the New Year and where she could help out. They also talked about their husbands, about how much they'd loved Christmas and Ava listened as they laughed and smiled at fond memories.

About five minutes from the revolution ending Joanna manoeuvred Ava to one side. She smiled at her and said, 'You know Blake's here, right.'

Ava nodded. 'I assumed he was.'

'You should talk with him.'

Ava gave a sad smile. 'I don't think your brother wants to talk to me.'

Joanna narrowed her eyes. 'You love him, right?'

Ava blinked and then laughed. Joanna was definitely a Walker—no subtlety. 'Yes.'

'So talk to him.'

Ava shook her head. 'He was pretty angry.'

Joanna regarded her for a moment or two and Ava felt as if she was being weighed up. 'Do you know the soldier that was killed the day Blake was injured was my husband?'

Ava's nodded. 'Yes. He told me when we were on the boat.'

Joanna looked taken aback. 'The last thing I said to Blake when they left for their tour was to look after Colin for me, to bring him home safe.' Joanna paused. 'He's not angry at you. He's angry at himself. That he's alive when so many aren't. That he *survived*. Every time he has fun or lets himself go, the guilt bites him hard.'

Ava's heart broke all over again for Blake. He shouldn't have to live his life eclipsed by guilt because he made it through when others didn't. 'I...didn't know that. I mean, I know he feels guilt about Colin...about the commendation...but not about surviving.'

Joanna grimaced. 'Well, he's not much of a talker. But I do know he was happy when he was with you and that he's never told *anyone* about Colin except for his shrink. I don't know if he'll ever be able to fully let go of the guilt and that's his *real* wound, not his leg. But I think if anyone can help him heal it's you.'

Ava couldn't agree more. But...'I can't if he won't let me in.'

The capsules were coming back down to the exit platform again and everyone was gathering at the door to clear the capsule in time for it moving on to the next platform where it would load again for the last revolution of the night.

'Well, they do say absence makes the heart grow fonder, right? And anyway, it's Christmas, it's the time for miracles.'

Joanna smiled and pointed to her brother standing rather grimly amongst the dozen people patiently waiting to get on.

Ava's gaze devoured him in all his tuxedoed glory. Who'd have thought a man who looked so good in a tool belt and a T-shirt could look just as good in a tux?

'Good luck,' Joanna whispered as she joined the exodus.

Ava sighed as Blake's gaze meshed with hers and he gave her a grim nod of his head.

She was going to need more than a miracle.

Blake had barely been able to take his eyes off her all night. Whatever capsule he'd been in, he'd tracked her movements, his sight starved of her for weeks now. And the second he entered the capsule and was offered a glass of champagne he took two and made a beeline for her.

He'd planned to patiently wait his turn and then make polite conversation with her, but as soon as the door had shut behind him the aura surrounding her grabbed him by the gut and yanked hard as a tumult of emotion flooded his chest.

What a fool he'd been.

He loved her.

And he didn't care how much anyone had paid for some time in her company, he was monopolising all of it.

'I've been an idiot,' he said as he elbowed someone else aside and handed her the glass of champagne.

Ava blinked as Blake's broad magnificence filled her vision. 'You…have?'

He nodded. It might have come totally out of the blue for Blake but he knew it as surely as he'd known he'd wanted to serve his country.

'Yes. I don't talk a lot and I'm not into staring at my navel and blabbing about my feelings. But I do believe in the truth and I've been lying to myself these past few weeks. Only I didn't realise it until right now. I thought I was doing so well and then I see you tonight and I realise that I'm in love with you and these last few weeks have been…*crap.*'

Ava looked around, pretty sure *everyone* was eavesdropping. 'You…love me?'

He nodded, wondering if she was going to stay monosyllabic for the rest of the night. 'Yes.'

'Oh.' Ava's heart tripped in her chest. *Well, that she hadn't expected.* Neither, she suspected, had Joanna.

It looked as if it was her night for miracles after all.

The temptation to let herself go and fling herself into his arms was enormous but there were still a lot of obstacles in their path and she needed to be sure. She needed *him* to be sure. 'What about the goldfish bowl?'

Blake sighed. 'I still can't live like that, Ava. But I was wrong a few weeks ago—*I do want it bad enough.* So I guess we're going to have to figure that one out. Compromise a little. Because I *want* this. I want you.'

Ava smiled at him for the first time, relief flushing through her veins making her almost dizzy. She reached out a hand and grasped his lapel, steadying herself. 'Well, I guess we could find somewhere to live that's more secure and not so accessible to the media?'

Blake slid his hand onto hers and held it against his chest. 'And you could stop feeding them gourmet snacks,' he suggested with affectionate exasperation, slipping his other hand onto her hip. 'And getting Reggie to report your movements to them so they know where you are every moment of every day.'

Ava nodded. 'I could do that. I could also set limits with them over you and your information. I've not done it before but I know others do and…I think you're a pretty good trade-off.' She grinned.

Blake pulled her in closer. 'And I promise to *try* not to punch every man who touches you during a photo shoot or a commercial or whatever you're doing for work.'

Ava felt stupidly teary at this concession. She knew how hard that would be for his Neanderthal, Bionic-Man streak. 'Thank you,' she whispered.

Blake smiled at her, wanting desperately to kiss her, to push her up against the glass and show her how much he loved her, but knowing they needed to talk first. 'And clearly, you can't live on a boat so I could sell it.'

'No way,' Ava objected. 'Keep that. I have very…' she ran her fingers under his lapel, feeling the firmness of his chest beneath the superb cut '…fond memories there,' she said, her smile widening.

He leaned in and nuzzled her neck. 'You're right. We'll keep the boat.'

Ava's heart dared to sing as she sank in closer to him.

'But is it going to be enough for you?' she asked, pulling back slightly.

Blake looked down into her yellow-green eyes. The whole Thames was stretched out behind her, the Houses of Parliament and Big Ben illuminated in a soft orange glow, a truly magnificent sight. But he only had eyes for Ava.

For the woman he loved.

'It's a start. And we'll get better at it. We have to, because I'm miserable without you.'

'Me too,' Ava admitted. But still her mind wandered to her conversation with Joanna and Ava felt anxious all over again. 'Joanna told me you feel guilty about surviving the war when Colin, when others, didn't,' she said.

Blake felt the usual punch to his gut at the mention of Colin's name. 'Did she now?'

Ava looked into his eyes because she needed to be sure that he understood what she was saying. 'I don't pretend to know what you went through, Blake. And I don't pretend to think it can be fixed through love alone. I know you're not a talker but I don't want you to shut me out either. I want to know *all* of you. Even the bits you don't want me to know. I can't be part of a relationship where you hide away all the dark bits…all the sad bits. I can't promise to know how to handle them, but I *do* want to try. I need you to promise that you'll *talk* to me. That *nothing* will be off-limits.'

Blake took a moment or two to absorb what she was asking. Opening up had never been easy for him, but he'd never met someone who'd meant so much to him either. He knew this woman in his arms and she was warm and sexy and giving and nothing like the woman he'd first thought her to be. She'd taken the risk and opened up to him, put her trust in him, surely he could do the same?

Because she was definitely worth fighting for.

'I promise,' he said. 'I don't promise I'll be very articulate but I promise to talk to you.'

Ava's heart swelled in her chest. She knew that couldn't have been easy for him. 'That's all I want.'

And for long moments they just looked at each other, absorbing all the details of each other's faces, trying to imprint this memory on their retinas for ever.

'You know there's going to be a bit of a frenzy to start with, don't you?' Ava warned.

'That's fine,' Blake said, lifting his hand to push the hoodie back off her hair. 'Let's just not feed it, huh?'

Ava nodded. 'Deal.'

Blake smiled down into her face. 'You're so beautiful,' he said. 'I can't believe it took me all this time to figure out I loved you.'

'I can,' Ava murmured. 'It took you a million pounds to even pay me any attention.'

Blake chuckled. 'I love you,' he said.

Ava sighed at the healing power of three little words as her heart felt whole again. And she was going to spend the rest of her life with her wounded warrior, helping him to feel whole again also. 'I love you too,' she said.

Their lips met and Ava felt as if it were New Year's Eve instead of Christmas Eve as fireworks popped and sparkled behind her eyes.

The sound of a dozen mingled sighs and the burst of spontaneous applause in the capsule added to the celebration as did the pop and flare of paparazzi lenses far below.

Best. Christmas. Ever.

* * * * *

Join Britain's BIGGEST Romance Book Club

50% OFF your first parcel

- **EXCLUSIVE offers** every month
- **FREE delivery direct** to your door
- **NEVER MISS a title**
- **EARN Bonus Book points**

Call Customer Services
0844 844 1358*

or visit
millsandboon.co.uk/subscriptions

MILLS & BOON®

Why shop at millsandboon.co.uk?

Each year, thousands of romance readers find their perfect read at millsandboon.co.uk. That's because we're passionate about bringing you the very best romantic fiction. Here are some of the advantages of shopping at www.millsandboon.co.uk:

* **Get new books first**—you'll be able to buy your favourite books one month before they hit the shops

* **Get exclusive discounts**—you'll also be able to buy our specially created monthly collections, with up to 50% off the RRP

* **Find your favourite authors**—latest news, interviews and new releases for all your favourite authors and series on our website, plus ideas for what to try next

* **Join in**—once you've bought your favourite books, don't forget to register with us to rate, review and join in the discussions

Visit **www.millsandboon.co.uk** for all this and more today!